ABOUT *INFANCY IN PARADISE*

Poet, essayist, and short-story writer Mercedes Cortázar tells the story of a girl from a family of educators who teaches herself to read and write at the age of three – and there begin her troubles. Her father's library lets her secretly immerse herself in science and the classics, while at school her teachers won't explain the difference between a vowel and a consonant. In the neighborhoods to which her upwardly-mobile family moves, she makes friends with children who have not yet learned to speak, let alone heard of Cicero, and others who are budding astrophysicists and poets. Developing a philosophy from the ups and downs suffered by her dysfunctional family and Caribbean homeland, she sees the light when her father begins to campaign for a seat in the Senate at the very moment this young republic starts to crumble. *Infancy in Paradise* is a novel of formation that makes the reader experience, through another world and another era, another reality that, far from a nostalgic glimpse into a childhood of the past, provides disturbing insight into the omnipresent political chaos of this moment.

BOOKS BY MERCEDES CORTÁZAR

El largo canto
(Editorial El Puente, Havana)

Deux Poèmes de Mercedes Cortázar
(Osmar Press, New York*)*

Astrogifts: An Astrological Guide to Gift-Giving
(Harper & Row, New York)

Orbes 1959-2016: Tierra/Agua/Fuego, Orbe Terrestre,
La Afrodita de Cnido, Razón de Eros, Naturaleza en el espejo
(Ediciones La Mirada, Las Cruces, New Mexico)

Orbs: Collected Poems
(Publishing Partners International, Dade City, Florida)

Images of the Divine Bird: Stories and Autofiction
(Publishing Partners International, Dade City, Florida)

Infancy in Paradise
(Publishing Partners International, Dade City, Florida)

Una Precocidad inverosímil (to come 2022)
(Publishing Partners International, Dade City, Florida)

INFANCY IN PARADISE

I see the awakening of consciousness as a series of spaced flashes, with the intervals between them gradually diminishing until bright blocks of perception are formed, affording memory a slippery hold.

–Vladimir Nabokov, *Speak, Memory*

MERCEDES CORTÁZAR

INFANCY

IN

PARADISE

Autobiographical Novel

Translated by Andrée Conrad and the Author

PPI

PUBLISHING PARTNERS INTERNATIONAL, INCORPORATED

DADE CITY, FLORIDA

2021

The author and publisher thank Rusela de Villena Liebgold
for permission to publish her photograph
of the author appearing on the back cover.

The photograph of the conch shell on the front cover
was taken by the author.

The font families employed in the typography of this book,
Garamond Premier Pro and Avenir, are licensed from fonts.com.

Edited and designed in the United States of America
by Publishing Partners International, Incorporated,
P.O. Box 318, Dade City, Florida 33526-0318

Library of Congress Cataloguing-in-Publication Data:
A catalog record for this book has been requested.

Printed in the United States of America

First edition

ISBN: 978-1-7347405-4-7 (pbk)
ISBN: 978-1-7347405-5-4 (ebk)

Contents

EARTH

WATER

FIRE

EARTH

1

WAVING ARMS
AS IF TO FLY

A BLACK CAR cruises slowly past our house. The vehicle is filled with men dressed in black, all staring at me from behind dark glasses. The man in the back seat at the window smiles at me, and I shiver with fear. That smile, revealing flashy gold teeth, is a brutish, macabre, diabolical smirk.

The sky has congealed into dark blue, gray, black clouds. The stifling air is about to collapse into a heavy downpour.

I'm sitting on the top step of our porch trying to hypnotize my new pullet, Pompadour, by lying her on her back and stretching out her neck. Armando, my father's driver, and Pancho Pistola, which is what everybody calls my father's bodyguard, are lounging in the red-and-white wooden armchairs on the porch, sipping beer. Armando has set his Colt .45 revolver on the white wooden table that separates the two armchairs, while Pancho Pistola cradles a Thompson machine gun on his huge thighs that look about to burst out of his khaki pants. Armando is a very white man with straight black hair trimmed in a bowl cut like a monk, except that he has a big mustache, which is full of foam and, to clean it, he sticks his tongue out with gusto. Pancho Pistola has a bullet-shaped head with broad brow, and close-cropped hair like a soldier. His milky, clean-shaven face is full of tiny holes like impact craters on the Moon. He drinks his beer with no sign of enjoying it, his snakelike black eyes scrutinizing all movement around him.

At last, Pompadour, lying on her back with her neck stretched out, sleeps.

"So," says Armando, "what do you think? Is the Doctor going to win that Senate seat?" He sets his beer glass on the table and crosses his hands behind his neck.

"Anything's possible," Pancho Pistola answers in his hoarse voice. "He has a ton of pull among poor Black folk in the slums of Atarés and Jesús María," he adds, laughing out of one side of his mouth.

Armando perks up. "So, then the Doctor moves up, right? And we'll be in Fat City! Aren't he and President Prío thick as thieves?" the driver asks.

Without answering, Pancho Pistola jumps up, gripping his machine gun so it doesn't slide to the ground.

"Shit! That makes twice this black car has gone around! Doctor! Doctor!" the bodyguard shouts, running into the house.

Armando grabs his .45, sprints to the garage gate, looks from left to right. Inside, the house explodes in commotion. My father, his gray hair messed up, comes out on the porch in trousers and undershirt, half his face covered in shaving cream and a razor in his hand, with Pancho Pistola right behind him.

"A black car, Doctor! First two minutes ago, and again just now, packed with suspicious subjects!" the bodyguard announces, very alarmed.

Just as I pick up Pompadour, my father grabs my hand and drags me into the house. Almaviva, the white country girl we just hired to be our maid, is wiping the dining room table with a cloth soaked in liquid wax.

"Take the girl and run, right now!" my father yells at Almaviva, the glow of a wild animal in his brown eyes, letting go of my hand and shaking the razor in his left hand.

"Run where, Doctor?" Almaviva asks, dumbfounded.

"To the bodega! To the bodega!"

"But to buy what, Doctor?"

"Buy Chicklets! Here's five pesos!" he exclaims, pulling a bill out of his wallet. "Take her running and stay there till I come get you! Get a move on, *now*! Dammit, *go*!"

My mother emerges in her nightgown from the bedroom she and I share, rubbing her hands together and quivering. My father disappears into his bedroom and in seconds is back with foam still dribbling off his face and a Colt Peacemaker .45 in his right hand. One glance at the weapon, and Almaviva is off at a run, dragging me behind. I dump Pompadour, wings flapping madly, in the middle of the living room, and we gallop half a block to Columbia Avenue, cross it, and go inside the bodega where the regulars are lounging at the counter drinking beer and talking politics. I order two Orange Crushes, Almaviva pays, and we stand near the counter to drink them.

Suddenly a black car screams by, its occupants shooting at the lemon-yellow mansion across the street from the bodega, a two-story stone building with a beautiful garden, surrounded by a wrought-iron fence painted silver. When the shooting starts, the men loafing in the bodega all drop to the ground as if they've been shot. Instead, I set my soda on the counter and run to the door so I can see what's happening.

The black car turns and heads down Columbia Avenue.

Minutes later, black cars and National Police cruisers arrive, tires squealing. The vehicles park everywhere in front of the mansion.

Agents in civilian clothes and uniformed officers bending over at the waist pour out of the cars, crouch behind bushes of the houses next door, flatten themselves on the lawns, and aim their machine guns, rifles, and pistols at the besieged house.

A man dressed in a finely-tailored gray business suit climbs out of one of the black cars. Smoothing his suit coat carefully, he heads towards the house, exaggerating the handsome stride that proclaims his power. A pistol appears in a second-floor window and fires at the man, grazing his left shoulder pad.

The man goes into a crouch and scuttles back to his black car.

In unison, policemen and plainclothes officers commence firing their machine guns, rifles, and pistols. Shouts from inside the besieged house are followed by barrels of several rifles and pistols emerging from the two windows of the second floor and spewing out gunfire.

On hearing the first shots, I throw myself on the yellow-and-blue tile floor of the bodega, making sure I can see everything in detail.

Almaviva, now, is flat on the floor too, protected by the wall that faces the besieged house, where stray bullets embed themselves when they aren't bouncing off the bodega's rolled-up iron grate.

I am excited by this danger, fueled by this thirst I have for childhood adventures.

After a while, a National Police cruiser parks in front of the bodega. One of the car's three passengers, in civilian clothes, gets out with his arms raised and heads at a run towards the house. As he's crossing the street, the other policemen spray him with machine-gun bullets.

The man falls backward on the pavement, waving his arms as if he wanted to fly or swim. A few minutes later he stops moving, while two liquid half-moons spill from his sides as if he's grown two large red wings.

In a window of the besieged house a stick with a white handkerchief appears. A husky masculine voice shouts: "Don't shoot! Stop shooting! Women and children are coming out! Cease firing!"

After a few seconds everything starts shaking. The streets tremble as if we are having an earthquake. I get up on my elbows to see better. Tanks and armored trucks of the Army of the Republic are advancing up Columbia Avenue. They turn at the corner, come to a halt in front of the besieged mansion, and adjust the aim of their huge cannons.

All firing ceases. A man wearing gray trousers and a white shirt opens the front door of the house and walks out into the garden carrying a tiny girl with a pink bow in her thin brown hair. She's been grazed by a bullet and is bleeding.

Two soldiers, armed with rifles, climb down from one of the military trucks to escort the man carrying the little girl to a car. One of the soldiers takes the wheel.

A woman in a flowery maternity dress comes out next, followed closely by two men. She is not tall and has masses of black hair. She walks down the garden path holding her big belly.

One of her companions opens the silver gate for her.

When she gets to the sidewalk, the woman reacts with terror at the sight of the man in the gray suit sitting in the black car.

He puts his hand out the window and waves, as if saying goodbye.

The cops' shots ring out in unison. The woman seems to jump through the air, then falls to the ground on her side. Blood flows as if from a siphon out of holes made by the bullets. From her thick thighs, cut lengthwise by projectiles, streams of blood ooze, blended with clusters of yellow fat. The wind wafts the sour, bitter smell of that body, whose intestines have crawled like snakes out onto the sidewalk. The men accompanying her carry her by her arms and legs as they try to escape, but after they take a few steps, shots ring out again. The men drop the woman's body to the sidewalk, and one of them collapses, face down, at the woman's feet, while the other flees in a crouch, trying ridiculously to take cover behind a small bush that can neither hide nor protect his body. Then he too falls, face down, at the curb of the house next door.

The soldier at the wheel of the car with the little girl and her father inside starts the engine and they flee at top speed under a barrage of police bullets.

A man looks out of one of the windows of the besieged house and shouts:

"Bastards! You sons of bitches! Murderers!"

A wave of shots silences him and leaves him without a face, erasing him from the window. The police throw tear gas bombs through the machine-gunned and semi-open windows of the house.

The shots from the mansion cease.

The soldiers point the cannons and guns of their tanks and armored cars at the police cruisers and black cars.

The police stop shooting, and the soldiers descend from the armored trucks with their shiny new submachine guns.

"You are massacring women and children!" screams an indignant army officer at the man in the gray suit as he confiscates his pistol.

The other policemen and plainclothesmen raise their arms and hand over their weapons to the soldiers. An army officer, very high-ranking judging by his decorations, followed by a squad of soldiers, shoves the man in the gray suit into one of the armored cars.

The downpour that the storm clouds of a few hours ago promised begins, diluting the blood of the dead and wounded, carrying it running, pink, down the gutters of the streets.

The smoke from the gunfire dissipates. The air smells of sulfur, fireworks, and those red firecrackers we set off when we play World War II.

Almaviva gets up from the bodega floor and, when I stand up too, she hugs me, trembling. The beer drinkers hoist themselves to their feet, shaking out their pants and shirts. The bodega owner, behind the counter ready to serve, throws his arms wide like he's trying to make sense of the size of the slaughter.

"What a tragedy, gentlemen! Like in the movies!" he exclaims trembling, trying to hide his fear with a smile.

This goes way beyond my childish games and those Chicago gangster movies I love watching at the Cine Avenida. The world breaks into pieces that don't fit together and can't be understood.

It stops raining. A man so extremely skinny that his wrinkled turkey neck seems to have a ball inside that goes up and down every time he swallows, runs with a movie camera and microphone, leaping over the dead and wounded. Likely he's the cameraman for the local newsreel shown every week in the movie theaters.

"Step forward, eyewitnesses! Eyewitnesses only!" he shouts, pointing his camera at Almaviva, who squeezes me closer, wrapping me in her dress.

A mulatta from the neighborhood who has come to gawk yanks him by the arm and says, "Hey, man, don't be such a vulture! Leave the girl alone, respect the dead! Can't you see all this blood and filth?"

"Take your hands off me, ma'am!" he yells, furious, freeing himself from the woman and bouncing towards me nimbly, as if he's made of rubber.

"Your name, young lady? Did you watch the massacre?" the cameraman asks, lowering his pimply face unpleasantly close to mine.

"What is 'massacre'?" I ask, playing the fool.

My father crosses Columbia Avenue at a run, passing between ambulances and around the wounded lying on stretchers. He talks briefly to the soldiers, removing all obstacles between him and us: the dead, the wounded, the stray dogs sniffing and lapping at the blood in the torrents of rainwater running down the gutters. Finally, he gets to us, sends the cameraman spinning with a commanding shove, and takes Almaviva and me by the hand.

The skinny guy catches his balance and glares at my father.

"Your name, sir?" he demands sharply, but without pointing his camera.

"I'm Tres Patines, you nitwit Procopius, and I warn you not to get all bent out of shape, because then your heart can't be operated on," my father replies menacingly. Almaviva laughs, revealing a black hole where an incisor once was.

As we cross the avenue, I turn and see soldiers taking away the guy's camera. He's arguing with them, gesturing impotently with his arms.

Back at our house, Armando the driver and Pancho Pistola the bodyguard flank the doorway, weapons in hand and on red alert, worried that my father will yell at them for lolling around and not being on the ball, even though the shooting has stopped. Inside, my mother, as usual sitting at the dinner table, sips the chamomile tea she always makes when she's nervous. Santana, the Black man who is my father's right hand, stands behind my mother, as if to protect her.

Toñita, our mulatta cook and semi-recognized relative, is parked in front of the kitchen door on a rustic wooden stool, resting her back against the corridor wall. "Don't worry, ma'am! Don't worry, ma'am! Don't worry, ma'am," she repeats, her usual litany to my mother, which stops as soon as we come in. My father dumps Almaviva and me at the dinner table in front of my mother, and, without changing out of his wrinkled guayabera and pants, he points a finger at Santana to follow him.

"Let's go to Ansola's, Santana, and see if the ex-Minister of Commerce is so terrified his balls are clanging together! You know how he is, as the 'pee-sychiatrists' say, a little 'neurasthenic,'" my father says mockingly, with a John Wayne air of calm heroism.

My mother resentfully watches them leave. The corners of her mouth turn down as she lights another cigarette.

"*Really*?" she says acidly. "Are they *really* going across the street to calm down *Ansola*? What a good neighbor he is, worrying about the ex-minister! What difference will that make? Meanwhile, his own wife could die of a heart attack! Not to mention his own children! He doesn't even bother to send someone to pick up his only son, your brother Septimio, from school! And, as for *you* – what a day to sleep late and skip school! And, to top it off, he sends *you* to the bodega! *Across the street from the shootout!*"

Toñita starts in again: "Don't worry, ma'am! Do not worry, ma'am..."

My mother, dressed in a white satin house robe in the style of the famous Hollywood actress Barbara Stanwyck, seems to be working up to a great scene.

"What rotten luck, being born in this shitty country – no beating around the bush about it, even in front of the girl! *Police* fighting against *other* police with *guns*! The Army sending *tanks* to murder police and peaceful citizens!

She forges on, hitting her stride.

"Has there ever been anything like this anywhere in the world? *Not even* the French Revolution! It *never* would have occurred to Robespierre, *not even* the 'In-corruptible,' would have done such a thing! If these trigger-happy gangsters had the atom bomb, they'd turn each of their enemies' houses into a Bikini Atoll! Here, no-body can live! We're delivering the country on a silver platter to the communists!"

She catches her breath and resumes, in a flat, doomed tone: "The plan of Stalin will be fulfilled! The Island's the key to communism in the Americas!"

Toñita flees to the kitchen.

Almaviva, still by my side to protect me, doesn't dare get up from the table, but I can feel her discomfort. I look at the ceiling, resigned to another of my mother's rants.

"I read the orders sent by Stalin straight from Moscow," my mother carries on. "They invited me to eat – how perverse is that? – the best French food, those Russian spies who stayed at the Hotel Nacional posing as American tourists and spending mountains of pesos. They made inroads with the media, the bankers, the universities, the writers. Even the grade-school teachers and priests, by God! They shoveled mountains of hard cash to get people to work for the Internationale!

"And now the man of this house, this devil, this cynic, is mixed up with these trashy leftist gangs! He will bathe this family in blood with his politicking! His po-litical enemies are going to bomb us, turn us into ash with their bazookas, these gangsters from the Ministry of Education. Is this the education they provide? Who do these jackasses educate? My hair is going to turn white overnight, like Marie Antoinette's. This man will crucify me!"

After a dramatic sigh, she adds: "My God, why didn't you give me the strength to resist his John Barrymore profile?"

Almaviva is collapsing with laughter, as if my mother were Vitola, Mexican cinema's greatest comedienne. And, more relaxed, the girl dares to get up from the table. My mother looks at her as if she were a cockroach jumping out of soup.

"You're still too young to understand this," she says to Almaviva. "A woman has the destiny a man gives her. You don't know how difficult it is to live," she ends tragically, taking another sip of her chamomile tea.

A lifeless light pours into the dining room, sunlight that passes through the windows' amber panes flanked on both sides by vertical purple panes.

I can't stand those dying flakes of purple on the floor.

I get up and turn on the radio. The announcer shouts:

"The two enemy gangs of high-ranking officers of the National Police force who met in a shootout at the residence of Commandant Antonio Morín Dopico, chief of police of the municipality of Marianao, have been brought under control by the Army.

"The attack occurred this morning in the Benítez quarter of Marianao popularly known as Orfila. Visiting that residence was Commandant Emilio Tro, director of the National Police Academy, and to whom Commandant Mario Salabarría, chief of the Extraordinary Investigations and Information Service, was delivering an arrest warrant accusing him of an attack against Police Captain Rafael Ávila. Tro and Morín refused to accept Salabarría's authority in the matter, and an exchange of gunfire ensued. The first victim was Police Officer Mariano Puerta Yergo, a friend of Morín Dopico, who appeared at the scene to try to stop the conflict but was halted by a burst of machine gun fire and fell dead on the pavement.

"Aurora Soler, Morín's wife, in the late stages of pregnancy, was shot dead directly in front of her residence as she attempted to evacuate the premises. Assisting her, also shot dead, was Emilio Tro.

"Miriam, her three-year-old daughter, escaped with a surface wound from the scene of the slaughter in the arms of her father, Morín, in a car driven by a soldier. The attackers, among whom was the known gang member El Colorao, are in custody.

"Commandant Salabarría has stated that he specifically ordered his forces not to shoot civilians, and that he made a gesture with his hand to halt the exchange of gunfire, but his troops mistook his signal, or decided not to obey him. So far, we have not been able to discover the extent of deaths and injuries."

"Change the station!" my mother shouts. "I've had to listen to an announcer narrating that massacre, live, minute by minute, like a baseball game. I do not want to hear another word about that horror show!"

I change the station, and the radio puts out the voice of the number one artist of Antillean song, the Puerto Rican Daniel Santos, singing, "Oh, Patricia, oh grieving woman!"

"Turn off that damned radio!" my mother shrieks. "I do not want to listen to that imbecile singing the story of my life!"

NIGHT HAS COME. I'm alone. I sit on my bed, lean back against the green wall of my room, which I now share with my mother. I touch my arms and legs to make sure I'm all there, haven't drifted away in rivers of blood running down the street. I am nauseated at the memory of that smell, sour and sweet at the same time.

Not long after the radio started giving the news, our neighbors ran to my house to comment on it. My family sat listening to the conversations without adding anything. We have kept silent. They sent to bring my brother, Septimio, home from school without explaining what had happened. My father made jokes. My mother sat at the table playing solitaire.

I cannot understand this day of so many dead. I hear in my mind the verses of Anna de Noailles:

> *The twilight will be long. The day is already growing.*
> *Daytime rumors flee and disperse.*
> *The trees are surprised, they do not see the night coming:*
> *They stay awake in the white afternoon and think.*

I lie on the bed and go back in my memory. Like Odysseus, I'm going to make a trip to my origin, to my beginning.

2

SHOCK

I FEEL THE DISCOMFORT of my wet diaper, the rash on my thighs.

I'm aware of a lukewarm wetness, now soothing.

I listen to a sound, or maybe it's a song.

I feel like I'm flying, like I'm an eagle spreading its wings in the nest.

Then the diaper turns icy and harsh. I burrow into the crib so that the wet part barely touches me.

Inside me, everything is dark, and the only sounds are *gong* and *tick-tock*. I have two rectangular windows where I see, over and over, the same image: a woman's blurry face.

Inside, it's black, quiet, comfortable. Outside, a tall hole in the wall lets the figure come and go, carrying something in one hand. When I grab it, I notice that it is hard and contains a white liquid. Sounds sprout from the figure's mouth. I can't make out those noises. I want to go through those two holes into the light, to that figure walking around out there.

Now other figures, not just the one, move their lips and make noise. Here inside, there are sounds but I can't pull them out of the blackness. I try to imitate the outside sounds, and my mouth laughs because my sounds don't match theirs. My tongue weighs on me, the sounds bunch together, and my gums hurt. Everything out there is so far away. It's hard to come up to the surface through the two gaps, so long as this black, endless void, this abyss inside, lasts.

Something hard spills a white liquid on my thighs.

The liquid is warm, calm, and makes little puddles on the sky-blue rubber mat where I am lying face up. I try to squash one of the puddles with my open hand and the liquid goes *plop, plop*. In a flash, the woman runs over with a cloth and sounds pour out of her mouth. She sits me up roughly and puts me on a dry corner of the rubber mat. With one hand she takes the bottle and with the other wipes the puddles with a cloth. My skin hurts where she grabbed me.

The noises she makes with her mouth grow louder.

I stay where there are no puddles.

With my forefinger and thumb I grab the little balls threaded on one of the railings of the crib. I move the red ball to the right, then the blue ball, the yellow ball, and finally the orange. I fall asleep on the mat.

I awaken to pressure on my chest and pain in my throat. Hands squeeze my neck and take away my air. The rail, one side of the crib, is down, and somebody has climbed on the blue mat to squeeze my neck. I kick and scream, but the fingers cut off my breath. I hear a torrent in my ears and everything I see fades into a gray mist. It's like I'm sinking into the ground.

A much larger shape slips between my body and the figure kneeling on my stomach. "Septimio, stop! You are strangling your sister!" the woman screams as she rips those hands off my neck. I cough. I can hear again, see, swallow, breathe.

It isn't long after this that the two holes of light join, and I can see through just one. The black inside is gone. Everything I see is what's out there, things that are far and near, their sizes, colors, depth. Things are no longer flat, now they have a body, bulk.

Now I know that the woman is my mother and it's she who's bringing me the liquid. Now I understand that the noises she makes are linked to the things I see. When she says "milk," she means that white liquid. Everything she says, I understand, or almost everything. I can't repeat the sounds, but I try, then I laugh because nothing comes out the same. My tongue still feels too heavy and my mouth doesn't move the way my mother's does. Sometimes my mouth even moves sideways and that makes me laugh.

My mother picks me up and carries me outside.

A sun shines yellow light ringed with purple that tastes like honey. The mockingbirds, now I know they are mockingbirds, fool other birds with their calls and leave white trails as they cross the sky. Their endless trills smell like the lilies out there.

My mother carries me to the corner where my brother and his buddies are playing with baseball cards. One boy shuffles them and turns them into two piles. "Which pile has the winning card?" my brother – Septimio – asks me. I point to a pile with my finger. My brother takes that pile and turns it over. The child who shuffled turns over the other pile. The one I pointed to has the biggest number and wins. We repeat this several times and Septimio always wins.

"I won't play anymore! If you bring your little sister, I refuse to play!" shouts the boy who shuffled the cards and made them into piles. Then he throws his cap on the sidewalk.

MUSIC OF VIOLINS, thunderous, and a flute that lingers on a high note. "Danzonete, play it, and go," sings the woman in a shrill voice, her broad mouth painted blood red and her white teeth open like a fan. The tiny white blouse she wears with its crescent-shaped collar is edged in red ruffles. Her vast skirt ends two palms below the knee.

The woman sings to music from the victrola and walks among the customers with her hand out, hoping they'll give her coins.

This music coming from the victrola at this beach restaurant is the same I heard at the house of the woman my father calls Godmother, the time she passed a dove over my father's head and mine. Godmother is a big lady with light chocolate skin, curly black hair shot through with white, fastened in a bun at the back of her head. She crosses the small room to greet us. She wears a white robe and a wide collar made of lace. I am afraid of the room's plaster Indians painted in bright ochre, red, gold, and blue, and life-size statues of saints, some with crutches and sores oozing a reddish liquid and others with white clouds above their heads and blue waves cresting under their feet, and a painting of a man with a lot of white in his eyes and yellow light behind his head looking up at the ceiling and holding a heart that's squeezed by thorns and pops out of his chest. Long dry yellow-brown leaves pop out from behind this painting. The house smells of pee, dirty laundry, and old furniture, mixed with the aroma of Creole fried meat, fresh lard, and sandalwood incense.

> *Danzonete, play it, and go*
> *I want to dance with you*
> *to the beat of the danzonete!*

sings a man, accompanied by music of flutes and violins from a large radio made of blond wood set on a table whose black paint is peeling.

"This is the girl!" Godmother exclaims as she passes some white pigeons over both our heads, my father and me. When she's done, she lets the pigeons fly out the window of the living room. She seems glad to see me, as if she already knew me. Satisfied, she jangles the brightly colored plastic bracelets stacked up on her plump brown arms. My father sits like a member of the family in one of the white wicker armchairs. His white guayabera, stiff with starch, is a little wrinkled at the elbows. He carefully straightens the sharp crease of his white dril 100 linen pants and admires his brown-and-white two-tone shoes, adorned with white holes.

"Before you were born," my father tells me, combing his mustache with two fingers, "she told me you were on the way. I remember Godmother's words as if she just said them today: 'A very peculiar spirit will be born in your house. This child is going to fill you with money and bring you luck. But this being is an *abicú*, a bird of passage. You must make sure she survives childhood.'"

I open my eyes wide to take in what my father is telling me.

I must remember all the details of this moment.

"Abicús are spirits who know things without having to be taught, who see farther than normal children do," Godmother explains to my father, in case he doesn't get it, although he says he does. "Abicús live until they decide to die and are almost always bored with life during childhood, because they are old people in the body of a child. You cannot spank this girl, and you must give her everything she asks for, otherwise she'll die and leave you bankrupt. You must dress her in white until she turns five, because, although she is a daughter of Yemayá, the goddess of the sea, Obatalá, the purest, the king of gods, has her head. Her being is so delicate that she can't stand colors. The spirits of evil did everything to keep her from being born and now, they are trying to take her in childhood. And she wants to go, because she can't stand it, *she can't stand it* . . . This will tie her to Earth," the woman says, and fastens a bracelet made of gold and coral on my wrist.

Godmother sits down on the couch in front of my father. She closes her eyes. Her face swells like a pumpkin, her cheeks inflate, she mutters something in strange words from another language, like sounds that I sometimes seem to hear in trees whipped by furious wind. Suddenly her eyes fly open, bright as if she had come back to life after a long, restful sleep. She's excited in a shocking way, but I can't pin down why. She scares me and makes my heart skip.

"Let's go into the room, Godson," she murmurs, herding my father toward a door with her hand. As she rises from her armchair, she supports herself for a moment on her thighs, as if she's suffering from great pain in her back.

Inside the room, I am surprised by all the objects it contains: pictures of saints hanging on the wall, even more statues on altars and on the floor; dried coconuts cut in half, showing their aromatic white pulp; orange papayas marinating their black seeds; scraps of red cloth lying everywhere. An encrusted anchor rests on the yellow tile floor. A large, rusty iron vessel fit for witches has strange instruments protruding from it: short spears, arrows, dark metal rods. The room's single large window high up in the wall extends almost to the ceiling. Through it, now and again, I see white, brown, and gray pigeons flying in a clear blue sky speckled with tiny clouds.

Godmother sits under the window in a wooden chair painted dark blue. She crosses her legs and reveals her plump, firm thighs covered in brown cotton stockings, kept in place by a knot. Fishing a dirty gray handkerchief out of her broad, wrinkled bosom, she opens it, and it's full of snail shells with brown spots on a white background, all with teeth and seeming to smile. She throws the shells on the floor and writes down some numbers. After repeating this process several times, she looks at my father in a scrutinizing way.

"Your son is strong as a bull, but *you*, you need to take care of yourself," she warns him, raising her voice. "Like any good son of Changó, you are a warrior, but you need to avoid the outbursts and tantrums. You think you're so smart, hmm? Don't be so curious – curiosity killed the cat! Get your affairs in order! Take care of this girl! Do not let her die! You'll get money, I see a lot of gold, enough metal to make candy with. Yes, I tell you, my Godson, everything is fine for you, but you must outdo yourself! Aspire to more! Work to get it!" Then she adds: "Also, watch out for that hard head of yours," she says, laughing with her whole body until she looks like she's having a fit.

I want to run out of the room, but I can't get out of the chair. Something like an electric current has frozen me where I am, and I tremble.

THE WOMAN OUTSIDE has stopped singing. I emerge from this memory and return to the restaurant where my parents and I are eating big loaves of bread with sausage, sitting at the only round table, which is covered by a red- and-white linen tablecloth.

The other tables, all rectangular, out on the gray cement that's darkened by wet footprints and lightened by small piles of yellow sand, are made of wood, painted bottle green, with splinters on the legs like roosters' spurs. Waterproof tablecloths smelling of rubber cover these tables with red and green floral designs. Among a few empty bottles are V-shaped glasses full of sparkling golden beer, like the lager my father ordered.

The restaurant is set on wooden pilings, around the bases of which the sea swirls furiously.

My father stares happily at all the women. On the stilts of their red and blue platform shoes, women dance with men who rhythmically move their wide trousers, white or sand-colored, and do pirouettes to the beat of the *danzonete* played by the jukebox. These are skinny, sun-toasted men lost in their loose-fitting guayaberas, neatly trimmed tiny mustaches over cigars hanging from their lips, squinty eyes, and huge aquamarines set in gold rings on several fingers of their hands.

The older couples dance doing gentle turns on a single imaginary tile. The blue-and-red victrola, framed by a plastic horseshoe through which bubbles rise and fall in a violet liquid, trembles with the beat of the high-pitched music. My father, a good dancer, taps his toe to the music.

My feet don't touch the ground and, to sit in the rustic wooden chair, I had to jump. My mother, across from me, wears her only "going-out" blouse, made of white silk with red ovals. Her long navy-blue cotton skirt ends at her feet, and her black shoes with square heels have an opening for her big toenail, painted red.

Today she has done her long black hair Greta Garbo style, parted down the middle and ending in loops that curl in on both sides of her head. She shows this off to my father as she eats, moving her face from side to side.

But he doesn't notice.

I watch my mother's long face, oval and pale, lips painted tomato red, teeth yellowish from smoking and a bit smudged with lipstick. She picks up her bread and sausage in her right hand, crooking her little finger.

She says it's a refined gesture she learned from a movie about King Louis XIV.

"They should have places like this in town so we wouldn't need to travel so far to enjoy them," she adds. The scent of the sea mingles with the spicy aroma of fried meats, the music, and the crackling sound of the Black cook's frying pan.

"Because, honestly, one shouldn't need to come all the way to a beach, to eat bread and sausage and listen to *danzonetes*. City people just haven't put their minds to thinking how to attract tourists with traditional, folkloric eateries. All you need is a palm here and a coconut tree there, and some typical Island food, and the Americans would come in droves."

My mother takes a quick sip of beer to perk herself up, and continues. My father eats in silence, his face expressionless.

"Now, the only places Americans are taken to is brothels. Instead, they could take them to typical cafés full of tropical vegetation and waitresses who dress like rhumba dancers and hand out tiny stuffed alligators as souvenirs."

To fill the silence, she adds: "This would be very popular and would make a ton of money."

My father puts his elbows on the table and looks at my mother as if analyzing her. He rests his chin on his intertwined hands and, for a few seconds, stops eating and drinking.

"People here have no imagination," my mother continues. "There are so many business possibilities! Amusement parks for the tourists' children, with bilingual clowns! Fireworks stores that open only on American holidays – for the rest of the year, those stores could house post offices, or hairdressers – businesses that never lose money! You need to think of something like that, Gus, something that helps us raise our heads, because, enough of eating nothing but corn mush the way we did during the Machado dictatorship! We need to get out on the street and begin to evolve!"

My father takes a toothpick from the little glass jar on the table and, digging at his teeth, continues to look attentively at my mother.

"Because, man, *this* nobody can stand. They say there's no evil that lasts a hundred years, nor any body that can stand it, but enough is enough. We don't have any money. You, with that rinky-dink job of primary school teacher that pays hardly anything, and I, who've lost my job as a clerk in the Ministry of Education."

Her face starts to glow. "Here's an idea, Gus. Why don't we get a loan from your brother the dentist so we can set up a hole-in-the-wall in town and sell *fritas* and *churros*? We could call it Flora and Augusto's Fritas! Septimio could take care of the business with us after school!"

After an awkward silence, she forges on: "Loads of millionaires began as children waiting tables in family holes-in-the-wall, then later became bank presidents or Hollywood actors." As if on cue, my brother, whose name is Septimio and who happens to be seven, five years older than me, and who has been running in and out of waves with other children he's found on the beach, dances into the restaurant, doing fancy steps and singing with great style:

> *When I was very little, I sucked the seed*
> *of the mamey and the mango.*

Now that I'm a cashew apple,
Cashew Apple purses lips and . . .

Seeing my father's expression, Septimio shuts up and sits in the chair next to my mother. Rivers of sweat run down his olive face, and his hair, black and straight, is plastered to his wet forehead. His face becomes very serious and his brow contracts in an unpleasant frown, as if something's really troubling him.

My father takes a sip of lager and sits back in his chair. "I'm registering at the university," he announces calmly. Savoring the beer foam on his lips, he adds: "I'm going to get a Ph.D. in Pedagogy."

My mother is stunned. A sip of beer leaks from the corner of her mouth and she quickly dries it with a napkin before it wets her blouse.

"After your sisters and your father, *another* pedagogue in the family? And, while you're studying, no money will come into the house!" she protests, very upset.

"Not so. My classes are all at night," my father replies without emotion, finishing his beer and getting up from the table.

"Come on, kid," he says jovially to my brother. "Let's go for a walk."

THAT NIGHT, impressed by the memory of the sea, I dream that my cousin Cleo takes me by the hand and we are walking on the beach. My mother and Isabel, one of her older sisters, are sitting on the sand. The day is gray, the waves seem calm, but, breaking against the reefs, they roar loudly, performing huge, foamy leaps.

I know the sea is full of fish and shells and conchs, and that green beards of algae twist and turn, driven by the waves. From the sea a murmur emerges like a song with no words, only whispered sounds. The song pulls me by the feet and, as we walk, it becomes harder for me to tear myself away from that magnet. The others ignore this and laugh. The strength of the song increases, and now it's stopped sucking at my feet, and is pulling at my whole body. I desperately clutch Cleo's hand, but must let go of her, the force tugging at me is that strong. I claw at the sand, at the stones, then take off and fly through thin air toward that dark immensity that now sings non-stop in its loudest voice, blurring the contours of people and things. The song and the roar of waves fill everything. When my terror is greatest, my feet hit the cold, viscous water of the sea.

Jumping in my crib, I wake up feeling punched in the stomach, as if I had belly-flopped into the sea. The house is dark. Only the green hands and numbers of the dining room clock on the sideboard stand out in that blackness. I get to my feet on the crisp blue rubber mat and fiddle with the colorful little balls on the crib railing, flicking them back and forth.

When my eyes get used to the dark, I see lights moving, flashes, and a woman walking around the room. She's just strolling, staring fixedly in front of her. She seems to be ignoring the lights, the phosphorescent green vegetation, the winged creatures jumping around playfully in the shadows.

I make signs to her as she walks past me. She looks at me and almost jumps from fright. What is she doing here? Is she a neighbor?

And, above all, how did she get in, in the middle of the night, with the front door locked?

Wrapped in a white robe, the woman approaches my bed. Her oval face has very fine features and pale skin, with blue, nearly violet circles from which her large brown eyes pop out and gaze at me sadly.

"Who are you?" I ask, hoping she'll quit fixing me with that weird stare. At first, she's startled, but then she returns to her distant expression. She moves her lips as if she's talking, but I can't hear a thing.

"I can't hear you," I say, upset. Again, she is surprised and moves her lips once more. The sound is like the wind whistling, and I must work hard to hear her. It's like she's talking inside my head, as if I've turned on a radio inside me.

"I haven't been able to eat for a while," the woman complains. "I come near food, and the food moves away. All I can think about is sitting down and eating; a well-laid table, with tasty delicacies, wine, dessert. I'm so hungry, so thirsty! Nobody hears me when I complain. They don't pay me the slightest attention. They look straight at me, pretend I'm not here – like I'm transparent. They just don't want to talk to me. And I am so hungry."

She keeps looking at me, pleading.

We barely have enough food for ourselves. Where am I going to find food for her? Besides, I don't know her. I don't even know how she got into the house.

"All we have is milk," I reveal, thinking maybe we have some milk left in the icebox after I fed the stray cats who always visit me in the evening.

The woman smiles and dissolves inside her white robe, turning into a moving gray cloud. Upon reaching the door, the cloud breaks up into many tongues that disappear completely through the seams in the wood.

3

THE SCORPION'S DANCE

I WAKE UP TIRED in my crib, but happy to know it's time to play in the street. I look forward to going out barefoot, wearing only nylon underpants to feel the warmth of the sun on my body and the cold grass under my feet. Then I fall asleep until late morning. When I wake up again, I decide not to go out.

After lunch I go back to sleep. At the end of the long siesta, I'm all set to return to my everyday routine and, when I stand up in my crib, there's my mother sitting on the floor, cleaning my booties with an old toothbrush and white paste from a flat round tin. To dilute the paste, she drips some water inside the lid and wets the brush with it, making bubbles and whitish whirlpools in the water.

Once the gray and black marks of wear are covered, the shoes turn white again, and even those creases in the leather that end in small cuts vanish under this wet mixture that smells like a new house. Slipping my feet into those cold booties after my nap is a pleasure that begins one more peaceful afternoon of my childhood, so delicate that it falls apart between my fingers, and convinces me I was born to enjoy it.

My mother combs my hair, perfuming it with Imperial Violets when there's money, and when we're hard up in the last days of the month, like now, she uses Water of Violets, a less expensive green liquid in a big bottle with violets painted on the label. But today, even though we're at the very last day of the month, she takes out her bottle of Imperial Violets because she feels generous. This golden, less pungent-smelling liquid lasts longer in the air.

"Also," she explains as she combs my hair, "water of violets, green or gold, makes you blonder," as if "blonder," being unlike other girls who have black or dark brown hair, is important.

With my hair combed and braided, I go out into the street wearing a new white linen romper with ruffles. My shoes look brand new and I smell of violets. This means the world and its spontaneity are forbidden to me. I'm going out not to perform, but to be seen. I cross the street looking three times in both directions, as my mother always tells me to do. However, when she goes out with me, she just stands in the middle of the street, clutching my hand and paralyzed with fear, while I scream as cars whiz by us on both sides, honking angrily.

That's why, when I go to Cusita's, I've learned to run fast, not giving cars a chance to materialize, almost jumping from one sidewalk to the next. Cusita's is right across the street from my apartment. Her house is big and faces the street, which seems a luxury to me.

Between her house and another masonry house of the same style runs a wide alley. This is paved with polished cement that's divided into large square tiles. On both sides of this alley are humble, single rooms that hint at squalor and promiscuity. Too serious for these dwellings is their street entrance, an ornate arch painted the same yellow as the big houses on either side of it.

Cusita's house is popular in this neighborhood because it has the only porch swing. Painted gray and pink, spotted with black from dampness, Cusita's porch swing is my favorite place. Entertaining Cusita, who is one year old, is the condition for my playing on her swing. I talk to her when I visit, but all I want is to feel the movement of her swing, the breezes it produces, the rhythm of its pendulum mixing with my thoughts.

When Cusita's family, the Cortados, go out, the swing sits on the porch abandoned, because no one is allowed to play on it. Now, they're out, and I can't. The Cortados' implied condition, that I must keep an eye on Cusita, controls my actions, introduces limitation in my life.

In the alley I see, leaning against one of the two small walls setting off the backyards of both houses, the mulatta Caridad.

At ten years old, with cinnamon skin and green eyes surrounded by long black eyelashes, Caridad is a mythological personage for me. For one thing, her hairstyle is different from other girls': it's parted into braids intertwined with strips of red cloth, and you can see her skull through the parts. For another, she's truly smart.

Judging me from head to toe, Caridad says: "See that dirt in the wall?"

In the middle of each of the two little walls are long narrow metal planters full of earth, but no plants, as no one's taken the trouble to plant anything.

"Yes. Why do you want me to look at it?"

"Right there, in that dirt, it'd be really easy to plant a money tree."

I look at Caridad. She isn't smiling and her eyes get bigger, focusing on me to emphasize the importance of what she's saying. Her smooth, serious face seems the epitome of honesty.

"A *plant* that grows *money*?"

"If you want to have money, you must plant it in dirt for it to grow."

I assume she's kidding.

She doesn't laugh but she's pinning me with her needle eyes like I'm a fly. A *money tree*? Impossible! But ... what if it's not? What if, in a week's time, I discover a branch barely peeking out of the earth, with a half-grown penny between its leaves? And later, after several months, thousands of pennies blooming and every-body admiring them, the whole neighborhood coming to look?

And me telling them, "This tree is mine."

"All you do is plant a penny, wait a few days, and you'll see it come up," she explains, reading my thoughts.

"So, why don't you plant one?" I ask.

"Me? I don't have any money. What about you?"

I quickly open a hole in the earth and into it press the penny I always keep in the pocket of my dress.

Now my capital is down to eleven cents. I've planted the cost of one round candy, half of a *carioca*, or a third of a *pirulí*. I flatten the pile of earth with my hands and wipe them on my new dress, and Caridad goes home.

I sit in the doorway waiting for Cusita for what seems like an eternity.

MY FATHER, DRESSED TO GO OUT as soon as he's read the newspaper and eaten what he calls his "little brunch" instead of "breakfast," announces he is tak-ing "the small fry" with him, as he calls me and my brother to his friends.

My mother, with an air of inevitable catastrophe, changes me into another white dress, puts my white booties back on, and warns me: "Do *not* get your white dress and booties dirty! Do *not* get your feet wet! Do *not* get your hands all muddy!"

In khaki pants and a short-sleeved white cotton shirt, my brother, Septimio, looks like what my mother calls "a miniature man." His olive-colored skin con-trasts with his red cheeks, which come from playing sports in the sun. He almost always puckers his purplish lips to remind everybody what a bad mood he's in, or how serious he is. But today, for once, he relaxes and stops being a jackass.

After lots of fluttering around me by Flora and the smoking of two premium cigars by Augusto while he reads and re-reads the newspaper, we leave.

I walk clutching my father's hand and discover that our street goes far be-yond where my gaze always stopped and made me think the world ended.

Now I try to recall how we got to Godmother's house, or to the beach res-taurant, or to the few other places I've been taken to, but I can't remember clearly.

Maybe then I didn't know what the world was, or just thought *That's all there is.* Traveling on the tram, I'm shocked to find that the streets don't end.

The tram seats creak when we sit down. They are made of woven wicker painted yellow and coated in transparent lacquer.

Also painted yellow are the three metal rods about a finger thick that go across the open windows.

The conductor, dressed in a gray uniform with a visored cap, takes my fa-ther's money, yanks a cable connected to a doorbell, and calls to the driver: "Go, passengers on board!" And houses begin to run by the tram's window: blue, pink, green, with red tiled roofs, wide porches, colorful gardens.

The sky, clotted with white clouds, follows us wherever we go, dizzying me.

Suddenly the movement of the tram turns my stomach into a carousel.

I feel my insides about to spew out of my mouth and nose. I lower my head and focus on the floor's dusty planks and black and gray spots, which I know is chewing gum because I stepped on some and it stuck to my bootie. Also down there are pink and yellow chewing gum boxes twisted before discarding, along with candy wrappers of every color. Heat rising from the floor smells of feet and dried spit.

My father notices that I am doubled over on my thighs, and hands me his cologne-scented handkerchief. All the disagreeable smells disperse when I duck my face into that square of lemon-scented threads. Closing my eyes stops the merry-go-round inside caused by the houses running by outside. The din of passengers talking becomes more tolerable.

Eventually my father gets up, shaking his wide pants. "Okay, kids, we're here!" he announces happily. Now we are on a small, narrow peninsula called La Puntilla, where the Malecón ends and the Almendares River flows into the sea.

Standing on the reef, I raise my arm to squeeze the sun inside my fist, and when I open it, the sun shines, smooth and yellow, on my fingers, but I can't grab it because it's far, far away up there in the sky.

We walk at the water's edge on the pointed rocks of the reef, which are all full of holes.

The sea enters some holes and spurts out of others in jets like a sprinkler, flowing over white snails with brown spots on their spiral shells. These cling to the rocks using a suction muscle, which I know because sometimes the force of the waves is so great that it can snatch a snail right off a rock, revealing that muscle, a black, grainy crescent that covers its mouth.

I pick up a few of these creatures and slip them into the pocket of my dress.

My father walks ahead of me with my brother, talking to a friend he bumped into when we got off at the entrance to the Pote Bridge, right next to the Fresquito Fresquet fish market.

The Pote Bridge terrifies me because the whole thing is metal, and whenever a streetcar crosses, the bridge sounds like it's collapsing and we'll all be floating out the mouth of the Chorrera to vanish in the sea.

My father's friend is about thirty, tall and thin. He hides his eyes behind large light green mirror lenses in a brown tortoise shell frame. He wears a guayabera and white dril 100 pants, which the wind whips around like the flame of a candle.

He and my father both look like my idea of teachers.

"Augusto, Flaco! remember when the police arrested us during the Machado dictatorship?"

My father says, "As if I could forget!" The stiff breeze cuts off his voice, and my tiny feet run to keep up with the men's long legs so I can hear.

My father's friend goes on: "You were lucky to get out so fast. I rotted in jail for days. They finally got tired of beating me with their sticks, and, before they let me go, they had to pour a whole jug of Palmacristi laxative down my throat," remembers the friend serenely. The wind drowns out my father's laughter, and again I must run to keep eavesdropping.

"They couldn't find a thing to detain me, Luis. We hid the anti-Machado pamphlets under the mattress in the boy's crib. He was sick with a high fever. They didn't dare look there," says my father, laughing again. I want to silence seagulls, wind, and sea so I can hear. My short legs are tiring from running after their voices.

"Augusto, Flaco, we aren't planning a revolution against Batista. He was duly elected, and yes, he's going to run again. But he must call for free and fair elections so we look like a real democracy – so we don't lose the Yankees' economic aid. Grau will beat Batista, I'm confident. You need to back Grau," Luis says, giving my father a friendly pat on the back. "We'll be able do a lot for the country when Grau gives us important positions in the Ministry of Education."

Walking beside my father, Septimio is looking at him worshipfully. He's proud that he's been taken out for a walk at La Puntilla.

I run out of breath and must stop on the reef. Meanwhile, my father, his friend Luis, and my brother walk on until they are lost in the spark of sun on the horizon. Some clouds open in a semicircle, white fans with golden edges on a background of dark red and light green sky. In my imagination, transparent walls come down around me and I'm surrounded by solitude.

The voices of my father and his friend, which had sounded like wasps flying in my ear, now claw at those invisible walls, intensifying their reality. The three shapes in the distance, wobbling like steam in heat, float on lights that lick the small waves.

A soundless movement in the water.

I turn, and a red-and-silver snapper pokes its head out.

Balancing on its tail, standing almost vertical in the water, it stares at me in astonishment. Its red eyes, ringed by whitish eyelids, fix on mine, and I come to a halt inside myself.

My lungs shrink, a whistling void enters through some slit in my stomach, everything is paralyzed: a scream trying to burst out of the open mouth of a mute.

No noise of waves anymore, nor of conversations – just silence and that great astonishment the fish and I share, trembling.

"Don't dawdle!" my father shouts, coming towards me, his dark silhouette growing against the golden sky.

His shoes squeak as he pounds across the reef, and the snapper in one move sinks back into the sea, concentric circles expanding on the water's now quiet surface.

"What happened?" my father asks, seeing my livid face.

"There." I point at the circles in the water made by the snapper.

I WAKE UP DAZED. The memory of the fish revives me, and I think about the penny I planted, the *kilo prieto*, as we children call it. Did my seed sprout?

I cross the street looking in both directions, dig into the dirt, and find no tiny plant of any kind. I dig into the other planter, thinking maybe I've misremembered which one I put it in. No penny tree here either. I lean against the wall of the corridor to consider what's happened. Why didn't the sapling come up when the penny disappeared?

All night I've been dreaming of the money tree, and now it doesn't exist. Something cold fills my stomach and I feel the floor open under my feet.

The mulatta Caridad has tricked me and robbed me!

I imagine her looking out her window, laughing, then yelling, "I fooled you!" She's made me feel like an idiot. I don't like this feeling, my burning cheeks, my arms feeling as if I've been put in a box and can't move.

I'll never again trust the mulatta Caridad. She lies to me the way my brother does. For example, Septimio once told me that, if someone covered my nose and mouth, I could breathe through my ears. Also, he told me that chocolate was cold mud and tasted like caca, to make me sick to my stomach so he could eat all my chocolate. I know grownups who lie just for fun, but this is the first time a lie has cost me a penny.

I have paid to be humiliated.

I take a deep breath and study the light blue sky, full of sun and white clouds in the shape of elephants, lambs, peacocks – even the profile of the Man in the Moon.

The wind smells of lemony *romerillo* and oleander. The scent erases my shame.

What I actually paid just a penny for was one entire night of dreaming a wonderful thing: a tree full of pennies, an image that gave me pleasure and made me happy. Caridad didn't deceive me, or rob me. She sold me a dream.

I lie down on my parents' wide bed to take my nap, and the breeze lifts the hairs on my arm. With the gentle wind, the strong light of twelve noon comes through the room's large window. The sun's rays, cut up by the metal grilles' floral designs, light up the floor tiles, creating whimsical black arabesques. I fall asleep.

AFTER A FEW HOURS, the air and heat of the sun lift me out of the midday torpor, out of that sleep where my being completely disappears, then returns with no memory of the past, like being born again.

All the things around me seem to be created anew, just now. Thoughts, in no hurry, pile up in my head. I hear myself and feel myself living. Although limited by my sweaty skin, I participate in the essence of the room on a deep level that I can't explain.

The yellow sun runs across me, awakening murmurs in my skin, leaps of blood under flesh refreshed by the breeze enveloping my body. Odors of lime, jasmine, and skin hot as freshly cooked bread pierce my sense of smell. The room reflects light, iridescent as in the depths of the sea, and the pieces of furniture float, acknowledging my consciousness, now awake with a rapture that makes those pieces expand in waves.

Shadow and light switch places, turning the floor tiles even more yellow as they catch reflections from the silver edges of the window grille.

"You're awake!" my mother exclaims. "Why didn't you call me for your bottle of milk?" She turns and leaves the room, not waiting for an answer. What answer could I give? I find my way in that silence and in that throbbing of things, the joy of being aware and noticing shapes, sizes, and colors of this multitude of things surrounding me. Silence gives them a dignity and a peculiar meaning, magnifying everything in jubilant disorder.

My mother returns and hands me a Coke bottle with a rubber pacifier filled with coffee and milk. The greenish glass is hot and makes the palms of my hands sweat. I suck on the liquid slowly, caressing it in my mouth, transforming it into a delicious nectar that warms first my throat, then my entire rib cage, then my intestines.

My mother leaves and returns in a bit to collect the bottle. I've drunk every drop of the milk.

"Come see a scorpion dance," she says, smiling and pointing at the patio door with the empty bottle in her hand. Without waiting for a response, she heads to the kitchen to make dinner.

I go to the patio and see a scorpion twisting, hanging by its tail tied to a thread looped around a nail in the wall. It struggles, it's alive, it's dark, kind of brownish, red at the edges where the sun hits it. Its skin is glowing so brightly that the tips of my fingers shiver. It's sending out a signal – "Back off!" – that I can feel all over my skin. This is the voice of danger.

My father moves the scorpion expertly using the thread. He laughs, maybe admiring the repellent beauty of the animal, or maybe mocking its disorganized, desperate attempts to regain control of its legs. My father lets it down to the cement floor of the patio, securing the thread with the toe of his shoe while he pours alcohol around the scorpion, allowing it a dry spot the size of a large grapefruit.

Then he pulls out his silver Zippo and lights the circle of alcohol, sending a blue-and-red flame and the smell of lighter fluid into the air.

At once the fire creates a circle around the grapefruit, corralling the scorpion, which advances and retreats, twisting and turning in every direction. Around and around the animal spins, until it knows it is trapped. Then it remains motionless in the center for a few minutes.

Slowly, with the elegance of a dancer, it lowers its pointed tail that ends in a poisonous stinger over the middle of its back.

It freezes for a split second, then suddenly, as if in a fit of rage, it plunges its stinger forcefully into its own back, arching upwards and lifting its two pincers and all eight legs at the same time.

My father blows out what's left of the fire. The scorpion twists in agony produced by its own poison, and my father laughs in admiration of its feat.

ON THIS LUMINOUS SUNDAY, when the sunlight is almost blinding, my father takes my brother and me to see the trains. My mother has often said that her father had an important position in the railroad company, and that this advance in transportation had been crucial to the Island's economic development.

When we arrive at the Central Railway Station in the Capital, I am amazed by its towers and façade adorned with shells and shields in the Spanish Plateresque style. The huge central clock, like the eye of a cyclops haloed with white clouds, yellow rays of the sun, and black Roman numerals, dazzles me. Inside the station, the trains look like gigantic metal animals, the "horn" atop their heads erupting smoke – black, acid, irritating, smelling of city – awful.

"The large iron wheels, powered by white steam, are joined by connecting rods," my father lectures, pointing with his index finger. "These are moved up and down by the steam-fed pistons, creating traction. These trains bring everything produced in the Interior to the City. Everything we eat is grown by our farmers and ranchers. The railroad is the cornucopia that spills all the treasures of civilization into our laps.

"And to think that the coal that burns in the locomotive's firebox produces the fire that boils the water in the boiler that creates the steam that moves the cylinders with their connecting rods that finally drive the wheels that spin on iron rails and propel the train with all its cars to their destination!"

He pauses to catch his breath and to achieve greater effect. "Perhaps this same steam, converted into a golden mist, hid the goddess Aphrodite when she rescued Paris from certain death at the hands of Menelaus during their duel in the Trojan War!" he concludes with an oratorical gesture, as men and women hurriedly board and exit trains, and porters carry their leather suitcases, large cloth bags, and round hatboxes.

And amid all the hullabaloo of shouting conductors, chatter of families saying their goodbyes, and rumble of metal wheels starting or braking on the rails, the hissing whistle of departing locomotives sharply penetrates my ear, like the inkling of a distant dream, now lyrical, and at other times sinister.

"Augusto, Flaco, I didn't expect to find you here!" exclaims a man who separates himself from the crowd and walks towards us with an uninhibited, determined air. When he's near, I see he's the same man we met at La Puntilla.

"Yet again, here I am, on an outing with the kids, Luis," my father says.

"Ah yes, it's so important to devote time to the family," Luis replies, smiling and looking at Septimio and me. "In fact, I've just come from my brother's place in Camagüey." He pauses as if he's about to make an important point.

"He has a cattle ranch with several thousand head and invited me to see if I wanted to go in with him" Another pause. "But I'm not made for that."

Luis and my father walk ahead of us, speaking in low voices. My brother examines the trains studiously, as if trying to figure out how the rods move the wheels. I walk faster to hear what the men are talking about.

"As I said to you last time, Flaco, we'll not be doing anything against Batista," Luis says. "He'll leave the presidency because the Yankees will pressure him to. We can't oust him the way we did with Machado. It would be a historic mistake, because Batista destroyed the officers who came from the upper class and promoted sergeants like himself to be general officers, so now the whole Army backs him.

"In other words, Grau has a chance to get elected because the elections must be fair. Batista won't be able to cheat."

After a pause, Luis concludes: "The Americans are the only ones who can control him – and they want stability in this country."

"I'm not thinking of doing anything subversive, Luis. I've gotten together with some Grau people to do politics," replies my father, giving the man a fraternal pat on the back.

IT'S A MISTY DAY. The silhouettes of my mother, father, and brother all mingle in the darkness of the house. Movement, chatter, hurried gestures, footsteps sounding on the tile floor fill the house. My crib vibrates with all this activity. Through my half-open eyes, and through the railing of the crib, I can see my brother in his school uniform and my mother adjusting his woven tie. I can smell starched khaki pants, pencils, rubber cement, the leather of my brother's brand-new bookbag.

I stay in my crib and, to my surprise, everybody is fine with that.

Why must my brother get up early, but not me? I keep asking until I'm told I'm not old enough, that I must wait until I'm five to be able to become part of this activity every morning. Two years – an eternity!

At ten in the morning, my favorite time, I usually sit in a corner of the living room to invent music, sounds that I mix into songs that I hum. But today I decide to change my routine. I sit on the threshold to our apartment, the second of four in the place where I live, and stare without blinking at the radiant blue sky until I penetrate it and can see small circles with balls in the center, bouncing and spinning in space. The circles of heaven, their nuclei, and their dances, fill my view and invade my mind.

"I'm three years old," I announce out loud. "I need to go back in my memory. If I wait one day longer, I'll forget what happened before I was born."

I see a young soldier sitting at a long wooden table with other blond young men like him. They're all wearing the same uniform. The room's walls are composed of gray smoke. They all drink wine or beer. Such excitement in the young man – what great plans he is explaining!

The big argument they are embroiled in is interrupted by a blurry figure.

"It's your time," the figure says, in a female voice.

"I've got to go, friends," says the young man, sadly. He doesn't want to leave, isn't exactly sure where he's going.

"Don't worry," says one of the soldiers. "We'll be down shortly."

That cheers the young man, and the scene fades.

Now everything opens. I feel no warmth inside me, but have arrived at a point around which everything known to me revolves, from which everything arises, and which, if I cease to exist, will turn images and sounds into impenetrable solids and create a deep, static, absolute hole. There I am!

In this other image, completely lacking heat, I exist in a state of laughter, as if all I've ever done is laugh. This is because, when I go from one place to the next, I turn into a line and suddenly I'm there. I see my hands: they aren't hands, yet I think they are.

It's me, and yet I'm not, all at the same time. You could say I'm a force in motion. At times I move so far and so fast that I vaporize, expanding and covering vast territories. I see everything all around, also within, me, landscapes with mountains and, sometimes, lakes.

Once this agitation ceases, I go back to being a small thing, like a dot, or a line. Or sometimes I'm a body – more or less. I can modify this at will. All I must do is tell myself, let the idea sound itself out inside me.

But there's another, closer, memory of stormy nights that traps me.

I feel a great cold and can go nowhere. There's no shelter from that cold. Mountains surround me, silhouetted against sinister yellow sky like darkness without dawn.

Hearing the terrifying, unceasing sound of a thousand thunderclaps from lightning bolts striking nearby, I float up and swiftly fly over trees whose branches wail as they're blasted by the wind.

Howling dogs of the night pursue me until one precise moment, when I think of palm trees and the sea. I'm in flight from terror over those palm trees, over a sapphire blue sea, resplendent in the sunlight.

Down below, on an island, inside luxurious mansions, hundreds of naked couples are lit up in red, making love. I insert myself between one of the couples and flow with the white liquid into a black and red cave that smells of blood.

The joy of having found refuge invades me. I fall asleep, totally protected from cold and storm.

After a long sleep, dreamless, inside this cave, I wake up to a horrible bellyache. My skin feels it's on fire. I start kicking. Blood begins to flow from wounds in the walls of my shelter.

I hear piercing squeals and feel shaken and flung back and forth until, finally, I can return to a state of calm.

"My husband doesn't come to see me, but my sister does."

I hear a voice that shakes the walls of my shelter. It's a foreign language, but I understand it.

"You've been irresponsible! You know perfectly well that the doctors said you can't have another child, that you and the baby are going to die."

"Now the poison you've taken to abort is killing you with hemorrhages," says another voice farther off. I feel my body trembling with fear of death.

But I know no one will die.

I will be born after eleven months, with long black hair, which then will turn almost blond.

IT'S STILL EARLY MORNING. My brother's gone to school, my mother fusses in the kitchen, I sit in my corner of the living room.

It's time to put furnishings inside my head, decorate it with meaning.

Through the open door, I see the hall with its strip of sunlight. The shadow in the house, its odor of damp stone, somehow proves my existence. A yoke exists between that shadow and me: I can't delete the one without nullifying the other.

This certainty has turned into one of the first pieces of furniture in my head.

My mind contains only white light.

Into that void, I must place furniture and objects.

I spend the whole day contemplating these objects from the most diverse viewpoints, linking them to other things run into in the same way, sometimes contrasting and setting them apart.

The most remarkable artifact is my age.

It is a red ball in the white space.

The red ball reflects light and rotates quietly on its own axis.

The Investigator, a miniature me that I insert into the white space, sits down to observe rotations of the red ball that has my age inside.

The Investigator inscribes the ball's characteristics on his body. The inscriptions are facts and details compressed into the contours of feelings that have great emotional intensity.

This allows me to become part of the red ball, but also to explore its external characteristics.

Sometimes the Investigator gets distracted and plays with his shoes, which float in space, in the white part, just by wanting it to be so.

Then the Investigator tosses the white space into the air like a net, to retrieve the shoes.

Meanwhile, the ball goes on spinning, producing a high-pitched sound, sort of like the whistle of a train, only richer.

The Investigator disappears inside the red ball.

The white space still exists, but now I can concentrate exclusively on the red, which has turned into a landscape and has stopped being a ball.

Inside the red, the Investigator becomes figures, copies of myself, incidents.

One of my images examines its hand against a violet-colored sun. It climbs stairs and falls into holes. Its voice fills everything, and repeats, with great urgency:

"I'm three years old. It wasn't very long ago that I was born."

Images of the past begin to appear in my memory.

"If I try to remember now, I'll find out what happened before I was born. Otherwise, I'll forget all of it."

Until a distant voice commands, "Eat this banana."

I emerge, dizzy, from the ball and the white space, and adjust my eyes to see the room.

My mother, in front of me, leans over with a banana. Her hands are wet because she has washed the banana in case I try to eat the peel.

"What are you doing?" she asks.

Her frowning face fills my visual field.

I can't see behind the wall anymore, or even the fringe of sun in the hallway.

"Nothing," I reply, moving my braids from one side to the other.

"You spend the entire day sitting in the corner or on the doorstep. Why don't you go out and play?"

"I don't want to."

The red ball and the face of the Investigator disappear.

Everything is gone.

This image in front of me drags me to the living room – to play.

For as long as I can remember, I've had the feeling that I had to hurry, that I had to understand the world. I had to work quickly to open my brain, because there was no time.

A lie makes my world disintegrate, it delays me for weeks, months, years. I recall the mulatta Caridad's *kilo prieto* and my brother's chocolate made from mud.

This figure in front of me doesn't care at all about – *ignores* – the destructive power of a lie.

I don't know where I am, or who these people are, or what they expect of me. When my brother told me that I could breathe through my ears, I thought I had reached a very advanced place, where organs had many purposes. Upon discovering the truth, part of the structure I had built in my head fell apart.

When I asked him how many sexes there were, because I noticed when he took a shower that his body and mine were different, my brother said, "Two." I collapsed laughing.

Clearly this was another of his lies, like breathing through your ears.

These people are making me regress. Why are they telling me lies and hiding truths from me? I must hurry to understand.

"Why don't you take a walk? Go play with kids your age." My mother is watching me from above, her face contracted with concern.

"I don't want to. I'm going to invent music."

"Are you going to invent a *danzonete*?" she asks, laughing and looking at me with fake admiration.

"No. Not radio music." I give the banana a bite.

My mother is getting into my head a lot. I don't know where to escape.

"You spend the day saying irritating things," she says.

"Go out and play like all the other kids," she says.

"I don't want to have a retarded daughter, singing in a corner," she says. "What will the neighbors think?"

"Go out and play now, and don't keep bothering me," she says.

Finally, I stand up, furious, and run outside. It's strange to be in motion, on my feet, balanced.

My anger dissolves at the joy of having a shape and being able to move things around. The morning is glorious. I walk along the sidewalk jumping, showing off in front of houses and dazzling the world of people.

THE ENDLESS DAYS in the early morning are like a ribbon of blue sky atop a porous yellow wall. I focus my gaze on that blue ribbon, trying to guess at the rest.

"These people don't deserve even to *stand* on this planet," my father exclaimed arriving home from work last night.

He was saying this about administrators, co-workers, teachers like himself.

I could not understand this very well because his words were blocks of stone in my head that I could only order according to their shape and size, but not their meaning.

My mother explained to me afterwards: "The 'planet' is a spinning ball called 'Earth.' You *stand* on this spinning ball."

That was how I deduced that the planet must be full of earth.

Otherwise, the planet would be called House, or Street, or Tile.

It's a ball of earth/dirt that spins around without making us dizzy.

Next, I find out that Earth is inside the Universe.

"What is the Universe?" I ask my mother.

She tells me to go outside and play.

Sitting on the threshold and looking at the blue sky, everything is there for me to see.

I still want to know what the Universe is.

The small dots of the distant sky appear, a multitude of dancing dots with halos of metallic gray that evaporate in the blue stripe.

From this amorphous matter, an image separates itself that enlarges when it reaches me.

Bright, golden circles rotate within other circles, spheres forming part of other, larger spheres. Everything rotates, becoming larger, producing, as they turn, a musical sound, like the wind when it comes in through the slits of windows, or like the coffee maker percolating with boiling water.

I get up and run to find my mother.

"I know what the universe is!" I exclaim, full of joy.

"The universe?"

"Yes."

My mother looks at me like she is waking up from a nightmare.

"The universe is circles within other circles, balls within balls, and lots of music," I explain.

She stares at my shoes and then at my forehead.

"Go play. Stop saying crazy things."

4

DO SOMETHING ABOUT YOUR DAUGHTER!

SHADOWS MOVE around my crib, and the noises of the morning, its incipient activity, as well as the tepid breeze with its slightly icy edge and its smell of humidity, like a torn leaf, are transformed into light. The light fills the room, my crib, and the pink blanket that covers me.

Under my body, I feel the creaky hardness of the mattress and its cover.

I lower the railing of the crib, and the red, yellow, and blue balls, strung horizontally on the metal rod, move to the right, then left with my hand, making a cheerful sound. I get down from the crib and run barefoot to the bathroom.

I hop up on a stool that I pull out from under the sink, turn on the faucet, and splash cold water on my face with my hands.

This cold is like a limit I put on sleep, obligating me to be present in my entirety.

"Every day is the same, the same boring things. Sing in the corner of the living room, eat the banana my mother gives me in the middle of the morning, sit on the doorstep, go back in my memory, then wait for lunch," I think in despair.

And still I put on my shoes and sit in the corner of the living room, where I can see the front door, which is always open.

All I have on is a pair of salmon-colored nylon undies, which the floor's cold pierces straight through, hardening my sensitive skin.

I sing, or hum, whatever passes through my head.

Each sound shelters another within itself and emerges in a chain that I can keep adding to, creating different combinations, until I get tired of it.

My mother tells me to shut up from the kitchen, where she is noisily scrubbing the dishes from breakfast. "My brother's books are in the bedroom," I whisper to myself, frustrated. "I'll take them and learn to read even though I'm supposed to wait till I'm older."

I can't wait. Time passes very slowly and I'm bored stiff.

Also, on Saturdays and Sundays, I won't need to ask my mother to read me the funnies in the newspaper.

In my parents' room are Septimio's textbooks, on the table where he stashes all his stuff from school. He's covered the books with a terracotta-colored paper that gives off a pungent odor of organization. The paper doesn't have that fur, irritating to the touch, it gets after the books are used for a long time, because these are new books. My brother just started third grade.

The glossy, smooth-to-the-touch covers, their titles written in blue ink, all appeal to me equally, and I don't know which book to choose.

The letters written on the covers are mute, reveal nothing to me – yet.

My mother sneaks up behind me. I can feel the change of air on my back. I turn around and there she is, glaring at me suspiciously, looking at the books.

"Give me some books. I want to learn to read," I demand, with great authority.

I sit at the dining room table with the book my mother chose. It isn't covered like Septimio's books.

With this book, my father, who is an elementary school teacher, teaches his students to read. It has a hard cover and lots of drawings inside. I flip through it, and a bird's wing painted in black ink appears on a page, with the letters A-L-A underneath. This dismembered wing on the page amazes and frightens me. Another page has a curly-haired woman in a short-sleeved dress with a V neck with the letters M-A-M-Á underneath.

These drawings popping out of the whiteness of the page terrify me: an eye under a bushy eyebrow, a smiling mouth, a nose – all these separate body parts painted, with letters underneath. My mother explains to me that the letters are the name of the drawing. "When you see those letters together, the image will pop into your memory," she tells me.

Controlling my terror, I turn page after page, copying the letters in an old notebook of my brother's. I begin by writing vertically with my left hand. Then I compare what I've done with the primer and realize that it's not the same. So then I write horizontally, but from right to left and, in the next line, I continue from left to right.

Now my mother sees what I'm doing and ties my left hand behind my back to force me to write with my right hand, which makes it very difficult to write anything at all.

I feel like I'm all thumbs writing with my right hand and make furious faces until it gets a little easier with practice.

"Every letter is a sound," I mutter, when I tire of writing. The letters together form another, different sound, and this creates an image. If I write that image in letters, I don't need to paint it.

Then it occurs to me, other people also have the image in their heads and see it if they look at the letters together.

I put the image on the paper so other persons can pull it out of their heads.

For a while these ideas whirl around me and organize themselves into all possible combinations. Sometimes my forehead and head hurt, and sometimes I drift off to sleep abruptly, and the pain is replaced by sleep.

Now, I stutter when I speak. Some mornings I want to leave my head the way I leave my shoes on the floor when I go to sleep – leave that resonant ball on the floor and lie down on the air, almost at the top of the wall in the alleyway, but without touching it, and look at the stars without the blackness of night, without music, see only with the low drumbeat of my own heart. I regret wanting to learn to read and write. My mother tires of answering my questions and leaves me alone in my encounters with those shapes, those words, with the anxiety of finding out what they are, how they sound, and how I can write them.

I learn with pain, because I must ask my mother and brace myself for a scolding when I ask her why writing must go from left to right on all the lines, and why the head of the letter "p" always points to the right, while the "q" and the "d" have their head and belly to the left. I must compare what I write with the primer and remember every minute what these rules are.

I'm crying, without realizing it, as I make this effort. The letters on the notebook page bleed blue on contact with my tears. It's very hard to write with my right hand. The pages of the primer laugh with their whiteness that's like teeth, and send me their terrifying images, like ships without an ocean, wings without birds, mouths without faces, and messages without images that I hear in my head: "Nené loves mama, mama loves Olalla, I love my mama." These are wells into which I sink my glance and that cause me anguish, like the picture of a child chained to a rock, surrounded by a stormy sea, which I find in my brother's more advanced reader. They scare me like bodyless feet walking over a desert of snails, with the sea above instead of the sky falling in an indigo-blue rain.

I hear myself screaming at night.

I wake up to hear myself better, to know that the night welcomes my cries and hides them from view in a box of stars.

ONE MORNING, AT LAST, I grab the pages with funnies in the newspaper and they open up for me. They are no longer mysterious images and symbols. I know what they say, there is no mystery. An extraordinary exaltation possesses me, raising me, in my imagination, a few feet off the bed on which I am lying, reading them. With the force and brilliance of lightning, the future opens to me. This moment is of paramount importance and its radiance fills the entire room. I throw the funnies to the floor and run to my brother's table in search of his school books. I examine them. Every single book is open to me now, except for one: arithmetic, because it has numbers.

How do you read numbers? What are they? I take the arithmetic book and sit at the dining room table to start over, trying to read the numbers, which, although they are not letters, are supposed to paint pictures.

My mother doesn't believe what she's seeing.

"What's this? Are you going to start studying again?" she asks me, exasperated.

"What are these weird letters called?" I ask, picking up my pencil and opening my notebook. My mother leaves without answering me, waving her arms to say I'm hopeless. As I try to understand the numbers by myself, life becomes like taking a purgative. I open my mouth and let life fill my tongue with repulsive heat and thick vomit. That ardor, that call in the form of a song behind the furniture that the books had made me integrate into my being, has disappeared. Life: days followed by other days, and nights running over them. I put my head over the sink to refresh it under the open tap, to let myself go with that water, away from the thorns of beings and images that have fallen on me like daggers.

SOME OF THOSE MORNINGS, I play with dreams, even if they burn. I build clothes, chairs, mirrors for myself, devouring my being at the same time, disappearing in the river that bursts out of my eyes and that separates me from my crib, turning my mattress into a puddle, a liquid tomb.

I don't know what I'm saying, or what I think. I raise my hands to the sky, calling to the nightingales, to test if they will come to me through the tube built by my sight, through my fingers making leaves in the light.

The birds are gone and so is the sky. Just a blue patch. Just a wall.

Just a small body abandoned among things and people.

I bang my forehead against the wall that had been the frame of my world, to shatter that ball of sounds that was beginning to reverberate in my mind and that I can't stop. I crush it with my fist to keep it from moving, so that it doesn't write symbols that others may have inside their heads but that I don't know, to stop it. The shapes and colors that surround me haunt me even in my dreams.

I've learned how to add numbers to other numbers, how to take away numbers from other numbers, and how to repeat them. This seems absurd to me. I know that a number is something closed, absolute, and cannot be transformed in any way, but I continue to entertain myself with these rules of addition, subtraction, and multiplication that my mother, finally, has taught me. I am about to start learning division when my mother hides the arithmetic book from me, takes me by the hand, pulls me out into the hallway, and sends me out to play.

Beside myself with rage because I am always being sent out to play, I run down the alley and cross the street without looking both ways, disobeying my mother for the first time.

Cusita, the little girl who lives in the house on the other side of the street, and with whom I often sit on the low branches of the leafy poplar in front of her house, is now sitting on the bench swing on her porch. Her black hair falls on her starched pink dress covered in flounces, like the ones I wear in the afternoon. Cusita slowly moves the wooden porch swing, I stop it, and join her on the bench.

"I want to be free," I declare, starting the swing moving again. I know she doesn't understand because she is younger than I am and still can't talk. Cusita looks at me with her sparkly black eyes, as if trying to guess what I'm talking about. "I want to be free of my mother – free of numbers and letters," I stress, defying her incomprehension.

Suddenly I can't stand that expressionless face, which seems to say: "That's how things are, there's no possible solution. That's life."

I want to smack that face, those eyes that are so brown they look black, that white skin, that soft skin never touched by the dagger of doubt.

I also want to strike at life, at meaningless phrases, at that dimension that has no words and has no answers.

I would like to do a lot of things, but I don't leave my seat on the swing.

Cusita stops the swing, stands up, trips as she steps down, falls on the porch's tile floor, and starts crying. I get off the swing and help her up. Cusita's mother runs out to the porch, takes her daughter by the hand, and brushes off the dirt her dress has picked up.

The girl stops crying.

The mother looks at me accusingly, as if I had pushed her.

"This happened because I left you alone on the porch!" she exclaims, furious. I turn my back on the woman, walk to the sidewalk, and run across the street again without looking, because now, for sure, I can't go back to those days of obeying rules.

"Where are you coming from, panting like that?" asks my mother emerging in the alleyway.

"From playing on Cusita's bench swing," I answer.

JULIA'S SILK SLIPS – Julia is Eduardito's mother – salmon, pink, green, and light blue, cover the king-size bed of our rich neighbors. Ubaldina, their maid, has just ironed them and folds them carefully, then puts them away in the bedroom wardrobe, while Julia and I watch her.

"What a lot of slips! My mom only has one!" I exclaim. Julia and Ubaldina laugh. Have I said something comical?

The maid looks at me with an expression of contempt. The mother covers her mouth with her hand while she laughs, as if she's ashamed to show her teeth.

What could possibly be wrong with having only one slip?

Full of shame, I escape to the dining room. The crystal fruit bowl is overflowing with intensely yellow bananas that have a few black spots, at exactly the point of ripeness that I like. Eduardito, in the dining room on the floor playing jacks by himself, gets up and yanks on my romper, jumping up and down because he wants me to play with him. I look at him the way his maid looked at me. He's ridiculous, so much smaller than I am though he's the same age, jumping and aerating his pee-soaked pants made of embroidered white cotton and attached by mother-of-pearl buttons to his matching nightie that is covered with drool.

"Will it upset you if I take your bananas?" I ask, knowing that he still doesn't know how to talk very well. "Since you haven't answered, I guess it won't bother you," I say, picking up the bunch of bananas.

Eduardito jumps up and down more emphatically as he watches me head for the door with his bananas.

"Robber girl! Robber girl!" he yells, not knowing what else to say.

"You shouldn't say that because you didn't tell me not to take them!" I answer, leaning over the boy, who yanks my braids with both hands, whining. I pass the bunch of bananas to my left hand, and with my right scratch his face. He lets go with a squeal as I escape to my house and decide never to play with him again.

"I TELL YOU, FLORA, you need to do something about your daughter. If she continues like this, she'll turn into a criminal, a gunslinger, a Dillinger. She won't respect other people's property, let alone their lives," Julia prophesies, sitting in the rocking chair of our living room, with her flowered skirt tucked under her thick thighs, making them look like hamburger wrapped in paper.

Julia is a fan of violent gunslinger movies, and, from time to time, she and my mother discuss the heinous crimes published in the red chronicle of newspapers and weekly magazines.

"Look, Julia, I beg your pardon a thousand times over," says my mother, distracted, smoking her cigarette, coping with the storm. "This girl – though she's taller and more advanced in her mental development – she's the same age as your son. She had no idea what she was doing."

"She might be the same age as Eduardito, but she talks like an adult. She should be able to distinguish between Good and Evil. This was armed robbery!"

Eduardito's mother insists that justice must be done. Her face is theatrical, she opens her eyes wide, shakes her head, pronounces the words with comic exactitude.

"She is a long way from being a child. She's like a grownup, she knows very well the difference between right and wrong, she knows the nuances, what's fair or unfair."

This is how Julia informs my mother, with pain in her heart, that she has brought a criminal into the world: me.

"Flora, it's not that I want to get involved in what isn't my business, but I think this girl already has the maturity to be in school. She needs discipline. She should go to a convent school where nuns can teach her good manners, religion, and, above all, the fear of God."

I run out of the house without waiting to hear my mother's response.

At the end of the hallway, I find my neighbor Elena, who's two years older than I am, sitting in her little rocking chair in front of the open door to her apartment, rocking her doll.

The girl's brown hair, cut in a page boy like Prince Valiant in the comics, frames her big, gray eyes in her round, pale face. Her apartment smells like floor wax and frying lard.

"Sleep, little baby, sleep, little baby," she sings sweetly to her doll.

"Dolls can't sleep because they're not people," I inform her, sitting down next to her on the floor. Elena sets her doll to one side and looks at me in amazement, as if I have violated some sacred commandment, the tacit agreement to pretend that dolls are babies. Then she stops rocking in her little mahogany rocking chair with woven wicker seat.

"They can't sleep because they're not alive," I insist.

"She sleeps because I tell her to. Right, baby?" she asks the doll, much to my amazement and exasperation.

We decide to move on to a less contentious subject, almost in unison.

"Do you want to see the ball I made with the metal paper from some chocolates? I made it boiling the paper in water. At the bodega they give you twenty candies wrapped with a postcard of The Phantom for each ball you turn in," Elena informs me.

"Why is that?"

"That's because of the war."

I still don't get it.

"Because there's this war, they need metal balls to throw at the enemy soldiers, and that's how they kill them. Then, because they're throwing the balls away, they run out of them, so they must get them wherever they can."

Elena moves her Prince Valiant page boy back and forth and starts rocking her doll again.

"The war? What war, you?"

I am dumbfounded. Nobody has told me anything about a war.

"*The* war, stupid. People who go *pow, pow*. They have weapons, I've seen them in the newspaper and in the movies, machines with a very long beak that throw out smoke. This is how they kill each another, they throw smoke and balls at one another. My father says the war might even come here. It's a *world* war."

"*World*, you?"

"Yes, the Earth, the world. They start a war and bring it from one side to the other. It doesn't stay in one place." The girl looks up at the sky like she's fed up with my stupidity. "Look," she says, showing me one of her plump little fingers, where she's wearing a silver ring with a tiny skull made of plastic.

"So, what's that?" I say, perplexed.

"It's The Phantom's ring. I won it last week with a premium postcard," she says, rocking her doll again. She's five years old, for me a very advanced age. She knows more than I do. She rocks her doll, now, with the authority of someone who knows about the war, about the world, about the metal balls people use to kill each other, and about The Phantom.

THE NEXT DAY, my mother wakes up worried about Eduardito's mother's visit. I realize this because she looks at me strangely and tells me to get ready to go out.

Is she going to take me to the doctor to make sure I don't turn into a gunslinger? I get dressed, and after she serves me and my brother breakfast at the dinner table, my mother shuts herself in the bedroom with my father.

I open the door and walk in, but my mother throws me out, upset.

"I need to talk alone with your father. You can't be here," she says, her face disjointed and her eyes jumping around nervously.

I decide to eavesdrop through the door.

Meanwhile, I drink my glass of milk. My brother looks at me, indifferent, so I assume he won't tell on me to my parents.

It seems what they are talking about is something related to me, that I am their problem. What have I done? What's wrong, I wonder.

My mother's voice sounds agitated. Her tone is sharp and hurtful.

"The child attacked Cusita and Eduardito! But the worst part is that she's taught herself to read and write, and now she's starting arithmetic! All by herself sitting there, at the table! It gives me the shivers! Really, it scares me to death! It's just not normal. Nobody believes me when I tell them what this girl can do, they think I'm making things up because she is my daughter. She asks me questions. She tells me things I've never heard. I don't know where she gets this stuff. Do you think I should take her to the doctor right away?"

My father replies in a tired voice: "She's a naughty girl, with a lot of energy, a total demon. Let her do whatever she wants."

"These things are not normal!" my mother, beside herself, exclaims. "We must take her to a doctor! She could have a brain tumor, maybe she needs a shot, they should give her a physical. She isn't even four yet, and she's teaching herself everything! I just answer her questions. In fact, I stopped answering, and she got used to figuring it all out on her own." She catches her breath, then adds: "All this, at an age that other kids are learning to walk and talk!"

My father paces back and forth across the bedroom. I hear the taps on his new shoes crisply hitting the tiles.

"You are not taking her to any doctor," my father patiently contradicts her. "If she wants to study, let her. What could possibly be wrong with that?"

"It's monstrous. It's a crazy person thing. It makes me tremble. We need to put her in school, get her out of here, so I needn't see her sitting there writing and doing bookkeeping. She's going to drive me crazy!"

"Look, it's time you stopped all this hysteria. You might as well put her in school if you're going to react like that. But which one? She isn't old enough to enter any of them. You must be five for kindergarten."

"I'll take her to a pre-kindergarten. At least there, they will keep her busy. She must realize that children her age behave differently. She can't just learn how to talk, read, and write as if it were easy. It takes a lot of work. She needs teachers. She can't learn just like it's no big deal. This girl is not going to respect the laws of the country when she grows up. She must realize that she is going to have to learn how to talk all over again. That there's a normal process of development. She must forget and learn all over again. Otherwise, she'll end up a phenomenon, a monster they'll exhibit in the circus. I've visited the pre-kindergarten teachers. There she'll learn how to play. I'm going to take her right now, this morning, this very instant!"

My mother barges out of the bedroom and almost breaks my face when she flings the door open, but I jump back in time.

My father stays in the bedroom adjusting his bright red knit tie, my favorite, and then combs his hair with a bone comb that he keeps in his pocket. In the living room, Septimio, who has finished his breakfast in underpants and T-shirt, quickly puts on his school uniform – khaki slacks and white shirt – and knots his black tie.

My heart pounds in my chest as I try to grasp what I've done wrong.

"Come, my little girl. I'm going to take you to a place where they'll treat you well. They'll teach you how to play with kids your age. They are good people." She speaks to me in her velvety tone, looking at me from above, as if from a trampoline.

I place the empty glass of milk on the table and try to get a grip on my imagination. The walls are throbbing like my eyelids. My cradle, wrapped in the early morning light coming through the window, is an animal covered in pink fur.

The stars that have no night, under the bed, twinkle and disintegrate into sparks and sounds, as if they're escaping from a punctured balloon and fleeing into the universe.

My brother smirks at me as we close the door to the house.

Once outside, my mother takes me by the hand. We cross streets and hurry along sidewalks. I want to think that it's the houses running dizzyingly, while we stand still on the sidewalk.

At length we arrive at a house surrounded by almond trees with fleshy leaves and pink flowers that have golden pistils like tiny parasols full of iridescent dust. I want to flow into the almond trees and hide inside their half-open fruit like reddish wounds, fall asleep in their solemn perfume, disappear in their iron-colored wrinkled bark.

I wish to live forever in those five raving pink petals of the almond blossoms.

I long to run across the ground, over the multiple tentacles of their roots, over their red-stained pods that smell of beets.

I need to fold my arm over my eyes and go to sleep.

We get to a room where there are children my age, or at least that's what the teachers tell us, but they're all littler than me.

I sit on the floor. I have a play dress on and don't feel the floor transmitting its icy electricity as when I only wear underpants.

My shoes bother me by not letting my feet touch the tiles.

The bow of my dress is tied too tight.

The teachers look at me from an immense height.

They turn their big faces down towards me, from those clouds. They look at me and laugh.

"Now, little girl, take these little blocks here in the corner and stack them on top of each other. See? Like so, one on top of the other. Each block has a letter on it, A, B, C, and a picture of an animal, and you put them on top of each other."

They laugh up there in the firmament, these goddesses uttering words full of honey and fake music. They nail me to the ground, they create pain in my heart with their A, B, C blocks, submerging me in the nullity of floor tiles and their own fear. Up there, their eyes shine like the outer skin of the scorpion reflecting the fire.

I pick up the wooden cubes with letters and drawings of animals in different colors: pink, blue, yellow. They want me to put them one on top of the other. So: cubes on cubes, circles within other circles, balls within other balls. The universe? These figures floating up there near the roof want me to re-build the universe, re-create my house, my family, myself, with these blocks.

Again, round wheels spinning with music and their rings that come unstuck and fly off to form multiple combinations that drive one insane.

There they are, still stuck to the ceiling, like an umbrella of vipers over my head, spitting out their words in a stupid tone between their silly laughs. And next to me, children play with the blocks, mixing letters meaninglessly with animals, colors, and shapes, not blinking, not blowing their noses, drooling, filling the world with saliva and "da, da, da."

Terrified, I jump up and run to the window, climb on a stool, and cling to the bars of the outside grille. I hear my desperate screams, my agony translated into sounds launching into space, flying across the air, and reaching my mother, who's walking placidly down the sidewalk that takes her to my house, to my crib, and to my bag of deflated stars under my mattress.

My mother, whom I can see tiny in the distance, turns around as if my cry is a hook that's caught her, a lasso that's turned her around. She follows the rope of my cry to its origin, and takes me out of that school, out of that abyss of cubic universes and tiny drooling children.

MANY STAPLES, OUR BASIC NECESSITIES, have been rationed owing to the war, because the island is part of the Allies and sends soldiers and victuals to Europe. A neighbor rushes to our apartment and tells my mother that the yellow laundry soap we use has arrived at a bodega she knows. Only one "loaf" five inches long is allotted per customer.

My mother takes me by the hand and we walk what seems an endless distance, but which is just three short blocks. My feet are too small to walk that far, but I don't complain because I know my mother needs soap to wash our clothes. I often see her leaning over the patio laundry basin, rubbing the bar of soap over my brother's khaki pants. The sweat runs down her face and her hands turn red, filled with sores from scrubbing his clothes so hard against the shiny cement ridges of the basin.

When we arrive at the bodega, not my father's friend Curro's that's nearby, a long line of people fills up the sidewalk where there's no shade, and my mother loses heart. I ask her for money and tell her not to worry, I will solve the problem. I walk to the front of the line and, standing on tiptoes so the counter doesn't hide me, say to the storekeeper, "My mom's the lady in blue at the end. She can't stand in line because she's so sick. Give me two pieces of yellow soap, one for her and one for me, because I also wash clothes in my house."

The women in line who hear this burst out laughing. The *bodeguero* also laughs, takes a big knife and cuts two large pieces of a long loaf of yellow soap that smells so rich, I want to eat it. "Take it, little girl, and don't work so hard," he jokes. I pay, very serious, and run to where my mother is. I proudly hand her the change and the two big pieces of soap.

THE PROBLEMS I CAUSE my mother and the neighbors continue. This causes my mother to take me to a school that Eduardito's mother has recommended. At the entrance to the school, there's a picture of a woman dressed in blue and white, with her heart outside of her body and a yellow light shining from the heart. The woman is grabbing this heart like an orange with her thin, sharp, very pretty fingers. Her oval, almost-transparent face is lit up by her clear blue eyes that roll upwards and almost disappear under her upper eyelids.

My nose reveals that we are in a real school: it smells like my brother's books, and erasers, and new notebooks. My mother takes my hand and we enter the world called School. To be precise, we're in the School of the Sacred Heart of Mary, as the image at the entrance proclaims. I am to enter first grade as an auditor, thanks to Julia's recommendation. My mother takes a seat in a rocking chair in the reception room, to talk to a woman wrapped in black veils who is sitting in another rocking chair. My mother says this woman is a nun, a religious person dedicated to Christ.

"Please make sure she's always doing something. Treat her just like the rest," my mother says to her about me.

After a pause, she adds, winking and lighting a cigarette: "Because she's ready to go into first grade." The nun, who's dressed like the woman in the picture at the entrance but in black, with a starched white breastplate and a silver pin with the image of a heart crowned with thorns, laughs heartily at some joke I don't understand. Her eyes become slits behind lenses mounted in gold metal.

"You are happy," sighs my mother, exhaling. "We outside are fighting against the world."

The nun's face contracts in an expression of displeasure, not necessarily because she's bothered by cigarette smoke.

Then she smiles, showing her own yellow teeth.

"Why yes, our mission is teaching. Our life is one of great discipline. However, we are happy because we strive to serve our Lord."

I haven't seen any men, but I think this "lord" must be the school's principal, whom they respect a lot.

The heat of this room violently enters the black cloth that covers up the nun's body: I smell the sour sweat it exudes. The face of the Mother Superior is lost in the voluminous veil fastened to her breastplate with pins finished in black heads. The top of her breastplate is like a starched white frame, which goes "crack" with each movement of her head.

Only her face and hands are evidence that there is a human being in there.

"Imagine, Mother, this child already reads and writes!" my mother announces with pride and contempt at the same time, igniting another cigarette and shooting a new gust of smoke up to the ceiling. She shakes her head in a mundane gesture, showing her secular freedom in the face of religious slavery.

"So, you can read and write already? You little angel!" The nun smiles anew, looking at me with eyes covered in a veneer of pedagogical goodness under which a deeper, supreme boredom is visible. I hear in my head a voice that says, *Yet another monster! And yet, another ten pesos a month...*

Out loud, she says, "We'll give you special attention, as you're so young in age."

Turning to my mother, she says, "Here the girl will feel at home."

"Yes, I know she will be happy here, among you holy women who are completely dedicated to religion and good manners. You don't even smoke!" She laughs theatrically and puts out her cigarette in the amber glass ashtray.

"Why yes, our life is like that. Total dedication," the nun confirms.

5

RELIGION AND LOGIC

IN FRONT OF THE SCHOOL'S DOOR, I remember yesterday's dialogue between my mother and the Mother Superior, but still have no idea where I fit in, what my role is, what I'm supposed to say or do. The entrance hall, with its windows giving onto a garden full of bougainvillea and roses, quietly refutes what was said then.

The sun could shine on those two women and transform that farce of words into placid sounds on which girls might walk without injuring their feet, without bleeding. The sun could cover those heads and fill those bodies with light, without cigarettes, without religious habits, without hearts dripping blood.

"Hail, Mary," says a girl in front of me as she enters the classroom. She's much taller than I am, and the long white socks of the school uniform reveal well-turned legs.

"Full of grace," replies another girl. This is how everyone walks into the classroom, in a line, saying things about this Mary I don't know and whose pierced heart seems to be so important in this school.

I'm having to give a lot of thought to what the difference is between Mary's heart and everyone else's, since my mother has told me that all hearts have the same job: they pump blood. Maybe Mary's does something extra, or is bigger, or must be impaled with daggers to beat.

Once we are all seated at desks, it becomes my turn to talk about Mary. All the girls look at me, concerned and a little scornful that I don't know what to say about her. I push back in the huge desk that I've had to climb into by jumping. The tips of my black shoes are straight in front of me, since my legs not only don't reach the ground, they barely reach the edge of the desk's seat.

"Not her," says Mother Superior. "She's the new girl I told you about. You know," she says, winking the way my mother did, "the new pupil."

"Blessed art thou amongst all women," says the girl behind me.

"And blessed is the fruit of thy womb, Jesus," continues another in front.

45

What a strange thing! Mary had a fruit in her womb? A banana in the belly? A mango? And why was this fruit blessed? Until now I had thought that fruits grew on trees and had nothing special about them; they weren't *sacred*. I had read this in one of my brother's books that talked about how fruit ripened on branches. Now I know, although I have a headache because it makes no sense, that we can have fruit in our belly.

THE FIRST DAY GOES BY LIKE THIS: talking about Mary. Meanwhile, the rest of the girls learn to read and write. I have my notebook and a pencil, and I write the letters that they write on the blackboard. They never call on me to write, luckily, because I'd need to climb on top of a stool to reach the blackboard, and then I'd be the target of the stares of those big girls who must bow their heads to look at me when we stand up.

When the bell rings, I know class is over. I feel a twinge of pain to be parted from this group with whom I can write and read and not be sent outside to play. The girls stand up and yet again repeat the story of Mary. Mary must have been the school's founder, or maybe a nice old lady whom the girls love very much. Outside, I catch up with the nun teacher, tugging on her habit.

"Who is this 'Mary'?"

"Ah! Mary is the Blessed Virgin. The mother of God."

"The mother of God!" I shout, dumbfounded.

"Yes, of the Creator of the Universe."

"Oh, of course."

Then, this Mary must be important, if she's the mother of the creator of the balls and circles. That's why they talk about her so much. But who's the father? This is what I'm wondering as I go outside and see my mother's head among the parents waiting at the entrance of the school.

My mother smiles and waves with her cigarette, fanning the smoke between her fingers.

"What did they teach you, my little girl?" she asks as I approach.

"Who is the father of God?"

She looks at me surprised, as if she were saying inside her head, "Is *that* what you were taught in school?" She squeezes my hand, and we walk on, leaving behind houses with porches, fences, gardens full of bougainvillea, roses, oleanders.

"God has no father," she says, tossing her cigarette on a lawn. Extinguishing itself, the butt lets out a faint squeal. The lawn's been watered and some drops still roll down the blades of grass to the soil. The wet imprint of the hose meanders on the sidewalk.

"Then how does he have a mother?"

"He doesn't have a mother either."

I am getting irritated with these evasions.

"The nun said Mary is the mother of God."

"Don't say 'nun,' girl, say 'mother.' Mary is the mother of Jesus Christ."

"And who's Jesus Christ?" I press her on this because I know she wants to talk about something else, light her next cigarette, go to the bodega to buy condensed milk. Anything but answer.

"Jesus Christ is the son of God."

"That makes Mary the wife of God."

"No, my little daughter, Mary is not the wife of God, but of Saint Joseph. Jesus Christ is the son of God, but God is three distinct persons and the one true God. Jesus Christ is the second person. God is the first."

Either I'm being tricked, or something isn't working right in my head.

"And who is this third person?"

"The Holy Spirit. A pigeon."

"What do you mean, a *pigeon*? How can he be a *pigeon*?" I cry, outraged at this absurdity.

"Hush, girl! A *dove*. That's one of the mysteries of religion," she scolds, with great solemnity.

We walk by Curro's butcher-bodega. Curro is a burly man who looks like Alley Oop from the Sunday funnies. On the sidewalk, Curro has set up a long wooden table, surrounded by several chairs covered in cowhides that still have their hair. Curro closes early some days to play dominoes in his undershirt with a bunch of friends, who all have ruddy faces and puffy cheeks. They all drink beer. Once they dump the dominoes, white with black dots, on the table, and mix them up noisily, they line them up in rows in front of themselves, protecting them with their hands.

The air smells of blood and guts.

"Let Augusto know we're waiting for him to play. Get him to come around," Curro bellows at my mother. He speaks in a weird way, as if it hurts to talk, like he has a sore throat.

"Curro's from Spain," my mother says. "That's how Spaniards talk."

Later, when I go to bed, it's hard for me to fall asleep because I can't forget the pigeon thing and I know I'm not allowed to ask questions about this topic. My mother must sing me to sleep with this simple song:

> *Sleep, while I cradle you,*
> *The spell of this song*
> *Will make the night pass.*

I DREAM THAT MY FATHER and I are walking along First Avenue. At the empty lot on the corner, a crowd has gathered. As we get closer, we see that my mother has been crucified in the center of the field. My mother is dying and her face is full of great pain and anguish.

47

Crying out loud, I command my father, "We must get her down from there!"

My father looks at me surprised, but also a little annoyed. "No, we do not need to get her down from there. That's how it is, that's how it must be. We must move on."

I wake up soaked in sweat.

Again, the moon is shining on my face, and its milky sapphire glow covers the white sheet. I stand up in my crib. Again, the night has been split in two by the "vigil," this horrified waking up from a sound sleep. I think I screamed in my dream; in the distance I hear a child crying that seems to be my echo. Everyday furniture does not exist; the night has devoured it all. The room is filled with lights of different colors, mostly red and yellow, flying back and forth. I hear a lot of people talking. I see things transforming into other things, animals coming out of green, phosphorescent waters. It's only the flora and fauna of night, always the same.

As my eyes adjust to the darkness, I see the pale-faced woman again, looking at me with sad eyes. She's wrapped in a white tunic of thin, vaporous fabric. It makes me so angry to see her looking at me, as if she expects something. This time she does not speak, but moves toward me.

I see her dead eyes, violet, very large. Inside, in her pupils, I see myself, a grown woman, dressed in white tie and tails, lounging next to a big grandfather clock, and staring at my pocket watch at the end of its gold chain.

It's eleven thirty at night. I'm in a very luxurious house, which I know now is in the French style, with large mirrors, elegant chandeliers hanging from the ceiling, walls covered in gold leaf.

A ball is about to start, and the couples arrive, lavishly dressed in *fin de siècle* evening wear, as I now know because I just saw it in the movies. The woman with the violet eyes is dressed in blue satin and sports a diamond necklace. She enters the room on the arm of a man with black hair and a pointed beard, dressed in tails.

"Aren't you coming to the dance?" the woman asks me anxiously. Her eyes reveal unspeakable torment, disguised by pride.

"After midnight, God willing."

That last bit is a joke and an insult, and I laugh out loud. The woman's face falls to pieces and her escort looks at me, smiling cruelly. They enter the room and begin dancing. The string orchestra plays a sweet, sentimental piece. I'm still laughing as I lounge next to the clock.

When it chimes twelve, the guests at the ball disintegrate in the air. I race through luxurious rococo lounges until I reach a courtyard like that of the Petit Trianon, a postcard of which my mother once showed me, saying that was where she wanted to live.

I lie down flat on the floor with my hands behind my head. I feel the stiffness of the coat, the starched bib, the tight, rigid collar uncomfortably rubbing my neck. The full moon, huge and bluish, hits me in the face. I let out a wild cry that carries through all the halls and cuts off the music of the string orchestra that, although the musicians have disappeared, is still audible as a distant, ghostly echo.

The woman is no longer staring at me. Everything is back to normal in my house. The furniture takes on its daytime appearance. The ticking clock with its phosphorescent green numbers is back. I throw myself on the mattress, drenched in sweat. I don't like to wake up my parents, but I can't stand this anymore. I lower the side of my crib and run to the bedroom. I wake up my mother and ask to sleep between her and my father.

"What are you afraid of?" my mother asks.

"Of fear," is all I can think of answering.

ONE BLUE EYE LOOKS AT ME, and the other looks the other way. I'm not sure which eye to look at, or even if both eyes can see me. I notice it more now because she's picked me up and sat me on her lap.

Before, when I was sitting on the floor and looking at her from below, I barely noticed her hump and her unusual way of walking, up and down, as if one leg were shorter than the other. Now, up close, sitting on her lap, I can clearly see her black locks stuck to the greasy, shiny skin of her cheeks, and I distinctly smell her fetid smile.

"This is Aparecida," my mother says, leaving me in her care as she runs an errand, adding softly so the woman can't hear it, "maybe because she's an apparition." Aparecida smiles, showing teeth mounted on top of other teeth.

As soon as my mother is out the door, Aparecida takes a small pair of scissors out of the pocket of her flowered yellow dress, which is a couple of sizes too big for her, and cuts my nails past the quick. I start bleeding. It's extremely painful, but I'm ashamed to cry.

At this very moment, as if she'd had a presentiment that I was in danger, my mother returns, saying: "I forgot to take my wallet to pay for the groceries."

Aparecida looks up, laughs, and gleefully shows my mother my hand, all covered in blood.

A FEW DAYS LATER, in the middle of the night, my mother comes with a candle in her hand. My parents' room, where I'm sleeping, is a blackness without depth or dimensions, and her candle's blinking flame timidly lights it up. She cups her palm around the candle to shield it from the wind, which is wailing in through slits around the door and window, threatening to extinguish the flame.

"The mother of all hurricanes is here," she says in a flat voice, "and the power's out. Your father and brother, when the wind let up a little while ago, went out looking for wooden boards to shore up the doors and windows, and now the wind's picking up again. I just hope this apartment doesn't blow away."

Outside, the wind shrieks. It's gotten biting cold, or, as my father says, "The monkey is whistling." The meteorologist on our battery-powered radio confirms that the hurricane has brought us a Norther. So, to make matters worse, besides a hurricane, we now have a wave of near-freezing cold.

The door to the patio shakes with each violent gust, and I imagine from one moment to the next that it will come flying out of its frame. Water is now flowing in from the patio onto the bedroom floor. My mother sets the candle on the night table as she throws towels on the floor. Once they've soaked up what they can, she wrings them into the aluminum bucket that she uses to mop, and the cycle starts all over again.

I love feeling the force of nature. I don't understand why my mother seems so alarmed and, in the candlelight, almost cadaverous.

As if to explain why she is so horrified, she announces, "Corrugated tin roofs have come loose in the air, like flying guillotines."

Now she adopts her prophetic tone. "If the door doesn't hold, we're lost. We have no basement, and we can't escape in the middle of the hurricane to Bella's, where we'd be safe. I knew it: the end of the world has finally come!"

She sighs and wrings one of the towels over the bucket, which is nearly full. "The radio said the hurricane was not going to hit the Capital. In the early morning, when we were asleep, it turned. We couldn't even nail boards on the doors. That's when I got you out of your crib to lie on the big bed. Water was pouring in through the window and you were going to get wet. Your father and brother went to get boards at Curro's – at the peak of this hell, and at night! I just hope he'll sell them some."

Sitting on the bed, I'm protected. The warmth of the blanket I've wrapped myself in contrasts pleasantly with the cold gusts coming in over the top and under the bottom of the door. The closed blinds are crying inconsolably. The rain lashes at them hard, horizontally, and the window glass that protects them is covered with tiny beads of water. The world is in total disarray, and I feel a peculiar exhilaration.

My father and brother arrive, loaded down with boards, nails, and hammers that Curro has sold them out of friendship, although his butcher-bodega, where he sells just about everything and above which he lives, is closed at night.

My father is soaked from head to toe. Even the improvised boat-hat he's made from a brown paper bag from Curro's is soaked. As he removes it, the water trapped in it pours down his forehead onto his chest.

He and my brother, also sopping wet, set about nailing the boards across the windows. The rattle of the hurricane makes music with the noise of the hammering.

Lit candles are everywhere, long tallow tapers and little votive candles of St. Teresa, which my mother lights every Thursday, the day of the Most Holy.

I'm vexed at not being able to look out the window now, at the height of the hurricane, because my mother told me that when it rains, the bogeyman we call "the cocó with the bicycle" comes out.

In fact, I've seen this cocó person every time it rains: it's a man wearing a black rain cape riding a bike.

My mother, whose aim in inventing the cocó on the bike was to stop me from going out on the street in these dangerous conditions, instead has inspired me to hope for rain just so I can go out and see the cocó.

To my surprise and excitement, the cocó turned out to be fat as often as he was thin, tall as often as short. Also, the colors of his rain cape might be white, black, or yellow, and lastly, the cocó had an extensive collection of bicycles of all colors and styles.

To my great annoyance, my brother tells me that "the cocó on the bicycle" is just pharmacy delivery boys who take medicine and other stuff to people's houses.

When my father triumphantly announces that we have nothing to fear now because all the boards are nailed tight, we hear on the battery radio, since the electricity is still off, that the hurricane has moved on towards the province of Pinar del Río, the westernmost tip of the island. What's left is light rain with a few harmless gusts of wind.

Then my father and brother go to work again, beginning the un-nailing soaking wet, without changing their clothes, muttering their annoyance. My mother heads to the kitchen to make breakfast. Maybe she doesn't want to see their furious frowns as they pull out nails, or listen to their furious howls when they crush their fingers.

Their complaints seem to be directed at the female sex for being, as my mother would say, so wimpy that they can't be counted on to help whenever there's hard labor.

After a few hours, and after we've had breakfast, the rain stops, but the sky still looks threatening.

I go out to see what's happened.

Some houses have been destroyed and others remain intact, but almost all the trees have been uprooted.

The most fragile ones, launched like projectiles, end up embedded in the windshields of cars.

Our street is paved with mud, branches, tree leaves, broken glass.

People emerge slowly from their homes, as if obliged to recover from a serious illness, pick up pieces of the jigsaw puzzle that is the outside world, and try to put them together again.

All this destruction everywhere around me excites me because I don't see it as tragedy, but as renewal. The end of routine and the destroyed houses let me see what people are really like.

My only grief is for my favorite tree, the poplar that grew in front of Cusita's house, where she and I had spent long moments of contemplation under its leafy crown. It's been plucked out of the ground and upended, exposing its red and brown roots. Now, its naked, sad guts try in vain to feed on the wind.

Its whitish-grey trunk, covered in green slashes, rests on the sidewalk, and its strong, proud branches with so few leaves left agonize in the breeze in a death I don't understand. How has something so strong been destroyed by wind? I count this as a personal loss. I had never enjoyed anything as much as climbing up this giant tree and engaging in a dialogue with it that no one, not even myself, really understood.

Near the doorway of her house, Cusita glides back and forth on the porch swing in a daze. I imagine that seeing the poplar separated from the earth and ruined is a painful experience for her. She beckons to me with her hand and I go sit beside her on the swing.

Her brother Henry, who's studying the debris pressed up against their front door, smiles at me. It's as if the storm has cleansed the bad blood of his anger, when he thought I had pushed Cusita and caused her to fall.

THE FIRST DAYS AFTER THE HURRICANE, the routine of our daily life is disrupted. I love getting up in the morning and not knowing what problems we'll need to solve.

For example, there's a shortage of coal for cooking. Because the hurricane has interrupted its distribution, it's a great event when the horse-drawn coal cart stops in front of our house. A tall, muscular man carries the coal on his back in a jute sack and drops it with a loud rumbling sound on the tile floor of our kitchen.

I'm surprised that a white can look Black: his face is completely covered in the coal he delivers.

After a few months, life returns to normal, and we buy coal at Curro's in small quantities, not needing to stockpile.

Also, when night has not yet fallen, the afternoon colors everything with a vibrant violet light that opens my heart and makes me feel the deep heartbeat of existence. I stand on the threshold to watch the colors change on the wall and in the clouds. Also, there is something unusual about the way my father, mother, and brother intersect around the dinner table.

One night, my mother nervously folds the newspaper she's reading at the dinner table as smoke wafts up from her cigarette in the glass ashtray beside her.

"He had to be crazy," she says, picking up her cigarette and drawing on it. "He went to the store every single day – imagine! – to visit this mannequin, to recite poems by Gustavo Adolfo Bécquer to it. Naturally, people stared. He ignored them – then one day he tired of wooing the mannequin and began to insult it, calling it a bad woman who didn't return his love. Can you imagine such a man?"

Then, when there's no response, she adds: "He ended up smashing the store window and demolishing the mannequin with an axe."

My father, sitting in his favorite armchair to study, raises his eyes from *Pedagogical Method*, his fat textbook whose pages smell brand new.

"And this has *what* to do with the price of tomatoes?" he asks, annoyed, making a gesture of irritation with his mouth that twists his mustache.

"I read it in the red chronicle, the crime pages." My mother closes her eyes as she exhales cigarette smoke, her expression dreamy.

"I repeat, what's your point?" says my father, looking directly at her, spreading his feet a little, resting his elbows on his thighs, passing his huge book from one hand to the other.

"It's news. One must make conversation. Yesterday Eduardito's mother told me a creepy, ghastly tale."

She emphasizes these last words by exhaling another breath of smoke, focusing her thoughts and grimacing.

My father's gaze is cold. The snapping sound he makes with his tongue, wiping his teeth and revealing his golden incisor, is like the warning a rattlesnake gives when it shakes its tail.

My brother, playing out a battle with his lead soldiers all over the floor, looks up at his father in fear. I'm standing on the doorsill, holding my breath.

My mother plows on.

"Eduardito's mother told me about this man who dismembered his wife and put her in a suitcase. He went to the bus station to buy a ticket to some city in the Interior. They arrested him on account of the trail of blood his suitcase left along the way."

A pause.

Then: "Can you imagine going on a trip to a provincial city with your wife in bits and pieces?" my mother asks.

"That's hardly news. It's identical to the case of a French criminal called Michel Eyraud, who hid here on the Island after having committed a similar crime in France, except that victim was a man." He gives this incident a little more thought, then adds: "The crime was solved by the famous criminologist Alexander Lacassagne – this is the well-known 'Case of the Trunk Full of Blood.'"

My father gives my mother a skeptical look, as if he suspects her of inventing the news.

Another pause with silence full of threats. "When do you plan to eat?" my father asks after a few moments, in an irritated voice.

"As *always*, as it is Christmas *Eve*, we are going to my sister Bella's."

Then, after yet another pause, she adds: "As *always*, Gustavo, her *husband*, who is an *excellent* chef, will *cook dinner*. As always, we will take the *children*."

"Or have you for*got*ten today is Christmas Eve," my mother finishes, now infuriated.

"Oh, I remember very well. But I can't stay long. I must go to the race track."

"*With what money?*" My mother's eyes explode open, and she seems to have re-entered reality. Sitting at the table, her legs crossed, her bony hands passing over the rubber tablecloth, she's coiled and ready to pounce.

"And after the races, tonight Santa Claus comes! Right, kids?" my father says to us with a great big happy smile.

Septimio, leaving his game with the lead soldiers, turns around, looks at my father, and smiles, relieved at this sudden good humor.

6

CHRISTMAS EVE DINNER

THE DINNER TABLE is rectangular, long, covered by a white tablecloth printed with large red Christmas flowers. Hanging from the ceiling and lighting up the table, there's a colorful stained-glass lamp with violet and deep purple grapes set in green leaves. Its band of velvet with wine-red fringes has almost completely faded. Aunt Bella, the most beautiful of my mother's four older sisters, was given this Tiffany lamp for her wedding and says she will never trade it for a new one.

My relatives around the table eat roast turkey, guinea hen, barbecued suckling pig that smells delicious and tastes of sour orange and oregano, black beans steaming in a porcelain tureen, and lettuce salad with radishes.

Awaiting the end of dinner in wooden boxes that smell like ships and Spain, the dessert is a variety of delectable imported Spanish almond nougats called Jijona, Yema and Alicante.

When my father stands up to fetch a beer from the kitchen, he makes his chair go "crick-crack."

The window that overlooks the patio is behind my chair, and my view is of the light green corridor that ends at the wall where a small wooden board painted yellow bears the house's vertical silver telephone with its black transmitter and receiver.

Also on this wall, next to this phone, a large poster shows a life-size Black man and a Spaniard wearing a beret and smoking a cigar, both men slouching against a thin crescent moon made of a piece of cardboard painted silver.

This is a relic of the 1920s, when Gustavo, Bella's husband, brought radio to the Island and began broadcasting his sitcom called *La Pitusa*, which became a smash hit.

Those were palmy years for our family. Bella's fortune was made when she married Gustavo who, in blackface, played the Black man depicted in the poster, the Al Jolson of the Island.

The show ran for years and years, and made piles of money.

One day, Bella, at the time more beautiful, richer, and more whistled at than any other woman on the Island, came home after hearing the great tenor Caruso sing the role of Radamès in an opera called *Aïda* at the National Theatre, threw off with a violent, theatrical gesture a lace shawl she'd bought in Paris, and declared: "I'm never setting foot outside this house again!"

Now, these many years later, Bella is presiding at one end of the dinner table. I want to understand, from this woman sitting here in front of me, the woman of the anecdotes who made the decision, which nobody could fathom, of never going outside her house again. Heavy, cheeks dabbed with rouge, laughing with half her teeth missing and the rest, stained yellow by nicotine and red by lipstick, Bella wears voluminous house pajamas, as she calls them, made of dark blue velvet with vermilion ornaments.

She's laughing heartily at a joke told by Bartolo, the widower of Aunt Dora, her older sister and the eldest of my mother's five siblings. Dora died young, of tuberculosis. She and Bartolo had Las Niñitas, the Little Girls, all three now in their twenties. Bella's laughter agitates her long black braids that are shot through with white and gray hairs and tied with red bows. Whenever she laughs, it makes me want to laugh.

Isabel, my mother's most forceful sister, is not present at this meal because she does not participate in family gatherings. "Isabel never leaves her castle in the Vedado to avoid exposing herself to the Island rabble," Emilio maliciously comments. Emilio and his wife, my Aunt Chavela, are the parents of my rabble-rousing cousins Emilito and Barbara.

My father returns from the kitchen with a bottle of beer, sits at my mother's left, across from me, and pours the liquid into his empty glass with utmost care and concentration. He's wearing a white shirt without a tie. His cheeks are redder and he laughs more than usual. His gestures are circular and expansive, as if to break the boundaries that these people, these in-laws whom he detests, seem to impose on him.

My brother, on my right side, plays with his fork, trying to gouge stripes in the tablecloth. He's still angry because *he's* had to wear a tie. Maybe it makes him feel like he's in costume.

My mother, facing right, with her crossed arms resting on the edge of the table and a little hunched over, is talking to her niece Cleo, the eldest of the Little Girls, sitting next to her.

"Imagine what a spectacle! I sent her home instantly!" my mother exclaims, raising her voice, and laughing and blinking a lot.

Flapping her long, skinny hands nervously, she continues the story.

"Picture this: I walk in from the street and catch her cutting off the girl's fingertips instead of her fingernails! The poor girl's hands covered in blood, dripping to the ground like strawberry jelly, like tomato sauce."

She shudders.

"The poor child! So brave – she didn't even cry! How was I to know this maid would do that?"

She pauses, as if giving herself time to consider what she's going to say, then continues: "She wasn't normal, I could see that, but not *that* abnormal! I mean, hunchbacks and cross-eyed persons aren't necessarily *crazy*!"

My father touches my mother with his elbow. "Would you like some turkey?" he asks, maybe to shut her up.

"Um, yes, no. I don't know. Serve yourself," my mother says, turning to Cleo. "I should *never* have left her alone with the child. She might have killed her."

Cleo, with her oval face and brown eyes with blue dark circles, flutters her upper lip like a candle and laughs, revealing her dark red, almost brown gums and long, horse-like teeth. Her heart-shaped mouth impresses me.

Cleo and her younger sisters Nadia and Chiquitina are always referred to as Las Niñitas, The Little Girls, although they are already in their twenties.

My mother, stroking the tablecloth with her fingers, lowers her eyes. Nadia and Chiquitina, seated to Cleo's left, lean into the table to look at my mother with curiosity, not daring to interrupt her silence.

"This dinner is like something from the court of the Sun King," my mother pronounces, addressing no one in particular, but raising her head regally and smiling, as if recalling that she had lived in the age of Louis XIV. "An Asiatic luxury, a Versailles. To go inside houses like that, even though it's just in movies, is a privilege, because you can touch, I mean really *touch*, that luxury and that life. Revel in it!" She closes her eyes and moves her head gently from side to side. "And Greta Garbo, that personality, without makeup!"

Her gaze is lost at a point in the void, the lines on either side of her mouth becoming more pronounced.

After a bit, she says, "When I like her best is when she works with John Barrymore. He has that profile! But in *sumptuous* scenes, because who wants to see poverty in a movie?"

My father turns towards her and pours some of his beer into her empty glass, taking care that it doesn't overflow.

My mother cuts the slices of turkey on her plate into perfect cubes and then eats them in order of size, starting with the smallest ones.

"In *Anna Karenina*," she carries on, "Garbo couldn't do anything because her role was that of 'good girl' up to the point when she becomes a victim of the passion of love. And though there was something of Russian luxury in the film, it didn't have that French or exotic flair. Now, *Mata Hari* had that, all those oriental idols with lots of arms – and those dances! Greta Garbo, yes, an interesting woman. Like all American women."

My father moves uncomfortably in his chair, and his mustache, uncombed and covered in a thin layer of beer foam, rises when he snorts.

"Greta Garbo is not an American woman," he contradicts her, irritated.

"That's so, Flora," Chiquitina agrees with him in a confidential tone, and adds: "She is a woman from Europe, or someplace around there. They took her to America and gave her perfect teeth so she could do closeups."

My mother seems surprised, but doesn't want to lose her train of thought.

"Imagine, John Barrymore for real, with Greta Garbo for real, living in a Swiss chalet! I see them sitting in front of the fireplace, wearing silk robes embroidered with noble coats of arms, toasting with champagne. And the world outside: photographers pressed up against the windows to take pictures through the half-open blinds, blimps circling in the sky. Inside: a waltz and a toast. It's kind of like the Sun King. Asiatic!"

"You mean John *Gilbert*, not John Barrymore," my father says.

Septimio cleans up his plate and looks at the others with a frown, rhythmically kicking his chair with his foot.

My mother fantasizes on, undeterred. Everyone watches her attentively.

"And then: gypsy violinists come in by the glass door that gives on the private patio that's surrounded by bushes! Greta greets them with princely kindness, then laughs, throwing her head back and showing off her glossy hair in a unique gesture. John Barrymore kisses her passionately à la Rudolph Valentino, with that personality, like the Sheikh's son – and the shine of her hair and the glow of her profile light up the screen!"

My father slaps the table, not hard but firmly. "Greta Garbo and John Barrymore are not lovers, not even in dreams! Also, you are talking about John Gilbert, who's gay and gets married just to promote his films. John Barrymore's a senile drunk who died last year. What does all that have to do with *you*? Here we are, sitting at this table with almost your entire family, the world is at war, there's little to eat, we have barely enough money to feed and clothe our children. The girl, finally, has her first pair of shoes and doesn't need to go around barefoot. And the boy, finally, has a new tie to wear to school and two pairs of khaki slacks. Enough of dreaming about American movies!"

Avoiding looking at my father and mother, Cleo concentrates on her slice of suckling pig and serves herself more salad.

"Is today when Santi Clos comes?" I ask, meaning to relieve the tension in the air, the rigidity that has taken over and almost choked us.

"Possibly," my father scoffs, looking at my mother. "If we're lucky."

Pouring herself red wine in a small brandy snifter, Bella intervenes, laughing: "'In the Possible there's room for everything, except for the Chinaman in the Shirt!' That's what Mother always said after she gave our Chinese laundryman all of Papa's shirts when he died, but the poor man couldn't fit into any of them, Papa was so thin!"

Gustavo, sitting next to her, rolls his eyes behind his glasses and snorts as he eats, his barrel belly pooching over his bent belt. His ruddy, plump cheeks and smiley crows' feet at the corners of his eyes create a genial, friendly impression.

"We must play poker," he says, and keeps on chewing with gusto.

The food we're eating, unheard of in wartime, transports this scene in my imagination through the air, covering it with crystals through which another, different scene, or another angle, is reflected. Seen through those crystals, Bella is at times a gigantic woman, with black braids and beauty marks, riding a horse at full gallop. The Fire Engine Horse, she calls herself, opening her eyes wide to terrify me and my cousins Emilito and Barbara.

Other family members are wax puppets moved by strange mechanisms, skeletons playing cards under the full moon.

After a pause, Emilio says, "This Island is doomed." Emilio has blue eyes, black hair, and a strong jaw. Next to him, Aunt Chavela, her black hair gathered in a bun, her black eyes small and bright as a mouse's, goes on eating with an air of concern, no doubt because they, too, have very little money.

"What do you think, Gustavo? Is this Island not hopeless?"

Emilio's voice reaches Gustavo, forcing him to lift his face out of his plate and look at him while he chews. "Because, think about it, what would our Christmas Eve be, if Bartolo hadn't got all this thanks to his wealthy family buying it on the black market?"

There ensues dead silence as everyone tries to ignore this mention of the black market, prohibited by law.

Bartolo, sitting at the other end of the table, makes comedic gestures of the elegant dandy, blowing on his fingernails and buffing them on his shirt to give them shine. Bartolo has a roly-poly face, very white with healthy, rosy cheeks, and he wears a fine gray three-piece suit – but no tie.

Emilio fans the tablecloth with his hand, takes a sip of beer, and sets the glass on the table a little too forcefully. The beer jumps out of the glass and falls on the tablecloth, forming a wet half-moon. His watery, faded blue eyes contrast with the reddish edges of his eyelids.

"If not for Bartolo, we'd be eating fricassee of shoe," he insists.

Bartolo laughs and picks up a thigh of guinea hen in his fingers like a king, and nibbles at it daintily. After a few seconds, he sets the thigh down on his plate and makes an operatic gesture with his eyes and hands, as if expecting applause for creating the food.

"This Island has no remedy, I repeat. We've declared war on Italy, Japan, Germany. We, who are this big!" Emilio continues, separating his forefinger and thumb by an inch of emptiness. "Who are we to declare war on anyone? And then, the rationing of goods! There's nothing! Everything goes to the Allied troops!"

Bartolo squints at Emilio, a spark of irony shining in his eyes. He removes his suit coat and, turning, carefully hangs it on the back of his chair. He unbuttons his vest and rolls up his shirt sleeves, ready to play poker. My father calmly gets up, goes to the kitchen, and comes back with a bottle of beer in his hand.

"'It is difficulties that show men what they are,'" my father quotes in a joking tone as he sits down again. My father's words create a void in the center of the table, through which all the guests gradually escape.

Suddenly everything is on another plane. There's another quality in the air.

Emilio, pressing against the back of his chair, feels humiliated by my father's levity.

"That's not true," Emilio mutters between his teeth, gripping his fork.

"Don't tell me, tell Epictetus. I didn't say that, Epictetus did," my father replies flippantly. He finishes off his beer, sets the bottle on the table, and looks steadily at my mother. "I'm off now, or I'll be late for the races," he says, standing up and throwing his napkin on the tablecloth. He puts on the white jacket hanging on the back of his chair, says goodbye with his hand to all the diners, and is swallowed up by the hallway to the door.

"*Going to the track on Christmas Eve*? When Batista's left me unemployed and we have no money?" The questions arise like a howl from my mother's throat, float over the dinner table like a giant jellyfish, and disappear the way smoke blows away or water evaporates.

I already knew that my father was going to the horses and my mother wasn't working, but that President Batista fired her is news to me.

Aunt Chavela, ignoring my mother, gets up to carry her plate to the kitchen. The creaking of her chair divides these minutes into an unreal interval. Bella follows her, collecting some glasses from the table, and the rest of the guests get up to take their dirty dishes to deposit in the sink.

Barbara and Emilito, until now quiet and almost invisible, have finished eating the dessert nougats they'd served themselves on their dirty dinner plates, and return to being children, jumping thunderously from their chairs to run around.

Septimio and I sit still at the table, even though we too have finished the nougats we served ourselves on our dinner plates.

A few minutes' lull goes by, and, except for Bella who says she doesn't want dessert, all the relatives return to the table with clean dishes. Emilio hacks off several chunks of the loaf of hard nougat from Alicante by punching it with a big knife and, along with thin slices of the two softer nougats, serves the adults.

My mother, nailed to her chair, her powdered face marked by fine drops of sweat running down her forehead, looks at me.

"Do you see how he treats me?" my mother asks. "Now tell me what to do! Give me a solution!"

She is pounding my head with these words. I hang suspended in this minute and this silence.

"I don't know," I reply, without looking at her.

"Don't tell me you're on his side! What should I do? You always have solutions!"

Cleo, who has been eating Jijona nougat with the greatest of pleasure, looks at my mother, surprised.

She touches my mother's arm and speaks softly, but I can hear perfectly: "Flora, don't you see that she's a three-year-old child in a romper? What possesses you to ask the girl for advice?"

Bella appears, coming from the kitchen. She's lit a cigarette and carries a small ashtray in her other hand. She sits down and ceremoniously sets the ashtray next to herself on the table.

"Who's up for a game of poker?" she asks chirpily, exhaling a cloud of smoke and admiring her cigarette, as if it were a cigar of the mellowest quality.

"Play poker on Christmas Eve?" my mother asks as if scandalized at this pagan suggestion, which is odd, given how un-religious she is.

"Oh, Florita! What are we going to do? Dance? We are all ancient relics. There: las Niñitas, get them to dance," says Bartolo as he wanders off to his room.

The whole family lives here, at Bella and Bartolo's, except for my parents and my aunt Isabel.

And except for my uncle Adolfo, the youngest of the six children and the only male, who lives in the insane asylum.

Bartolo returns with a green felt tablecloth, a round wooden carrier with colorful chips, and two packs of playing cards. He's dancing and singing like Count Danilo in *The Merry Widow*:

> *To Maxim's restaurant at night I always run,*
> *and there with the coquettes await the morning sun!*

Chavela clears the table and spreads the green felt tablecloth. Everything, somehow, is closed, is moving on to another stage. I feel the wings of the next moment slapping at me.

To avoid the emptiness I feel, I jump down from my chair and run out into the patio.

It's already night, the sky teems with stars, and crickets are chirping. The moisture from the afternoon rain is still on the grass and in the porous walls.

From the patio, the dining room framed in the open window is a movie set. The velvet-fringed Tiffany lamp, its reddish light like living blood, the people settling themselves at the table say it could be a gangster scene.

My brother comes outside to pick up some rocks and pitch them at the wall.

"Children! You are *not* to go out in the street!" Chavela shouts at us, aware suddenly that none of us are in the dining room.

On the side of the patio illuminated by the hall light, Barbara is running after Emilito with a baseball bat in her hand.

They are heading for the porch, Emilito screaming and dodging the blows his sister aims at him.

The smell of basil comes in on the breeze.

Up above, the pulsating lights of stars impart a strange sense of silence, of peace. If I stand still, I will float towards those lights like bright dust.

Bartolo and my mother come out to the patio, their arms around each other. My mother has had far too much to drink and can barely stand up.

"I'm going to suffocate the kids with a pillow and set myself on fire!" she vows.

My brother stops throwing stones and looks at me, terrified.

My mother adds, almost screaming: "I'm going to come back as a ghost to torment Augusto and his whole damn family, until each of them dies in slow agony and fear, with no help at hand."

"Stop poisoning yourself with anger, Flora," Bartolo advises my mother.

My mother, reeling and stumbling, sings at the top of her lungs:

> *With what sadness we watch*
> *a love we are losing*
> *a piece of the soul*
> *torn away, unpitying.*

Crying, she leans on her brother-in-law, who looks at her, embarrassed.

7

THE ACCIDENT

SHE'S DRUNK, yet my mother manages to walk home without collapsing in the street, and once we get to the apartment, a block or so away, she locks herself in the bedroom. My brother gets undressed and climbs into the bed in the corner opposite my crib. I throw my romper on the floor, take off my sandals, and lie down in the crib, wearing only my underpants.

Through the window, next to my crib, I look out at the starry December sky. A cool breeze comes in, scented with night-blooming jessamine and gardenias.

Tonight, Santa Claus is supposed to come, and I've been told that if I'm awake, he won't leave me any presents. Also, because this year Santa Claus is dirt poor and will bring whatever he can, I've been told not to ask for a thing, so I didn't. What I really want is The Tree, a small artificial pine with colored balls that Eduardito's family promised to give, once Christmas Eve was past, to the poorest kid on our hallway.

Very early the next morning I wake up to noises in the hallway and I think Santa Claus has arrived with his sleigh pulled by reindeer. I don't hear sleighbells ringing, but maybe this year he doesn't have any because he's poor too and has had to pawn them, like my mother who pawns stuff when she's short of money at the end of the month.

I make myself go back to sleep and don't notice when I lose consciousness.

In the late morning I climb down from my crib to find my brother already playing quietly with the shiny new set of lead soldiers Santa brought him.

My mother, recovered, sort of, from getting drunk last night, hands me a little truck painted yellow and a black doll as big as I am, and informs me that these are my gifts.

Seeing that black face with lips painted red and large gold rings in the ears and red headscarf, I run around the living room screaming in terror, "The Cocó Doll! The Cocó Doll!"

My mother laughs, picks up the doll, and heads for the bathroom.

I follow, curious. She seats the doll on the potty chair, which only I am allowed to use. She says, "Go to the living room for a bit and come back here when I call you." I go to the living room. My brother abandons his toy soldiers, smirks, and runs to the bathroom to find out what my mother is up to with the doll.

After a while, my mother calls me, saying it's all right to come back now.

"Lift the doll from the chair and see what she's done," my mother tells me, smiling. Septimio, next to her, looks at me, trying not to laugh. I lift, even though it scares me, and I see something black in the potty.

"The doll made caca. See, it's like a girl, isn't it?" my mother says to reassure me.

With my hand I pick up the black thing in the potty and show them it's a hunk of coal, then hurl the coal against the bathroom wall and hand the doll to my mother.

"Go trade this doll for Eduardito's tree," I order, furious.

"They gave the tree to Elena because she is poorer than you are," my mother explains gently. I run down the hallway to Elena's apartment and find her sitting in the doorway, switching around the balls on the twigs of the tree, sorting them into red, blue, and green groups.

"Do you like my gift from Santi Clos?" she asks proudly.

I see that I have been told the truth. I don't answer and run to my house to play with the little yellow truck that, now, I like much better than before.

When my mother hands me the doll to get me to play with it, too, I hurl it against the wall.

"She's not a real girl!" I shout, incensed by this lie.

I DREAM OF BLACK FLOWERS that open by making the noise of a gong, then afterwards exhale a column of purple smoke through their pistils. The silver moon, which has scales bordered in blue, hangs cut in slices from the sky. The black sky is broken, and its fragments have been stitched together with red thread. The dark trees, interwoven on the horizon with the yellow nimbus of a city shining behind their crowns, are like a wall of monsters.

My feet walk on ground that's been divided into squares, like a checkerboard. Almost without transition I leave solid ground and sink into greenish-brown bubbling mud, which stretches all the way to the horizon. Sinking deeper and deeper, I move forward, struggling to pull my feet out.

I see myself in a cross-section of the Earth, fighting to get free of the mud that's swallowing me, but it is really doctors in white lab coats who have long nails and diabolical looks, and they are pulling on my feet to drown me.

The desperate struggle intensifies, concentrated on a single point, which at its peak and in a shriek brings me in an instant to consciousness. My sheet is soaked with sweat. I move in the crib. The springs creak.

The night, through the window, seems peaceful. The sky, intensely black, quivers with stars. The moon, huge, lights up the mattress with lavender clarity.

I lift my pillow, and see my tooth still resting underneath.

Septimio told me that if I left it under my pillow, at night a mouse would come and trade it for a peso. I make a hole in the center of the pillow to lay my head.

From the sky, a song falls like rain. I hear it with the ears inside my head, not my outside ears. An accordion, far off. Somebody says something about the circles the night creates and that then disappear on the sharp edges like knives that streets have at their tips. I look at my hand with the moon behind it, illuminating its edges. Against the sun, my hand looks red; against the moon, my hand has a silvery, bluish glow around the edges, but in the center, it's all shadow.

The ticking of the alarm clock in the living room echoes through the house. My parents' snoring intertwines with crickets chirping.

Septimio is silent, and if I cried out in my dream, it didn't wake him. The walls exhale the tropical heat, like a tender warm steamer. The wind comes in waves from the window bringing visions of white, fleshy nocturnal flowers with green stems that drip dew. I breathe deeply. Everything turns into a block, a geometric figure floating in space, made of light and shadow, smells and sounds. I play with my hands to measure that figure, and with my feet I feel its palpitations, as the palate feels a ripe fruit diluting itself in juice.

Numbers and hands of the clock on the sideboard have a greenish, sometimes violet glow.

It's three in the morning. Nobody's awake. The silent corridor holds memories of footsteps and people. If I stare at it long enough, the people who have walked there during the day are reborn, gray as storm clouds, propelled by my gaze, freed from the shadows where time has trapped them.

Yesterday is staged for me again – everything that happened in the hallway, and everything that happened in the apartment.

When I get tired of reviving these images, they vacate the space, but in a few moments, from this apparent emptiness erupt many winged creatures of my size, jumping around in the hallway and from chair to chair inside our living room. Strange vegetation, phosphorescent trees made of human flesh. Lagoons full of aquatic plants, and steaming miasma. I stand up on the mattress. With my eyes wide open, I observe, at times laughing, the dissolution of the room and the hallway into a landscape where the only thing left of the daily world is my cradle, like a yellow island amid a world of mind-blowing visual profusion.

TODAY IS SATURDAY. Every Saturday, a peculiar peace reigns in the house. My brother sits at the dining room table studying, my father reads the newspaper in his armchair in the living room, I cut out paper dolls on the floor, next to the open front door that lets in the morning air.

The refreshing shade felt inside the house contrasts with the hot rays of sun hitting the outer hallway and wall. The smell of disinfectant and vapors that arise from the wet tiles unite in the special, deep feeling of consciousness that is linked, for me, to the word "Saturday."

This Saturday, I'm cutting out dresses that come in a book of paper dolls, that is, flat dolls made of cardboard. I take special care when trimming evening dresses and the small white rectangles that pop out of the clothes to fix them to the flat doll. The most difficult to cut out are hats, because they are very small and have odd shapes. Hats tend to fall off heads, especially in action scenes, like when the doll is a spy for the Allies.

My mother cleans the floor.

She swipes the rag mop across the floor with energetic pendulum movements.

To clean the house, she always wears the same dress, a red-flower print whose white background has turned yellow from so many washes. She wears tennis shoes, which she calls espadrilles. They are gray from use and broken through at the tip, where her big toe pops out. The sole, very worn out, is almost flat and sometimes slips a little on the wet floor.

My father opens and closes the pages of his newspaper, creating sounds of impatience. Septimio disappears behind the book he's reading. He is angry at the books he must study and sometimes raps the table with his pencil's eraser.

My mother picks up a rocking chair and turns it upside down near me, to be able to mop a wider space. The chair's rockers, half-moons finished in sharp ends, reveal their black undersides, which emit a smell of dust and stuck chewing gum. In this instant, not knowing why, I think, crossly: "She's going to fall. If she keeps mopping in those old tennis shoes, she is going to fall."

These images grow like an annoying internal organ in my body, representing an organic anger that I can't explain. I don't say a word.

My mother mops with great energy, and the pendulum movement that she traces with the mop handle grows wider and wider. Sweat runs down her forehead. She makes gestures of worry and annoyance.

Suddenly, she makes an abrupt movement with the mop handle and slips in a small puddle of water. Her body falls straight forward with a dry sound and her chest is skewered on one tip of the chair's rockers.

Screams and run-run. In one brief second Saturday changes. No one has consulted me to make this happen, and I feel it as an aggression against me. My father carries my mother, who can't stop screaming, out to a hired car and they go to the hospital.

Hours pass and my father comes home to announce that my mother has several broken ribs and must stay in the hospital until she's well again. There's no one to take care of us, so my father drops my brother off at Bella's, to be with my mother's family, and takes me with him to his family's house on the Calzada de Concepción, in the municipality called La Víbora – the Viper – more than an hour's bus ride from the place where we live.

8

THE WORLD AS SEEN FROM LA VÍBORA

THE NEXT MORNING, I wake up at my grandmother's house in La Víbora, where all my father's sisters, the teachers – the "pedagogues" – live.

From the bed, I see the sun shining faintly on the amber-colored marble column in the living room. Lying on these clean, scented sheets, I ask myself, might this column be something more than a piece of stone? Is the sun, just beginning to shine over the city, something more than light, something like breath that springs from exhausted lips, or like water filtering through porous earth to reach roots – or is it like a soap bubble before it pops?

With my imagination, I can touch this marble column that, reflecting the light invading it more completely by the minute, seems to smile – or does it reveal something that needs to be deciphered, something I must pass on to others?

But how to do this?

This mixture of all things makes me ecstatic, and yet this joy somehow underscores the gloom of not waking up in my crib and in my home. This confusion of feelings as I contemplate this classical column with its beautiful capital, gradually beginning to glow as the sun moves up in the sky, is the first symptom of being in my grandmother's house. Everything that happens during the day, the flock of voices jabbering in the kitchen, the marbles and murals of the bathrooms and sinks, my constant bumping into the furniture when I run or ride at top speed the tricycle that my father has managed to convince my grandmother is needed for my daily exercise in this vast house, are all contained in this radiance that begins to illuminate the column at dawn.

Another sign of daybreak is the pigeons cooing, the murmur and rustle of their flight in front of my bedroom window, the noise of their feet scrabbling on the windowsill, their beaks grooming their feathers.

My father, in boxer shorts and T-shirt, sleeps beside me, snoring gently with lips part open. The house is sort of deflated by the tyranny of sleep, and reverberates only with the joy of nature, not with human sounds.

So, I go back to sleep and don't think about everybody waking up with questions, poking their heads in at the door, hustling and bustling.

Between dreams, I hear the ring of the fence gate bell at the bottom of the entrance staircase. The gate opens with a wounded moan and closes with a metallic rumble, followed by more sounds that begin the human day: footsteps of the cook and her son, Lucianito, walking down the hallway; the hubbub of my aunts waking up with great energy; my cousin Daisy being dressed and groomed; everybody's ablutions in bathrooms; and, finally, the fey voice of my Uncle Papo, forever embarrassed that he's the black sheep of the family, though no one wants to come out and say why. Proudly sporting his yellow bowtie, Papo peeks in the door of our room in his shirt and pants, his thumbs hooked in the black suspenders that hold up his gray trousers, to say hello to my father, who climbs out of bed making athletic gestures to fight off early morning cold-air currents that graze the skin like blades of sharp knives.

The house is set to begin a brand-new day with all the brothers rising like a well-disciplined Spartan army, determined to build their destinies. I can get into this sensation of the house: waking up like it's crystalline currents of water in which one can swim energetically – or one can just float and relax.

Then Aunt Amelia stealthily appears at the door of the room with a plate full of suppositories. Her obsession is to make sure all the household children – she has no children of her own, except for her pupils at school – are "regular." She has made herself high priestess of a rite in which she inserts a suppository that requires children to go to the bathroom early in the morning, before breakfast.

I take this nuisance to be an essential, ceremonial aspect of the rigorous, Prussian-style regime that rules this Basque household. Mercifully, it takes only one efficient minute, during which I see up close the brown spots that darken Aunt Amelia's cheeks, likely caused by problems with bile, according to my mother.

To escape from Aunt Amelia, I wander off to a bathroom where I can study the ceiling full of reliefs of dolphins, tritons blowing on conch shells, and sirens with long hair and crowned with seaweed. The green and blue tiles convey an ambiance of marine depths, and let me make believe I'm under the sea. A few minutes of peace go by, away from watchful eyes, without being forced to report results or give explanations. The locked door creates a parenthesis for me, a strategic retreat. Outside, one must wait for the day, for adults with their rules and obligations; inside, I can make these dolphins on the ceiling move, swim, leap over tritons and ruffle the weedy hair of the sirens.

I leave the bathroom, and there is Aunt Amelia.

She demands to know if I did anything in the toilet.

"Of course. That's why I went to the bathroom."

"Then where is it?"

"What do you mean, 'Then where is it'? I flushed!"

"Next time, don't flush and let me see," Aunt Amelia warns me in a venomous tone, full of ill humor and distrust.

AFTER A FEW DISMAL DAYS of learning the ways of my father's family and of seeing almost nothing of my father, who gets in after I've fallen asleep, my grandmother asks, "Would you like to see the pigeons?" This, inviting me to see her nests of pigeons that coo in the patio at the end of the long hallway off the dining room, is a change from the old woman's usual reticence.

The dovecote consists of wooden and cement houses, surrounded by lots of clay pots planted in fragrant basils and red roses, ranging from the brightest red to the darkest crimson. The pigeons enter and exit through their houses' round doors, crooning *cucurucú, cucurucú, cucurucú.*

"Here they are," says this plump, black-eyed, brown-skinned woman with short-cropped curly white hair. I interpret her tone as affectionate, but have no way to judge, as she's not spoken to me before. "Choose the tenderest – the ones you like the best."

I carefully pick up the loveliest fledglings, docile and trusting, with two hands. One is white with light brown spots, another green with a bright red neck, another two are white with bright yellow bills and no spots. I gently hand them to my grandmother to set apart for me, imagining they'll grow up in my own little dovecote we'll build in the patio at my house to protect them from the neighborhood cats and other creatures that eat pigeons.

My grandmother walks into the kitchen and, very gently, hands the docile birds to the cook, who, I assume, is going to put them aside for me somewhere. My grandmother sends me off with a neutral "Now go play."

I run up to the terrace. I see streetcars passing by at this hour, around eleven o'clock in the morning, almost empty. Also, a few cars – *fotingos,* my father calls them – cruise by. The sunshine glitters on the streetcar cables. The air is fresh and light, and makes me want to take a walk down to the street.

I skip down the staircase to the metal gate, which isn't completely closed, push it gently to keep it from making its easily recognizable noise, and slide through the gap. I slink down the spotless, polished marble flight of steps that smell of disinfectant, of cleanliness, and arrive at the street that I have been staring at with longing from the terrace.

Now, there it is, right in front of me, the street with its life-size houses painted yellow and roofs displaying ribs of red terracotta barrel-tile.

My aunts have mentioned a Chinese store down on the corner that sells the best fruit ice cream in the entire city. The tart scent of pineapple, the sweet odor of mango, and, less often, the serious, sharp smell of guanabana guide me to the store, which is decorated with posters filled with vivid, colorful images of the

Caribbean's most delicious fruits, red mamey, yellow mango, white, fleshy guanabana flaunting its black seeds like tiny bright eyes. Also, colorful drawings of these ice creams served in transparent glass cups or brown waffle cones.

The white marble countertop has a few mysterious holes, stained black. The cones ascend inside their dispenser, one atop the next, as if trying to reach the ceiling. Waxed paper cups – the glass cups are only for show – are also stored one inside the other in tall columns. When I enter, an empty cracker tin is overflowing with little wooden taster spoons inside cellophane wrappers, but within minutes, the Chinese servers in white aprons must refill the cracker tin from a big metal box of these spoons that's stowed behind the counter, and refill the paper cup and waffle cone holders, and replace empty cardboard tubs with ones full of ice cream. Each time they remove an empty tub, the scent of its fruit is aroused and wafts deliciously through the air.

I perceive the mango ice cream that a young customer is licking with such obvious pleasure as a sun – yellow, clear, fragrant – atop a toasty brown cone.

It's pointless to stand here with no money and unable to buy a thing, so I head back to the house. At the front gate, I find a stray dog scratching his ear with a rear paw. He's a puppy with a pink belly, and his stiff, short, grimy hair was once white with black spots.

His black snout, wet and shiny, points towards the roof.

How I long to bring him inside! But I know I can't. Without realizing it and without knowing why, tears run down my cheeks. As I'm finding out, my only recourse in this house is to run up to the terrace and try to entertain myself by watching streetcars and people who have the joy of being adults, freely walking down the street and doing whatever else comes to mind.

Shortly, somebody calls me to come to the dining room. The family is sitting down to lunch. I want to continue marveling at the landscape of city houses and sky covered in bulbous white clouds.

"Can't you hear when you are called?" shrieks Aunt Amelia, furious, materializing on the terrace, napkin in hand.

I run down to the dining room and jump into my chair, causing it to make a loud noise. Except for my father, his whole family is seated here, even my uncle, the dentist, who's visiting. They all look at me with damning eyes. I wish I didn't need to eat, and could skip sitting at this table with these grumpy, critical people.

The cook serves me a soup that I start to slurp, making lots of noise with the spoon and with my mouth. I'm hungry. The others sip their soup in silence. The reason they're not making noise, I fantasize, is that they're all dead.

Aunt Amelia looks approvingly at the cook and says: "Chencha, your soup turned out very well today."

"That's because your mother always chooses the tenderest pigeons," replies the cook modestly.

"Pigeons? This soup is made of *pigeons*?" I ask, horrified.

"Yes, girl. Do you mean you can't eat pigeon soup either? Must we make special soups for you?" asks Aunt Amelia, irritated.

I scream and cough convulsively, grabbing my throat with my hands. My aunt Catalina, alarmed, thinking I've choked on a bone, stands up and smacks me on the back. Unable to control myself, I vomit on the fine white lace tablecloth, which produces a general howl of revulsion.

"Now you will go without lunch," Aunt Amelia rebukes me, dragging me to the bathroom to spot-clean the vomit that's soiled my white dress, worn for the first time on this morning that began so brightly.

I retreat to the living room and go to the window. Several pots planted with malangas crowd the windowsill. I squeeze the malanga leaves to watch their sap run. These are plants that I've seen Aunt Ernestina, the youngest of the sisters, carefully water. I like feeling the leaves on my fingers, knowing I can break them.

That's one of the pranks I've found to annoy Aunt Ernestina, who's always sitting down with great solemnity to play the piano. My other prank is to raise the height of the piano's dark wooden stool, which is changed by spinning the round seat. Ernestina is very short and must lower the seat so her feet can reach the pedals. I look elsewhere when she asks, furious, who the person is who fiddles with her stool.

She knows it's me, but doesn't say so, to make me feel guilty.

I walk to the dining room and see that my grandmother has finishing eating her soup quietly and without looking at anyone. The rest of the family looks at me with disgust. Although I'm very hungry, I decide to hold out until dinner and leave, without asking them to pardon me for throwing up. I return to the balcony to escape this suffocating house and regret that the rest of this family does not have other leafy plants for me to mess with.

I DON'T KNOW HOW LONG I've been at my grandmother's house, but it seems an eternity. Tonight, like every night after dinner, everyone heads to the living room. I watch to see what happens, standing aloof, leaning against the wall beside the window. I don't want to sit among them. I want to be invisible.

My third aunt, Catalina, looks particularly attractive in her white cotton dress with large red poppies that contrast with her large green eyes. Her bulging abdomen makes her walk with her legs apart. She wears low-heeled shoes of the sort used by women expecting a baby. She sits in an armchair, and her husband, tall, thin, with a blond mustache and blond hair, stands behind her, hugs her and seems very caring.

The rest of the relatives sit in the highly polished mahogany rocking chairs, bobbing back and forth almost noiselessly. An air of complacency invades them as they digest dinner under the chandeliers, their beveled crystals cut into leaves and tears that glitter near the ceiling. A pleasant, diffused yellow glow comes from lightbulbs that look like thick flames atop what look like melting wax candles but are yellow ceramic tubes that hide the wires of the chandeliers.

The men smoke cigars. The only man not smoking is my uncle Papo, his sunken black eyes from time to time throwing off what seem to be ironic sparks.

The international situation is discussed. The family is discussed. The international situation once more. Then the family. I don't want to listen or talk. I miss my own house and have no idea when I can go home. I go out on the terrace. It's suddenly become dark. The fronts of houses and the Calzada de Concepción itself are lit by a shiny ribbon of electric lanterns in the center island that seems to go on forever, getting lost among tiny roofs and dark trees off in the distance. The sky, dark blue and porous, has a silver glow far away where I imagine my house to be, and, here, it frames the terraces and tile roofs, which now have turned purple. The menacing black of telephone and electricity cables cuts across the avenue. Other, thicker cables hang along the middle of the road. There is where the upper wheels of the streetcars run, sending off menacing sparks.

Many streetcars pass at this hour, crammed with men wearing fine Panama hats. They spill out onto the platform, or hang from the metal grab handles inside the cars, or from handles on both sides of the front and rear doors. Each streetcar arrives like thunder, shaking the street's cobblestones that look like so many blue crab shells. A dry, metallic blow strikes the rails before the cars screech to a stop.

Inside the cars: light and people, heads of men sticking their noses out the windows to breathe in the fresh night air.

Outside my grandmother's house, men with newspapers under their arms step down from the streetcars and walk, shadowy, elusive, agile, under the street lamps, casting long, sharp-pointed, threatening shadows. The streetcars start up again with a bang and get lost among the few automobiles circulating at this hour.

Of all these men descending from streetcars to head home, none is ever my father, and I don't know any of the other men. They're other children's fathers, or maybe they don't even have children.

My father studies late at the university and I extend bedtime watching the streetcars stop, hoping he will come before I fall asleep. When the street is empty and the light does not illuminate anyone, I see small flying spots, like fireflies, orbiting the streetlights, interrupting the light with gray and pink lines. The icy tile floor numbs my thighs and legs. I hug, sleepily, the equally chilly balustrades of the balcony.

MY COUSIN SOFIA comes to visit this Saturday, accompanied by Novo, her father, and her mother, my aunt Virginia. The morning begins with Sofia's parents trying to converse with the resident relatives over the racket of Sofia jumping around in her white piqué dress with flounces. This uproar is a happy interruption of my grandmother's house's weekday monotony.

Novo has promised to take us exploring somewhere, and after talking it over with my aunt Luisa and my grandmother, he takes Daisy and me by the hand and leads us out into the street. Sofia follows closely. With him, we are allowed to descend that forbidden staircase, leave the cage that is now always locked as a result of my unauthorized excursion to the ice cream store. Now we can walk down the street that, for a week or more, has tormented me with the allure of an impossible dream. This morning, by gently herding us with his hand, carefully planning our jumps, and premeditatedly causing our spontaneous laughter, Novo gets us out of the house.

Novo's plan is to take us on an excursion to the hill of La Víbora. It's like a tower from which you can see the entire municipality. After contending with obstacles such as streets overhung by black streetcar cables, electric and telephone wires, and crowds of women dressed in silk prints accompanied by men in gray three-piece suits sporting polished reed canes with gold knobs, we climb the hill.

Green and quite steep, the hill at its top shows us that distance is a transparent, tender bluish mist, that yellow, pink, green houses grow like mushrooms between the gray lines of streets, and that the meandering flow of the clothes of passers-by vibrates like a river of colors. The sky is turquoise blue and clear, with some snowy, blurry cirrus and bulging cumulus clusters that sashay by, prodded by the wind. Up there among the clouds, the occasional kite sneaks in and shakes like a flying snake that has a tail of red or blue ribbons.

"There are the colonels!" shouts Sofia. She points her finger at spectacular large, kites that almost always have razor blades fastened to their tails, meant to cut enemy kite strings when a "war" starts. The breeze at the summit musses up our hair, and I dream that its whistle is like the wing-beat of a gigantic bird from whose open bill the treasures and splendors of nature pour out, like a cornucopia.

Daisy, away from the oppressive frame of the walls of that house, becomes free, evolves. Her obesity is no longer disturbing, but makes her seem like a fresh fruit swollen with juice as she rolls around on the grass. At the crest of the hill, our crazed running around stops, and we dedicate ourselves to serious contemplation of the landscape. What springs from this instant is something like triumph, and I see it arriving from the horizon on that breeze, inside that fragrance of grass and earth saturated with dew. When I come down from the hill, I erase myself from time and space to preserve that peak as a plenitude, a fullness that encapsulates the sum of days and justifies them.

THE WEEK PASSES QUICKLY and it's Saturday again. Because Sofia is here, we have permission to play in the street. Sofia is our age, but in the aunts' opinion, she is more responsible than Daisy or me. The three of us run downstairs as if escaping, incredulous at this sudden freedom.

In the house next door lives a German couple that our aunts call the Kartoffels because when they go shopping at the bodega, they sometimes get confused and ask for *kartoffeln* instead of *papas*. I have heard in dinner-table gossip that they could be German spies. Sofia jumps excitedly on the sidewalk and starts planning how we will invade the Kartoffels' house.

In our imagination we are Allied spies, trying to uncover how they send messages to their Nazi bosses.

"We must pick a top-notch spy," suggests Daisy, who is very serious.

"A spy who's not afraid to die in combat," says Sofia cunningly, and suddenly chicken.

I feel my mission in life has arrived: to be an Allied spy and to uncover the Kartoffels' treachery. I must take great care, go slowly, uncover their nefarious methods without arousing suspicion.

In front of the house there is a red garden full of geraniums, protected by a metal fence. I open the fence decisively. A way off, Sofia and Daisy watch me, torn between excitement and fear. I go up the small concrete path that leads to the porch, which is full of pots containing large malanga plants.

The picture window beside the door has pots on its sill planted with basil and other fragrant spices that I can't identify. The living room looks empty.

At the entrance there's a small plaque painted in navy blue with a white cross in the center. These words in Spanish appear in white paint: "With God everything, without God nothing."

I knock on the door hoping that no one's home. Sofia and Daisy run off. I'm unsure what I'm doing here and am about to run away like my cousins, but then a lady with very white, wrinkled skin, white hair, and blue eyes ending in crows' feet opens the door.

She smiles. She wears a sleeveless cotton gown printed with lavender flowers that stand out against a white background. She smells of nice soap and cleanliness.

"Madam, I live next door, and I've come to visit you," I say as quickly as possible, stumbling over my words.

The woman smiles again and, to my surprise, invites me in. Inside, the house smells of humidity and old junk. In the large living-dining room there is a cream-colored sofa with two matching armchairs at the sides, several wicker armchairs with tables beside them, a large dinner table of light-colored wood covered by a white lace tablecloth and surrounded by four chairs, a sideboard of the same style containing cut-glass beer mugs, blue-and-white tableware with Tyrolean designs, ceramic beer jugs painted in bright colors with metal lids, and, hanging on the wall, a cuckoo clock.

I plop myself down in one of the armchairs.

The coffee table to my right overflows with old sepia photos in elaborate metal frames. I look at one of a couple hugging: a young woman with large clear eyes, who gazes toward the horizon with a faraway expression, accompanied by a man sporting a handlebar mustache and dressed in a black three-piece suit, who stares straight at the camera. The dedication is written in Spanish, with sepia ink and very flowery calligraphy: *A Helga: Recuerdo de Berlin. Rudolf.*

Another photo shows aviators about to enter a plane that seems the size of a mosquito. The pilot in the foreground, smiling, has a leather cap with flaps on both sides of his head, like the long ears of a hound. In the background, a young woman sits on a bench. Behind her there are trees and bushes of a country place. It has no dedication.

I don't know what I'm doing in this house. My determination to be a spy falters in the face of these innocent, sentimental images. I regret coming.

"Would you care for a cookie?" Without waiting for a response, the lady gets up, finds a box of cream-filled María cookies, and offers me one. "Do you go to school?" she asks affably.

I hear an insistent chatter of canaries, a fluttering of caged birds.

"Not right now. I'm visiting my grandmother."

The woman, sitting in front of me in another armchair, clearly is expecting me to carry the burden of the conversation. After all, it was I who knocked on her door. I hadn't foreseen this and I say the first thing that enters my head.

"I'm told that you're in favor of Hitler. Is this true?"

She smiles and leans toward me kindly. "And you know who Hitler is?"

"No, but he has something to do with the war."

"Hitler puts children like you in school. He is the leader of Germany."

She gets up and leaves the room, coming back with a photo album. She opens the book and hands it to me, smiling with pride. It's full of clippings from daily newspapers and Sunday supplements. There is a man with a mustache who has his right arm outstretched and an arm band with a weird letter Z. The lady says it's the swastika cross.

She goes on: "As for war – why is there war? It's because the world has humiliated Germany, imposing draconian war reparations on it in the Treaty of Versailles. All because the world envies German superiority."

She takes me by the hand to a room in the interior of the house. Here are several cages with canaries, shelves with old radios and books, photos glued to the walls, all very neat and clean. The woman opens a closet and shows me a soldier's uniform and, on the top shelf, a helmet finished in a spear tip.

She says, "This was Rudolf's uniform, from when he fought in World War I. That was when Germany was humiliated." She trembles with anger, but recovers and takes down one of the cages to observe its canary occupant.

This woman's feelings are as embarrassing and sticky as those of any of my relatives. I feel trapped like an insect in molasses.

"I'm leaving," I announce abruptly.

As I walk through the room towards the door, I hear her say to my back: "Come often. I'll show you more photos and give you cookies."

THE MULATTO LUCIANITO, son of Chencha, the Black cook, is two years old and has kinky blond hair. He's jumping up and down naked in the kitchen to entertain my cousin Daisy. I'm leaning against the sink because I'm being made to drink cholagogue tea every morning to "cleanse my liver."

Daisy, dressed in pink organdy, has a glass full of yellow liquid in her hand. "Drink it!" she commands Lucianito. "It's tasty. It's just cider."

Lucianito keeps jumping and his tiny penis goes up and down with every move, as does the golden chain with the image of St. Lazarus hanging from his neck.

His hair is getting even curlier, and his face, tarnished by streaks of dirt, expands into a smile.

Chencha is out shopping for groceries at the bodega, and her son is alone having to deal with this glass that he doesn't want to touch.

Daisy, seductive, insists that he take the glass. "It's cider! It's very tasty, and good for the stomach," she assures him by rubbing her fat belly with a circular motion of her hand.

Behind us, Aunt Luisa, Daisy's mother, laughs. Her silhouette is a cut-out in the morning light coming from the dining room.

In my tumultuous perception, the white tiles of the kitchen, the marble of the sink, and the pungent smell of crushed garlic emanating from the mortar all join Lucianito's jumps and his smile.

Now Daisy, imperious, grabs Lucianito's chain and fixes him with a look. Lucianito stops smiling, shrinks in the kitchen, disintegrates. Daisy gets bigger as she senses her mother behind her like a mountain.

From that pinnacle, Luisa opens her eyes very wide, scaring both me and the cook's son.

Daisy rips off Lucianito's thin chain in a calculated, meticulous gesture, throws it on the floor, forces the child's mouth open, then pours the contents of the glass inside him. Lucianito must swallow to breathe and keep from drowning.

With the glass now empty, Daisy looks at me, triumphant.

"It wasn't cider, it was pee! It wasn't cider, it was pee!" she screams, ecstatic.

My aunt Luisa, a teacher, or so I'm told, laughs, then claps her hands at her daughter's antics. I look at my cousin, appalled.

Aunt Amelia enters the kitchen with a military air. "What is this racket? Let this beast alone! Can't you see he's filthy and almost certainly has worms?" she scolds with a metallic voice. She has no idea what the girl has done.

Aunt Amelia takes Daisy by the hand, and Luisa, like a naïve lapdog, follows her older sister, the martinet, and her daughter, the delinquent, out of the kitchen.

Lucianito sits on the floor, his chin and chest dripping urine.

His green eyes travel around the kitchen as if to absorb and memorize everything. His body, the color of raw sugar, crisscrossed with black stripes that blur with sweat and urine, has turned into an assault of dirt on the immaculate white floor.

I want to pick up his chain to give it back to him, to try to fix everything broken in this kitchen. But, before I can move, Lucianito boy crawls over, scoops the chain off the floor, and struggles to put it back on his neck.

I help him quietly, but it's too broken for me to fix.

I place it in his hand with a gesture of sorrow and shame.

NIGHT ARRIVES. The doorbell rings, the fence squeals as it opens, and makes a muffled gong sound as it closes.

From the shadowy staircase into the illuminated room come the two Delgado sisters, twin maiden ladies, distant cousins of ours, who wear identical simple sleeveless black cotton tunics with a V neck.

Both have large dark violet circles under their eyes. They know their place, and enter the living room hunched over, as if ashamed because they are very poor, smiling with just the right side of their mouths, which raises the black mole that both have at the corner of their lips until it is almost on a line with their nostrils.

The Delgado sisters' emergence from the darkness of the staircase, now somewhat illuminated by the yellow glow of the night lamps, cuts the evening in two, stops conversations, ends the snapping noise of the rocking chairs that had become, after an interval of irritating speeds and sudden movements, melodious counterpoint.

"We brought you this little gift, Nike," the two announce to my grandmother, smiling from under their black felt hats with small black veils that obliquely cover the tops of their faces, revealing only the left eye, a squinting, ironic beacon behind all that modesty and circumspection.

As twins, they've opted to do everything in unison. It is difficult to know who is Lila and who is Lola, as the only difference is Lila's slightly squarer face and greater shyness than Lola's.

Lila supports Lola every time Lola expresses an opinion.

Their little gift is a box with vetiver bags for my grandmother to place in linen sheets stored in her chifforobe, to give it a pleasant odor.

"We are talking about the disasters of this European war," summarizes my grandmother, to avoid the usual tiresome questions, as she gets her chair back into a good rocking rhythm, her face somewhat retracted into her brown neck, striated with turtle-like wrinkles.

"It's awful to bring children into a world like this," says Catalina, unconsciously touching her bulging belly, shaped like those enormous ostrich eggs I've seen in books. Catalina's husband, standing behind her and placing his hands on her shoulders as if approving her statement, exclaims: "If Hitler had simply annexed Austria – after all, he *is* Austrian – but invading Poland and the other countries is just too much. This is the end of the world!"

As if to dilute the poison of prophecy, my grandmother opens her sandalwood fan, painted with the image of a nineteenth-century woman riding in a *calèche*, and fans herself. The fan disperses a scent of sandalwood to calm the unease aroused in the listeners by this topic of conversation.

"God's punishment," Lola says, and Lila repeats.

"They don't let you live," Catalina complains again.

"Hitler's problem is pathological. He's crazy, he's a monster, he's going to destroy the civilized world," her husband prophesies.

Aunt Amelia moves in her armchair, uncomfortable, and the brown spot that covers part of her cheek darkens more.

I imagine that all the participants in the conversation are either hanging from the lamps or flowing from them. The golden marble columns ending in beautiful arabesques, the windows filled with the painful mauve horizon splattered with the red dot of the dying sun, the music of metal streetcar wheels wafted in by the breeze through the wide-open door to the terrace, all this together makes it possible for these people and their words to exist.

Like a plant, I have been cut and transplanted to this living room, and so flounder like a still-floating shipwreck between all the objects inside this house and the words of these relatives.

"Germany was betrayed by the Treaty of Versailles!" I finally shout defiantly. Catalina's husband looks at me like I'm a cup floating in thin air. Everyone's eyes open inordinately wide and focus on me, and I can't stop myself.

"The world doesn't want to recognize Germany's superiority and that's why they humiliated it with the abusive Treaty of Versailles! That's the cause of this war!" I assert insolently. I've managed to get all eyes to converge on me, and I burst out of the morass of things and words in which I have been plunged, into a light that's more benevolent – into *existence*.

"And who is it that's putting these ideas in the head of this little girl?" Luisa asks Aunt Amelia, with infinite contempt, insinuating that the blame rests with my mother, whom they hate.

"Only a savage could think like this," replies Aunt Amelia, very annoyed.

"A person without Christian ideas," adds Lola, and Lila echoes her.

"Look at her there," Ernestina points her finger at me, and continues with her complaint: "Sitting in that chair, talking about the superiority of Germany and the World War. When has a tadpole ever been seen talking? My brother has raised crows, and his eyes will be plucked out."

Everyone seems to agree, and they all nail me to my chair with their eyes.

"Never say those things!" my grandmother scolds between violent flaps of her fan. "You're going to end up in hell."

"Those ideas are going to lead you to destruction! Keep it up, think like an animal!" Amelia condemns. Catalina's husband is the only one who doesn't try to fry me with his eyes. I find this refreshing, novel.

"Where have you gotten these ideas?" he asks me, without any tone of condemnation. "Who told you that?"

"The lady next door."

"She must mean The Kartoffel!"

Everyone is outraged.

The Delgado twins laugh as if they had guessed it.

My grandmother fans herself more quickly, and the night seems suddenly to end with a clap. Rather than watch its painful journey to the grave, I escape to the terrace where the street lanterns still await me with their luminous halos and the hope that my father will come, squeezed out of some streetcar full of men with straw hats.

I DON'T YET KNOW how many days or months I must stay at Grandmother's house. Very early in the morning, when the sun is still shining on the amber column of the living room, the image of my real house, where I used to live with my parents, crosses my mind.

As if from between shadows, the images creep forward, living room and armchairs, dining room and table, crib ... bedroom with the patio door open and a tongue of light on the tile floor.

It's a dream. Reality happens in this house, my grandmother's, where her beautiful pigeons are fed barley so they can have their necks wrung and then become soup at her long dinner table.

As it's Saturday, Sofia appears again, ready to rabble-rouse, followed by Virginia, her mother, who sports an elaborate hairstyle that ends in two large curls on her forehead, like car lanterns. I find out later from my mother that they are copied from the actress Joan Crawford.

Sofia wants to play stars, so we go with Daisy to Aunt Cora's room, which we almost never visit because it's dark and damp. It's also full of pictures of saints, Christian martyrs whose wounds from martyrdom terrify us.

"Air! air!" Sofia shouts, throwing open the windows. "This is the den of Dracula!" I am always surprised by Sofia's sharp wit, her knowledge of the world, and her confidence to act at every moment to modify her world. Sofia possesses a unique range of motion in this house that's so tied to traditions and fixed forms of behavior.

No one dares oppose Sofia, for example, by reminding her that she is very young, or impugning her motives with suspicions of malice, or repressing her exuberance of thought and action.

With the finesse of a magician, Sofia pulls a box of toothpicks out of the air, extracts five of them, bends each one in the middle, and lays them out next to each other on the floor, leaving a small gap in the center.

She then runs to the kitchen, returning instantly with a glass of water. She lets a drop or two fall in the center, and the toothpicks open to form the tips of a star.

"Magic! The magic of the star! The whole world can do it, even Aunt Cora, who's a little slow," Sofia teases, laughing and jumping like a rabbit.

"Let me try!" Daisy screams behind me, as I run carrying the glass of water behind Sofia.

"Try to get it, fatso!" I shout, dodging to stop her grabbing the glass.

We run in a circle until I turn around and give the glass to Daisy, spilling some of the water on her hair, wishing it were urine.

Daisy, drying her hair with her hand, sits on the floor and repeats what Sofia did: she bends the toothpicks with her pudgy hands, pours the drop, and, little by little, the star opens again when its points are filled with water.

I do mine next, and watch, absorbed, as the star grows on the ground, and don't hear Aunt Cora creeping up behind my back.

Cora, all dressed in black, wears black shoes tied with black laces because she's still in mourning for my grandfather, who died ten years ago.

"They have come to collect you," she announces to me in her voice from beyond the tomb.

"They? They who?" I ask, knocking over the sticks, making the star overflow, and creating a mud puddle on the floor with the soles of my shoes.

"Your mother. Who else would come for you?"

I run through room after room. When I get to the entrance stairs, I see my mother, outside the gate.

They haven't invited my mother into the house.

She's emaciated.

A long black skirt with wide folds hangs from her waist.

A light black wool jacket imprisons her sunken chest.

Her pale face, her fire-red lipstick, her extinguished, sunken black eyes, her flat, sparse, lifeless black hair, all accentuate the look of death in her face.

"Give your aunts a goodbye kiss," my mother tells me, exhausted.

Luisa and Cora are behind me. I can smell decay, as well as Cora's books about saints.

"I don't want to!" I shout resentfully.

I run down the stairs jumping and open the gate, which shouts insults as it closes, and we walk away. I don't care what I am leaving behind.

My mother tells me she's just left the hospital and that she headed straight here to pick me up and take me home.

She reproaches me for not saying goodbye to my aunts or thanking them for taking care of me all this time.

"They didn't ask you in! They treated you like a maid!" I shout.

"It doesn't matter how they treat me or you. They took good care of you all this time while I was in the hospital. They didn't leave you lying in the street. You must be grateful, but you *are* going home now, and you *will* be there with your parents."

"So, I still have a house?"

"Yes, from now on you're going to live in your house."

This is a revelation.

That place, which I remembered when I woke up with a dry blow to my stomach for so many mornings, still exists.

AS WE LEAVE, I see several policemen marching the Kartoffel couple away in handcuffs. A crowd of gossips clusters in front of the house and on the street.

"They're spies for Germany!" shouts a woman zealously.

"At last, they've been caught! They've been communicating by telegraph with a German submarine sailing off our coast!" others shout.

"You know what's in store for them," says another woman, smiling, and making a gesture with her index finger on her neck, as if chopping a head off.

We make our way through the bystanders. My mother feels weak and keeps a hand on the wall as she walks. She disappears inside her clothes.

At the corner where the streetcar stops, there's a small kiosk that sells combs, pencils, and candy. My mother buys me a small plastic wallet, blood-red like her lipstick. I open the gold metal closure to see what's inside: flimsy paper, like what they use at the bakery to wrap bread, wadded up to give the wallet the appearance of being full. Other than that, there's nothing inside, just seams sewn with red thread. I remove the paper, and my mother drops a five-cent coin into my new wallet.

"Take it, and make it last. That means don't spend it right away," she says.

As we leave the kiosk, my mother slumps against the wall. Drops of sweat run down her livid face.

"Let's duck into the cinema next door and rest in the air conditioning."

We buy two tickets at the box office and walk into a huge, very dark room. I can't see a thing except a screen with brightly colored flat images. When my eyes adjust to the darkness, I can make out seats upholstered in red velvet, where a few people are sitting. We sit near an exit, in the middle of an empty row. I notice that everyone looks at the screen. I get that you're supposed to do that, but I don't know why. Then the flat figures speak words I don't understand, but under the images I can see sentences in Spanish, which change very quickly, making it hard to read the whole thing.

I read one text on the screen that informs us that the pianist of the film has been invited to play for a very important personage, but that the pianist's mother and sister can't come because they're poor and don't have the right clothes. I feel sorry for them, because I imagine that my brother is the pianist, and that I cannot attend the concert because my mother and I also are very poor. The concert guests dress in a strange and luxurious way. There is an ornate golden piano. On it, the pianist, who is called Chopin, plays a music that I have never heard, composed by him. It sounds like what I hum in the mornings, but it's prettier.

The bright colors of the film wound my heart and I can taste them. The dark, intense, playful reds taste like pineapple and smell like roses. Dark blues that play with light taste like guanabana and smell like pine. I feel the velvet of this color like a caress on my hands. The golden gowns are like mango juice diluted on my tongue, and they have the scent of rice and chicken with a lot of cumin.

A woman dressed as a man wearing a top hat appears on the screen. I almost jump out of my seat. Everyone greets her very cordially because she is famous.

She is the writer George Sand. I enter the whirlwind of that flat world called Paris and observe its dazzling luxury.

Near the end of the movie, the pianist plays a piece that excites me a lot. It's a Polonaise, my mother informs me. The pianist coughs and a few bright red drops fall on the white part of the keyboard. The air goes out of me and I can't bring myself to ask my mother what those drops mean.

Leaving the cinema, my mother has recovered, but I am trembling because of the experiences I've lived in the dark. Before climbing up the streetcar's steps, I look back. My grandmother's house is the one that now submerges in sleep, in the distance, in the fog that buries things in my head.

9

RETURN TO LA SIERRA

COMING HOME is like starting over. All combinations are possible, things come closer, are well delineated and recognizable all at once, but at the same time, they keep a polite distance, and I can take a deep breath, take a comfortable view of things, treasure them, and improve them when I feel like it.

The three months of summer vacation are over.

I am told, however, that for now I won't be returning to the nuns' school. Today we visit my mother's family for the first time since she had her accident and got out of the hospital.

The green hall of Bella's house goes past at high speed as I run, mussing up my new dress and undoing the sash tied in a bow behind my back. Behind me, noon reverberates on top of the patio's huge mango tree with leaves edged in red with brown dots.

I'm running toward the end of the hall, toward the vertical telephone and the poster of Gustavo, my uncle-in-law, where he appears in blackface. To the right, the green wall makes a turn and there's the living room, a large space with furniture upholstered in dark copper brocade. I'm chasing my cousin Barbara, and her brother Emilito is chasing me. Breathless, I'm fully focused on this race and determined to win. I want to recapture something I lost at my grandmother's house, something that existed inside me but has vanished.

As I hurtle past the hallway's large open window, something violently stops my head, like a knockout punch. My neck moves back and forth, the blow and rebound scrambling my brains. A hot liquid pours down my forehead like a red curtain over my eyes. This sticky substance runs over my lips and teeth and down my neck. I laugh and smack my forehead. My hand is all wet, and red.

I was sure I could run under the window. I could do it last year, despite the latch hanging down in a rusty T, traces of white paint stuck to the metal.

"My child, you're covered in blood!" screams my mother in the living room.

In a state of total panic, continuing her terrified shrieking, she comes running over to shake me, as if that could stop the blood or reverse the moment. She grabs my arm with hands that turn into iron from hysteria, which I always hate to feel, because I've made a fatal mistake, I've killed myself. I've sliced my life in half with a malevolent knife. All around me, my relatives are screaming. I can barely see them through the red waterfall.

"We need to take her right now to a clinic, to the emergency room, to the hospital!" my mother screams, as if waiting for someone to do it for her, or as if they were all trying to stop her from doing it.

Or maybe she's expecting to be told what to do, but nobody says a thing.

After a few minutes of indecision, my mother yanks me by the hand out of Bella's house and drags me through the streets. I have a few seconds to wipe my face with my skirt, but so much more blood gushes out that I'm amazed. I didn't know I was so full of that red sap.

In our frantic march, houses and streets blur together, splashed with my mother's breathless wheezing and the anguish she expresses not in words but through her pincer-like fingers gripping my fragile wrist. I feel ashamed that people are looking at me. I want to give my mother a kick, but what right have I to do that? I always need a reason for everything I say and do.

How could I explain myself to adults? Is it the fact that she is holding my wrist so tight that it hurts a compelling reason to kick her? Or that she's panting with rage and expects me to get her out of this jam by turning back the clock and avoiding the window latch that ripped my forehead open? I feel an elemental turn in my intestines that makes everything clear. My viscera reason better than my brain, better than my premature explorations in the art of logical thinking.

In my mother's mind, which I hate to penetrate but must, moved by this primordial nausea, I see her thoughts at war with one another, moving themselves around like pieces of furniture that don't fit into the decor. I'd like to bleed to death, leaving her with her furniture in her head and her expectation that I can fix everything.

I want to die. This seems the perfect moment to leave this hard life full of upsetting and incomprehensible moments.

THE WHITENESS OF THE DISPENSARY yanks me out of these thoughts. Then, a hunk of cotton and cold water remove the sticky mask from my face. The dispensary is salvation. My mother hands me over to be repaired. The doctor on duty is an intern, young, with olive skin and chubby cheeks that are inclined to laugh at anything. He takes my arm and injects something into me. Tetanus antitoxin serum, he informs my mother afterwards.

He dabs on mercurochrome, wraps my head in gauze and tape, and out I go, repaired, surprised to be able to see clearly again, minus the red curtain, the asphalt, and the fronts of houses, their baby-garment pinks and blues cracking and peeling under the repellently ferocious midday sun.

When I return to the darkness of my house, the furniture and floor look different, as if my eyes had been living behind a curtain of oblivion. My mother, trying to straighten up the house a bit, seems weightless, turning herself into bubbles. I can't grasp what's happening to me, or the lightness inside of me, or the difference between my eyes, what they observe, and what's boiling inside my head. There is something of chaos in all this.

I touch the backs of chairs to steady myself when, suddenly, wings sprout from my feet and begin to flap. My head keeps repeating: "A year ago I could run under the window latch."

And this mixes with the cold shadow inside the house, contrasted with the shimmering sun outside that makes you cry as it strips all things bare.

I can't put my finger on what's wrong with me. I can't say "This is it!" because I can't hand "it" over like a gift, because who do I give "it" to? Who can I talk to? I think "it's" hilarious, although I must hold on to keep from falling because the wings want to take flight and the armchairs are running around as if they're trying to hide from me, as if I'm chasing them, as if I could catch up to them with my head in its current state. I can't grab them – it's the farthest thing from my mind, because my feet are on fire, my head's swelling and filling up with water, my ears buzz full of bees, my eyes burn.

My face is tingling and I open the front door to get a breath of fresh air. I smile. "This time yes! This time is it!" I think without knowing why.

I'm going to leave from one moment to the next.

I'm going to take off and fly past this sun and these clouds, to a place that I imagine to be blue and benevolent.

My mother has gone outside to dump the garbage. Turning on the sidewalk, she sees me and runs, terrified, towards me, closing in from the alley, taking on mass and contours, banging the garbage can against the wall as she moves it, producing a crank, crank, crank sound that makes my hair stand on end.

"You're red! You're all swollen!" my mother hollers like a madwoman from the alleyway.

She rushes inside the house, hurls the empty garbage can across the living room, picks me up like a bundle with her typical nervous violence, and gallops out of the house with me.

"My little girl is dying! My little girl is dying!" she yowls, immobilizing me over her shoulder in a bear hug as she runs her marathon past almond trees, past oleanders with their poisonous leaves and their pink flowers open and waiting for I-don't-know-what, as she trots beneath royal poinciana trees with their bouquets of red flowers so huge that when they fall to the ground, their pistils explode and spray yellow pollen everywhere.

My mother repeats her cries in her race towards the nearest clinic. The sight of her trotting, breathless, with her daughter over her shoulder immobilizes everyone she comes across.

I feel embarrassed again. I'm crying, not because of how tragic my mother wants this scene to look, but out of shame at her lack of silence, the way she flaunts her pain in front of everyone. The surprised glances of passers-by sharpen the desire I feel to sink into the sidewalk, to vaporize. Arriving back at the dispensary doesn't seem like salvation but like return to a cemetery, a graveyard run by inexperienced medical students. My mother comes close to beating up the intern, who quickly injects me with insulin, as he later informs us. After a heated argument between my mother and the intern, I am carried home and deposited in my crib. I desperately want a door to be closed on all these facts with a sign saying: 'It was nothing!' I want to erase everything. I fall asleep to prevent the drama from continuing and to quiet down the muttering of demons growing in my head by the minute.

MONTHS LATER, hives still cover my body from my allergic reaction to the tetanus antitoxin serum. I sleep naked on the rubber mattress cover, drenched in talc. My skin is full of welts, some of them developing into pustules from scratching myself. When I scratch the welts, they produce a colorless, viscous liquid that disgusts me. Eating eggs or chocolate makes it worse.

Finally, my mother takes me back to the place where it happened, the house of her family that she hasn't wanted to visit out of a superstitious fear that I would have another accident. As soon as I arrive, I'm playing with my cousins as if nothing had gone wrong. I chase after Barbara to take the baseball bat away from her, and, as before, she runs after her brother Emilito to beat him up.

"Faggot! Thief! Faggot! Thief!" shouts Barbara.

Emilito stumbles over a loose brick in the patio and falls to the ground. Barbara gets set to smash his head in with the bat, but I grab her arm. She turns and decides to smash my head. Running is the only alternative because Barbara is bigger and stronger than I am.

"I'm going to crush your skull!" Barbara threatens with her "big landcrab mouth," as Aunt Chavela, her own mother, calls it.

The children next door perch on top of the wall to watch us fight. Some bet on me and others on Barbara. They all clap and cheer. I run, Barbara follows me, and Emilito, who has gotten back up, picks up his brick and runs after Barbara. Chavela appears at the patio door, drying her hands on her dress, adding to the water stains around her belly.

"Demons! Maniacs! Children! You make me sick to death!" shouts Chavela.

The children next door burst into applause whenever Chavela appears, like she's some great actress making her entrance on stage.

Noticing the commotion of the children next door, Barbara stops dead and throws the bat to the ground. Emilito also drops his brick, and they walk arm-in-arm toward the street, talking calmly, as if they were the best of friends.

Barbara calls me to one side. "Don't get mixed up with those kids next door," she warns me in a low, protective voice.

"Why?"

"Because they have lice. They're slum kids. They've turned their house into a rabbit warren."

Her face contracts with revulsion saying this.

"What do you mean? What's a 'rabbit warren'?"

"They've divided up the house with cardboard and made lots more rooms. Poor families live there and they have dogs with ticks."

These neighbors, these children, climb down from the wall and run out into the street.

"The Devil take the hindmost!" Barbara shrieks and runs toward the street, away from her mother's eagle eye, as Chavela goes into the house. I see her walking down the hallway, through the open door, in the large window, silhouetted against the green wall.

When we get to the porch, we sit in the big rocking chairs, we're all gasping. I raise my head and notice, on the porch roof, a few lizards that look like salamanders, some brown, some black, some green, and a few whitish, transparent, with alert red eyes and covered in brown spots like freckles.

I imagine their silence hides some secret, that they are magical animals.

The poplars on the sidewalk in front of the house, leafy and whispering, stir in the breeze.

The houses across the way, their porches now lit by the yellow glow of insect-repelling bulbs because the afternoon is nearly over, the sound of footsteps on the sidewalk, the whoosh of car wheels, form a curious hodgepodge of images and sounds.

From time to time, adding a melancholy note, some stray dog barks. The smell of jasmine floods the almost-night, spreads with the breeze.

"Let's go to the bodega," Barbara commands. "To get *dulce de leche*."

Bella appears in the window in her blue pajamas, printed in red, green, and black, which makes her look like a fortune teller.

"Don't go out, kids, or you'll get caught by the Black *ñáñigos*. This is the night the Abakuá ñáñigos come out to kidnap children and drink their blood," she warns us in a voice from beyond the tomb.

Barbara gets up from the rocking chair, goes down the porch stairs, opens the garage fence gate, and swings on it.

The children next door come to see her swing.

She ignores them and raises her nose, giving herself importance.

WHENEVER I GO OVER TO ANITA'S HOUSE, I look carefully at the fig tree growing in her yard. Her green house, although a little discolored by the rains and stained black by humidity, is surrounded by flowering plants of all colors and leafy trees, and the fig tree, the largest of them, stands out.

I sit in the grass under it, leaning against the trunk, when I want a little silence. Now I'm under the tree to think about my grandmother's house, the accident I had at Bella's house, and the hives that torture me, especially at night when I end up scratching myself without realizing it, re-opening my hives.

Anita, white with brown eyes and dark brown hair cut in a page boy, is four years old, my age. Seeing me in the yard, she comes over, gives me her hand, and helps me up from the grass.

Together we cross through the corridors and rooms of her house.

Large conch shells on the tile floor secure all the doors to prevent the breeze from slamming them shut.

The shape and structure of these mollusks, with their pink, curled mouths, make up an important part of the silence whispered by the fig tree in the yard.

We lie on the floor, underneath Anita's parents' iron bed, to watch the light gliding over the yellow tiles.

We are waiting for something, with our bodies stuck to the cold and dust of the floor, staring up at the dusty springs of the bed frame.

"Conch shells are the safekeepers of the sound of the sea, and if you hold them to your ear and listen to them long enough, you yourself go to the sea."

The girl reveals this to me in a mysterious voice. "The song of the sea carries you away," she adds. This seems a short route to get to the sea, but am I ready to follow it?

"Once I'm inside the conch shell, how would I get out afterward?"

Anita laughs at my comment and opens her arms and legs. This is not for adults to see. She is being herself, a child, in a way that does not allow interrogation by others, especially grownups, who might ask, "What are you doing under the bed? Why are you lying down like that?"

But for me, the same age as she is, her gesture is very clear.

We look forward eagerly to something happening out there, and, in the meantime, without anyone suspecting that we are down here, we see the world.

"I don't want to miss Oscarito's bath," she says, coming out from under the bed, taking my hand and leading me to the house next door, which also has lots of shrubbery, but it's better cared for.

Even the treetops are shaped, like upside-down cups and lollipops. The porch is shaded by curtains made of narrow white wooden slats that hang horizontally between rails of the same color on top and underneath them, raised and lowered by pulling on a cord.

These curtains, a novelty in the neighborhood, come from the United States.

Oscarito, a little boy about one year old, sits inside a bathtub filled with water and bubbles, playing with a floating duck-shaped soap so yellow and so like an egg that I want to eat it. The mother furiously rubs the boy's skin with a real sea sponge the color of coffee. The child's skin, normally pink, flattens out like rubber with each pass of the sponge, then pops back to its normal shape, but turns fiery red.

Oscarito is focused on the light reflected in the bubbles and tries to grab them with his hands. The scent of the perfumed soap fills the air. The mother, pudgy and kind-looking, with a wide face, green eyes, and huge, black pupils, works quickly. Each movement she makes transmits great energy, a belief in the superiority of cleanliness and order. Oscarito is the son of a famous journalist, and the fact that his last name, Bolaño, appears in the newspaper every day confers special prestige on his family in the neighborhood.

I feel it's a privilege to be in this house and to see the child bathe.

After a few minutes, Anita runs off without saying goodbye, as she usually does, but I stay to watch the bath ceremony.

The mother goes out to the bedroom for a moment, and I sit on the edge of the white bathtub, which is supported by lion's feet that clutch crystal balls that rest on the tiny blue tiles of the bathroom floor.

Oscarito throws the duck into the water, then reaches in to fish it out. The duck has been in the water long enough to lose the sharpness of its contours. It still retains its orange bill, though its eyes, black circles, can no longer see.

The mother returns from the bedroom with a large yellow plush towel that makes me dream of yellow *romerillo* flowers and of the roaring summer sun.

The mother pulls the plug to empty the tub and uses the towel to dry Oscarito, who stands in the tub jumping and down, while the gray, lathered water glug-glugs down the drain pipe.

Like Anita, I leave without saying goodbye.

THE NEXT DAY, Sunday, a few girls have gathered in the patio at Anita's house to play the Wheel, and we sing:

> *To the wheel, the bread-and-cinnamon wheel,*
> *give me a little kiss and go to school.*
> *If you don't want to go, lie down to sleep*
> *in the soft grass, or on your bed in your room.*

The end of the song is the part I like best, as it's also my mother's belief: "If you don't want to go, lie down to sleep."

However, I know that the world is not like that.

I can't just go to bed. Every morning I must struggle against this idea as well as my laziness and force myself to go to school, because the holidays are over and the new school year has just begun.

The fact is, I enjoy sitting at a big desk and copying down what they write on the board. Already the big girls have gotten used to me, and none of them give me mocking looks anymore.

I also like to sing and dance in a ring holding hands with girls like Anita and others older than me, like the girls who go to the Oblate Sisters of Providence School. My mother has told me that white girls are not allowed to attend that school, which takes only Black and mulatta girls.

Some people despise them for this, but Anita and I think they are very important, attending such an exclusive school.

We dance around and sing, looking at the sky. The day is clear and bright, the sky blue, yellow butterflies are flying among the red Mar Pacífico flowers. Suddenly the sound of summer interrupts our pleasant morning: the engines of an airplane passing over our heads.

Summer and engine noise are synonymous for me, because that hum underscores the heat of the sun with a line of sound.

"What are you playing, little girls?" asks Guillermito from the sidewalk, in front of the patio fence.

Guillermito looks like Henry of the comic strips, with a long neck, an almost hairless head, a chickpea-shaped nose, and a pooching belly. He always interrupts the games other kids are playing. At Anita's house they are building a second floor, and in the patio, there's a mound of sand and another of cement. Guillermito can never avoid the temptation to pick up a handful of sand. That's why when he appears, we disappear, as grownups say.

"We were playing Dead Dog," I reply, stopping the round.

"I don't see any Dead Dogs, just white girls running around and singing with pickaninnies," he replies mockingly.

The boy opens the garage fence gate and walks right up to us in the yard. He squints, pretending that the sun bothers him. However, he told us during a previous intrusion, what this gesture is supposed to do is make him look handsome, like cowboys he's seen in Westerns at the Cine Rivoli who squint when they get in gun duels at noon in the deserted streets of the American West.

Guillermito thinks he's the fastest draw in the neighborhood, but he has no gun, only what we call a *tiraflechas,* a slingshot, a Y-shaped split branch with a rubber band tied to it. With this you can fire off stones and break anyone's head. It is said in the neighborhood that Cat Whiskers, a tough kid who's a friend of my brother's, put a boy's eye out with his slingshot.

"We're playing Dead Dog and if you can't see that, you're more of a dog, and deader than one," insists Anita ferociously.

"And a hairless dog too!" one of the Black girls from the Oblate Sisters exclaims, laughing. Guillermito raises a hand to his bald head, scratches it, and looks at the girl. I think he's trying to size her up as a fighter, but also, probably, trying to remember whether she has brothers to defend her.

"A bald dog like me?" he asks, mocking her, touching his head.

"Hardly. Like you there is none other," I answer with contempt.

"Let me play with you! I can play 'father' or 'doctor.' Also, I can play 'priest,' if you lend me a robe."

Guillermito laughs, trying to look innocent. His hands are in the pockets of his shorts. From his right pocket hangs the orange rubber of his slingshot.

"There's no father or doctor here, no priest. Go away and stop bothering us. This is my house," Anita scolds, facing him without fear.

Guillermito backs up, turning slowly and walking towards the fence. When he passes the pile of sand, he scoops up a handful, turns quickly, runs, and throws it at us with all his strength.

"Take that from Dead Dog! See if you can catch Dead Dog!" he shouts like a person possessed by the devil. We try to protect our eyes with our arms, but for me it's too late. My eyes are full of sand, and the minute I blink, I can feel the grains scratching my cornea. Almost blind, I run across the street. It hurts to open my eyes, and I guide myself home with my hands, touching walls and fences.

When I get to the door of my house, I collide with my father's pants. I cling to them because they give me security, because they are so light to the touch and so floating.

"Who did this to you, so I can beat the crap out of him?" my father asks, furious, holding me with his clenched fists.

"No one did. We're at war," I reply quietly. "This is part of war," I add. I cannot bear the thought of my father attacking Guillermito, or my brother defending me.

This, to me, is *my* war. Who defends you in a war? You win or you lose, forget about defenders.

My father pulls a chair into our alleyway, to see better in daylight. He sits down and lays me across his thighs. With little cotton balls to gently extract the sand, he drips olive oil into my eyes.

Each drop captures grains of sand, the cotton absorbing the oil and taking with it the abrasive kernels. Gradually, I can half-open my eyelids, see patches of blue sky or pieces of white roof.

Inside the house my mother is screaming: "This Guillermito! He's crazy! Don't play with him anymore! He's always throwing sand in kids' eyes. I'm going to complain to his parents!"

Ignoring my mother's tantrum, my father continues patiently to remove grains of sand with cotton balls. I smell the cigars he always smokes, mixed with cologne. My mother never uses cologne. My father always does. He likes to dress well, wear elegant ties, carry linen handkerchiefs with his initials embroidered on them, meticulously trim his mustache, dye his hair to an elegant steel-gray color. My mother finds this upsetting and says my father is as vain as a banty rooster.

Bit by bit the sand is gone and I can blink and open my eyes without scratching them. Everything looks new. I was blind for a few minutes, but now I can see colors, things are visual surprises, as are people and the blue shadows of empty spaces.

My father smiles and gives me a piece of advice: "Don't fight clean against those who don't respect rules. If you do, you lose. Do you want to keep losing? Next time, throw sand at him first!"

"THE BOYS," MY BROTHER AND HIS FRIENDS, Cat Whiskers, who has no whiskers, and Ping the Chinaman, who has oblique eyes and is sometimes mockingly called Ping Pong, are playing ball on the empty lot at the corner, which we children call "the field." Despite the tropical heat, the boys wear gray flannel baseball pants with elastic ankle cuffs, and shirts that copy original uniforms of professional players. On the fronts of their shirts, they've sewn a large navy-blue A intertwined with a scorpion, emblem of the baseball team called "Almendares," named after a neighborhood in the Capital. The Almendares team always wins the Island's baseball championship.

We girls, the mulatta Caridad, Anita, and I, watch sitting on a bench, to the left and behind the catcher, far enough away so the ball doesn't hit us.

My entire family is Almendarista, meaning they ferociously support the Almendares team. That's why, as soon as I had use of reason, I declared myself a rabid fan of The Capital, named after the actual Capital.

The Capital is Almendares' arch-enemy and most serious competitor.

The Capital's symbols are a lion and the color red.

My mother keeps trying to convince me to become Almendarista, saying that only Blacks root for The Capital, and it's just because red is the favorite color of the lower depths.

"Well then, I'll be Black and of the lower depths," I reply defiantly. I am particularly proud not to give in to such pressure because, in a family of Almendaristas, someone must back The Capital, to go against the tide. Also, red truly is my favorite color because it is the color of vibrant blood, and the lion is my favorite wild animal, for his majesty and courage.

The Capital baseball team, though it always loses, has unmatched spirit, and I'm convinced that, one day, we will win in spectacular fashion and embarrass all the cocky jackass Almendarista fans everywhere on the Island.

Cat Whiskers is at bat, Septimio is the pitcher, and Ping the Chinaman the catcher. Cat Whiskers knocks dirt off his shoes and practice-swings with the bat.

Ping the Chinaman makes some finger signals and my brother throws a fastball. Cat Whiskers hits what looks to be a home run.

Septimio chases after the ball, while Cat Whiskers runs the bases, digging his cleats deep into the red dirt. But just as my brother is about to retrieve the ball, Guillermito appears and snatches it away, smiling with his face all sweaty and the few blond hairs on his head messed up by the wind.

"Hand over the ball, you!" orders Septimio.

"What's that you say?" asks Guillermito, hiding the ball behind his back.

"The ball, asshole!" demands my brother. Cat Whiskers comes over, huffing and puffing, rearranging his testicles inside the baggy pants that are narrow in the crotch.

"Give him the ball, faggot! Your mother's cunt, bastard! You think you can just come here to mess with our game?" Cat Whiskers shouts, furious, grabbing Guillermito.

My brother steps away from the two boys, fixes his uniform by tucking his shirt in his pants, dries the sweat on his forehead with a handkerchief that he takes out of his pocket, throws an imaginary ball into the air, catches it with his glove, and ambles off. Cat Whiskers and Guillermito, who are rolling around on the ground punching each other, are unaware the pitcher is leaving and the ball is rolling through the grass.

Caridad walks over, picks up the ball, and holds it in her hand like an apple she's about to eat, white with red seams, like a war trophy. Without changing the calm expression on her face, Caridad kicks Guillermito in the back so hard that it immobilizes him.

Guillermito curls up like a wounded spider. He hasn't made a sound.

Cat Whiskers stands up, brushing the dirt off his pants. "Get up, you son of a bitch!" he orders Guillermito. Guillermito doesn't move. Cat Whiskers lifts him up, holding his arms from behind and preventing him from using his hands. "What does this coward deserve, girls?" he asks us.

We all look at each other. Caridad asks, "What do they do in the movies?"

Then she answers herself: "But this is real, a real person to punish, who will really bleed, no tomato sauce."

Guillermito does not dare glance up. Now Cat Whiskers is starting to look all grandiose and magnanimous, preparing to consult his people, getting them to participate in the punishment.

"I think we should try him," says Caridad.

"Well thought out. We are all witnesses in this case. The witnesses must all state what they saw, and then the jury will decide what needs to be done. The witnesses will be the jury, of course, because there are no other people here," explains Cat Whiskers, looking at Anita, who has stood up and is fiddling with the hem of her dress.

"Guillermito is always harassing us. He throws sand in our eyes without provocation, without a word of warning. He's a coward," Anita condemns. Her voice is surprisingly secure, irrevocable.

Cat Whiskers gives Guillermito a look of contempt and punches him softly in the stomach, like a subtle prelude to what comes next.

"A coward, huh? Throwing sand in the eyes of helpless little girls?"

Caridad nods her head, as if to say that she was just about to say the same thing as Anita, so there's no need to ask her.

Cat Whiskers looks at me.

An imaginary blow, like a huge leaden hand, descends on my head. The expectation of others crystallizes what I was going to say. It's as if they've put the spotlight on me and everything else has suddenly disappeared. I feel naked, like they are trying to get words out of me with a hammer. I move over close to Guillermito and see how afraid he is, trembling spastically like a fish out of water.

"He, well, why don't we let him go? I don't know, sometimes he . . ."

Without letting me finish, Guillermito raises his head and looks at me with bright black eyes that pierce me with loathing. He smiles scornfully and spits in my face.

A red curtain descends over my eyes. Everything becomes sounds and black shapes like slithering lumps. I feel a murmur, a strange air at the end of a tunnel, a landscape at the end of a hole that smells of blood and screams. When I can see again, Guillermito's curled up on the floor, foaming at the mouth.

"What happened to him?" I ask Cat Whiskers.

"You punched him in the stomach," he replies, which does nothing to allay my astonishment, because I have no memory of doing this. Cat Whiskers, with great speed and without waiting for the jury's verdict, removes Guillermito's clothes, revealing his whitish skin, like a rice worm. Ping the Chinaman, the catcher, who until now has not intervened because he rarely speaks or acts, looks at Cat Whiskers, understands what he wants, and proceeds to open Guillermito's legs as if they were a pincer. Cat Whiskers, stroking his fist like a boxer about to make a knock-out punch, socks him in the testicles.

Guillermito howls, then shudders like a headless chicken.

Cat Whiskers looks at him with a sneer as if Guillermito were a disgusting thing, a repulsive object he will make sure to avoid for as long as he lives.

Guillermito, blinded by tears, gropes around in the dirt for his trousers and shirt, but the mulatta Caridad has hidden them among the field's scrawny bushes.

I go home still not understanding how I could hit Guillermito without seeing him or feeling it. Also, I don't understand why he spat at me when I felt sorry for him.

As night falls, I wonder why I didn't quit the game before the violence started, the way my brother did.

A FEW DAYS LATER, Caridad tells me that she saw Guillermito walking along First Avenue, hand in hand with his mother, and that when he recognized her, he became frightened. Then he became very mannerly and greeted her with great respect – he, who despises mulattos and Blacks.

The lesson served him well.

But it left me with a bad taste in my mouth.

Maybe the other girls feel the same way I do and that's why we haven't gotten together anymore to dance the Wheel.

Now, playing hide-and-seek with Anita in her yard, I'm no longer afraid of having sand thrown in my eyes. But I am frightened by a voice that calls to me from the end of the streets, stretching out the last two letters of my name until they become a scream, finishing in a sigh, like a lament: "Mercccyyyyy."

I come out of my hiding place and walk toward the sidewalk.

I look off to where the streets end at a point of trees and houses.

"Did somebody just call to me?"

Anita, who has emerged from somewhere behind me, laughs, scratching her nose and moving her head back and forth to say "no."

"Someone called me from there, where the street ends. The voice came from there." I point my finger.

Anita sits on the curb because at this hour no cars go by. I stand in the street, in front of her, as if waiting for an answer. I see her white panties and the small rolls of fat on her thighs. Her page boy, parted down the middle, hangs on both sides of the ears like a frame.

The afternoon smells of fritters, and the breeze also brings the crackle of a frying pan coming from some neighborhood kitchen.

"I'm done playing," declares the girl, opening her eyes, as if to make me fall inside them. Everything stops. As soon as she sits down, Anita cuts all the strings that united us in the game and kept us in that circle, gasping and full of sweat. Now I pay attention to the houses, to the leaves of the trees dancing around in the breeze.

And I sit down, next to her, on the rough curb heated by the siesta-time sun.

"Somebody called to me. Other times I've heard this call and I've looked, but it wasn't anybody."

Anita plays with the gold bracelet with a tiny heart in the center that goes around her chubby, white wrist.

"Over there, there's no one, nor any thing," she replies, annoyed.

I cut a non-existent cord and fall into a strange place, cold and without walls.

I need to give some answer quickly, climb up to the Land of Anita where there's no one at the end of the streets. I need to get out of this cold and this absence of walls, this nothing under my feet, this something banging inside, like a hammer in my ears.

"It wasn't my mother. It was someone over there. Another voice."

The girl laughs with disdain and continues playing with her bracelet and moving the pebbles in the gutter with the toe of one of her shiny black patent leather shoes that have straps fastened by black pearls.

"We're going inside my house," she decides, taking me by the hand.

The fig tree in her garden is laden with bulbous fruit, some of which has fallen to the ground and burst, giving off a sweet smell of decaying flesh.

We go inside.

Anita picks up the conch shell that acts as a doorstop for her parents' bedroom, and we scoot under the bed. She raises the conch shell to her ear.

The light coming through the window facing the garden vibrates on the yellow floor tiles, but Anita doesn't see it because she's closed her eyes. Her pink ears, which smell of soap, seem to swell, to become gigantic. Drops of sweat make her face shine. She's lost in the conch shell.

"The sea is inside it," she assures me, handing it to me.

To put my ear to the conch shell is to take a dangerous step, something that compromises me. I don't know what it means to Anita, but there's something sticky about the situation, something that clings to me and makes all my actions meaningful – even inaction.

The girl moves on the floor to a place where she can observe me closely.

"I don't know what you're saying. How is the sea going to be *inside* this shell?" I ask, suddenly skeptical. I'm trying to slow down the moment with words, by seeking clarifications. I stretch out the space between the conch shell and me. I expand the time between indecision and the adventure of hearing what is inside this conch shell and its huge violet-and-amber-ridged tongue that, whirling, sprouts from its inner white spiral.

Anita touches my arm to give me confidence, and at the same time with the complicity of someone who is revealing some arcane perversion.

I bring my ear closer to the calcareous surface, and the murmur of the sea comes gushing, boiling out, cleansing the bad taste I have in my mouth. My childhood enters the inner fire of the conch shell.

The girl moves her hands over the ground. Her sweaty palms caress the cold floor that has the wounding smell of the creolin disinfectant that's been left, here and there, in humid traces like snail tracks.

The fuzz under Anita's nose vibrates with her choppy and anxious breathing. She thrashes on the ground. She wants to show me a part of herself only expressed in movements.

Distances have disappeared. Anita has severed all the cords, but, instead of the emptiness of minutes ago, I have fallen into her intimacy. For her there are no limits. She fills the entire floor under the bed. She is in her element, under the sea, watching the dust of light spread with each return of the wave.

She takes off her clothes, as if this were the last gesture of liberation.

I give her the shell, no longer as a separate person, but as an echo of her own being that, gratefully, returns the shared pleasure to her.

I CROSS FIRST AVENUE, which is two-way, with lots of traffic. It's four o'clock in the afternoon of the next day, and I'm wearing, as usual now at this time of day, a white piqué dress with flounces and lace.

Sitting in a rocking chair on Ping the Chinaman's porch, I see the avenue suddenly empty, unusual at this hour. No one knows I'm here, and this gives me a secret joy. I crossed the avenue "just because." I wanted to go as far as my feet would take me. This is a way to celebrate the pure joy of existing that right now swells in my chest. I absorb life in every way as if it were honey and the pleasure experienced by all the cells of my body makes me feel light, able to fly if I try. I am drawn to Ping the Chinaman's house because it's gray. These days, I relate gray to mystery, to music of serious tones, to the smell of musk and the taste of ginger.

I discovered musk and ginger at Eduardito's house because his mother uses musk perfume, and their cook, who sometimes prepares fish with ginger Chinaman-style, has given me a taste of that root. My senses become confused when trying to capture things, to discover their most hidden meanings.

The house has a large garden in front, including pines with twisted branches and even twisted trunks, unlike any pines I have ever seen. Strange dark-green glazed shingles like river moss cover the roof, whose four points end in beak shapes so bright that they dazzle my eyes. I get up from the rocking chair and pat the rough surface of the gray walls of the porch, stimulating my sense of touch. Blue and yellow tiles, with a few touches of green, cover the floor, and I feel their colors under my feet like a caress, although I'm wearing my white booties.

Against the wall, and between the rocking chairs of the portal, a rectangular fish tank imprisons a dark green lamprey, so large that it has a hard time turning to swim in the opposite direction. The motionless fish, with its black spots and gaping pointed mouth, watches me without blinking an eye. Maybe it's asleep with its eyes open, dreaming of a place where it could turn around without having to fold up its tail. The lamprey haunts me because it seems very old and wise.

Maybe it knows why I, unknowing, do things, and why people spit at me when I want to help them.

A gentle sun outside accentuates the warm shadow of four o'clock in the afternoon that's falling, blue and purple, behind objects, like music. It's as if everything is of a piece, and I've fallen into the sea with this piece in my stomach. I try to surface despite the lump inside me that's making me sink, but I can't.

The sun moves on in the sky and its light gets weaker. At this moment I can do whatever I want. I am truly free. I could break the fish tank, turn the rocking chairs around, shout, run, ring the doorbell. So many acts can be contained in the moment. That's why it weighs so much. I could run into the street and throw myself in front of a streetcar.

Then I'd never need to wait for nighttime, and food, and my mother to sing me to sleep.

However, I decide to contemplate this big fish with fixed eyes and listen to sounds that spring from the house: women's voices, the radio broadcasting a soap opera with thunderous music that highlights the dramatic moments.

The people who pass by on the street don't know that I shouldn't be here, that it's not my house but that of a Chinese kid, a friend of my brother's, and that this fish isn't mine either. Passers-by don't notice and don't look at me. Nobody looks at a girl on a porch who, in turn, is looking at a fish. There is nothing to see, in this case. It's not at all strange.

But I do find it stupid that they don't realize that I don't belong to this elegant house with its pagoda roof – that, really, I live across First Avenue on the same alley as poor people, in an apartment that, instead of overlooking the street, has a patio we share with screaming neighbors.

Here, when my mother washes our clothes out there, because it makes her feel cosmopolitan, she sings the *Internationale* at the top of her lungs, giving it all she's got:

> *Arise ye prisoners of starvation*
> *Arise ye wretched of the earth*
> *For justice thunders condemnation*
> *A better world is in birth!*

All the neighbors hear her and assume she's a communist. Some have stopped greeting her. It's bad now to be a communist and, apparently, it's considered as contagious as a dread disease, because when those neighbors see her, they plaster themselves against the wall and won't go near her, as if she were about to explode with communist germs from one moment to the next.

My mother doesn't sing other songs, because boleros make her cry, and she refuses to memorize lyrics.

Also, she believes that the *Internationale* is elegant and proves that she has traveled, though she's never left the Island. She would like to have lived, like my revolutionary uncle-in-law Alejandro de Nájera, in Russia, or in Germany between the two wars – not now with the Nazis. Alejandro is the dead husband of her sister, my Aunt Isabel.

My mother would also have enjoyed being like Isabel, who shocked the German women with her nylon stockings and her silk undies because you couldn't buy these things in that country during the economic crisis of the Twenties and Thirties.

SUDDENLY Ping the Chinaman comes out of his house.

He closes the door without slamming it, not making the slightest noise.

He passes in front of me without paying me the slightest attention.

He has a baseball in his hand and a new mitt with a player's autograph on the thumb.

He stands on the porch, practicing catcher moves, and smacking the ball against the glove.

The lamprey watches Ping out of the corner of its eye.

I skip down the porch steps, open the fence gate and turn to look at him.

Ping the Chinaman sits on the steps and looks at me without talking. Caridad says that's because he doesn't know much Spanish, and that's because his family comes from China, where they speak some other language. At first, he had a hard time getting other children to play with him, but then they let him in when they got sick of him staring at them all the time without saying a word.

It was Septimio, my brother, who said, "Let this pest play, or he's going to give us the evil eye." I can understand the other children's fear, because those slanted eyes impress me too, along with his weird fish and the pointy roof of his house.

Ping the Chinaman leaves the ball on the ground and smacks the new glove with his fist to give it shape with his punches.

He doesn't ask me what I was doing on his porch.

No cars or trams are coming, so I run across the street to my house.

AT SEVEN IN THE EVENING, after we eat dinner, I go out with a saucer of milk, which my mother has reluctantly given me, and climb up on a chair to set it on top of the wall.

I wait for the gray cat with black stripes, who always walks on top of the wall at this hour to get his daily ration.

In a few minutes the cat appears, meowing, followed by two others, one striped and the other black. They walk single file, and seem to smile when they meow.

I run to the house and ask my mother for two more saucers of milk.

"We can't feed all the cats in the neighborhood!" she hollers as she fills the saucers with milk.

The first finishes its milk and sits on the wall to lick itself and clean its whiskers. The others, the burly black one and the skinny striped one, are waiting for their own saucers.

I set them on the wall in front of each of them, and they lap up the milk, snapping their tongues. When they're done, they give out a little meow, like thanking me, and walk back and forth on the wall, rubbing against my hands. Then all three leave, single file, the way they came.

My mother waits for me at the door with her arms crossed.

I run past her with the saucers and put them in the sink. "I need just one more saucer of milk. To put under my crib," I say timidly.

"A saucer under your crib? For whom?" My mother sits at the dining room table, crossing her arms and looking at me, as if judging me.

My father is getting dressed in the bedroom to go to the horse races. My brother, lurking at the street door, is eating an orange.

"The plate is for during the night."

"What cat comes into the house at night?" my mother asks, losing patience. "Do you think we're rich? Feeding cats at sunset, then at midnight? We have no food! We have no milk!"

"The plate isn't for a cat. It's for a lady."

Septimio laughs from the doorway and comes over, eating his orange.

"How many times have I told you not to tell lies?" my indignant mother asks me. "God the Father punishes you! The noses of children who tell lies grow like Pinocchio's! They put a ring in their nose and they turn into donkeys!"

My brother, still eating his orange, spits a seed in my face as a joke, and laughs like crazy.

My mother lights a cigarette and pauses, her face dark as night. The smoke billows out of her mouth.

"Right now, you are going to bed," she orders, furious, and she undresses me with a stern expression, depositing me in the crib.

I hear my father's voice singing in the room:

> On the trunk of a tree
> a girl swollen with pleasure
> carved his name...

I smell the perfume of his colognes and hear his shoes' tiny iron taps clicking on the tile floor.

When he finishes dressing, he leaves without saying goodbye. My mother growls and makes an angry gesture.

"Mama, please give me a plate of milk for the lady," I insist from my crib.

"No, girl, stop this nonsense. You are living on the moon. Don't you know that your father is going to gamble his salary on the horses, and if he's unlucky we won't make it through the month?"

"If you feed the lady, I know he'll be lucky."

"Go to sleep!" she tells me, exasperated.

I pretend to be asleep, and lie waiting for the violet-eyed woman to appear at three o'clock in the morning. Seeing her walking through the living room, I climb out of the crib, careful not to make noise, to keep from waking up my brother. I go to the kitchen, open the icebox, take out the bottle of milk, and fill a saucer for her. The woman licks at it desperately without consuming the liquid.

"Please make my father not lose money on horse racing," I beg the transparent woman, who smiles and dissolves in a gray cloud.

PRECISELY SIX MONTHS LATER, during which time I have not seen the ghost woman once, and apparently nothing special has happened – except that my father has made money in horse racing – I arrive home, tired of playing hide-and-seek with Anita, and, to my surprise, I find my mother and brother putting clothes in cardboard boxes.

"What are you doing?" I ask, alarmed.

"Your father was graduated with a Ph.D. in Pedagogy from the University, and he has been given a very well-paid position with the new Grau government. His friend, the pedagogue Dr. Luis Pérez Espinós, is now Minister of Education and has appointed him head of Primary Instruction," my mother explains, not looking up from her packing.

"So?"

"So, we're moving," she says.

What is this? I didn't know my father had finished at the university. I haven't been paying attention to my parents. I didn't know what was going on in the house.

"What's this about moving? Why must we move?" I ask.

"We're moving to Almendares. The apartment faces the street, not an alleyway like this, and you'll have a room that you'll share with your brother. You'll have a real bed, like a grownup. I'm giving your crib to your cousin Chiquitina, who is expecting a baby."

I don't understand how we can just pack up and go somewhere else.

On the other hand, it's nice to find out that the apartment is not on an alleyway, meaning I won't need to walk in front of the mulatta Luzdivina's apartment.

Luzdivina always has her radio turned on, playing rhumbas, which is wonderful, because when there's no one in our living room, I can dance there to my heart's content.

Once, my parents surprised me doing the rhumba and were amazed, because no one had taught me. "It's like Natasha's dance in Tolstoy's *War and Peace*. She has the rhumba in her blood," my father said to my mother.

The bad part is having to pass in front of Luzdivina's door, where her gigantic grown-up children look out and stare at me, just to embarrass me. When I try to ignore them and go on my way without giving them importance, they say to my mother, "She's turning into a little snot." What is it that makes adults want to embarrass a four-year-old girl?

Other things that make me glad we are moving: no longer will I need to pass by Eduardito's house and ignore his cries to play with him, or avoid looking at Elena when we are in the hallway.

MY FATHER COMES HOME LATE, when Septimio is already in bed and I'm in my crib.

Now my father is a big D doctor and he's going to be rich.

But he brings home the same white bag with *minutas*, or pieces of fish breaded and fried, for dinner. Also, as usual, he loses his temper with my mother because she can't find the kitchen knife. And, as always, he sits down at the table to eat in his T-shirt and underpants.

Standing up in my crib, I look closely at him to see if a "Doctor" looks any different, but I don't notice the slightest change.

When I look down at the ground, I see the shadow of a dragonfly flying, like the ones I try to catch in the field at the corner. But when I look for this dragonfly that's casting its shadow everywhere, I can't spot it. The shadow flies all by itself, in the air, one foot above the ground.

WATER

10

ALMENDARES

WE'VE LEFT AN OLD APARTMENT that faces an alley, and a few minutes ago we arrived at our brand-new apartment that faces the street and has a small balcony in front. Everything inside the house smells new. In the light-yellow kitchen, a white porcelain stove rests on the red tile floor. I turn a nob that lights a burner and am fascinated by the blue and purple coronet of fire that automatically spews out with the sound of an explosion, giving off a pungent odor of gas.

The bathroom glistens with blue and black tiles. The radiant white grout of the tiles' interstices gives off a serious, cold scent of chalk. The brand-new medicine cabinet has a mirror with no black corrosion spots, but it's covered in a thin layer of white dust, remnant of building this newly-painted apartment.

I've just carried in the last bundle of clothes. I sit on the cold yellow-and-white tile floor of our new living room. Facing me, slumped under the little window overlooking a small interior courtyard shared by the other apartments, my brother rests his head against the wall, drops of sweat inching down the blue veins popping out on his neck. We are surrounded by lots of boxes and packages. Soon the new living and dining room furniture will arrive. The bedroom furniture is already here. These heavenly spaces, clean and bright, will fill up with our new life.

Through the living room window a gray light enters, along with the odor of fresh cement coming from other new houses in the neighborhood. From the little window to the interior patio, I hear a shrill, fluty voice crying: "Where are you? I can't see you in the dark!"

Amazed, I look at Septimio for an explanation. "It's a parrot. A talking bird," he clarifies.

Through the window come sounds of someone dragging furniture around, and the choppy conversations of neighbors.

"Where are you? I can't see you in the dark!" the parrot cries again – and now answers itself: "I'm way over here, in Maceo Park!"

My brother picks himself up off the floor to help my mother unpack boxes.

I stay sitting on the floor, alone, with the little patio window facing me and the sun angling in to shine on the yellow wall of the little patio.

"I'm four years old, I'm sitting on these new tiles, and this is my first new house. Here is where I will grow up," I murmur with great seriousness.

Something pointed, like a knife, touches my heart.

I have left behind the other place and my friends. Elena, Anita, Cusita, the mulatta Caridad, Cat Whiskers, Ping the Chinaman appear like ghosts inside me, filling my mouth with a bitter liquid. I believe that I will never see them again. The joy of this new house hollows itself out, and through this opening something different emerges, like a relative who walks off down a long road and doesn't even turn to say goodbye.

I'm overcome by worry: What if there are no kids on this block? If I'm the only kid, how am I going to live in a world of older people who don't like to play?

The next day, I get up early to see what morning is like here in the new neighborhood. I enjoy having my own bedroom and sleeping in a real bed like a grown-up, without the railings of a crib.

Septimio woke up minutes earlier than I did, and is in the bathroom. His bed is unmade and I hear the noise of water. I don't want to wait for him to come out, and quickly pull on my overalls. a brown jumpsuit that my mother bought me because the neighbors in the other neighborhood were saying that I went out naked to play in the street, even though I wore my nylon panties.

I put on my sandals, because, here, in this new place, I'm not allowed to walk barefoot. I don't feel like having breakfast. I'll brush my teeth and wash my face later.

I go outside, and am greeted by a mob of yellow butterflies that fly and perch on the five-petaled red hibiscus flowers called "Mar Pacífico" that have been planted under our little balcony.

We're on the ground floor, but there's a small staircase of red tiles I must climb down to get to the sidewalk.

The yellow walls of this big apartment building glow with the first rays of the sun. I stroll down the sidewalk to find children, but all I see are adults. I walk over to the avenue on the corner to look at cars.

In this neighborhood cars go by much faster and more often than they did in the other.

I don't see any of my friends from the other neighborhood because we've moved far away. Even so, my eyes look for them. I hadn't really realized that I wouldn't see them anymore because I thought I would just be getting away from the ones that bothered me.

I knew these things, but I didn't feel them. Now, I feel them and am sad, but what can be done? I can't go back and play in the other neighborhood.

Distraught, I go inside my house and collide with my brother who's rushing outside to explore the new neighborhood. Septimio is nine years old, and some time ago decided he belongs to the superior caste of adults. So now he almost never speaks to me. Another thing: my father no longer beats him when he does something wrong. This makes me happy because now I don't need to cry and beg my father, on my knees, not to whip Septimio with his belt when he gets furious with him.

I never understood what my brother did to be punished so, but I couldn't bear it. Now, because I am an *abicú*, I can think of many things that my father must do because I say so, other than to stop beating Septimio.

My father comes out of his room smelling of cologne and wearing one of his white suits made of *dril 100* that he's just bought at a very expensive store. He carries a Mexican leather briefcase embossed with an eagle perched on a cactus called a *nopal*. I would like to have this briefcase to take to school, but I know better than to ask my father for it.

And not just because his assistant, a skinny little man with steel-rimmed glasses whom my father calls Doctor Shop Window because he's a scaredy-cat and breaks at the slightest political disturbance, has appeared at the door to carry that very briefcase for him.

They leave in a hurry, heading for the Ministry of Education, I guess.

IN THE MORNING, when I leave the apartment, I run into a very white girl with gray-green eyes, long blond hair parted in the middle and cascading in curls alongside her rosy cheeks that remind me of the Venus in *The Birth of Venus* by Botticelli.

Except she's jumping around the sidewalk on one leg.

"What are you playing?" I ask with curiosity.

"Hopscotch," she answers. "Do you want to play with me?" she asks.

The girl continues to jump only with her right leg on numbers written in chalk on the sidewalk.

"I don't know this game," I confess.

"It's really easy. You throw the crushed can as far as possible over the numbers one through ten drawn in the squares. Try not to make it fall on any line. You jump with one leg on the single numbers, and you rest with both legs on squares that sit side by side. Then you pick up the can and jump back to the starting square."

I am surprised at how well this girl can explain things. She must be much older than me, although she is not taller.

"Who wins in this game?"

"Whoever has the highest score in each throw," the girl informs me, giving me the can, without waiting for me to ask for it.

I think it's a stupid game, but I don't say that because I don't want to get on the wrong side of this girl, who is my first friend in Almendares. I throw the can as far as possible to get the highest score. The can falls on number nine.

"What's your name?" I ask as I pick up the can and start jumping back.

"Elena."

"Then you're Elena of Almendares. There's another Elena in La Sierra."

"I know what your name is, because my dad works with yours, and my dad told your dad to move to our building," explains the girl, starting her turn. She jumps without running out of breath from the effort.

I'm upset that my father hasn't said a word to me about this.

"Does your father tell you everything he does?" I ask with annoyance.

"My mom and dad tell my brother César and me everything during dinner," Elena explains proudly, as she picks up the can from the ten and hops back, giving the can to me.

"My dad works very hard and doesn't have time to tell anybody anything," I say, annoyed, and toss the can on the sidewalk to stop playing.

EARLY SUNDAY MORNING, I go outside and run into Elena again, sitting on the steps at the entrance to the building. She wears a yellow cotton dress, adorned with lovely white lace, and she's reading a book with great attention.

I'm wearing a white skirt, also made of cotton, printed with violets, and a matching bodice that knots in the middle of my breasts, if there were any in childhood. My mother bought me the outfit so I could alternate with my brown overalls and not always go out in pants like a tomboy.

Not taking her eyes off the page of her book, Elena announces cheerfully: "I'm going to read to you from this book. 'Sett El-Hosn, daughter of the vizier Chamseddin, appeared amongst his female servants, and shone like a houri.'"

The girl reads very well, continuing:

> *Compared to her, the others were nothing more than satellites that made up her court, like stars that gather around the Moon when it leaves a cloud. She had scented herself with amber, musk, and rose, and the locks of her hair shone under the veil of silk covering her face.*

"What is that book?" I ask. I am utterly amazed to find a girl who can read, and who wants to share her reading with me.

"It's called *A Thousand and One Nights*. It's a book I found in my parents' room. Don't you think it's wonderful?" she exclaims.

I sit down next to Elena on the stairs, and smell her jasmine-perfumed soap.

"Your mom lets you read?" I ask, horrified. "Aren't you afraid you'll get TB? My mom says that reading books, and, worse, writing them, gives tuberculosis."

"No!" the girl exclaims, laughing mockingly. "That's a lie. My mom doesn't want me to read this book because it tells you what grownups do in bed at night. That's why I'm reading it on the staircase, and I hide it when I go back to my apartment."

"What do grownups do in bed at night?" I ask, afraid to look like a fool.

I don't understand what this girl is talking about, and I want to know how she thinks, to be able to gain her friendship.

This Elena is different. She doesn't play with dolls. She reads books.

In the light of the sun, her lemon-colored dress, her blond hair, and the golden fuzz covering her very white and shapely arms create a profusion of yellow. I feel the warmth of her body next to mine like a music that comes from a faraway and very longed-for place.

"Sex," Elena replies brutally. "That's what grownups hide all the time. I hear my parents doing it at night. In the morning they don't want to talk about it."

"Let's get out of here!" I say, scared. "I don't want my brother, who tells my mom everything, to leave the apartment and surprise us reading a book and talking about these things."

"My family sleeps all morning and my brother is the last one to wake up," the girl replies, holding my hand and getting up from the steps.

We walk down the sidewalk without saying a word. Elena keeps holding my hand, and this physical contact surprises me. Perhaps because I can feel her pulse under her skin, a strange complicity arises between us.

At the corner, we find an older woman of medium height and a little overweight, with big blue eyes and white hair gathered back in a bun, dressed in blue overalls and a sleeveless white shirt. She is watering the plants in her garden with a large green metal watering can.

"Good morning, Adela!" Elena greets her with ease and without introducing me. "How are the roses doing?"

"Good morning, Elena! The roses are quite wonderful this year!" the woman responds. "I fertilized them with a powder made of algae some friends in Chile just sent me that has a lot of proteins," she explains in a didactic but friendly tone.

She adds: "Some Araucanian Indians use it in their fields to make everything grow bigger. In Chile I've seen zucchinis the size of my forearm. The algae of the South American Pacific, you know, are very rich in nutrients because the ocean floor is volcanic and contains lots of minerals."

Adela leaves the watering can on the grass and gestures for us to follow her to the porch, waving us to sit in white rocking chairs that flank a white table, atop which are several metal tubes "the size of my forearm," as the woman says.

"These are kaleidoscopes that I bought for my grandchildren. Look through the hole and turn the tube," Adela says, settling herself in a third rocking chair.

I'm the first to pick up one of the tubes. I turn around and point it toward the sun. Several colored crystals combine into multiple geometric shapes.

"Inside the tube, you have three long mirrors joined in the shape of an equilateral triangle, and, at the opposite end of the hole from your eye, colored crystals that move every time you turn the tube. Their reflections form mandalas," explains the woman.

I don't dare ask what "mandalas" are. Anyway, I'm too fascinated by the colors and changing shapes.

AS WE LEAVE ADELA'S HOUSE, to my surprise Elena thanks her for letting us see the kaleidoscopes and for the refreshment she served us.

This girl behaves like an older person. I feel clumsy next to her.

"This woman talks like a book," I say to Elena when we are out on the sidewalk and Adela can't hear us.

"Well, she'll always be a teacher, though she's retired now. She taught elementary school and that's why she's so kind to us. She misses the contact with kids."

"Does she, too, avoid talking about sex?" I ask, as we walk down the sidewalk again holding hands.

"I don't know. I've never asked her. She's a teacher. I'm not close enough to her to deal with that issue."

Elena brusquely releases of my hand.

In front of my apartment, I say I must go in to lunch. It's a lie. I'm not hungry even though I haven't had breakfast. I just need to be alone.

Elena hides her copy of *A Thousand and One Nights* inside the top of her yellow dress, doesn't say goodbye, and runs up the stairs to her apartment.

As soon as I walk inside my apartment, my mother emerges from the kitchen and looks down at me with her piercing hawk eye.

"You're very happy. Who did you meet? Who did you talk to?" she asks, staring me in the eye to get inside my being.

"Nobody." I lie, holding her gaze, to spare Elena and Adela from her hurtful comments, to keep her from destroying my emotions, and filling my head with negative ideas.

I'm a child, but I've come to realize that I must protect myself from my mother's jealousy and her tendency to see it all black.

I go to my room and lie on my bed. My brother is out and, fortunately, I can be alone with my thoughts.

Meeting Elena has touched me in a strange way.

I'm not used to people I've just met getting so close to me, and I don't know how to understand it. Males avoid this bonding with me and with other males.

I have learned it's a weakness to show emotions or feel them, but Elena shows me affection without embarrassing herself. I close my eyes and try to remember the girl's face, but to my surprise, I can't do it.

I don't know what her face is like and I just remember the intense yellow of her dress and the jasmine fragrance of her scented soap.

THIS SECTION OF ALMENDARES is so important that it has a main avenue, from the corner of which, on this bright afternoon, I see a parade of wooden carriages and floats with dancers, tightrope walkers, magicians with black capes, and ferocious animals in cages.

"The circus has arrived," announces the lady next to me who's watching the parade, like me. Looking at her big blue eyes, I realize, with surprise, that it's Adela, the retired teacher. I am also astounded by these people dressed in colorful clothes and outlandish designs. I think they're very different from the people I have met so far. That's because they don't want to do what other people do, and show it by their clothes and actions.

Maybe the circus is destiny knocking at my door.

Maybe it's with these people that I belong.

The caravan of trucks towing garishly painted floats, with strong-men dressed in animal skins lifting weights, and women dressed in green-, red-, and blue-sequined bathing suits and leotards swinging on trapezes, parades past the apartment buildings on 12th Avenue, to the applause and shouts of the enthusiastic neighbors.

Several children chase after the floats, imitating the performers' dancing, smiling, and waving goodbye to the crowd. The music that gushes from the loudspeakers is raucous, exciting.

"The circus expresses our most hidden desires," reveals Adela, smiling with complicity and as if she had known me forever.

IN THE AFTERNOON THE NEXT DAY, I lift a small flap of the enormous gray tent and find myself inside a big circle in darkness, ringed by wooden bleachers painted white. Already a large crowd of children and adults are seated. The dirt floor of the ring, covered with straw and yellow sand, smells of animal pee. No one has seen me sneak into the circus, which put up its tents over the weekend on a large weedy lot two blocks from my house.

My brother, sitting in one of the upper tiers of the grandstand, didn't see me come in. As he smokes a cigarette, his attention is focused on his friends, the neighborhood thugs with whom, in just a few days, he has stoned adorable chubby green-and-yellow tanagers to death, picked lizards off fences with a BB gun, and set fire to the tails of cats.

I sit almost in the front row, between two girls accompanied by their respective parents. They are wearing yellow and white piqué party dresses. Their hair is tied up with satin ribbons of the same color on their heads. I settle into the empty space between them and ignore their disdainful glances at my overalls.

Who says that I must dress up to sneak into the circus? Or why I must pay admission?

The lights dim in the big top.

Then, a powerful spotlight focuses a blinding circle on the tall young ringmaster, who runs in flamboyantly, in elegant tails with a shiny top hat and a huge, glittering diamond that glows on his white bib.

Cracking his menacing whip in all directions, the ringmaster kicks off the show with his huge voice:

"Ladies and gentlemen, the fabulous Circus Maximus returns from its triumphant tour of Egypt to the elegance of Almendares! To lead off our our troupe – our firmament! – of unequaled and resplendent stars: Nataranya! the emaciated fakir of India who sleeps on, and rises from, a bed of pointed knives! Soraya, the bearded woman from Morocco! Rama, the Burmese virtuoso who plays the handsaw as if it were a melodious violin!

"And many more! Maryse, the acclaimed rhumba dancer, tightrope walker, acrobat, and gymnast from Guadeloupe who can dance on the neck of a bottle! Ivan, the Bullet Man from Kiev who is shot through the air from a cannon dating back to the time of Napoleon! The Brothers Tabak, sensational Turkish horsemen who do risky rope tricks while riding high-spirited colts from the Sahara Desert! And the world's most dangerous animals: Kenya's four most vicious lions, and the ferocious white Bengal tiger tamed by the famous Armenian trainer and lion tamer, Captain Samarkand!

"And you will quake with fear before the feats of Mandrake the Malaysian, the sinister magician who once caused the Eiffel Tower to disappear from Paris! And Olga, the rightful tsarina of Russia, our royal acrobat who swings from the trapeze using only her strong teeth! And many, many, many more extraordinary persons and exotic feats and attractions!" Finally, seduced by the perfume of distant lands and spectacular feats, the audience bursts into delirious applause.

Next to be announced in an exaggerated and bombastic way by the ringmaster is a child my age dressed in an old-fashioned suit made of white satin. He makes his entrance into the circle of light, followed by a stagehand carrying a marimba, a bench, and a stack of phone books. The stagehand sets the marimba in the middle of the brightly-lit area, then, in front of it, the bench. Finally, he plunks the stack of phone books on top of the bench, somersaults backward, picks up the tiny child, sits him down on top of the phone books, blindfolds him, and lays a green cloth over the marimba. The child then plays wonderful music while smiling angelically. His little hands, as skinny as mine, wield with graceful ease the marimba sticks ending in red balls, moving them everywhere over the green cloth, tapping the resonant metal keys.

I feel for this extraordinary child, forced to work in such terrible conditions. Why do they put obstacles in his way, when it's enough of a feat to play the instrument so perfectly?

At the end of his act, the audience bursts into wild applause, and the little boy makes a graceful bow before disappearing into the shadows.

Now, to liven things up between acts, clowns enter screaming, riding on unicycles, juggling brightly painted wooden balls and bowling pins, making miniature poodles jump through hoops of fire. I can't understand why this makes people laugh.

Clowns, their faces painted white, their lips red with crimson running down to the chin, circles around their eyes as dark as night, and costumes beyond bizarre, make me sad.

They want to make us laugh, but I see great bitterness in their dead eyes.

For the last act, the ring is surrounded by the bars of large cages. The trainer enters through a door in the bars, along with five golden lions and one white tiger. A stagehand closes the gate. I relax, assuming those ferocious animals can't jump to freedom over the small fence that separates the ring from the tiers of the grandstand where the audience sits. By dint of threatening lashes in the air, the trainer manages to make the beasts jump up on drums of varied heights painted blue with white stars. How is it possible that animals so strong, so ferocious, so proud – rulers of the jungle! – obey this little man wielding the whip? Although when I look carefully, I see that only one of the lions is obeying the trainer's command to stand on two legs and jump around the ring. The others growl menacingly when the little man shakes the whip in front of their noses.

The tiger, especially, is studying the trainer with malevolent eyes.

Then the trainer makes provocative gestures in front of one of the grumpy lions, who has not stopped roaring and showing his fangs whenever the man passes in front of him. He's pushing his luck, I think. He wants the audience to believe he's brave. This arrogant Tom Thumb wants to get them to applaud.

He gives the lion a slap, the animal bites his arm and, jumping on him, pulls him down to the sand.

Another lion joins the fray and bites the trainer in the thigh. The audience howls with terror. Children cry and women scream.

The stagehands open the cage door and run in with firehoses, aiming jets of water at the two incensed lions, which abandon their prey, back off, and shake their manes.

The other animals, sitting on the drums, keep their glittering eyes focused on what's happening in the ring.

Now the trainer stands up and whirls his whip around in the air, smiling despite his tattered clothes. The rebellious lions go back to their drums and roar so menacingly that my blood freezes in my veins.

The trainer walks around smiling with open arms before the audience that gives him a delirious standing ovation.

As I leave, somebody taps me on the shoulder.

"Where'd you get the money to pay for the ticket?" my brother asks, removing his hand from my shoulder.

He looks me dead in the eye to see if I'm going to lie.

"I snuck in and nobody saw *me*. But I did see *you* smoking a cigarette," I reply defiantly.

I'm counting on him not tattling on me to my mother who doesn't allow him to smoke, even though she herself smokes like a chimney.

If he tells on me, I'll tell on him.

"You did well," he approves diplomatically.

I escape to see the other circus attractions without my brother spying on me. There are dozens of kiosks, decorated with bright wads of crepe paper, where they sell yellow and blue balloons, resplendent red caramelized apples on wooden popsicle sticks, peanut brittle, green *pirulís*, multicolored caramel *chambelonas*, popcorn, ice flavored with lemon or anise syrup, and pink strawberry-flavored cotton candy.

I don't buy anything because I didn't bring money, but what I see dazzles me and makes my mouth water.

A little man about my size takes off his hat in front of me.

"Don't miss the Hall of Mirrors," advises the tiny man mysteriously, bowing politely. He wears a Tyrolean costume: green corduroy trousers with suspenders, yellow shirt, and a green felt cap with red feathers. In every respect he looks like a normal person, except that his legs are very short. What has life been like for this man, whom cruel people call a dwarf? I imagine the taunts, the insulting looks, the hurtful comments he has had to endure in this world that demands normalcy. I'm glad he got this job in the circus because I don't think he could stand to work anywhere else.

I walk to the Hall of Mirrors, followed by the look and smile of the little man. I don't need a ticket. It's a free attraction to interest kids in the circus, and I enter without a second thought. I see my image everywhere and walk, arms outstretched, touching the mirrors with my hands, trying to find the way out.

After a few minutes, I despair. There's no way I'm getting out of this maze of images of myself.

I see myself dying of thirst, running in panic, blinded by lights and reflections. After long years my bones will be found and no one will know it's me.

I'm ashamed to scream for help. I'm making faces in front of the mirrors to try and calm myself down, when I see the head of a boy with curly brown hair. After a few seconds, he finds his way and is standing next to me.

"The trick to getting out of the labyrinth is to keep turning right," he instructs me, without being overbearing like my brother.

I follow him without talking.

At the exit, the boy walks towards the Ferris wheel set up at the center of the tents and kiosks. I head towards a tent that has a woman painted at the entrance. It's a young woman, with long blonde hair, naked, like Lady Godiva. She's tied to a large X-shaped steel cross. A tiny man, with a hunched back and sparkling, diabolical eyes, squeezes her nipples with black pincers.

"Come inside to see the most gruesome instruments of torture from medieval times!" exclaims another hunchback, this one dressed as a jester. His red, peaked hat has a green tassel and his yellow felt shoes with pointed toes end in bells. Some men go inside the tent.

Others, with huge black mustaches and cruel smiles, contemplate with pleasure the agonized face of the painted woman at the entrance.

IN THE MORNING, WHEN I WAKE UP, I notice my brother doing cartwheels on his bed. I join him and the two of us make cartwheels in tandem.

"I present The Siblings Septy and Mercy, international contortionists and gymnasts, performing their dangerous and risky number for the first time in America!" I announce.

I'm doing a handstand in the air, Septimio's holding me straight up, with just his hands.

"Clearly you were adopted, daughter of circus gypsies, Delgadina," he says maliciously, destroying my concentration and the perfection of my balancing act.

NIGHT IS FALLING, but a faint pink glow still lets you see everything clearly. The inflated full moon shines, yellow and hypnotic, in the violet sky. Elena reads, sitting next to me on the pavement of the building's roof, the continuation of Sett El-Hosn's story from *A Thousand and One Nights*:

"'And Badreddin lay next to Sett El-Hosn, gently passing his hand under her head, and she also surrounded him with her arm . . .'"

"What did the beautiful Sett El-Hosn feel at that moment?" I ask Elena, who seems to be living what she narrates.

"She felt as if she had no more questions, as if she didn't need anything else in life," replies the girl, her eyes lost on the moon, as if, there, the emotions she'd just invented were clearly visible.

The pink glow makes her face gleam and take on the look of a grown woman, distant and yet close at the same time.

"Sett El-Hosn has achieved, apparently by magic, what she wanted: to look closely at the handsome Badreddin, to sink into his eyes as they reflect her," Elena goes on, now looking at me as if the story were about the two of us.

I close my eyes to understand this instant.

The door to the roof opens with a squeak, and out comes a tall, thin, roughly ten-year-old boy with curly brown hair. He wears navy blue baggy pants with knit cuffs, and a short-sleeved red shirt.

To my surprise, he is the boy from the hall of mirrors. He's carrying an apparatus on his shoulders, and he sets it on the roof, opening its metal legs.

"Don't let me interrupt you, girls," he says, urbanely. "I came up to see the full moon with my telescope."

Elena closes the book and stands up, approaching the boy smiling. "Dieguín, this is Mercy, the new girl in our building," she explains, pointing at me with the book as I stand up.

"Very nice to meet you, although I believe we have seen each other before," the boy reveals politely, extending his right hand to me. I shake his hand, full of surprise at his formality.

"Dieguín is our scientist and intellectual," reports Elena. "His parents are university professors and he has a big library in his house. You can ask him anything. Also, he has a parrot that talks a lot and is very mischievous."

"I hope my parrot doesn't bother you," the boy apologizes, smiling. A yellow spark of malice passes through his dark green eyes.

Those eyes are fixed on the book that Elena has in her hand. "Ooh, *A Thousand and One Nights*!" he exclaims enthusiastically.

"It's wonderful that you're reading this classic of Oriental literature," he goes on enthusiastically, "even though some adults don't approve of it for children because they consider it erotic.

"However, my parents believe reading stimulates intelligence and imagination – thus, because the vizier's daughter, Scheherazade, was an imaginative storyteller, she escaped being beheaded by the king."

The boy peers through the telescope, adjusting it to point at the Moon, and backs away, making a gesture for Elena to observe the Moon's progress. Elena takes over the telescope, smiles, and gazes into the eyepiece.

Dieguín walks away from her and looks me over from top to bottom.

"Are you interested in astronomy?" he asks mockingly, and continues talking without waiting for an answer. "I believe the future is in space. We will go to the Moon and visit the planets. My father, who's a mathematician, has told me that the difficulty lies in the many mathematical operations that must be carried out for flights not to be disastrous, but I'm convinced that we will find a way to make space-ships faster."

"I'm interested in the sky, the Moon, and the stars," I reply, a little shy in the presence of this boy who knows so much.

"I don't think we will ever go to the Moon," says Elena, abandoning the telescope and staring at me as if expecting me to support her opinion.

"*Of course,* we are going to go to the Moon!" I exclaim, defying Elena's assertion. "That's the easiest thing in the world!"

"And how do you know that?" the boy asks me, scoffing. "Have you already been there, riding a large cannonball?"

"No, I just remember it. Sometimes time passes so quickly through my mind, that seeing the future is already the past. I remember that it's possible to go to the Moon and to the planets, though I don't know if you go on, or inside, a great cannonball. I myself have gone in my dreams to other places, to a land where nightingales sing very beautiful songs, ones that teach about life and death, and melt the heart," I answer in a declamatory voice, as if reciting a poem.

"'Melt the heart!'" repeats Dieguín, doubling over with laughter. Elena also laughs out loud, and I decide to laugh so that the mockery is transformed into joy and camaraderie among the three of us.

I PULL ON MY BROWN OVERALLS and leave the apartment just as Morning's daughter, rosy-fingered Aurora, colors the sky a deep blue.

The cold breeze of the first hours of the day causes a shudder along the whole length of my spine, pampering my face and electrifying my nose with the life-giving perfume of the earth wet with dew, of grass freshly mown.

My eyes are dazzled by the yellow of the butterflies that flutter and perch on the Mar Pacífico hibiscus flowers.

My ears vibrate joyfully listening to the jubilant cackles of the rowdy blackbirds.

I feel I'm becoming lighter. Like Achilles, he of the light feet, I seem to ascend towards the bulbous white cumulus clouds playing in the celestial vault. My chest expands with joy, and I go out determined to discover the treasures of the world.

On the staircase I stumble upon Dieguín sitting on the steps, looking closely at a flower.

"What are you doing?" I ask him, surprised at this contemplation, and I sit down beside him.

"I'm studying a sunflower," he replies, absorbed in the flower.

"Are you hiding on the stairs because you're afraid your parents will catch you studying?"

"Not at all! My parents like me to study. I'm sitting on the stairs waiting for you to come out to show you something very curious."

"Are you going to make fun of me again?" I ask him, a little afraid of this smart kid's sense of humor.

"No. My father scolded me for laughing at you and told me that only stupid people make fun of poets. What you said was poetic. Do you read poetry?"

"Yes! I secretly read my father's books, because my mother won't let me read. She says reading gives you TB. That's if it doesn't drive you crazy," I answer, whispering so no one listening at the door in my house can hear me.

"You're right not to believe your mom's superstitions. I too read my father's books, and an encyclopedia that contains the entirety of human knowledge entitled *The Treasure of Youth*. I don't need to hide to do that," Dieguín says.

"What did you want to show me?" I ask, impatient.

"See this sunflower?" he asks in a mysterious voice, raising the flower to my eyes. "Notice its extraordinary symmetry? From the middle out, the seeds go in interlocked spirals, twenty-one seeds on the left and thirty-four on the right."

He waits for me to say something, but I have no idea what he means.

"That's two consecutive numbers of the Fibonacci Sequence!" he shouts.

I open my eyes very wide because I don't understand a word of what he's describing. The child scrutinizes me with his dark green eyes, without light, like those of an adult. He realizes that I don't understand a thing.

"Leonardo of Pisa, called Fibonacci," he recounts, "was this Italian mathematician who described the sequence of natural numbers 1, 1, 2, 3, 5, 8, 13, and so on. Fibonacci revealed it as a solution to a problem about breeding rabbits, but since then, it's used for many other things," he explains in the tone of a teacher, the way I suppose his parents talk. He goes on: "The numbers in the sequence are the result of the sum of the previous number with the subsequent one. So: 1 plus 1 is 2, 2 plus 3 is 5, 3 plus 5 is 8, and 5 plus 8 is 13, and so on, successively. This sequence appears everywhere in creation, in the number of petals of flowers, in pine cones, in sunflower seeds. This shows that the gods are mathematicians."

"*What* gods?"

"The Greek gods, the only ones I like."

"Such as?"

"Zeus the Thunderer who throws lightning bolts. Pallas Athena, who wears the aegis and flies using golden sandals."

"Aha, the gods of my father's books!"

The boy's brown hair smells of lemon. Maybe he uses lemon cologne to lighten it the way my mother does me with water of violets. His white, smooth knees sprout from his navy-blue shorts. They are not tanned and scarred like mine. I'm beginning to get that this child never climbs trees or gets into fights with boys.

"Do you fight with boys? Do you get into punching matches with other guys?" I ask him to make sure.

Dieguín looks horrified and moves a little away from me, as if he senses that I'm about to hit him.

"No! I don't like to play with boys. There are some that I'd like to stick with pins, and pins, and pins!"

I think this child, despite being male, older in age and taller than me, is very fragile. I'll need to protect him from the bullies that surely live on this street.

Behind my back I hear someone coming down the stairs quickly. I turn around and see Elena just as she grabs me by the arm. The girl pulls me away in a friendly way, and walks me down to the sidewalk.

Dieguín follows us with a sad look, moving the sunflower like a fan.

"Don't go and fall in love with that child," she warns me when we're far enough away that he can't hear us. "He's a fairy."

"A fairy?"

"Yes, a flit, a fruitcake, a pansy, a nancy boy who likes guys."

"Actually, he told me he doesn't like to play with guys," I contradict her, uncomfortable with this gossip.

"He might not like playing with guys, but he falls in love with them instead of girls." It's as if she takes this as a personal offense.

"And you know this because?" I ask her, shaking away her arm and squaring off in front of her.

"Because he told me so. He's in love with our neighborhood poet, Hercules, who's so skinny we gave him that nickname. You'll meet him."

Noticing my displeasure at this revelation, Elena takes me by the arm again and walks with me, skipping with joyful anticipation. We go to Maximino's bodega, which is on the corner, where, if you buy two *boniatillos*, sweet potato candies, he will give you a third, which Elena gives me, perhaps to have the sweet dilute the bitterness of our conversation.

I HEAR ON THE RADIO that tonight, there's an eclipse of the moon, so I run up the stairs to the rooftop to see it better. There, as I hoped, is Dieguín, standing beside his telescope. He is talking to a skinny, ungainly teenager with straight blond hair that covers his forehead. He's wearing a very loose-fitting white shirt and pants.

"Let me introduce you to my friend, Hugo." Dieguín beckons me with his hand, smiling kindly.

"Better known as Hercules," says the young man, unwounded by the mockery of his nickname, and shaking my hand very seriously.

"You can talk to Mercy like an adult because, although she is very small, she reads books like us," Dieguín informs Hugo.

Hugo smiles showing perfect, white teeth.

"Are you coming to see the eclipse?" the young man asks amicably. "Do you know that, once upon a time, eclipses of the Moon were feared by all mankind? Even now many Hindus fear them because they believe the demon Rahu is devouring the Moon." No wonder Dieguín has taken to explaining everything to me according to Hindu mythology — Hercules is his model.

"The demon Rahú," the young man continues, "passed himself off as a demigod entitled to drink the nectar of immortality at the time when they were handing it out in heaven. Chandra, the god of the Moon, denounced him to the supreme god, Vishnu, who hurled his disc, cutting off Rahu's head. But the demon already had the nectar on his tongue and therefore could not die. Since then, Rahú's head has remained alive, floating in space, and from time to time he devours the Moon, as revenge. The Hindus make sacrifices so the Moon can come out of the demon's mouth, even though bloodied by Rahú's bites. That's why, at the end of eclipses, the Moon may look reddish in the sky. And *colorín, colorado*, my story is over!"

We remain silent because the eclipse has started.

Taking turns to see through the telescope as the Moon gradually darkens, our silence is intense, but I think I hear a music that comes out of nowhere. Perhaps it's the music of our enchantment at the secret of the Moon, the planets, the stars, and the universe.

"Mercy remembers that going to the Moon is the easiest thing in the world," Dieguín tells Hugo when the eclipse is almost complete and a dark red blanket covers the surface of Earth's satellite.

"No one has gone to the Moon, so Mercy must be remembering the future," Hugo clarifies, without mockery.

"There are people, prophets, who can predict the future. What if we all try to remember the future and, when we meet, compare our memories?" Dieguín proposes. "We might concentrate on the twenty-first century to the twenty-fifth, five hundred years of memories," he adds cheerfully.

"But we're all going to be old or dead!" I protest.

Silence reigns for a few seconds.

"In the twenty-fifth century we are all going to be dust!" I insist.

"Yes, 'dust we shall be, and dust in love," jokes Hugo, explaining, with a friendly smile, that he's quoting from a famous sonnet by Francisco Quevedo.

"I like the idea, Dieguín," the young man continues. "Of course, as we are all limited by the obscurantism of the twentieth century, we will express those memories with the iconography, with the images we know. In the same way that, in order to be understood, that ancient enlightened Buddhist, Padmasambhava, also known as Guru Rinpoche, over a thousand years ago spoke of the airplane as 'the great metallic bird that flies through the sky,' because the people of that time did not know the theory of lift, the law of action and reaction that makes the flight of an airplane possible."

"When we accidentally find ourselves on the roof again, we will compare our memories of the future," agrees Dieguín categorically, as he folds the legs of his telescope, indicating that the observation of the sky is over.

I DREAM TONIGHT THAT I AM AN ADULT and that I'm wearing a pearl-gray tailor-made suit, very elegant. I am surrounded by three young men, also well dressed. We are absorbed in studying the plan of a building on a light table. The room we're in has glass walls, and all around us is a landscape of phosphorescent green vegetation and hills that shine like smooth domes under the tender light of the morning sun. We are full of enthusiasm and are animatedly discussing the plan in front of us.

I look at my reflection and say, "Something's wrong."

I approach the young woman depicting me in this scene, and, with the edge of my right hand, cut the image in half at the waist and from top to bottom.

The young woman opens in four parts, like a ripe fruit.

I am surprised to see that she has no organs inside, but rather machines the size of matchboxes or even smaller. These machines are working very hard, making a monotonous noise like cats purring.

AT SUNSET, and still remembering my strange dream, I go to the rooftop in search of Dieguín and Hugo. As if they had guessed that I was going to show up, they both greet me with a smile of satisfaction and launch into asking me about my memories of the future.

"I remember writing with just my brain," I say. My eyes are closed and I'm trying to recall memories visually.

"How are you going to write with your brain, given that it doesn't have hands?" Dieguín, the future scientist, criticizes.

"Wait, Dieguín! Keep in mind that we're remembering the future, and things won't be the same as they are now," Hugo, already a philosopher, admonishes him.

"What tools do you use to write?" the boy persists.

"I connect things inside my head, and the letters are written on something that looks like transparent glass. Later, I manage to write directly with my eyes on the glass. And finally, I write with my eyes on the air."

"She is talking about a progression of discoveries," Hugo explains. "At first, the Faraday electrodes are connected inside the head, which is mindboggling. Then the brain transmits electrical impulses to a screen, which looks like glass. Later, they put a device on the screen that records the electromagnetic impulses being transmitted through the eyes. And, lastly, it's discovered that air can store letters by the same means as it can transmit sounds in the Hertzian waves that radios capture."

Dieguín looks admiringly at Hugo.

I, too, am amazed at the ease with which he deciphers the things I remember.

"Another thing I remember, too, is that we make our own clothes with a little machine that looks like an electric razor," I continue.

"There aren't electric razors, only metal razors!" Dieguín objects.

"What are these electric shaving machines like?" Hugo asks, ignoring Dieguín's comment.

"They're made of a hard material. They fit in the palm of your hand, and they work connected to the wall outlet, or with their own energy."

"In other words, plug-in or battery-powered. Keep going with your memories," Hugo encourages me.

"Clothes are like tree bark, or like a second skin of multiple very fine layers. The machine creates them when I touch some tiny lights on its surface."

I continue with my eyes almost closed, imagining the future with them.

"Each layer is designed to protect us against different environmental threats, and to maintain a perfect temperature and a pleasant level of humidity in the body. The layers also protect us from those of the Sun's rays that kill.

"We'll also have wearable pupils that adjust to the Sun's intensity and let us see like insects, or owls."

Both are deep in thought.

"Is it very hot in this future?" asks Dieguín.

"Yes! the sun's rays have dried up the oceans to such a point that you can go from one continent to another easily by highways, railroads, and regular bridges."

"If the sun has evaporated the oceans that much, it should mean that the Earth is covered with clouds and fog, and there won't be much heat," Dieguín corrects me, with scientific logic.

"No. Actually, after that, we *lost* the water," I reply, without explanation.

"Have you read lots of science fiction?" the boy asks, mistrustful.

"No, Dieguín! She may be accessing the collective subconscious, or the Akashic archive that the British Theosophist Annie Besant refers to, where the past, present, and future are stored and accessible to some people. Keep going with your account, Mercy. What are houses like?"

The young man's interest again encourages me.

"They're like membranes, like transparent bubbles that breathe. They clean the air and adjust the interior temperature and humidity."

"What is public transportation like? For example, trains," Hugo asks.

"They're flat, because people travel lying down owing to the high speed. The cars have two rails, one on top and the other underneath."

"Like streetcars?" pursues Dieguín.

"No, The trains float in the air, between the two rails, one above and the other below. That's why they can go so fast."

"In other words, you're saying there's little or no friction," explains Dieguín. After a pause, he adds, "But what makes them float?"

"The rails are magnets," I reply, not quite sure what I am talking about.

"Yes, they can be electromagnets," Hugo explains, "that is, magnetized by electricity, given the same polarity as the wheels so they are repelled, and that's how the trains that travel above and under them *float*, in a magnetic field where the force of gravity has been nullified."

"Sticking with this idea, maybe in the future we'll travel to space in a spacecraft made of an alloy stronger than steel and lighter than a feather that is at the same time a negatively-charged electromagnet, like that of the Earth," reasons Dieguín.

"Perhaps, too, negative electromagnetic fields and gravitational fields will be used for propulsion," says Hugo, meditating. "And, if the spaceship travels from West to East, it gets thrown into space like a ball – that's the direction of the planet's rotational movement," he adds, as if we might not get it.

After a silence, Hugo, whose father is a medical doctor, asks with sincere curiosity what medicine will be like.

"Barbaric operations with knives won't exist," I say immediately.

"You mean 'with scalpels,'" Dieguín corrects me.

"Everything will be done with lights and colors, and manipulations of cells, atoms' orbits, and the body's energy fields. Extremely small bits of organic gold will also be used."

"Organic gold – you mean that this special kind of gold is neither mineral nor chemical and that, in future, gold can be manufactured based on the biological structure of living beings," Hugo continues. "This will transcend the craziest dreams of the alchemists!"

"Yes, cures will be at the level of cells, molecules, atoms, in biological structure, energy, vibration. Old age and death will be diseases that can be cured." It all seems so obvious, and I don't want to leave out one other idea:

"We'll only die, I think, when we want to completely change our physical interior and exterior, dimensional reality, in search of new learning."

"Moving on from medicine, focus on the very distant future and tell us what you remember."

"I remember traveling in a ray of light. I moved very quickly from one place to another." I swim in this memory in a monotonous voice, as if I am asleep. "But I don't think that was in the very distant future. It happens now."

"You mean," Hugo clarifies, before Dieguín can ridicule what I'm saying, "that we are going to be able to transform our bodies from solids to energy, so that we can travel in photons, that is, inside the particles of light, as if they were vehicles. Matter increases greatly in volume as the speed at which it travels approaches that of light, so no solid can do that."

My mother's voice, calling me to eat, pulls me out of the trance. I am exhausted from the effort I've been making to remember the future, but the idea of dinner revives me. I leave the rooftop, saying goodbye with my hand to Dieguín and Hugo, who seem upset they can't ask more questions. And I'm upset they haven't told me a thing about their own memories of the future.

WHEN I GET TO THE APARTMENT, a plate of food is waiting for me on the table: beef stew with potatoes, white rice, and black beans with a lot of cumin, the way I like it. My mother, who's playing solitaire at the dinner table, doesn't raise her head when I sit down to eat, but clears her throat to start talking.

"Your brother is eating at a friend's house," she explains. "Your father hasn't come home yet, and I have no appetite. That's why you're eating alone," she says, concentrating on her solitaire. "I get bored with food when I must cook it, and it disgusts me afterwards to eat it. We are going to hire a cook and a maid, to help me with the housework. Now that your father is in fat city, he can afford them."

I eat quickly and watch my mother make faces.

I suppose this has to do with the things she's thinking.

"Mami, what is the speed of light?"

"Girl, why do you care about that? You're talking about weird things the way you were in the other house, when you had no friends to play with," she scolds, raising her eyes from the cards and looking at me as if for the first time.

"If you don't know the answer to my question, why don't you buy me *The Treasure of Youth*? It answers all the dumb questions children like me ask."

"Very well, I'll tell your father to buy it for you. Maybe, now that he's head of primary instruction at the Ministry of Education, he can even get it for free. I have no idea where you'd buy such a thing. I'm sick of your father's books and wish one day I could burn them all.

"Anyway, the school year is about to start and you want to learn, so I'm going to send you to the nuns' school of the Apostolate of Vedado. I'll enroll you as soon as I get organized. I'd already given it some thought before we moved, since you can't go on 'auditing' first grade at Sacred Heart of Mary, which, anyway, is a school for middle-class girls."

"Why not? I like that school!" I protest, annoyed.

"You're old enough now for pre-K," she declares. The Apostolate is a school for rich girls. Now that we have money, you need to rub shoulders with the cream of society."

"I don't want to change schools!" I object, upset.

"Also, I'm going to send your brother to the Baldor School, which is Catholic, but without priests." She keeps talking, ignoring my objections. "I must get him out of the Belén School which is for rich kids and is very good, but Septimio can't stand it. Those priests have yanked both his ears as punishment so often, he looks like Dumbo the elephant," she adds, laughing.

"I don't want to go to pre-K. I want to go to second grade!"

"You can't go to second grade, because of your age. You can't even go to first."

"I know how to read and write. I know how to add, subtract, and multiply! I'm better at arithmetic than anyone in first grade!"

"You're not old enough," she replies, impassive. I realize that my mother has come to a decision and that there is no way I can sway her.

I spend the next few days avoiding my mother, except for meals. After a while it occurs to me that I've never once thought about what kind of person she is and why she makes the decisions she makes. In the books I read, writers are always describing how their characters think, whether they are invented or real. I don't know how my mother, or my father, or my brother thinks. Maybe remembering the future has suddenly enlightened me and I can escape the present where I am trapped, and see people with more distance and clarity.

My mother seems to me a person interested in money and what everybody else thinks about her. That's why she wants me to go to a school for rich girls. She needs the support of my father, her own family, and society to be able to exist. She isn't coherent. No sooner does she say one thing, than she says the opposite, and every time I do what she tells me to, I get confused, and I upset other people.

One day she tells me that only bad guys succeed in life and, if I want to succeed, I must become a bad person.

The next day she tells me that the good sleep peacefully because their conscience doesn't trouble them. Then I spend the whole night awake, examining my conscience to find out whether I'm good or bad.

She always says that reading books gives you tuberculosis – but look how easy it was to convince her to get me *The Treasure of Youth*. Does she want me to read it so I get TB? It's because I can't trust her that I think and I read, even though I'm not supposed to be old enough to do either.

Recently, my cousin Gisela visited us and said to my mother: "This girl thinks. She has an inner life, and children do not think or have an inner life." She also told my mother how she was surprised that, just after I was born, I would lie quietly in my crib, watching everything. "Children cry when they are newborns and do not open their eyes immediately," she said.

After thinking about it further, Gisela added: "This girl is not like any other child. She is very weird."

I may be weird, but Dieguín is like me, and so is Hercules.

They think and read.

I'm not the only one, alone in the world.

Tonight, I finish eating my food and get up from the table. My mother continues self-absorbed, playing solitaire, and, clearly, she does not want me to keep her company, so I go to the bedroom to read surreptitiously *A Thousand and One Nights*, which I found in my father's library.

I want to be able to talk knowledgeably about it, if Elena happens to read it to me again.

THE NEXT DAY, on the sidewalk in front of the house, Elena is whipping a rope over her head with both hands. I go out to see this up close.

"What are you doing?"

"I'm 'dancing the Swiss' – jumping rope," she answers without looking at me, concentrating on not skipping over her *suiza*, a rope woven from blue and gray twine with navy-blue wooden handles.

"Why do you jump?"

"Because if you step on the rope, you lose, stupid," she replies, rudely.

I sit on the steps of our building to watch her jump without grasping why, out of the blue, she is being so hostile to me.

"Did you finish reading *A Thousand and One Nights*?" I ask, as a pleasantry to start a conversation. "I'm reading it now. My father had it in his library," I add.

"Who wants to read that dumb book? There's nothing in it but eunuchs and shipwrecked sailors," Elena says disparagingly, and keeps on jumping.

"Well, Dieguín says it's a famous classic of Oriental literature," I respond politely.

"Who cares what that fairy thinks!" Elena says, gasping for breath, but she doesn't stop jumping. I don't answer because I don't understand what's happening to Elena. She's the only girl I know in this neighborhood, and I don't want to lose her friendship.

I scour my mind for something to say that will take her out of this nasty mood.

"I met Hugo! Hugo, Dieguín, and I got together on the rooftop to remember the future. It was fun!" I exclaim, laughing.

"Hugo? Oh, you must mean 'Hercules,' the other fairy. Be careful, or queer dust will stick to you, too," she spits with fury and stops jumping.

"You were the one who introduced me to Dieguín and Hugo," I reply.

I'm wounded and confused, and don't understand why I can't say anything that she won't turn around and use as a weapon to attack me.

"You can talk about people without sticking to them," she admonishes me contemptuously, rolling up her jump rope and dashing up the stairs to her house to end the conversation.

I sit on the stairs perplexed, with a feeling of emptiness and cold in my stomach. I cannot imagine what has provoked this girl's rage.

Then, after a while, it occurs to me that, for days, I haven't sought her out.

Elena is jealous. She was jumping rope in front of my apartment to see if I'd come out, to then turn her back with disdain and leave me high and dry.

TO ESCAPE FROM THE POLITICS OF CHILDREN, I open one of the twenty volumes of *The Treasure of Youth* that my father has just brought me. Lying on my bed, I read that the speed of light is three hundred thousand kilometers per second. According to Hugo, we can't travel at that speed with our material bodies because we would grow enormously.

So, in the future, we will have to be able to dematerialize our bodies.

Or maybe not. The ghosts I have seen have a body that's visible, but not material, because they can go through walls. It is possible that we have not just one body, but several, as I read in an item in this very encyclopedia about the Russian philosopher Helena Blavatsky.

What we *can* do, then, is leave our physical body and travel in our astral body as a ray of light. Blavatsky, however, teaches us the body travels at the speed of thought, which is instantaneous, without the need for any vehicle.

This explains why I pay attention when I hear a noise coming from the patio below us, which belongs to the mansion of an old woman who always wears black.

Although our apartment is on the ground floor of our building, there is a drop in the terrain, and this woman's house is lower than ours.

One day, when we walked by on our way to Maximino's bodega to buy sweet-potato candies, Elena informed me, "That's General Bermejo's widow who lives there. The front door is always open, and she's always sitting on the couch. She dresses in black because she's been in mourning for her husband for two years now. She talks to herself and is a raving lunatic."

Now I go over to the window to find that, in fact, the noise was made by General Bermejo's widow.

She was tossing large empty aluminum containers against the wall of her house, after planting whatever came in them.

Now, she's taken out her gardening shears and is cutting white roses to make a bouquet.

A sneeze escapes me, and the widow looks up.

I hide quickly so she doesn't see me, and when I look out the window again, the widow is no longer in her patio.

I go outside, sneaking past my parents' room so as not to wake my mother, who is taking her siesta.

On the sidewalk, Elena is back, jumping rope again. I ignore her and walk to the house of General Bermejo's widow.

"Where are you going?" Elena asks, running after me.

I don't answer and walk away quickly. Elena stops following me, annoyed.

When I get to the house, I climb the wide marble stairs to the side of the open door where General Bermejo's widow, sitting on the couch, can't see me, but I can see her. Also, people passing by on the sidewalk can't see me because I am hidden behind a large oleander bush in her garden.

The white roses she's just cut are now in water in a glass vase on the long coffee table in front of the sofa.

Sitting in the armchair next to the sofa, a gray-haired man, dressed in a three-piece white suit, smooths his lush gray mustache with his hand.

General Bermejo's widow smiles at him. "Mario, my dear late husband, do you like these roses? They have a delicate fragrance," she says.

"I can't smell them, Patria. You know there are certain things I can't do now," the man replies sadly.

"I cannot imagine what life must be like for you now! How is it?"

The man doesn't answer and looks at the floor, despondent.

General Bermejo's widow lets out a sigh and shakes her head back and forth as if she's frustrated.

"I remember a time my father took me riding in the savannah," she says after a pause, happy to have chanced upon a topic of conversation. "You know he named me 'Patria' because I was born on the battlefields during the War of Independence against Spain. My mother nursed the wounded in the tents, and my father fought with a machete and a rifle. Ah, my father was not a career general, like you, but was made in the savannah by the blade of his machete. He didn't wear your epaulettes, sashes, and gold braid – he wore rags! In rags he went to war against the best dressed, best fed, best equipped army in the world!"

"Don't dredge up those things, Patria," the man begs in a wounded tone.

"Never will I forget the day the national flag was hoisted over the Morro Castle!" the woman continues fervently. "I was just a child then, but the cannonades, rockets, fireworks, and firecrackers still resonate in my ears! The crowds gathered in front of the Plaza de Armas and roared with ecstasy at the change of command and the inauguration of the first President of the Republic, who swore to defend the Country and our Constitution. People wept with joy! Women hugged! Men blocked out the midday sun, throwing their black bowler hats high in the air!"

"Erase those memories, Patria," he pleads again in a mournful voice.

"Why? Our joy was short-lived," says the woman, now spiteful. "My parents had burned their mansions, their mills, their cane plantations to keep them from being co-opted by Spaniards. They freed their slaves. They donated their entire fortunes to finance the War of Independence. Then, when the Republic came, they were given a ridiculous pension that kept us in poverty.

"By contrast," she continues, "*your* family, Creoles who supported the Spaniards, *you* got to keep your mansions, your cane fields, your fortunes – above all, your wits! Not only that, but your father held high positions in the new government created by the Americans!

"And, later, you managed to grow your own fortune with your dirty businesses with the dictator Machado! From such a stick, such a splinter! Then again, I must admit that if I have money today and don't live in misery the way I did in my youth, I owe it to *your* family's treason and *your* family's opportunism."

The man looks up at the ceiling. He shakes his head from side to side as if he's sick to death of the woman's harangue.

"I'm going to eat a chocolate bonbon filled with liquor," the woman says in a superficial tone and with an angelic expression on her face. "They're the ones you used to like the most, remember?"

The widow of Bermejo opens the red-velvet-lined box.

Very deliberately, she sets the box on the long coffee table in front of her, and picks out a chocolate, gazing at it avidly.

"Oh, how delicious this bonbon looks!" she exclaims, with a voice of satisfaction. The man pounces on the bonbon and, in a flash, pops it in his mouth. He's done this so quickly that if I hadn't been looking at him, I wouldn't have seen it happen. His portly face swells with bliss. But, after a few seconds, tongues of fire emerge from between his lips, his eyes seem about to leave their sockets, and his mouth opens, letting out a squeal of intense pain. The man spits out the burning chocolate and stops squealing. The bonbon has either dissolved in the air or, as I now can see, the woman still has it between her index finger and thumb.

"You know perfectly well that you may not eat unless I offer you the food. You can't steal, husband, the way you used to, at the slightest opportunity. Nor can you display greed, avarice, or lust. Nor can you eat or drink if I don't offer it to you.

"Remember how you laughed at me when I undressed? You thought it was ever so funny that you could count all my ribs. I'd become emaciated was so skinny because my family had almost no money to eat. You used to say, as a joke, that I looked like a survivor of one of those concentration camps created by the Captain General of the Island, that evil Spaniard, Valeriano Weyler.

"You compared me to the poor peasants that devil imprisoned in the cities so they couldn't help the Liberation Army, so they would fall to the ground like flies, starving."

"It is not good for you to dwell on these things, Patria," advises the man, panting, as if to refresh his scorched mouth with cool air.

"You're right," the woman agrees, kindly. "You may eat this chocolate now," she adds, seductive.

The man takes up the treat gingerly, as if it might be a trap, but puts it in his mouth without any unpleasant consequence. I can sense the joy he feels as he closes his eyes and savors the bonbon, emitting exclamations of pleasure.

AT NIGHT, LYING ON MY BED, I can hear my brother, on the other bed, breathing in a deep sleep. The memory of Bermejo's widow keeps me from falling asleep. Witnessing that scene with her dead husband has made me nauseated. I interpret it as a message about hate. The widow of General Bermejo is trapped in her hurtful memories.

I set to thinking what I will be like at her age. Will I too have gone through tragedies that will fill me with hatred? I decide not to fall into something like when "darkness comes to the Island and the armies of Mahomet and the Only Sons annihilate the world," as my mother says when she starts ranting about the future. I want to fly above all hatreds because I see as in a lightning flash that spite is a millstone that disables our wings and condemns us to crawl on the earth.

I'm not sleepy, so I pick up *The Treasure of Youth* and turn the pages. There, in the light of the full moon coming through the window, I see an engraving of Orlando the Furious.

He is dressed in battle armor with thick leather straps and is smashing his sword on a boulder at the peak of the Pyrenees. I read Ariosto's verses:

Unjust love, why do you with such greed
our desires crave to orchestrate?
Why, perfidious being, with pleasure so dear,
do you lodge in two souls discordant hate?

As I set the book on the night table, a noise of wings draws my eyes to the wall in front of my bed. I sit up and see a winged creature gently swinging on clothes hung from a nail on the wall, to the left of the window where the night is coming in. Its skin is between gray and dark brown, and smooth as a bat's, not just smooth but shiny. The creature looks like one of the gargoyles on the cathedral of Notre Dame in Paris, and it's making faces at another creature of the same kind, swinging on clothes hanging from the nail on the wall on the right side of the window.

The two creatures jump in unison, with great agility, trading positions and grimacing all the while. The room glows with a phosphorescent green coming from a lawn that stretches down to a stream of silvery water.

On the right, a narrow waterfall shines like diamonds and makes a high-pitched musical sound as it falls on moss-covered pebbles in the stream. Blue fish with pink wings fly above the waters. Green and yellow frogs, dressed in tuxedos or tails, jump from one pebble to the next, and a golden dragonfly circles endlessly above the waterfall.

Clusters of mushrooms, their caps red with white dots, grow at the foot of bushes that have round, fleshy, exultant green leaves. The bushes, planted next to a low wall of porous stone, white with yellow and brown veins, stir gently in the warm breeze ruffling the surface of the water.

A young woman the size of my hand flies past me, her long blond hair crowned with daisies. She's dressed in very thin white gauze that's printed with tiny pink buds. A shower of bluebell flowers, chiming with a high-pitched but pleasant sound, falls from above, as if to celebrate the young woman's arrival.

The atmosphere is subtly scented with sandalwood, roses, and another pure, delicate essence in the background that I don't recognize – but it fills me with a yearning to discover this distant and unknown something.

This fragrance interweaves worlds, painting landscapes in pastel colors that I become more aware of through the pores of my skin than through the pupils of my eyes.

A pink flower emerges from the stream, its color intensifying at the edges of its petals. The young woman slowly descends and perches on its calyx and the current carries her off to somewhere I can't see.

Other girls like her, but dressed in yellow, fly after her carrying linked garlands of golden daisies. A bird of paradise with long feathers of colors as varied as the rainbow, and crowned with a golden circlet, flies in front of me and dances gracefully in the air.

Everywhere I direct my gaze, something new emerges: dazzling colored jewels, white, yellow, orange, pink, and purple orchids floating in the air and spreading their pollen like gold dust, fantastical animals playing in the river or on the moss, elegant and whimsical insects that ski down the leaves of the bushes and throw themselves into the river, producing a twang, like striking the strings of a harp. I savor the delicate honey that falls on me like dew, and touch the fine velvet skin of the night. My chest swells with joy at witnessing this flamboyant scene to the point that I think my heart will burst.

11

CHANGES

I WAKE UP IN THE MORNING, still euphoric from last night's experience, and run to breakfast. My father presides, sitting at one end of the rectangular dining room table. My brother, seated to his right, drums on the tablecloth of fine embroidered linen.

I sit safely across from him, to the left of my father.

My mother comes out of the kitchen, pushing the door with her side, and carrying in her hands a silver tray with the cups of *café con leche* and plates with rounds of French bread, toasted and buttered. She places the cups and the plates in front of us and sits at the other end of the table, with her own coffee cup and bread plate in front of her. I look at them all, trying to detect in their faces some sign of the impression that last night's extraordinary spectacle must have made on them. I keep expecting them to start talking about it, but everyone just chews on bread and drinks *café con leche* in silence.

My father smiles at me as he bites into his bread, expressing wordlessly how much he likes the taste of crispy bread in his mouth, not to mention the butter, which makes his lips glisten a little. My brother eats without looking at anyone, and my mother looks up at the ceiling as she sips her café con leche.

Suddenly I realize with a shudder that none of them saw anything, not even Septimio, who sleeps in the same bedroom. Clearly, I alone witnessed these things.

It's also clear that I'd better not say a word about this experience because my mother will drag me to a psychiatrist or just dump me in the nuthouse, the way her family did with my uncle Adolfo. People who have unique experiences that nobody else has are nuts – "neurasthenic," my mother calls it – and need to be locked up. I know I'm not crazy, but it's doubtful that I could convince anyone of what I've seen.

Not even my mother, who right now is looking at something lost in space. "Now that the school year is about to begin, I'm going to enroll the girl in that nuns' school, the Apostolate of the Vedado," she says, savoring her café con leche. None of us react to her announcement, so my mother speaks louder, looking again toward the ceiling, as if addressing the Greek gods who live in Dieguín's apartment on the third floor. "And I'm going to enroll Septimio in the Baldor School, which is Catholic, but *not* run by priests."

She continues sipping her coffee, without looking at anyone.

Not belligerent, just looking straight at my mother, my father asks, "Why not enroll them in public school?"

My brother and I focus intently on our cafés con leche and bread and butter.

"Now that we have some money, I don't want them mixing with the rabble that goes to public schools," replies my mother, still looking at the ceiling. "When we didn't have a cent, we made sacrifices so that Septimio could go to Belén and the girl to Sacred Heart. In private schools, where you must pay tuition, the children rub shoulders with the cream of society."

"I went to a public school," my father proudly reveals.

"So did I," replies my mother, staring at my father intensely. "But that was because we were both starving to death. Now, we have moved up the social ladder."

"My family was *not* starving to death," my father protests. "I have lots of siblings, and we all have doctorates from the university or medical degrees or teaching certificates. Very important people have been educated in public schools. It's good to mingle. That's how you learn how to defend yourself in life."

"Some of my friends at Belén are transferring to Baldor because of abuses by the priests," Septimio interrupts. He's lowered his head and is blushing.

"*What*? What abuses are these? I'll tear the faces off these men, even if they do wear cassocks!" my father shouts, suddenly furious.

"Don't get angry," replies my mother, fearful. "They yank Septimio's ears and spank him on the butt with rulers. Imagine, priests without women, full of complexes," she adds, in a superficial tone.

My father clenches his fists and stares at my brother, choleric. I sense he might use his bare hands to rip off the head of any priest who dares to touch his son. Guessing his thoughts, my mother says, "Don't even think about taking action or making a fuss. You occupy an important position. The last thing you need is to make headlines by killing a priest. Let it alone and we'll transfer Septimio to the Baldor School."

My brother gets up from the table, making a big noise with his chair, and, his face bright red, heads towards the door without finishing breakfast.

"Where are you going?" my mother asks, half surprised, half frightened.

"Out," Septimio replies, slamming the door.

"I want to stay at Sacred Heart, in first grade, or move on to second," I plead, breaking the silence left by my brother's abrupt departure.

"The girl is old enough to attend pre-K," explains my mother, looking at my father. "Girls of the best social class go to Apostolate."

"I know how to read and write, and I can do sums in arithmetic," I protest.

Glaring at me as if she were my teacher, my mother stands up and insists:

"You need to be with kids your own age and learn how to make boats and swans with colored construction paper."

"Origami," my father corrects her.

"I'll be so bored," I whine.

"Bad Bug, what do you think of *The Treasure of Youth*?" my father asks, smiling.

"I like it a lot!" I reply. "I plan to read all twenty volumes. Then I won't ever have to go to school with babies."

"Don't read so much! It'll make your head explode!" my mother warns.

I get up abruptly from the table and, like Septimio, head for the door.

"Where are you going?" my mother demands, irritated.

"To study butterflies," I lie, annoyed.

IT'S ALMOST NIGHTTIME and I jump, with one foot in the air, on the numbers one to ten that someone has re-drawn with pink chalk on the sidewalk. I lean over to pick up the squashed soda can I'm using as a token, and I keep jumping until I get to "Home," where I can stand with both feet on the ground. Dieguín, sitting on the staircase of our building, watches me. His curly brown hair seems more erect and electric than ever.

"Want to play the Squashed Can Game?" I ask, coming over and sitting next to him on the stairs.

"Actually," Dieguín says, "the game is called 'Chicken and Rice,' or 'Pon,' or 'Hop-scotch.' Roman soldiers played it wearing full armor and carrying all their military gear to build strength and speed in their legs. No, I don't want to play it because I'm going to be a scientist, not a soldier. But also, it's a truly stupid game," he replies, contemptuous.

"What game do you like that isn't 'stupid'?"

"None. I can spend that time reading, thinking, or listening to the radio. Today I heard on the radio that the Germans are losing the war. I'm glad!"

"The Germans aren't good?" I ask with surprise, remembering how the Kartoffel had praised them.

"The Nazis are the bad guys. But bad as they are, they can't wipe out the memory of good Germans, like the mathematician Kepler, the physicist Planck, the philosopher Kant, the musician Bach, the writer Goethe, the poet Schiller, and many other names in science and the arts who have made that country great in the world of culture."

I memorize those names to look for them later in *The Treasure of Youth*.

"The Nazis believe that we Caribbeans are inferior because we're not pure Aryans. They believe that we're a mix of slaves brought from Africa and aborigines the Spaniards found when they arrived in our lands. If the Nazis win the war, they will make us slaves."

I shudder at the thought of being the slave of the Kartoffels.

"That the Nazis are losing is good news, but I'm not up for games today. My friend Hugo just won a prize for a book of poems, and moved out of his parents' apartment. He wants the bohemian life of the poet, to live alone."

He adds, desolate: "I'll hardly see him anymore, which makes me very sad."

I'm amazed that Dieguín talks about his emotions so openly, and that he's not worried about getting dragged to a psychiatrist.

I can't talk like that in my house without worrying that my mother will explode and take me to a doctor because she thinks normal children should "play" – as opposed to reading, writing, thinking, or feeling strong emotions for others.

"Apart from Hugo, what are you thinking about now?"

"I was thinking, why isn't the sun's energy consumed, even though it's burning all the time? What is that energy?"

"The fusion of matter produces such a high temperature that it turns all matter into helium. It will take five billion years to burn it all," I answer, giving myself the importance of a know-it-all.

"How do you know that?" the boy asks me, ever the skeptic.

"I read it in a book."

Dieguín says to follow him to his house because he has something to show me. We climb the stairs to the third floor, and, on entering his living room, I am stunned to see every wall covered from floor to ceiling in bookcases crammed with books. The impact is so great that it almost paralyzes my heart.

Beside the window overlooking the inner courtyard, perched on a bar inside a large gilded cage, the boisterous parrot watches me with malicious eyes. I marvel at the bright greens, reds, and blues of its plumage.

"Look at these images of the Sun," the boy says, pulling a big book from the bookshelf and showing me a color photograph.

I see a yellow ball with firestorms. I tremble at the thought of the people who might live among these flames, even though I know there can be no life at that temperature.

A girl comes out of the kitchen and, without greeting me, places the plates and forks in her hand on the dinner table that's covered by a white tablecloth edged with lace.

A woman wearing eyeglasses brings out a bowl full of black beans and sets it in the center of the table. Then she puts out bowls of white rice and chicken fricassee.

"You must stay to have lunch with us," says Dieguín, taking me by the hand and making me sit in a chair he pulls up next to his, on one side of the table. His mother and father sit at both ends and the girl in front of us.

"Dad, Mom, and little sister Aurelita, I've invited Mercy to eat with us," he announces.

"Of course! Welcome!" the father answers, smiling. The mother smiles too.

Aurelita realizes she must fake a pleasant expression, but I can tell she doesn't like me.

"What did you learn today at school, Dieguín?" the father asks in a professorial tone, while he ladles the food onto his wife's plate.

"The five postulates of Euclid, which I already knew. It was interesting to review them, but it boggled my mind to learn that, when he was twelve, Pascal discovered, all by himself, that the sum of the angles of a triangle is 180 degrees," the boy replies calmly.

"Yes! Let Pascal serve as an example to you. *His* father did not want him to study mathematics until he was fifteen, but he discovered geometry all by himself when he was still a child," says the father, who wears grey trousers and a long-sleeved white shirt with the cuffs rolled up so they don't get dirty. His appearance is tidy and well-groomed. His long face and Dieguín's curly hair, together with his glasses that have gold metal frames, give him an air of authority, but also of kindliness.

"What does the young lady think of Pascal?" Dieguín's father asks me very kindly.

"That it would have been better for him to invent calculus, the way Newton and Leibniz did almost at the same time, because geometry had already been discovered centuries before," I reply with cruel pedantry.

"Excellent that you know Newton and Leibniz!" the father exclaims, sincerely cheerful. "But you are very severe. You must remember that, in addition to making other valuable contributions to science, as a teenager Pascal invented the Pascaline, one of the first mechanical calculators, to help his father, who was a tax collector."

From the living room comes the parrot's high-pitched voice: "In a right triangle, the square of the hypotenuse is equal to the sum of the squares of the other two sides."

"Did you teach Loulou the Pythagorean theorem?" the father asks Dieguín.

"No, Loulou was listening to me memorize it, to prepare for an exam. So now she repeats it just to make fun of me." The boy is perfectly serious, while we all laugh.

"What did you learn today at school, Aurelita?" asks her father, ignoring the parrot's chatter while making up his daughter's plate.

"I made friends with one of the girls who gets the best grades in the class. She is the daughter of the brother of the headmaster of the school."

"If she's nice, you can invite her to spend the whole weekend in the house," the mother politely suggests.

The father serves Dieguín and looks at his wife. "How was *your* day?" he asks with real interest, because she is a teacher.

"We are trying to implement these new guidelines for school reform that the Ministry of Education has sent down. The idea is to make education here more like the American system. That's all well and good, as long as we aren't required to shorten the afternoon session." The mother looks at me and adds, graciously: "Your dad must know a lot about this because he is head of Primary Instruction."

I have no way to respond to this. I'm suddenly thrown, absolutely terrified by these people talking openly about forbidden things.

I'm glued to my chair. I don't know how to get up and run away.

Miraculously, I hear my mother's voice on the staircase calling me to dinner. I get up and run around the table, dropping my napkin on the tile floor.

"I have to go," I say, choking, slamming the door violently behind me.

NEXT MORNING, I leave the house with my spine curved and my chest collapsed like a swimmer who, gasping for air, surfaces from the depths of the Hellespont.

Elena is playing with some kids on the sidewalk. The sun is shining like a blazing ball of gold that, combined with the exalted green of the garden's bushes and the leaves of the trees planted along the sidewalk in front of my house, intoxicates me in a whirlwind of amber and emeralds. Before I can make any sign of displeasure at seeing her again, Elena smiles at me, as if there hadn't been the slightest row between us, comes over, and takes me by the hand. "Let me introduce you to Mercy," she proclaims in a charming voice, leading me over to the children. "She's the new girl on the block."

The children look at me, expressionless.

"Here is Ricky, and his brother Cristín," Elena says, touching a small, blond child on the head first – that is Ricky – and then touching another, also blond, taller than me, on the shoulder – Cristín. Both wear short-sleeved shirts and light blue shorts.

"And this is Laurencita, Laura's daughter," Elena continues, touching a girl taller than me on the cheek. Laurencita has short black hair in ringlets.

"And you will meet the others when you play with them and they tell you their names," Elena concludes, running out of steam. "The others" are three girls and a boy that I do not see in detail, but as a group, because I can't distinguish them by their names.

"Now we are playing Hide and Go Seek," Elena announces.

"What's that game?" I ask, though I know what it is.

I feel a little silly in front of all these kids I've never seen before.

"See this cross that I've made with chalk on the sidewalk?" Elena asks me in a superior voice, as if I were an idiot. "This cross is called 'the base.' Standing on it, I'm going to close my eyes and count to ten. You all go hide. If I find you, you must walk over to 'the base,' which is 'jail,' and stay there. Whoever can run and touch base first, without me catching them, is free." She adds, for the benefit of anyone who might not have played before, "The last person to touch base frees himself and saves all the prisoners."

Without another word, Elena closes her eyes, turns her back on us, and begins counting out loud. The kids run in all different directions. Watching Elena in case she cheats, I run down an alleyway on one side of the building and hide behind some large trash cans. From here I can see Elena without her seeing me. When she gets to ten, Elena opens her eyes and walks along the sidewalk, passing me very close, without even looking at the trash cans. I keep an eye on where she's going, and notice the sun is projecting two shadows from behind a large poplar tree. Elena runs around the poplar.

"Caught you! Go to jail!" she shouts. Cristín and Ricky must go to jail.

Ricky, excited, hops up and down on the chalk cross and pees in his pants. "Pig! Go home and change!" his brother Cristín orders, furious and embarrassed.

Ricky runs home, and Elena finds Laurencita behind another tree.

In a few minutes, Elena has discovered all the kids except me.

I suspect she peeked.

Ricky looks down at us from his balcony wearing a clean pair of white shorts. The others are in jail, standing on the cross of the base, and it is fun to watch Elena pretending to look for me everywhere. It's not worth it to save just yourself, and that's why I've waited to be the last. Orlando de Roncesvalles, Alexander the Great, Napoleon, or Joan of Arc would have done the same, I think. When Elena is at the farthest point away from the base, I run to the cross, step on it, and rescue the screaming, jumping children. Ricky on his balcony jumps up and down and screams, "You won!" Elena runs towards me and gives me a bear hug that embarrasses me in front of all those kids.

MY MOTHER FINISHES EATING LUNCH and removes her dishes from the table, annoyed. Making a big racket, she dumps them in the kitchen sink, and comes back with her deck of cards. She sits down at the table and, without looking at me, deals out the cards for a game of solitaire. I keep eating, because I like to take my time and enjoy what I eat. My father is at work and my brother has left, so we're alone.

"I'm so tired of cooking!" she exclaims, making a face like she's going to throw up. "My food tastes like disgusting ground stone!"

"But this *picadillo* is wonderful!" I reply, surprised.

"Your Aunt Bella is going to send us a very fat cook who also cleans," she answers making a gesture to indicate how little importance she gives to my praise.

I shut up and focus on what's left of my picadillo, rice, and fried ripe plantain.

"That blonde girl you were playing with this morning is Little Bone's daughter," she informs me without any intonation, looking at the cards and frowning. Her black bangs fall on her gray forehead, and her aquiline nose snorts with displeasure.

"Who's Little Bone?" I ask, knowing I'll regret it. I am afraid of her answers whenever she talks like this, as if she gives no importance to the words.

"Little Bone is one of your father's flunkies at the Ministry of Education. An assistant," she clarifies, in case I don't understand the word "flunky." My mother laughs mockingly, continuing to play and not looking at me. "He's the guy who brings the office girls coffee," she adds.

"So why is he called Little Bone?"

"Because he's a fatso who doesn't fit in his pants, with a belly like this." She shows "this" by raising her open arms in front of her as if she were grabbing a huge globe.

"Well, his daughter Elena is very nice," I angrily contradict her. She's made me feel like a spoiled brat, the daughter of the boss that Elena must flatter and humor.

I rush to finish eating so that I don't need to listen to her disparage Elena or her father, and go to the bedroom I share with my brother, which is now gloriously empty.

I persuade myself that the room is the bottom of the sea, and that I'm wandering among the resplendent seashells to the rhythm of a waltz, and playing with the green and fluffy seaweed fronds that caress me. I fish *A Thousand and One Nights* out from under the bed, lie down on the comfortable mattress, covered by a clean, scented sheet, and read aloud the story of Sinbad the Sailor: "I observed that the banks of that river were strewn with stones, rubies, gems of all colors, cut stones of all forms, and precious metals. And all manner of precious stones abounded like pebbles in a river bed. The ground sparkled with a thousand reflections and lights, so many that the eyes could not bear the splendor."

Images of enchanted islands brimming with brightly colored jewels flash before my eyes, silver jets emerging to spurt scented water over black marble fountains, flocks of robins swooping through a tame, endless afternoon, across a violet sky that mingles with the sea in a long crimson wound bleeding into the waves. Strange chords produced by heavenly string instruments resound in the curved sky that I can reach with my hands and transform.

Out of the corner of my eye, I think I see a face at the door peeking into my room, and an icy finger runs down the center of my back from the nape of my neck to my waist. The face returns and I see another, bigger, face peeking over the smaller one.

My mother and my brother are spying on me. I freeze, not knowing what to do.

After a few seconds, my mother walks over to me, alarmed, and yanks the book from my hands. Septimio follows her in silence and, very seriously, stops in front of my bed. It was he who told on me. "You should *not* be reading this book!" my mother shouts. "This is not a children's book! It talks about things that only grownups should read. I'm going to hide it so you won't read it anymore," she says, and she grabs me by the arm, violently lifts me out of bed, and pushes me into the hallway.

"Go play! Girls your age play with other kids!"

I DO NOT ALLOW MY MOTHER'S PUSH to make me angry, but instead let it serve as an inspiration. I leave the house with the best intentions of exploring the afternoon world, discovering its wonders at the turn of noon. The light is now a yellow whiter than in the early hours of the morning and the shadows a blacker blue. The air, exhausted by the weight of humidity and heat that the boiling rays of the sun pummel us with, is denser and more difficult to breathe. The hairs on my arms shiver with pleasure when the warm breeze smelling of earth, dust, asphalt, meals seasoned with garlic, cumin, and oregano, flows across them with the delicacy of a caress.

There's nobody playing on the sidewalk, maybe because the afternoon sun is so intense now that they are sheltering in front of portable electric fans in their homes.

But there is one kid sitting on one of the little walls near the staircase that leads down to the alleyway where the poor people's apartments are. In our building's shade, this boy seems to have light chocolate skin that contrasts pleasantly with his dark yellow shirt and shorts.

This is the first time I've seen a child like me with skin this color. My friend Caridad, from the other neighborhood, had milky brown skin, while my other friends' skin was white like my father's or yellowish like my mother's and brother's.

White-skinned children, I've noticed, become red when they run or play, whereas those with yellowish skin turn greenish. My skin, grayish white, only looks good when I get plenty of sun. Then it turns golden. When my mother is in a good humor, she says that the skin of Islanders is yellowish because we are all bilious: we eat the heavy meals of Spaniards, who came from cold climates, and in this heat that food gives us liver ailments. When my mother is in a lousy humor, she says yellowish skin comes from us being mixed with Chinese and Black people. I'm not sure if this is true, but Isabel, my aunt on my mother's side, does have oblique, Chinese-y eyes.

Nike, my grandmother on my father's side, is Black-ish, the color of cinnamon.

This child is playing with some colorful glass balls. I approach and sit on the little wall in front of him, to watch his game. The child shoots a ball using his thumb and forefinger at a bunch of them. Every ball he hits, he places to his right, which means he won it. Of course, they all belong to him.

"Will you lend me a ball to play too?" I ask as if I've known him forever.

"Okay, but all the balls you hit are mine. Plus, they are called *marbles*." The boy seems annoyed, as if suspecting some trick from me.

"How about the first *marble* I hit belongs to you, but the others should be mine because you only loaned me one."

"Okay, but your mom can buy *you* all the marbles you want, and mine can't," he reasons, upset at having to reveal that he is poor.

He's right. I don't want to strip this kid of marbles he can't get back. I also lived on an alleyway before, and haven't forgotten that I had very few toys. Now that my parents have money, I don't want to be like those rich kids who rub poor kids' noses in it.

"Okay," I say. "All the marbles stay yours."

We play in silence. After a while, a female voice shouts from the alleyway: "Zaro! Zaro! Come help me fold clothes!"

Zaro straightens his back and hunches his shoulders. I can feel that he's annoyed at having to go to work even though he's still a child. Also, I feel he's ashamed because I found out his mother is a laundress.

The woman in the alleyway is short, and her yellow dress is all wet around her stomach. Her skin is a darker shade of chocolate than Zaro's. She wears a handkerchief, also yellow, tied like a hat on top of her head. "Hurry up now, Zaro, I don't have all day to wait for you!" the woman shouts, irritated. "I have a delivery this afternoon!"

Zaro picks up all the marbles, jams them into his shorts pocket, turns his back on me and, without saying goodbye, runs toward the woman.

LOOKING TO THE RIGHT, I see Ricky and his brother Cristín in the garden of their building. Ricky is running with something colorful that spins. Cristín, sitting on the staircase facing the street, makes soap bubbles by blowing through something.

Ricky stops when he sees me. "What's that thing that goes around?" I ask.

"It's a pinwheel," he says, handing it to me to look at. "It's a wooden rod with a star made of white paper with colored stripes, nailed to the tip. The star rotates propelled by the wind," he explains proudly,

"Very pretty," I tell Ricky, returning the toy.

I approach Cristín and sit beside him on the stairs. "

And what are you doing?"

"Blowing soap bubbles with stems from a pumpkin vine."

Cristín dips the stem into the pot with foamy water on his knees, and blows on the stem. A sphere sprouts slowly, reflecting the colors of the rainbow: red, orange, yellow, green, blue, indigo, and violet. When the bubble is fully inflated, the boy gently shakes the stem and the bubble comes off and floats up through the air. Cristín blows again and two soap bubbles emerge at about the same time, joined on one side. They float towards the Sun, propelled by the wind. This mysterious union shakes me. It's as if two galaxies, or two universes, collide and intermingle at their edges. I've seen frightening photos of galaxies colliding and I imagine the apocalyptic conflagration and the cries of terror of the inhabitants of the planets, swiftly silenced in the indifferent blackness of space.

"So, these are your games?" I ask, concealing my emotion. "Why don't you play Cowboys and Indians with revolvers? It's much more fun."

Cristín smiles at me pityingly, like I'm an idiot. "Because that would be killing," he responds, as if this were the most obvious thing in the world.

I smile back. "Don't be ridiculous! They're cap guns! They don't kill anyone."

"But they teach you how to pull a trigger. My mom won't let us play with toy guns because they're violent – nor with dolls, because they're just for girls." The boy stops blowing bubbles and sets the pot of foamy water with the pumpkin vine stem beside him on the staircase, so he can pay attention to me.

"Dolls? Wouldn't you get bored with dolls?" I ask in a paroxysm of amazement at having this conversation with a boy.

"No, my brother and I want to play with dolls. We make rag dolls and hide them inside our toy chest, so my mom doesn't find them."

I gawk at this boy, who's as white as the Moon and as blond as the Sun. I can't believe what I'm hearing. Is he making fun of me? His light blue eyes, which don't reflect light but instead project it like two stars, are jewels that shine in the tame light of the afternoon. They have a clear, glittering bottom, like the sea. I detect no mockery in these eyes, just sadness.

"We like to play with girls because they are quieter. Boys are forever beating each other up," he complains.

"I play with boys because their games are much more interesting than girls' games. And, so what if I must give or take a punch? That only makes me stronger. Don't you realize you're a coward?" I ask him this with real annoyance while boxing him, softly, on the jaw. Cristín, to my surprise, covers his face with his hands and bursts into tears.

"Really? As if I hurt you!" I exclaim. I cannot believe that this child, who is bigger and stronger than me, is crying because I rubbed his face with my fist.

I try to comfort him because, suddenly, I feel very sorry for him. "You'll learn to defend yourself when some boy tries to beat you up."

"No, no!" Cristín exclaims, his voice breaking up as he cries.

"What do you mean, 'No, no'?!" I ask him, disturbed.

"With them it's worse, because they are the same as me, but they look more like you," he reproaches me, pointing his finger at me and wiping away his tears with his other hand. After some moments of silence when I don't know what to say, Cristín picks up the pot with the foamy water and the stem from the pumpkin vine, stands up, and climbs the stairs to his house.

140

12

SCHOOL TROUBLES

"WORTHLESS DRONES! LAZY SLOBS! LOATHSOME THIEVES! Gangsters! Assassins!" General Bermejo's widow shouts from the sofa in her living room, gesticulating at a man in a white suit sitting in an armchair near her.

The coffee table in front of the sofa is laden with a large silver tray bearing a fine porcelain tea set of a handsome pattern, and a serving dish of the same design heaped with a small pyramid of golden cookies.

I'm again spying on this couple from behind the big oleander bush.

"Our brilliant president, *Medical* Doctor Ramón Grau San Martín, wanted to *inject* gang members into government ministries and even into the Police and Secret Service to neutralize the *germ* of gangsterism. But all that's done is *infect* the lot of us with the deadly disease of terrorism!" the woman rants on, not looking at the man, more like addressing an invisible crowd in a great hall.

General Bermejo's widow lets her head fall onto the backrest of the sofa as she raises her arms and waves her hands around in despair.

Long, thin dark clouds cover the ceiling, black and gray snakes undulating, crisscrossing, devouring one another, howls of terror coming from all directions.

"Swallow that somber darkness, Mario!" the woman commands. "This Island's darkest times are not yet here, the era when the arch-devils Belial, king of hell, the most vicious of all demons, and Proserpina, sovereign princess of evil armies, will rule. Today's politicians steal millions of pesos from the public treasury – but in the future they will steal the whole island and all its people! Castor and Pollux from the Avernus, Romulus and Remus from the Abyss of Eternal Death!"

The snake-clouds spin in a whirlpool and descend to a point like a tornado, disappearing into the enormous open mouth of the man, and the screaming ceases.

The green scales of a reptile cover Mario's body, and his elongated face swells and turns red with rage.

"I've told you repeatedly: do *not* drag the horrors of the plane where you now abide into the living room of my house!" the woman scolds.

The man's appearance slowly normalizes, his face pacified, becoming kind and gentle.

"If you can't behave in a civilized way, I won't invite you again for tea and biscuits. *Then* what are you going to drink and eat, wretched soul?"

"Thank you, Patria, for feeding me and giving me drink," whispers the man.

"Don't thank me, you hypocrite! I know you aren't capable of gratitude for anything! What you feel towards me is hatred and desire for revenge because, now, I have the upper hand."

"Let go of those old grudges! Forget those wounds!" the man begs.

"I'm going to enjoy my tea," the woman announces, fastidiously picking up the teapot with both hands and pouring the steaming liquid into the cup in front of her. After inhaling the aroma, she sips the tea daintily in an exaggerated display of pleasure.

"There's nothing better for you than Chinese black tea. You always said it was sheer snobbery to drink tea, rather than coffee, the Islanders' favorite beverage. The custom has been in my family since the days of British rule. My grandmother told me that it started when we invited George Keppel, third Earl of Albemarle, who at the time ruled this Island, to have tea in our noble mansion in the Capital's central plaza. That's how," she continues with a certain reluctance, "the family could be certain that my female ancestors would be invited to the spectacular balls Keppel hosted. Despite our subsequent penury, we kept the custom of drinking tea, as we did that of washing our bodies with fine French scented soap, even when we had not a scrap to eat."

"Your family is certainly of the most ancient lineage," the man whispers.

"Stop talking like the actors in the radio soap operas! Men always think women are stupid and that you can handle us with praise and sentimentality."

The man smiles and lowers his head as if accepting what the woman says. "I would like tea and cookies," he begs in a cowed voice.

General Bermejo's widow fills a cup with tea and places it in front of him.

"You may eat and drink, provided you mind your manners," she says. "Don't behave like a beast." She stacks cookies on a plate beside his cup and saucer. "Belgian biscuits, of the best quality, and the tea is the best from China. Breeding, you see, makes the greyhound, and I only consume the best."

I back away from my hiding place when I hear my mother calling me home for dinner.

THE WHISTLE OF A DISTANT TRAIN wakes me. I imagine the train carrying the animals of the Circus Maximus, lions with gorgeous golden manes, white horses bedecked with red feathers, fat, shiny green snakes from the Amazon. The train moves off, and the night breeze comes in through the window carrying the intense fragrance of night-blooming jasmine from the garden of the widow of Bermejo. It's a warm wind whose waves filter in gently, like a caress.

I get up stealthily from my bed and tiptoe barefoot, so as not to wake up Septimio, who breathes rhythmically in his bed, sleeping like the famous dormouse.

Looking out the window, in the full moon's faint white light and the patio bulb's yellow light, I can't tell the roses from the night-blooming jasmine, or the regular jasmines, or the gardenias. Only smell distinguishes the sharp, wounding perfume of the gardenias from the fleshy and caressing odor of the jasmine. I think I can single out the other jasmines' loud scent in the background when I wiggle my nostrils to suck up the air, the way rabbits do.

I look up at the night sky that shimmers with points of light, nighttime bonfires that run away from the Sun and are, in fact, other, distant suns that I will never see up close. This obsidian, velvety-black firmament, with its white, yellow, red sparks and its dust-cloud of light makes me bigger at the same time as it dwarfs me.

I grow by realizing that I can observe the sky and think about it, that I am conscious and aware, but I shrink by observing how small I am in the face of the immensity of the universe.

The night is tender, even loving, and kisses my eyes with a deep, celestial silence, which invites me to penetrate this moment of life to its bottom, which makes me drink this intoxicating liquid of existence to the last drop.

I wish it were possible to live with this intensity under the voluptuous rays of the Sun, which tear at your skin like the claws of a bloodthirsty animal.

I wish tonight would never end because tomorrow I must face harsh reality: my mother has told me that in the morning we must buy my uniform for the Apostolate of the Vedado. I must go back to school, be in a classroom with children my age who drool on themselves and pee their pants, like Ricky, or Eduardito, the boy from the old neighborhood.

Something is beginning that scares me, and I can't sleep.

"IMAGINE HAVING TO BUY GLOVES for this tiny child. White gloves, blue wool cape, and beret in the Antilles!" my mother exclaims as we enter, late one morning, the third store that supposedly sells gloves for tiny hands.

Luckily for us, they also sell the other pieces of the gala uniform, including the navy-blue cape and the beret with a visor like that little boy's in the Buster Brown Shoes ad.

Although we already have acquired the uniform for daily use in this nuns' school, my mother has worked herself up to the height of anxiety in her quest to obtain all the gala garments that I supposedly must wear tomorrow because we've been told that, on the first day of school, there's a tremendous ceremony in the chapel. So, come the first morning of the new school year, my mother insists that I must wear the cape, the gloves, and the cap to make an impression.

For that reason, dressed as if I were going to the North Pole, I stand on the corner waiting for the school bus in the raging sun.

People passing by in cars yell at me: "Where's the costume party?"

Easy for my mother to say "What uncouth people! Such disrespect, gentlemen!" but I'm the one who has to suffer the motorists' lack of manners in silence, rivers of sweat dripping from my temples.

Eventually the milk-chocolate-colored bus arrives, its dark chocolate stripe down the side filled with letters painted in white: APOSTOLADO DEL VEDADO.

The bus approaches carefully enough not to run me over and comes to a halt with a piercing squeal of brakes.

The bus's humped roof looks like a black canvas whale and reeks of tar.

I clamber up the two high metal steps and, as I search for somewhere to sit, the dozens of girls in rows burst into gales of laughter. I go crashing from one row of seats to the next, disconcerted at being the focus of general amusement. Even the supervising nun pulls out a white cloth handkerchief to hide her laughter.

One of the big girls, sitting by herself at the window seat to the right of the nun, calls to me and tells me to sit beside her.

Before I sit down, she removes my cape, cap, and gloves, and quietly tells me, "You put all this on only for chapel."

The giggles eventually subside. I deeply regret that I allowed myself to be led by my mother, by her obsession to impress.

The nun sticks her hankie in a black purse that she has in her pocket of her habit and shouts sternly: "Silence! Don't make such a fuss!"

As soon as she says this, she can't control herself and starts laughing again.

Her black veil, almost transparent from the thousands of washes it has withstood, moves spasmodically with her laughter, and her starched breastplate produces a crackling sound with each spasm.

I do not find this amusing. I'd like to see my mother facing a little of this laughter, and see for herself what "make an impression" means. What is her idea of life? More and more, everything she tells me seems inappropriate in the outside world. Who can guide me? I know nothing about the world, but might it be better for my own ignorance to guide me, rather than her fantasies?

"How old are you?" the big girl with the voice of a saint asks.

"Four tiny years old," I reply, showing her four fingers to play stupid.

She laughs and puts her hand on my head sweetly. She has a very white, round face, blond hair, light blue eyes, and the strange, almost unearthly beauty of a Virgin by Giotto – but I hear a false, two-faced, dull tone in her voice.

"What made you get on the bus all dressed up?" she asks, curious.

This big girl wants to keep the comedy going, but I'm tired of this game of pretending to be an idiot. I don't want to go on talking like a baby, or following the protocol and hierarchies I already learned at the last nuns' school.

"First," I reply with great seriousness, "my crazy mother told me I needed to make an impression, and I was just crazy enough to believe her. Next, this will teach me not to trust her anymore. But, third," I add, "I think the people on this bus are stupid, because there's nothing funny about this. Instead, it's just pathetic."

The older girl jumps in her seat as if she's just seen a snake. She moves away from me and stares at me with her eyes wide open.

"Shove forward on the seat, so there's room for three here!" she orders me brusquely. She turns and says to a girl behind us, "Miriam, sit up here next to me, so we can talk."

Miriam sits, and I must move way up on the seat in between the two of them so I don't get squashed by the newcomer's fat thighs.

"This little girl said something really strange to me. Do you think she's crazy? She talks like a grownup."

The big girl looks at me closely with her big snouty face. She looks, as my mother would say, like a brown-eyed nautical figurehead, her long brown hair parted in two pony tails secured by pink plastic barrettes shaped like bows. Her long aquiline nose and her cheeks are covered in shiny fat and acne.

"So, little girl," Miriam squeaks, "what's the Earth like? Is it flat or round?"

She's testing me. If I answer, will she shut up and leave me alone? Or would it be better for me to shut up? Or do I cook up some childish nonsense?

I withdraw inside myself. The thick fabric of the uniform produces a lot of heat. My new shoes are too tight. I feel my head swelling.

"Round," I answer, heaving a sigh of impatience.

"Then how come we don't fall off?"

I laugh. It happens that I'd just been discussing this with Dieguín, so I decide to astonish the big girls with what we discussed.

"Because of the force of gravity. The Earth draws us to it with that force, so we don't fall. The Earth revolves around the Sun, which has circles of gas churning inside its center and is a fireball that never burns up because its atomic explosions will go on for millions of years."

Fortunately, I've memorized this information. If she'd asked me last week, I couldn't have answered. I'm parroting the wording of the encyclopedia where Dieguín and I read the facts after having a furious debate on the subject.

The two older girls look at each other with their eyes wide open, and push me farther forward.

For the rest of the bus trip, they talk in whispers and don't ask me any other questions.

We go up to the second floor of the chapel. The rest of the big girls are already seated downstairs, in the nave, and everybody is singing:

> *O Mary, mother mine,*
> *O spiritual comfort,*
> *protect and guide me*
> *to the heavenly homeland.*

The chapel thunders with the hymn and shines with the glow from lamps, tapers, and votive candles. The scent of lilies mixes with glows and sounds, creating a mixture that exalts and confuses my senses. We, the little girls, come in from one side and get to see everything by stretching out on the railing of the choir's balcony. After the hymn, they move on to prayer: *Our Father, who art in heaven.* I don't know the words, but I'm beginning to find it very strange that these people are always talking about fathers and mothers. My father and mother are at home and are not the parents of anyone except my brother and me. I have no idea which fathers and mothers are the ones up there in heaven.

All I can see in the sky are blue circles with black dots inside that go around, but no father or mother.

The girl next to me jabs me with her elbow to get me to repeat the words because the nun is staring at me. I look at the girl's lips and try to imitate what she's saying.

Then a man in a black dress comes in, who must be yet another father, and he starts talking. It seems only fathers can speak from the pulpit. Nuns cannot speak because they are mothers. The father raises his arms and, in Curro's Spanish accent, says: "You, Daughters of Mary, must continue your apostolate. The mother of the Crucified never lost her purity. Do not fall into sin! Preserve the lily-like purity of Mary. Even you, little angels up there on the balcony, can be tempted by the weakness of the flesh and be cast into the eternal fire."

This is how he explains what he has just said: "Because you already have the use of reason, the Evil One can tempt you with concupiscence."

I'm having trouble following him, but I get that we can fall into sin and that it can burn us. I don't know where sins might be that I could fall into them without realizing it. I've never seen one, I don't know what they look like, where they are, or why they burn. Maybe they're in the kitchen, because my mother has burned herself there a lot, though she hasn't fallen.

Also, in the kitchen we keep flesh, like meat, in the icebox, but whether it's weak or strong, I can't say. Maybe sin in the kitchen is different: though it may burn, you can't fall into it.

At the end of this sermon, the big girls stand up, walk in a file, and kneel at the railing in front of the altar. The father has in his hands a metal cup that shines like gold, and he pulls out of it with his right hand a white wafer, round and thin, which he inserts into the mouth of each girl. Then the big ones get up, staring at the floor like they're looking for something. The nun behind us says: "They are taking the host. Communion is a sacred sacrament and you, when you grow up, will also take it. The host is the body of God."

I tremble. The body of God's host is a round wafer!

O Mary, Mother of Mine is sung once more, and the chapel shakes anew.

The odors of mahogany from the pews, new shoe leather, fabric of uniforms and capes mingle with the lilies' perfume.

The nun sneaks up behind me and pinches my tiny arm, exclaiming in an angelic voice: "Sing! Sing!"

THE DAYS THAT FOLLOW have not been very pleasant. Nuns have pinched me because during recess I went to the empty English class, climbed into one of the cars the kindergarteners get to play with, and sped down the hall with nuns tripping over their habits and their big black rosaries trying to catch up with me. Another day, also during recess, in the same class, I was surprised and pinched by a nun because I bit into an appetizing wax apple that the English teacher always waves around when she says "apple." Then, a week later, when we were in line to be vaccinated, I got frightened by the girls' screams and cries, so, before my turn came, I stepped out of line holding my arm as if I'd had my shot. A nun got suspicious and asked me if I had been vaccinated, and when I said yes, she pinched my supposedly vaccinated arm very hard.

After several months of being routinely pinched, I show my mother my bruised arms and tell her I refuse to go back to school. Her reaction is to quickly switch me to the Baldor School, which is Catholic but not run by nuns or priests. It's the same school my brother attends.

THE NEW SCHOOL is on Avenida de los Presidentes, which ends at the Malecón, where the equestrian statue of Calixto García, a major general and hero of our Island's Liberating Army, loses its blind gaze in the sea. The avenue is wide, clean, white, divided in the center by the graceful royal palms that are symbols of our country. The flags of the school and the country fly in the tower where the punished must stay after school.

This tower seems to have turned into my favorite place. Because I don't know how to hide my faults, since my arrival at this school I've accumulated almost more hours of punishment than I could fulfill in the nights and Saturdays of an entire school year. I spend my time talking or daydreaming in class, because everything they are teaching, I already know. The teacher is forever asking me to repeat what she just said, and punishing me if I can't. As I never know what to say because I've not listened to a word, the tower welcomes me with its two showy flags every night and Saturday morning to do my penance.

An unexpected event has interrupted this routine: I twisted my ankle jumping off the school bus before it had come to a full stop. The kids laughed thunderously when they saw me limping towards my house. Since that day my mother carries me to school. Every day, always late, we gallop into the broad-tiled courtyard, run past the Apostle of the Fatherland's bust with his mustache and goatee, cutting through the big girls' surprise and mockery.

These almost-adolescent girls, their chubby bodies stuffed into the tight measurements of the school's white uniform, cover their mouths with their hands to laugh, or do so shamelessly.

This depends on whether they've reached the stage of development I call borderline shamelessness. When I limp into the first-grade classroom, all my classmates are already seated. Renata, the teacher, does not scold me for being late but smiles, showing a perfect denture, and turns to the blackboard, displaying her gigantic butt and thick calves that spill down from the short beige skirts she usually wears. In squeaky white chalk, the teacher writes the letters of the alphabet on the blackboard, separating them by eyelashes that she calls commas. Then she explains capital letters and lower-case letters, calling them "majuscules" and "minuscules."

I've already learned this alone.

Outside, the morning goes by, reflecting Sun on the walls and shifting the shadows' places. To amuse myself, I imagine we're all at the bottom of a well, and we're frogs transformed into girls, and, at some point, we will discover our real identity, jump on top of the desks, and start croaking. I invent different combinations of things, animals, and people.

Sometimes I convince myself that we are pencils that have forgotten the power of writing, and that we've come to class to re-learn that process. As we learn to write with various instruments, we try to remember how to write with our selves, on an unstable surface such as air or fire.

From time to time, the teacher yanks me out of my thoughts by asking me about something that, of course, I haven't been listening to. The other girls, with their chunky arms and legs covered in blond hair, bright eyes wide open, braids secured in white ribbons, laugh at my ignorance.

And then I must spend yet another hour in the tower writing "I must pay attention in class" one thousand times.

This goes on for months until I realize that I already have more hours of detention than I could serve during the rest of my years in school. What would they do with all those hours of punishment if I died suddenly?

If I were stabbed to death, like the child martyr Maria Goretti, by my father's political enemies, how could they force me to write millions of times "I must not speak out in class" and all those things they make me write until my fingers harden and my desk is smeared with the gooey sweat dripping from my cheeks and pouring off my hands?

I don't know why I must pay attention in class, or keep quiet, or listen to the whistle-like voice of this teacher hammering the inside of my head. Why must I focus on those letters and those numbers that she writes on the board? Are these people crazy?

I've fallen into a place of madmen. I'm dying of boredom. I want to sleep during class and never wake up again.

The teacher mercifully hides her butt from us by sitting down. But then, while still smiling, she asks me to explain what a vowel is. I stand up, growing taller than that entire classroom full of golden locks and curls.

I can no longer hide inside my imagination because I am standing, inside my little white shoes, smelling the morning and the pencils' erasers, listening to the school principal announcing over the intercom: "Attention! Sixth Grade A! Sixth Grade A! Distinguished Students of the Month are excused from class to come to the Office to organize the Civic Act!"

I imagine these kids with decorations on their chests, a strip of gold metal covered in blue paint from which hang little stars with the number one, or two, rising proudly from their desks and marching to be congratulated because they have been chosen to carry the national flag. This Friday, up on the platform, they will carry the mast and display the flag before which every other student in the school must parade and respectfully salute like a soldier.

I'm also thinking of the small museum next to Sixth Grade with its display cases of stuffed sharks, with their idiot noses and their stripes on both sides of their mouths. And the hammerheads with black eyes at each end. There, too, are the turtles with their golden checkerboard stomachs, made shiny by embalming liquid and shellac. These are creatures that sometimes appear in my nightmares.

Outside the school, statues of our presidents are placed along the avenue, all standing, pointing a finger into space, or turning their back to the sea, toward which this avenue flows.

Our heroes, mounted on horseback, are plastered with political posters: "Vote for Castellanos," "Castellanos for Mayor."

Sharks, turtles, presidents, and heroes on horseback – all beset me as the teacher demands that I define a vowel.

The silence is spoiled by whispers and giggles.

"A vowel is the uppercase 'A' and the lowercase 'a'," the teacher finally explains, triumphant in demonstrating her knowledge.

"Yes, but what *is* a vowel?" I ask her in turn.

"The uppercase 'A' *is* a vowel and the lowercase 'a' *is* a vowel," she repeats, with an indulgent smile. Do I say it, or not? I wonder. Words fill my head but I'm not sure of my ability to express them, plus I don't want more hours, more towers, or more laughs. "The 'A,' capital or minuscule, may well be a vowel, but *what* is a vowel? Why is it different from a consonant?" I surprise myself by asking.

The classroom explodes into laughter. The teacher stops smiling and tells me that I have an hour of detention during which I must write a hundred times "The A is a vowel."

I collapse on my desk. Now my mother must talk to the assistant principal of the school, who's in charge of detention. I can't be serving punishment for the rest of my life, especially now, with my foot twisted.

The class continues with its vowels and I dream of recess because, although it's a small death because I have no friends and I'm always alone, at least it's a break from the danger of being assigned detention.

CLASSES END with the school's bell, and we go in a procession of two abreast to another classroom. I have been excused from serving the hour of detention so

I can attend this extra class to prepare for first communion. For several weeks we will undergo intellectual and spiritual preparation for this highest Catholic ceremony. Though this school's faculty isn't made up of priests and nuns, it provides Catholic education. The classroom is cleaner than the one for first grade. It's painted light green and has a real-black blackboard, freshly washed, while all the others are gray because of the chalk that adheres to their surfaces after lessons are just smudged away by an eraser.

Sitting in the teacher's chair is a very white young woman with an oval face and black hair. She's from Catholic Action, she informs us. Her name is Miss Camps, and, with a sweet smile, she invites us to take a seat. The class feels at ease. There's a pleasant air of informality. Not felt here are the military discipline, the oppressive duty that reign in this school.

"Taking first communion is a very important thing. You must be prepared. First, there must be perfect trust between you and me. If you want to ask anything, even the most lurid questions" – she smiles and her eyes shine when she pronounces the word *lurid*, which I must look up later in the dictionary – "you may ask me during class or afterwards. If you are ashamed, just write your question on a piece of paper and I will answer you in class, without telling the name of the girl who asked."

I can't believe this relaxed atmosphere, this smiling young woman who goes to the blackboard and writes with the coordinated movements of a swimmer. The other teachers move like tanks or cows, are not vital athletes, seem weighed down by the burden of Pedagogy, Religion, or Society.

Miss Camps, her lips painted fire red, is a modern woman, a Progressive Catholic, who doesn't worry that the two words might be contradictory.

No, it's possible, I'm seeing it.

Her youth and sympathetic ways make the girls forget the "unwritten laws" (the ones you must write a thousand times if you end up in detention), such as "Do not speak in class unless called on," "Do not interrupt the teacher," "Do not go to the bathroom without asking for permission."

The class comes to life and everybody is sending Miss Camps bits of paper with, possibly, "lurid" questions written on them, although, like me, they may not know the exact meaning of "lurid." Now we'll know everything! What are we going to find out? I'm not sure, but I've heard the big girls talk when they gather in small, exclusive groups during recess, things that "little girls shouldn't know." And they shut up when any of us approach their group.

You can tell who the big girls are, because not only are they in more advanced grades and taller, but they pull the belt of their school uniform so tight that it gets ragged and threadbare, sometimes even breaking the uniform's pearl buckle, all because they want to show off their "wasp waists," as the older girls call it. In addition, on the right side of their chest they have a visible lump which is concealed on the left by the school shield embroidered on a pocket intended for a white handkerchief. Then, too, they paint their lips pink, or "natural" color, as my mother calls it.

Above all, big girls adopt a peculiar cynicism that says they've reached adolescence. I've seen some girls' personalities transform from one day to the next. That cynicism and blasé-ness signal the death of childhood to me.

"To take communion is to receive the body of Christ," the teacher asserts.

I raise my hand and Miss Camps smiles at me.

"Where is the body of Christ?" I ask, showing I'm paying attention.

The teacher moves in her seat and makes a gesture that I interpret as approving. It's a good question.

"The body of Christ is inside the host, and that is why we cannot chew it, because it is a sacrilege to chew Christ. You must suck it."

I laugh and the other girls laugh too. "You can't chew, but you can digest it, and then poop," I reason out loud, laughing.

In this atmosphere of freedom anything is possible.

It's as if I were home and my mother were to ask me what she should do with her life.

I would point out to her the most logical path, because inside everything, there is logic, as I've already read in my father's books, and you must use intelligence to find it.

My mother once asked me, when I was crying very loudly, *why* I had to cry. Unable to discover the reason, I stopped crying and shut up.

What reason is there, then, for that story of the body of Christ?

This time the teacher gets serious and moves uncomfortably in her chair. The class is still laughing. The girls in the front row turn to look at me mockingly.

"There are things in religion that can't be understood. The mortal mind is incapable of understanding the divine mysteries. You must have faith. Faith moves mountains. Men are ignorant, and, sometimes, prompted by the devil, they look for reasons!"

The class suddenly gets serious.

"But I am not prompted by the devil," I protest. "And I'm not a man," I continue. "I want to understand how Christ can be in the host, why they don't want us to chew him but just to digest him, and why we must eat God."

Miss Camps opens her black patent leather purse, pulls out her glasses case, puts on her glasses which are round with a black frame, and stares at me.

"What is your name?"

I answer, without rising and standing beside my desk. Everything is supposed to be informal, like in my house.

"Good. Leave the class now. You don't need preparation for communion."

I stand up supported by everyone's gaze. It's a triumph. I know so much about religion that I don't need to prepare.

Maybe my questions are good ones. Maybe the teacher is on my side.

Out in the hallway, I drink water.

The afternoon is cooling down a bit. The sky is full of red and yellow ribbons. The trees lining the sidewalk move with a breeze that smells of sea and comes from the end of the avenue. I sit in one of the large wooden armchairs of the school's porch to wait for the bus that takes kids home when they've had to stay an hour later for detention. I put on my navy-blue school sweater. I am at the pinnacle of glory. I'm going to take my first communion without having to prepare for it.

WEEKS LATER, when I find out that Miss Camps suspended me for not being old enough, I am stunned. I don't believe the age thing. She's a young Catholic, modern, progressive. What did I do to offend her? What laws have I violated?

She laughed with me the whole time, told us to ask questions, be ourselves. There was something that didn't fit.

Or was it me? Was I inspired by the devil?

Then the devil is my mother and father, because they've always demanded that I give a reason for crying, or asking for something, or doing something. Have I misunderstood?

I'm the only one in class not taking first communion.

The teacher and her class break apart like pieces of a puzzle.

For months I'm playing with those pieces.

WE ARE IN RELIGION CLASS – nothing to do with Miss Camps' class – and the teacher, it seems to me, has not prepared the lesson and is improvising. "I'm going to teach you unwritten religion," she says in a mysterious voice. "We are not going to teach sacred history today, but give a realistic class about Christian piety."

She stands on the platform where the teacher's desk is, opens her arms abruptly, and poses herself on an imaginary cross, and begins: "Christ died on the cross for us."

Dressed in black, with matching tiny hat and half-veil, the teacher seems to have transported herself, in a trance of mystical fervor, to an invisible cross where she's nailed. Black shoes, with fat heels and laces, hit the platform, producing the deep sound of a drum. The blackboard, behind her, frames her in black. Though it's daytime, I imagine the profound darkness of a stormy night.

"*We* killed him! So did *every one* of you!" She points a finger at us. We little girls tremble in our seats. "Yes, you too, little angels. *Even you* have killed the Son of God. They shoved a spear right in *here*!"

She strikes her right breast, which sounds like a drum.

The class lets out a unanimous cry of horror.

Ringed by curls and smelling of milk, our rosy-cheeked, tender little faces tremble as now the teacher nails herself back onto her imaginary cross, arching her breast and looking at the ceiling, as if seeking divine protection.

After a few seconds, she closes her eyes and mumbles something like a litany. We little girls trade glances of amazement. Some of us are still trembling.

"O ingratitude of the world! We have crucified you in our ignorance, in our lust, in our disgusting pleasures of the flesh!" A great silence comes over the class, and she continues: "We must also think of the Evil One, of Satan, who pushes the flesh to sin and make us lose our souls."

Camila, the number one student in the class, sitting in the row in front of me, turns with a gesture of elegant indifference because she is ten years old and considers herself above it all. She nails me with her sparkling amber eyes and a gesture that says, "Need we hear this today, *really*?"

The teacher, who's calmed down a bit, sits in her chair at her desk covered with religious books, and looks up and down and from left to right at all the students. "Today," she says, "I'm going to tell you a true story. This really happened." She takes a deep breath. "There was this sinful woman who, despite the good advice of her virtuous friends, persisted in sin."

At this moment, a lightning bolt strikes close to the school. The building's foundation shakes and the windows vibrate. A torrent of rain is unleashed. The entire courtyard, which I can see through the open window on my left, disappears behind a gray curtain of water.

"This woman *persisted in sin*!" she repeats to be heard through the rain's din. "And one night, as she slept in pleasure after having surrendered herself to concupiscence, the Devil appeared to her and told her that he was going to take her away.

"The Devil grabbed her by her right wrist and dragged her to the door. Then the woman uttered, for the first time in many years, the name of Christ – and the Devil released her, fleeing in terror! The next morning, there were footprints burned into the carpet in her room, and the impression of fingers burned into the woman's wrist.

"To hide the burn, this woman, from that moment, wears a silver bracelet."

The teacher stands up shoving her chair back, which produces an alarming screech. Before the stupefied class, she raises her right arm, slowly slides down her silver bracelet, and reveals her wrist with its horrendous burn.

The little girls again tremble. This time, they let out screams and cries.

"Don't be afraid, little girls. If you are good, you will go to heaven."

Another thunderbolt comes even closer. Instantly, lightning illuminates the entire classroom, which had gone dark. Everything trembles with the bolt's strike and the girls let out a heart-rending howl.

Outside, the entire neighborhood appears to have lost electrical power.

"And do not be fearful of lightning either," the teacher says, after a pause.

Then she adds: "If a bolt strikes this class and chars us all to cinders, you will all go to heaven because you have all just taken your first communion."

Now I'm the one trembling.

I'm the only one in the class who hasn't communed, thanks to Miss Camps.

WHEN I ARRIVE HOME FROM SCHOOL, I open the door carefully so nobody can hear me. My mother never locks the door so I don't need to use a key.

That way, I make less noise.

This is important to me, because, in my family, it's always good to know what's going on before you make your presence known. I don't want to go in if my mother is having a fight with the cook, or talking to herself about Louis XIV while she's sitting at the dining room table playing solitaire.

Also, if I don't make any noise when I go in, I can leave my bookbag beside the door and escape to the street to play.

Now, I hear voices coming from my parents' room and sit on the pink silk sofa to eavesdrop.

They're not whispering, and I hear the voices of my mother and her sister Isabel.

"Florita, if you have migraines, it's because you aren't taking care of yourself," Aunt Isabel, with the authoritarian tone of an older sister, scolds my mother. "You never go to the doctor and you never take your medicines. This disease is not cured so easily."

"I've always had migraines," my mother defends herself. "I suffered from them long before I met Augusto," she adds in a whiny voice.

"This disease," says her sister angrily, "your husband gave you without your eating or drinking it, and it can bring all kinds of disorders. Thank goodness you didn't die giving birth to Mercy, as weakened and bleeding as you were."

She goes on. "And it's a miracle the baby herself wasn't born infected."

"And me with only half a uterus," adds my mother to change the direction of the conversation. "That's why her father calls her 'Bad Bug.' Because, as people say, 'Bad bugs never die.'"

"How irresponsible you were to let yourself get pregnant!" Isabel continues with even greater harshness in her voice. "The doctor warned that you and the baby were likely to die. That it was impossible for both of you to come out alive. A nine-hour delivery! Who can survive that?"

My mother, beginning to get irritated, says: "Well, at the end of the day, everything turned out fine, did it not?"

After a pause, Isabel says: "Gisela wants to study piano in the United States and it's very expensive."

At last, Isabel has changed the topic of conversation to the real reason for her visit.

"Do you need money?" my mother asks with a tone of reaching for her wallet to give it to her.

"I need a fellowship for my daughter," Aunt Isabel replies. "They are very difficult to get, and they must be given by the Ministry of Education." She speaks in a neutral voice, without asking.

"Do you want Augusto to get it for you? You know he hates doing my family favors. Whereas he does them for anybody who supports him and his political party."

Now Isabel exclaims, with great resentment: "After infecting you, after sleeping with God knows what dirty women, the least Augusto can do is give you whatever you ask of him. He is a loathsome man! You may forgive him, but I won't, not ever! Nobody does such a thing to a sister of mine!"

"The girl's about to get home from school," my mother answers, meek in the face of her older sister's anger, but now they are going around in circles..

I get up from the sofa, open and close the front door making a lot of noise, and walk into the bedroom with my bookbag in hand.

"I'm going to take a shower," I say, without greeting anybody. "It's hot as the devil outside."

"Well, I need to leave," says Isabel, I suspect because she doesn't want to continue discussing her personal affairs in front of me.

"Goodbye, then, and I'll let Augusto know what we talked about," says my mother to Isabel's back as she glides out the door.

My mother, on the bed in her pink robe speckled with coffee stains, looks at the ceiling and sighs.

"I've a migraine. Bring me a little alcohol in a handkerchief to sniff, and a bucket to vomit in," she asks me, annoyed and suffering.

"THIS CHILD LIKES FUNERAL MUSIC," my mother tells my cousin Cleo, the eldest of The Little Girls. We're in the living room. Cleo's sitting in an armchair in front of me, cutting her nails with scissors, and we're listening to the radio, a big wooden appliance with a needle that moves along three parallel lines, one of them red, with numbers on a yellow background to indicate frequencies.

At six o'clock in the evening they broadcast waltzes by Johann Strauss, which I never miss.

Especially on this day, when a hurricane is attacking the Capital and the world seems to be coming to an end out there, the violence of the elements adds a touch of drama to the music.

There's something special about mixing the playful champagne waltz rhythm of *Tales from the Vienna Woods* with the dramatic reports from the Meteorological Center, prepared by the Lieutenant Commander of the National Observatory, who seems to take delight in periodically interrupting the music. Especially since, for the first time in a long while, the report isn't "Skies cloudy or partly cloudy, breezes from east to west gently strengthening from time to time, with occasional rain scattered throughout the national territory."

Instead, he's talking about a "low-intensity" hurricane that will arrive "in the first hours of night."

Already we are beginning to feel the apocalyptic force of "low intensity."

155

The heavy rains that precede the hurricane are slapping at the row of newly planted, rickety trees in front of our building. Cleo, a serious hurricane aficionada, wears sneakers and clamdiggers that come down to her calves. She's tied a red cotton bandanna around her hair and has come to our apartment in search of news, as well as to have lunch with us, or sponge a meal, as my mother calls it.

Several times since we moved here, I've dreamed that I was flying over those very trees the wind is beating up. In my dream flight, these trees were wrapped in a soft white layer like the angel hair we trim our Christmas tree with to reflect its colored lights in concentric circles. I didn't know what that dream meant, but whenever I woke up, I felt a lightness, a very pleasant freedom.

My mother, playing solitaire at the dining room table, seems to be putting her life in order. Cleo, done trimming her nails, sits with her legs in the lotus position, showing off her white sneakers and a stretch of hairy leg between these and the hem of her indigo-blue denim clamdiggers.

"Funeral music!" says my mother. "All well and good for when you die – but girl, given that one is alive, all that *tan, tan, tan-tan*! There's no melody, in my opinion, not a danceable sound! I don't know who this girl takes after, listening to this communist music! She'll end up like Rosa Luxemburg, sitting in Clara Zetkin's lap! So tasteless! And at the end of the day, raped and murdered by bayonet while being transferred from one prison to another! Live and learn! And, after dumping on poor old bald Vladimir Ilyich, oh dear, what did she expect? Lenin was a Mongol and he had those snake-in-the-grass eyes that came from reading political journals in Zurich, poor wretch! Everyone was in Switzerland then, before the Great War, when people could travel without passports. What a time that was! The time of the Dance of the Millions, here on the Island! Even Caruso and Galli Curci came here, to the Capital. Sarah Bernhardt said we were Indians dressed in frock coats!"

How could that be, I reason, with no Indians on the island? They were exterminated by the diseases brought by the Spaniards and forced labor, entire families committing suicide.

The light in the dining room accentuates my mother's paleness, and makes her face look as if it were covered in white powder.

While spouting off her monologue, she's also concentrating on her game of solitaire. She pauses theatrically, throwing her head back, as if freeing her brain from vermin. "My brother-in-law Alejandro and the good Doctor Almanzor got together to hear funeral music. Our communist Galen said: 'We are going to hear good music. I have records at home,' and Alejandro went, with his honey-colored hair and his restlessness, his almost-St.-Vitus-dance jumpiness. Not even photos could fix him in time and space. He was always jumping to the next moment.

"It seems that Almanzor's funereal music had something to do with Gorky's *The Mother, And Quiet Flows the Don* by what's-his-name, the three-volume *Pedagogical Poem* by Makarenko, and Mayakovsky's poem *Cloud in Trousers*, required reading of Party comrades. What a mess, girl, those men reading, and leading, the country into chaos! Martyrs of the Comintern! Not at all like the Catholic martyrs, with their marvelous sense of the morbid! – but instead restrained, scientific – and yet, in the end, the very same suicidal madness! The Spartacus Group calling Social Democrats 'lackeys of imperialism'! Rosa Luxemburg writing flattering letters to Romain Rolland! How did she not know Rolland admired fakirs? What has *Das Kapital* got to do with Indian fakirs? Then the debacle began. Armageddon. After the Great War, did anyone have an ounce of common sense? Not Simone Weil, refusing to eat because The Poor were starving – so *she* starved her*self*, without even having to go live in India! and the whole time being able to eat French food, imagine, the best in the world! Yes, she was a Ph.D. when women were nothing but housewives. Yes, she wore round steel-rimmed eyeglasses – in short, she was a high-strung Jewess with an ideal of justice for all! And, of course, she embraced her mother, a fat-bellied old woman who believed she had given birth to a phenomenon! Shadows in History, the rejected anonymous, all her daughter wanted was to be a Ph.D., move away, rent an apartment, in short: emancipate herself!"

Laughter gushes from her throat like a bag of blood.

The wind whips at the door, and the rain finds openings around its edges, the spray sketching small treetops on the walls and a half-moon on the ground. *Tales of the Vienna Woods* gives way to the *Blue Danube Waltz*, which I first heard as background music for an episode of a radio program in which a woman lives obsessed by that waltz, thinking it beckons to her from the sea – so she ends up walking into the waves as if she were going somewhere, then loses her footing and drowns. The episode made an impression on me. It brought back the memory of one of my earliest dreams.

My mother laughs sarcastically, affected by the nostalgic music, as if she were smelling the silk of the coffin, the gladioli hidden behind the smoke from the candles, which, for me, that melody evokes.

"And then they come to me with stories! When I met Augusto, he was as skinny as a skeleton in his black suit that danced on him, and his vest of the same color with silk in the back that hung on him, and his Charlie Chaplin mustache – a graduate of the Normal School, a Mr. Nobody whose ears stuck out like Dumbo's. He was a zero to the left in his own family, on a par with his brother Papo, who's known for mysterious nights out and sporting garish-colored bow-ties. Acid-tongued gossips say Papo has a Black mistress, that he picks up young men at bus stops ... Only God knows what Papo does at night in La Víbora!

"Then, we marry, Septimio is born immediately, with his crying jags and his hernias. But he's the son Augusto wanted, and so did I. To carry on the name.

And then, five years later, along comes the girl, who should not have been born because I was missing half a uterus (I did everything I could to prevent it), but there she is, born against all odds.

"How often I prayed for her to dissolve inside me, not to be born, but just to go back where she came from! But instead of bringing death, my death, our little angel brings money, she brings us luck. No one died, neither she nor I, and the doctor told us that we could both leave the hospital dancing the can-can. What a cheeky doctor! But, you know, for sure he spent a million hours at the operating table and, when he left, my sister Isabel told me that he was covered in sweat but smiling because he had won the battle against Death *twice*. The same doctor who'd said it was impossible for us both to live! What he won was a short-lived battle, one of those in which all doctors engage – it was a postponement.

"In the end Death, the Bald Lady, grabs us all by one leg, and we go straight to the grave. Doctors can win battles, but in the end, they lose the war."

Cleo turns to look at my mother, like she's tired of her chatter.

My mother smokes and flicks ashes into the glass ashtray next to her on the table. There's a semblance of order in this.

"Flora, it sounds as if now the hurricane is beginning in earnest," says Cleo with poorly disguised glee.

"Let the hurricane take us. Me, and this entire accursed Island!"

The door creaks, pushed by the wind. The waltz is over, and I turn off the radio. The hurricane has arrived. The night will be filled with howls of wounded dogs chasing their own shadows. The scrawny trees in front will fly like witches' broomsticks in this wind, cars will be pierced by bullets of water, and the sea, rising in huge manes of foam, will furiously pound the Malecón a long way from here.

Cleo slept with us, and when I went with her the next morning to check out the hurricane damage, we were disappointed to find that, except for a few branches and leaves scattered on the ground, everything remained the same. Even the scrawny trees that had just been planted were still standing.

We haven't suffered anything catastrophic enough to interrupt our boring daily routine.

13

THINGS THAT FALL FROM THE SKY

MONTHS LATER, today, Saturday afternoon, I haven't gone out to play. For a while now, I have been cutting down on outings because I'm obsessed with the idea that I must think up something truly important.

I don't know what, but I must make something clear, understand it, break it down. Something essential must incubate inside me.

The incessant activity of my games with my friends, my conversations with Dieguín, but, sadly, no longer with Hugo, my spying on the Widow of Bermejo, suddenly seem frivolous. They serve no purpose!

Now, today, Saturday, after trying all morning to reflect on something important, I give up, and, lying on top of the cherry-colored silk spread that covers my parents' big bed, I read the Trucutú comic strip, our version of the Americans' Alley Oop, in the newspaper.

My brother, sitting on the same bed, reads a Prince Valiant comic book.

"Tico, tico! Tico, tico!" screeches Loulou, Dieguín's parrot, in her sarcastic, mocking falsetto.

Septimio lunges out of bed, runs into the living room, sticks his head out the window to the inner courtyard, and, unconcerned about Dieguín's feelings, yells several times: "Shut up!"

The parrot shuts up for a few moments and then attacks with her second theme: "Royal parrot, go you to Spain and I'll for Portugal."

Septimio gives up on the parrot and I hear him shut the window, not considering how hot it gets when the flow of cool air is interrupted. He announces that he's going out to play with friends, maybe to escape the heat, maybe to get over the frustration of being unable to silence the bird.

After a few seconds, I hear the door slamming. I get off the bed, go to the living room, and open the window because the parrot doesn't bother me a bit.

On my way back to the bed to read the comics, I glance at Choli and my mother lounging in the armchairs, each reading sections of the newspaper that interest them.

Choli has come in place of her older sister, Kika, the light-chocolate-colored young woman who helps us from time to time with house cleaning. Choli, with a rounder face and darker skin than Kika, went to the Ursuline nuns' school, but she isn't religious or serious the way Kika is, and she'll laugh at just anything. Strangely, she doesn't care for the funnies. but loves the morbid red chronicle section, having acquired my mother's taste for crimes of violence.

My mother, however, is poring over the page where the national lottery numbers are announced, and comparing them with the numbers on the tickets my father bought this week. As my mother bends over the newspaper, her nose sharpens, as if she's a hound hot on the scent of the number she's seeking.

Her face seems particularly tragic to me, clinging to the illusion of the game.

She wants more money – more than the fat rolls of high-denomination bills she has at this very moment in her wallet, which my father gave her this morning to deposit on Monday in the Authentic Party's bank account. Often my mother carries more than five thousand pesos to make these deposits in the bank.

She answers people who ask her if she's afraid of being assaulted: "Who's going to steal from me? I look like a beggar!"

My mother's gaze jumps back and forth between the newspaper and the lottery tickets at an accelerated pace. She's like a sparrow pecking at seeds. I stop reading the funnies and sit up to get a better look at her. The jumps of her eyes increase and I see the blood leave her face. She's livid.

"Oh, ohh, ohhh!" she shouts, raising her arms and then crushing the sheet of lottery tickets against her chest.

"Ma'am, what's the matter?" Choli asks, alarmed.

"Oh, look, Choli, look. Is this number on the lottery tickets the same as this one in the newspaper?"

Choli's eyes jump from one number to the other, and, after a bit, she says, carefully: "Yes, ma'am, they are the same."

My mother hands me the newspaper and the sheet of lottery tickets, and makes me compare the numbers. "You look, girl. Tell me if they're the same!"

I too conclude that they are the same.

"Oh, it's our turn for El Gordo! We won the jackpot!" my mother shouts, flapping the sheet of lottery tickets in her right hand.

Dieguín's parrot for some time has been gurgling, whistling, and muttering to herself.

Now the bird shouts, over and over: "Royal parrot, go you to Spain, and I'll for Portugal!" Does that bird know that my mother has in her hand only half of the entire sheet, that is, fifty tickets? When she announces that we have won the grand prize of the lottery, valued at one hundred thousand pesos, she informs us that this might have been a real fortune if Augusto, during a meal this week that ended if not in total inebriation, at least in beer euphoria, had not given the other half to one of his political friends.

"Fifty thousand pesos, suddenly, rained from the sky, are not a trifle," I say in a calm voice.

"Yes, imagine," agrees my mother, "you can buy a three-bedroom house in a nice neighborhood in the city, for only ten thousand."

My mother now starts jumping around enthusiastically and phoning my father, her family, friends. Very soon the apartment is filled with neighbors and relatives who scream, wave their arms a lot, and burst into laughter. People have gone crazy. I remain impassive. Every now and then someone looks at me as if to reproach me for lying on the bed, silently witnessing this uproar.

When my father arrives home, followed closely by my brother, my mother goes to the living room to greet him at the door with shouts of jubilation. I follow her, quiet. My father, dressed in his usual white suit of dril 100, walks in with his elegant dance step, carrying a couple of bottles of his favorite champagne, "The Widow," he calls it, in his hand. He is surrounded by sycophants from his office, his driver, his aide, and a few pretty women from party headquarters who drove in their own cars to celebrate the success of this politician with a future.

"Money attracts money, gentlemen!" my father shouts, opening one of the bottles. The cork shoots through the air and the bottle spouts foam. A few people toast with some Baccarat flutes that my mother recently bought at El Encanto, others must settle for drinking from the ordinary jelly glasses we have always used. The neighbors, mostly people I have never seen before, whites, Blacks, mulattos, Chinese, blonds, redheads, and those with brown and black hair, as well as assorted relatives, are superstitiously glad to be splashed by my father's good luck.

My brother, red-faced with pride, looks at my father admiringly, as if he's accomplished a major feat, and reaches out to shake his hand, but my father dodges my brother's gesture, and instead gently pats my head, saying quietly, "Keep giving me luck, Bad Bug."

"Money brings money! We are rich! We are rich!" my mother chants, hugging Choli, drinking champagne, and crying.

"Fifteen men on a dead man's chest, yo-ho-ho, and a bottle of rum!" the parrot squawks.

Everyone screams, hugs, and cries. The aide turns on the radio and the chorus of a *son montuno* is heard:

> *Castellano, how good you dance!*
> *Castellano, how good and how sexy you dance!!*

Hearing the voice of the singer Benny Moré and the rhythm of his Giant Orchestra, my father laughs, flashes his gold ring with its huge aquamarine surrounded by tiny diamonds, a traditional symbol on the Island of political success, and draws all the prettiest girls in to dance. Others pick a partner and dance animatedly around the room. I sit in an armchair to watch the dance. After a few minutes, driven by the joy of the music, by the enchantment of singing, my father dances alone, with the others forming a circle around him.

Castellano, how good you dance!
Castellano, how sexy you dance!

They all chant the chorus, while my father shows off, doing his graceful solo in the center of the circle.

I'm the only discordant note in this scene. This eruption of joy doesn't infect me. This is all for show – laughter, gestures, screams. Within me, a void opens where this joy doesn't fit. I don't know why, but I think the future will be the negative of this positive, and that everyone will look back with nostalgia, like Adam and Eve when they're expelled from Paradise.

For my part, I know nothing will change in my life. I must continue going to school, and on my birthday, I'll receive many white boxes of different sizes from those who seek favors from my father, containing everything the imagination can conjure up.

Above all, I'll get socks and handkerchiefs of all colors. I'll be able to wear something new every day for the rest of the year.

Money is pouring into the house. Why do we want more? I'm nauseated by my family's desire for more money, more stuff. To lessen this unease, from now on, I'm going to retreat into myself.

Monday I'll go to school, calmly, as if nothing's happened.

"YOU ARE ENDLESSLY BADGERING ME, always making me do things for your damned family!" my father shouts, flaming with anger, walking from one side of the bedroom to the other.

"Your family is a passel of freeloaders who've never done a damned thing for you!" My father gesticulates violently, raising his arms, stamping his feet on the tiles. "Hear me well: they haven't done, and never will do, anything for you!"

My mother, lying on the double bed, wearing her salmon-colored silk house coat that shines under the light of the ceiling lamp, wipes her tears with a handkerchief, but they continue to pour down her contracted face, furrowed with premature wrinkles. Her fine, sparse black hair clumps wet with tears on both temples.

Septimio, sitting on the floor of their bedroom, propped up against the wall opposite the bed, is whiter than chalk. His brown eyes bulge out, bloodshot, and his hands, crossed over his legs in the fetal position, are shaking.

I'm sitting on the bedspread at the foot of the bed, watching my mother cry, unable to comfort her.

"You are a bad man! You are a bad, bad man! The misfortune of me and my children! Bright light of the street – dark shadow of the house! Everything for your friends and your girlfriends – and you let your family starve to death!"

Septimio and I look at each other in surprise. No one is starving. On the contrary, we live much better now that we won the lottery.

My father becomes more enraged, approaches the bed, wags his index finger in my mother's face in an accusatory gesture, and shouts: "I'm going to tell you what you are: *nobody*! A big nobody, because you have never done anything you wanted to do, only what others told you to do. Your family is your pretext for *not* existing."

"Any day now, I will suffocate your children in their sleep and set myself on fire!" my mother screams back, turning her face to evade my father's finger. "Then you'll realize what you had!"

My brother and I look at each other in terror.

I get out of bed and quietly tell my father that he had better leave, that he must quit arguing. I take his hand to get him out of the room.

"And the worst thing is that you're taking my children's love away from me!" my father reproaches my mother, turning his head towards her before I pull him out of the room.

After my father leaves the house, slamming the door, Septimio gets up from the floor, sits on the bed next to my mother, and dries her tears with his clean handkerchief. My mother seems to be in a trance state.

I just stand there, watching the scene.

IT ALL STARTED WITH A NORMAL CONVERSATION that turned into a discussion about things I don't quite understand, though I heard the words "women" and "money" repeated.

Then I realized that my mother had worked herself up to ask my father to award Isabel's daughter that fellowship to study in the United States.

Coincidentally, some member of my mother's family told her that my father was going out with another woman, and had seen them together in a restaurant.

"I'm going to divorce him!" my mother declares when she realizes that my father has left the house. "I swear by this" – she says, making the sign of the cross with the forefinger and thumb of her right hand and kissing it violently– "that I will divorce this man!"

After a few minutes, she confesses, "But I can't, because of my children, be-cause of the two of you. I sacrifice myself for the two of you. As it always has been. Like when I ran the errands for Mother and never stepped on joints or cracks in the sidewalk. I never once stepped on a crack! If I stepped on a crack, they said, Mother would die. Mother always loved Dora more, because she was the daughter of her first love. Not us – five other children, and Mother didn't give a damn about any of us. Bella had her beauty, Chavela had her practicality, Isabel had her ability to deal with life – but what did Adolfo and I have? Adolfo, a madman who pulled his hair out, measured each hair, and wrote down the lengths in a booklet! Scientific madness, you would say, mathematical insanity! I never once stepped on a crack, and yet Mother eventually died.

"Adolfo went nuts because he was gorgeous – he was a man but, amid all his sisters, he looked like another woman. He even sang in a soprano voice! In our games he was Mademoiselle Fifi, Isabel was Mrs. Smith the millionairess, I was Florencia Pocopelo, the Almost-Bald, and Adolfo was the diva who danced at the Moulin Rouge in Paris.

"But then Adolfo went crazy! When Septimio was born, I didn't worry about stepping on cracks anymore, because, then, Septimio was the one who could die, and I knew I couldn't kill him by stepping on a crack, because that only kills mothers. I protected him by bathing him in near-boiling water so that he wouldn't catch cold, until Isabel told me that I was going to peel him like a suckling pig. The child turned purple from so much crying when I put him in boiling water, and that's how he got the hernia in his groin, from so much crying.

"I'm going to divorce this man, who is bad, who doesn't deserve the children he has!"

My brother brings her some alcohol to sniff so she'll calm down. But she waves it away and keeps talking.

Septimio and I look at each other, as if agreeing that we must let her talk, cry, do whatever she wants. It's like being with a dead person, someone who is no longer in this world and whom you can't make come back to reality.

"'Florencia Pocopelo' am I! But with money! with cash in her wallet, with a husband, two children, and a house! I have succeeded! I control all things and Adolfo is in the insane asylum and Mother is in her grave!"

She cries even more uncontrollably. My brother and I escape to the dark living room. Sitting on the floor, our backs against opposite walls, face to face, we gaze into the void. After a few minutes, my brother stands up and turns on the ceiling light. Black moths, which came in through the open window at the front of the apartment, make circles around the light. Night, too, enters through the window: noise of cars, murmurs of conversations of neighbors out on their balconies, laughter of children still out playing on the sidewalk.

My mother goes on talking to herself in the bedroom.

WEEKS AFTERWARD, forgetting the fights she has had with my father during this time, my mother is boiling over with good cheer and proud of discoveries she has made.

"Gus, the dressmaker – I went to her studio! She has her fitting room on 12th Avenue. I need to go for another fitting because today she only took my measurements with a tape, like Coco Chanel. She comes very highly recommended. They say she studied with Dior. Women were lined up at the door to see her, and her phone never stops ringing. She is a fat mulatta who has made quite the career for herself. She even gave me the name of a spiritualist!"

Enedina, our new maid and cook, serves dinner in her dilapidated alpargatas. Her feet, which support well over two hundred pounds of obesity, splay out, sprouting through holes in the gray canvas of her alpargatas.

My father rests his bare elbows, free of his white shirt's rolled up sleeves, on the table, and moves his fork with its tiny bit of steak to his mouth.

Septimio plays with his soup spoon in his soup, bored, resting his head on his hand.

My mother, dressed in a white ensemble adorned with shiny black sequins, pleated at the padded shoulders, her fine black hair fluttering electrically with every turn or vertical movement of her head, seems to be trying to bring to Earth some message from outer space as she ignores the plate of food in front of her.

I sip my soup in silence. My father scratches one ear, perhaps thinking about problems at work as he cuts what's left of his steak into small pieces. My brother finally finishes his soup, and Enedina removes the soup plate and replaces it with a clean dinner plate. My brother serves himself a steak and a mountain of white rice and black beans.

Enedina heads to the kitchen, disappearing behind the crick-crack of the automatically closing door.

After a few minutes, Enedina returns with *tostones* on a dinner plate, since we only have two serving platters, for steaks and rice, and a bowl for beans. The rest is served on plates.

This is the new simplicity of the house. My mother, who boasts of not letting the money and power that have suddenly flooded into her life go to her head, is making a speech defending her atavistic ties with her past of deprivation.

Combing his mustache with his finger as he eats a *tostón*, my father casually announces, "I'm going to Santiago," as Septimio serves himself *tostones* and I continue to slowly savor my soup.

My mother's reaction is, somehow, predictable. "What on earth for? To do politics? I'm sick of politics! You and your henchmen, your guns, your gangsters – Death! Dirty, rude, base scoundrels! Damn politics to hell! Cursed be the day you had the brainstorm of getting into politics. You were fine being a school-teacher. We could have been so happy! Now we are wretched, fearing for the lives of these children. Worrying whether Policarpo Soler or El Colorao will come, whether they'll murder us with a bomb or some other thing, or kidnap us!"

My father finishes eating his *tostón* and rests his chin on his clenched fist. He looks at my mother calmly, as if measuring distances, or considering how to make something clear.

"I'm going to the province of Oriente to fulfill my promise to the Virgin of Caridad del Cobre," he explains in a neutral voice, getting up and leaving much of his food untouched.

He puts on his white suit coat of dril 100 linen, tucks into his trousers of the same material his shirt of the finest white cotton, and knots his knit tie of red silk yarn with the easy gesture of a wealthy man with a future.

"You know the song, kids! It says: 'Should I die on the highway, don't pile flowers on me,'" my father sings, taking a few dance steps.

I get up from the table dancing and singing:

And if you go to El Cobre
I want you to bring me
a little Virgin of Charity.
I don't want flowers.
I don't want a poster,
what I want is the Virgin of Charity.

I follow my father, dancing, to the door and watch him, almost in a single leap, get into the car, the latest model Oldsmobile, in two shades of blue, navy and sky, presented to him by the friend to whom he gave the other fifty lottery tickets from the whole winning sheet that paid out 100,000 pesos.

"The Virgin of Charity of El Cobre!" my mother cries, insulted, from the dining room when she knows my father can no longer hear her. "Gus's going to thank the Black Ochún, the Yoruba goddess of money. As if I didn't know about Black things! True, I don't have a mulatta mother like his, but, instead, descend from very white nobles and grandees of Spain. From rich Creole patricians with sugar mills, cane fields, and hundreds of slaves–" she makes a dramatic pause – "all brought down by the excesses of the corrupt politicians of the Republic."

IN A FEW DAYS, my father returns from Santiago laden with gifts and statuettes of the Virgin of Charity of El Cobre. He arrives hooting and laughing.

"Kids! *Fiñes*! Here are enough little gifts to make sweets with!" he shouts, piling them on the big table in the dining room. My father lights up his fragrant cigar and sits down to smoke it in an easy chair in the living room, his body surrounded by the pink damask of the lounger like an enthroned king, as he unbuttons his coat and loosens his tie.

Along with the perfume of his fine French cologne, I smell the sharp odor of sweat mixed with the leather smell from the car's upholstery where he's been sitting for the long drive back to the Capital.

"It's not what you have, but how you use it," my father instructs us. My brother and I encircle him, smiling and relieved that he didn't die on the road.

"I went to El Cobre with my car given to me as a present, driven by a chauffeur. Others went on their knees and bled all over the steps of the Sanctuary. They destroyed their knees for Ochún. Who goes to see some Catholic virgin? They are there to see the Black Goddess, the goddess of love and money. And do you think

Ochún gives them money for crawling on their knees? No, she gives it to me. And not because I have a university education, a library with classical books, or a good physique, but because I have *this*."

He touches his forehead with his index finger, meaning intelligence. "But also, you must do good, help people. For just one example, I've made every effort to ensure that corrupt officials do not steal the money that pays for school supplies and school breakfasts."

Seeing her opening, my mother, sitting in the other armchair, retorts: "Nevertheless, they steal shamelessly," adding: "Children in rural schools go more to be fed than to learn. You can't memorize multiplication tables on an empty stomach." She adds, as if it were the most obvious thing in the world: "In any case, public education is a mess. That's why I have the kids in private school."

"We have made many advances in this government. Of course, 'There's none so blind as those who will not see,'" replies my father calmly.

Both Septimio and I ignore my mother's words and, still standing, look at our father with adoring eyes. I turn my gaze to the gifts on the table: yellow towers of sugar cane wrapped in crinkly transparent yellow cellophane, bottles of cane syrup or *melado* with their colorful labels, *dulces de leche*, boxes of the finest cigars for my father to smoke or for him to give to friends, since none of us smoke cigars, though Septimio secretly smokes cigarettes.

"Never care overmuch for your lives, *fiñes*," advises my father. Sitting in the easy chair, he opens his arms as if he were giving a political speech.

"In life you must have balls – courage – but not be stupid, of course not, but there are times when you must stand up for yourself."

His new assistant, because Mr. Shop Window couldn't bear my father's fraught-with-danger life, is a dapper Black man called Santana who, like us kids, is standing nearby, observing.

Santana leans against the frame of the front door, smiling broadly, his contrasting teeth white as lime. He approves of his boss's wisdom.

Of course, he's paid to approve, but he seems to be engraving my father's words in his memory.

"That's very good, Doctor. That's the way!" Santana says, laughing and, with his sclerotic-yellow eyes, studying us, "the Little Doctors," as he calls us to please my father.

My brother, carried away by the exaltation of the moment, shouts: "I'm going to be President!"

My father looks at him, pleased, certain that after his death he will leave a worthy dynasty.

"You do have the name of an emperor, son," he says. "Your name, Septimio Severo, is the name of a Roman emperor, but you yourself must turn it into 'Septimio Augusto'."

Septimio, his large ears very red, laughs.

My mother folds her wings like a powerless bird of ill omen, overcome by the irresistible force of my father's optimism and recklessness. One minute she looks like the scariest of the Furies, and the next, she's the tiny wife next to the gigantic Egyptian pharaoh.

"And your sister carries the name of Obatalá. The Virgen de las Mercedes is Obatalá, and he is the purest of the gods. He is the source of luck. Thus, the two of you can create a world. Don't be chickens, like all the spoiled brats. When I go to visit my university classmates, those Mister and Miss Doctors with two and three Ph.D.'s, I see them peering through the blinds trembling. They don't even dare leave their homes. I fight gangsters every day, and I win. Of course, I never come home by the same route so they don't get the chance to blow my head off. You must use your intelligence. But don't put much stock in books. I was always a bad student, and look where I am! At the head of the Ministry of Education!"

My father exaggerates. My brother and I laugh, admiring him, and again Santana smiles, looking at him meekly.

"That's very good, Doctor," approves my father's assistant. "Say something like that at a rally in the neighborhood of Atarés, or Jesús María, and you'll get every last one of their votes. That's what people want: to *get* there, to *be* more, to *have* the good things in life! They want to be in Fat City, Doctor!" He accentuates the words "Fat City" comically.

All of us, even my mother, laugh.

"Socrates has spoken through you, Santana. *Everyone* wants to be in Fat City. Let's not preach to the people anymore about ideals and sacrifices. Sharks may bathe, but they must splash! There are sweets for everyone! Let everyone have their big car, their fine cigar, and their little fun on the side, because we are not monks . . . but fun *with order*, gentlemen!" my father declaims.

In an original way, ancient Greek philosophers unite with the Creole hoi polloi to create an island dialectic, a kind of political song-and-dance. This is the latest word in vernacular political philosophy. Both my brother and I assimilate these pearls of wisdom offered to us by this man of action who's been crowned with success.

But secretly, we know we'll never be able to match his charisma, his cunning, his gift with people.

DAYS LATER, my father enters the house in a lather, laughing and shaking out his coat and pants, grotesquely wrinkled around his thighs after a long day of inspecting rural schools and traveling by Jeep.

He takes the cigar out of his mouth for a moment to repeat what's become his slogan: "I'm friends with my friends!"

"We've been waiting for you," my mother tells him, grabbing him by his coat sleeve. "We want to eat out, at that restaurant near the Capitol."

My father looks mystified.

"Oh, Gus, don't pretend you don't know! The air-conditioned one, where you can watch the fountain with the Indian Maiden statue and the billboard with the Little Jantzen Doll."

My father approaches Septimio and me, messes up our hair as if expecting a photographer to be nearby to preserve the moment for all eternity, and asks in a festive tone: "So, how do the small fry vote?"

"The Little Jantzen Doll!" I scream, jumping up and down and adding my excitement to the scene.

We are outside the apartment in a flash and on the sidewalk piling into the car. My father wants to capture the spontaneity of the moment, "the peak of jubilation" as it might have been called by Tibulus or Macrobius back in Roman times – if it had occurred to them.

My father, who'd selected this car as a gift from someone to whom he had given a much larger gift, wanted the car painted with the two colors of his white-and-brown shoes, but that wasn't an option, so he settled for two shades of blue.

Likewise, he wants life to have two colors, classicism and popularism, the wisdom and way of the people, as a counterpoint or dialectical game: sonata and rhumba.

The poetry of politics and the art of ingenuity, liveliness. These are the arts of many islanders, formed in the distillery of the country, pure and unadulterated by foreign mixtures. Of course, in a country where milk is mixed with water, where everything is spoiled by heat and laziness, what triumphs unpolluted is improvisation, and disrespect for the law. Executing the *danzón* on a single tile, on one foot, that is the dancer's challenge, the feat of the Island's ingenuity, the contribution to its history.

Then, too, instead of Cicero's Catiline Orations, we have the *trompetilla*, the rude noise recognizable as the raspberry. "What more can we ask?" my father says. "Here, only the tiresome, the bore, the bloody nuisance starves to death. The shark bathes, but he also splashes!" repeats my father, again echoing the motto of the politician who immortalized the popular saying. My father splashes at this moment, gives away his joy so as not to look tiresome or bloody or stingy, in order not to starve. He gives one hundred pesos each to his driver and assistant to celebrate, to buy their own bottles of the Widow's champagne.

And, in a moment of great self-confidence, my father orders Santana to go home. He doesn't need his aide to go eat at a restaurant.

We glide in the car along the Grand Promenade, under the green roof of the interlocking trees.

The Capital, full of flashy, cheerful neon lights, is populated by skinny, sun-tanned, hunched-over men wearing white guayaberas and wide pants that flap like flags in the wind. Children, adults, and cars dazzling with their lights and polished enamel bodies, all move happily along the Gran Paseo. It is as if they are following the orders that cops give to beggars: "Get a move on! Don't loiter, circulate!"

We pass in front of the broad flight of granite steps flanked by the pair of large bronze statues of a muscular man representing the Progress of Human Activity and a robust woman called the Holder of the People's Virtue.

This is the National Capitol, a building designed and erected in a harmonic neoclassical style. It is from here that the Island's Congress steers the ship of state. The sixty-five-foot-tall golden statue of the goddess Athena, with helmet, shield, and spear, symbolizes and guards the Republic.

We leave behind the Ionic columns, the great dome, and the national flag, waving and proclaiming the joy we have at being a free and independent country.

14

UNPROTECTED

ARMANDO THE DRIVER drops us at the restaurant we chose, next to the Capitol. The wicker chairs on the sidewalk are nearly all taken by families having tropical fruit ice cream and snacks, or succulent dishes such as paella and casseroles.

A little girl dressed in red, wearing red shoes, smiles at me as she savors her mamey ice cream.

"Can we sit outside?" I ask. "It would be nice to eat here, in the open air!"

But we go inside because my mother wants to be in the cool air conditioning, which we don't have at home.

The city vibrates quietly outside the panoramic window that protects diners from the heat of a fiery summer's-end afternoon.

The air conditioning cools the immense window, producing a condensation that covers it, blurring everything into the imprecision of a mirage.

Barely visible are lottery ticket vendors passing by out on the sidewalk, their strings of tickets flapping like tapeworms, some fastened to the brims of their straw hats by clothespins.

Each one is shouting that this time, for sure, they have the tickets with the numbers for El Gordo, the Jackpot, for sale.

My mother chooses a table back by the bar. My father, brother, and I follow her.

Outside, through the glass, the lights of the five rotating reflectors located in the lantern of the Capitol dome intersect in the mauve, green, and garnet sky of the early hours of a romantic Antillean night, creating a vast mural.

The waiter who approaches our table is a Spaniard wearing a white apron that does nothing to disguise his potbelly.

"Just a fruit cocktail," my mother says.

"Lobster Thermidor," my father orders, laughing heartily and displaying his gold tooth. He must show off his Pantagruelian appetite to offset my mother's delicate stomach, he says.

Septimio and I order ham-and-Swiss-cheese finger sandwiches.

Armando, who's taken forever to park the car, sits at a table behind us next to the bar, despite my father's insisting that he come and keep us company.

Armando orders nothing but his *sudadita,* his cold beer in the bottle.

From my chair, I can barely make out, through the restaurant's foggy glass wall, the neon advertisement for Jantzen swimsuits. It shines in the distance atop a big building. The Little Jantzen Doll in her red swimsuit, her head encased in a white swim cap, climbs onto a yellow diving board, leaps into the air, and disappears into an unlit abyss. I don't get bored watching the doll repeat the same moves over and over.

It's the first time we on the Island have been treated to a moving figure in neon lights that disappears into the absolute void. This glowing commercial reproduction of the myth of Sisyphus has stirred the imagination of the city's entire population, especially that of children.

"We're becoming a replica of Paris, and it's not even fifty years since we won our independence from Spain! Imagine! A mere fifty years since we became a true Republic!" my mother exclaims as if she's had a revelation.

She goes on: "Here is this luxury restaurant where you can order the most exquisite delicacies, and there's cash to pay for it! When I was little, I would stain my blouse with egg yolk so everybody could see that I'd had an egg to eat. Then, we barely had corn mush to eat. Now, with the high price the Americans are paying us for sugar, also because we've modernized ourselves in every way, there's money by the bushel. Sure, some people are poor, but they are the minority."

Through the window, I see two men deep in conversation as they saunter across the street in this hour's light traffic. They are headed for our restaurant. The older one points upward with his index finger, and the younger one stretches out his open right hand. It reminds me of a painting in one of my father's books: Michelangelo's *The School of Athens.* If these two men were wearing robes and had books in their hands, they might be those very men in the painting: Plato and Aristotle.

"Now," my mother continues, "we are visited by the greatest symphony orchestras, Russian ballet companies, German pianists, Italian opera companies, tenors from La Scala, even sopranos from the Metropolitan Opera. When have we ever been more prosperous, more civilized, more independent? The old mansions of El Cerro and the new ones in the Vedado are furnished in the style of Louis XV, with tiles of Carrara marble, Persian carpets, Limoges and Sèvres china, ornate cutlery of gold and silver, Baccarat and Bohemian crystal.

"Antique Göbelin tapestries embroidered in France with scenes from Greek mythology and the *Iliad* hang on our walls. Americans come to spend their dollars and want to stay because they live better here than in the United States.

"We are the Golden Demitasse of the Caribbean! We are a golden chariot!"

All at once, a dazzling golden light hides Plato and Aristotle. The Virgin Mary is about to appear, as at Fatima, when she is always preceded by a great glow!

Everything happens in slow motion. Septimio, his face spectral in the glow, opens his mouth like a stupefied grouper. My father smiles like he's in front of a photographer's flashbulb. My mother looks at her nails, reviewing the thread of her aria. Diners left and right raise their arms as if worshipping the god of the Sun.

Glass projectiles reflecting light fly by like luminous voracious insects.

A cloud of smoke with a sour, irritating smell moves in through the window, chasing after the sharp fragments, leaving diners deaf from the sound of a thousand thunders.

A hot wind, smelling of gunpowder, enters last to scrape my face and head, while a gigantic hand violently shoves me backwards.

On opening my eyes, I'm sitting on the floor, my back against the wood of the little bar. I appear to have flown without feeling it.

I touch my face and the rest of my body to see if I'm all there. I'm not hurt. I haven't broken a single bone. My skin is covered in hot dust.

Septimio, sitting next to me, has messed-up hair, and his white shirt is covered with the same dust. He looks around, bewildered.

My father, standing by the bar, his white suit darkened from the dust, has a stunned expression. My mother, kneeling on the floor, covers her mouth with one hand, as if she has said something unseemly.

Armando, my father's driver from the Ministry, remains stolidly seated at the only table where the tablecloth, the glass of water, and a bottle of beer have been perfectly preserved. The bar area behind him remains intact, bottles of rum, whiskey, gin, vodka still erect and as full of liquor as they were when we arrived

The rest of the restaurant is rubble – pieces of tables, chairs, tablecloths, napkins, plates, and broken glass all jumbled together on the floor with bloody remnants like a butcher shop that's been vandalized.

I get up to see what became of Aristotle and Plato, who a few seconds ago were crossing the street. Where they had been before, there are only dying blazes and columns of dark gray and black smoke.

Wounded men, sitting on the floor of the restaurant, silently wipe the blood from their faces and hands with handkerchiefs and napkins. Wounded women clean themselves with hopeless little gestures while screaming and crying.

Avoiding stepping on the wounded, my father pushes us to leave the restaurant quickly. Outside, we jump over dead and wounded.

My eyes are fixated on a little red shoe lying bloodstained on the sidewalk.

Everything smells of burnt flesh and of gasoline. Sitting in the middle of the street, a portly woman, her white dress half burned and her thighs gashed open with long wounds, raises her arms to heaven and scolds: "What have I done to deserve this? Why have You sent me this punishment?"

I look up to the sky where the black columns of smoke are thinning out, and realize she's talking to God.

My eyes fill with tears from the smoke.

Also, even though I didn't know them, I become aware that the tears are for those who were just here and are no longer, especially the little girl in red who got her wish to sit outside.

My father forces us to rush because he doesn't want journalists asking him questions.

"Good thing you parked far away and the car didn't get fried!" my father comments to Armando on seeing that the car isn't damaged.

"Really, Augusto, must you be such a callous monster!" my mother scolds him, as she climbs into the car.

"Thank God we didn't sit outside," Septimio says through his teeth, looking at me with suspicion, as if I had been the one who planted the bomb.

15

In Paradise, disgrace rules

THE NIGHT OF THE BOMB at the restaurant I dream that Elena, she of Almendares, and I are walking along a beach the sand of which is gold dust, with round diamonds polished smooth as pebbles glowing here and there with all the colors of the rainbow as they reflect the late afternoon sun.

We're walking barefoot on the sand toward a dark blue rowboat rocking in the azure waters. It's splattered with copper reflections of the sunset, an end-of-afternoon castle that stands in all its rosy splendor on the distant horizon.

The girl and I climb into the boat. I take the oars and start rowing to get us to the castle. The waves are flowing in reverse, from the sand towards the sea, which helps propel us. Marine birds glide over us singing:

> *Mambrú went to war*
> *What pain, what a pain, what shame.*
> *Mambrú went to war*
> *And will never come home again.*
> *So do, re, mi. Sol fa, re, do.*
> *And will never come home again.*

Elena and I shoo away the seagulls, toward the coast.

When we arrive at the castle, we don't see walls, towers, or turrets, but instead the golden domes of a palace. This emerges self-contained from the darkest blue of the deepest ocean. Its walls, of a delicately pink marble, stab the heart like the tip of a dagger.

I climb out of the rowboat and secure it to a piling that rises out of the water. I ask the girl to guard the boat, and go alone into the palace. The ceiling within is made up of small marble vaults. Golden reflections from the sea play across their surfaces, light and shade weaving together in the silence, gently interrupted by the lapping of the waves.

There's an odor of salt and roses. Aware that the palace is empty, I can feel the presence of courtiers who've just gone and hear the musical silence their voices have left, can smell the perfume of their garments, dispersed by a light breeze from wide windows and narrow jalousies.

Through the air like an arrow flies a grackle cawing raucously, its squawks multiplied and distorted by echoes. At once entire flocks of grackles pour through the windows like black clouds, shrieking under the vaults and staining the white and pink walls of the palace with their excrement.

Horrified, I run to the boat, only to find that Elena has rowed off and almost reached the shore.

She's so far away that she looks like a tiny doll. Everywhere around me, great frothy waves beat against the palace, roiled by the grackles' shrill cawing.

I wake up bathed in sweat. My brother is asleep in the other bed. I hear his strong breathing. The room is dark. It must be past midnight and I force myself to go back to sleep.

AFTER A FEW DAYS the nightmares stop. My family doesn't talk about the bomb at meals and closes its eyes to articles published in newspapers and weekly magazines. But I did see the hair-raising photos of people blown to pieces, chosen apparently on the principle of "the more atrociously gruesome, the better," which our Island journalism shamelessly embraces.

Yet neither journalists nor the police can find anything about the cause or perpetrators of the explosion. My father is not mentioned as the potential target, but I did overhear a conversation he had with Santana, his assistant, in which he said he suspected that the attack was meant for him, but the bomb went off prematurely, or in the wrong place, so we were spared.

The reason for the attack, he said, could have been his refusal to pay an exorbitant sum of money to the notorious gangster and murderer, Orlando León Lemus, called El Colorao because of his red hair.

I'm really trying hard to get all of this out of my mind. Death and life are overly intertwined on this Island. It's all part of the war of life that, in my house, never interferes with our following a normal routine.

MY MOTHER SITS at the table drinking a freshly-made *café con leche*, combing her hair with one hand, lost in thought. La Gallega, whom together with her sister, La Isleña, we call The Twins, is sitting across from my mother. The Twins sometimes help us clean house when Enedina has a lot of work in the kitchen. They are daughters of the manager of our building, who was born in the Canary Islands. My mother has given them these nicknames because in her opinion the names fit their personalities: La Gallega is very "Spanish" in looks and manners, whereas La

Isleña looks and behaves like us. The eldest of the sisters is Rina, the second in the order of birth is Margarita, and the youngest is called Reina, whom we nicknamed Chinesca because she has slanted eyes. Although she is ten years old and much bigger than me, sometimes Chinesca plays with me. We both have treasure stashed in the Cave of Ali Baba, a hole in the sidewalk for the electricity company's wires and equipment that we fill with empty soda bottles swiped from Maximino's store on the corner of 12th Avenue. Whenever we have enough bottles, we trade them in for sweets and hard candies at the same store.

Behind the kitchen door, Enedina moves back and forth making dinner. I can see her through the door's porthole from where I'm sitting, to my mother's left at the dining room table.

"Don't delay, Gallega," my mother advises in an imperious tone. "Find yourself a good match, a man with piles of pesos. But to do that, first you need to clean yourself up."

Gallega laughs, embarrassed. Her perfect white teeth, fed with milk from the goat she keeps in the backyard of her house, shine in her face, which is now red as a tomato.

"Oh, Flora, not everybody can do that! All I want is a little house with a room just for me, where the old folks don't need to sleep on a cot and all my sisters on top of me."

"Yes, and let's talk about the smell in your house! Clean it with pine solvent, girl! Then you can invite a decent prospect to visit."

A car horn honks several times and my mother gets up, excited, and heads for the door.

"Here's Gus and the big machine!" she shouts. The three of us go out on the balcony. The car stops in front of our building, and Armando gets out to open the door for my father, who emerges dressed with his usual elegance. The driver follows him, carrying his alligator-skin briefcase, full of Ministry of Education documents.

"How goes it, family?" my father asks, ascending the stairs in graceful leaps and dance steps. He picks me up and we go into the house.

He smells of cigars, sun, and fine French cologne. In the dining room he sets me on the floor, throws his tie on the table, sits down, and unbuttons his jacket to get comfortable. My mother and I sit to the right and left of him, and La Gallega across from him.

Armando comes in and greets everyone shyly, setting my father's briefcase on the floor by his feet. Without looking at him, my father says to him, in an odd tone: "Tell Santana and Pancho Pistola they don't need to get out of the car, we'll talk tomorrow."

Then he adds, maybe to make it clear to Armando where he stands: "Drop them at their houses before you head home. I won't be going out tonight." The driver takes his leave with a humble tilt of his head.

He's still not back in my father's good graces after his oddly shy behavior at the Capital.

As soon as the driver is gone, my father's good spirits burst out again, with a very big surprise for us.

"The house!" he crows. "I just signed the papers. At last, we have our own house! It needs some small changes because I want it to be authentic Spanish colonial style, with Arab orange floor tiles, black lanterns, and everything Spanish I can put in," he announces, ecstatic.

Standing next to him, Enedina, her hair gathered up with a few pins, dries her hands on her wet apron.

"Doctor, would you like me to bring you your beer?" she asks, terrified.

"Yes! We're going to celebrate," he replies, smiling.

My mother's face lights up, then clouds over. Suddenly she looks overwhelmed, as if a concrete block had fallen on top of her.

"So, we're moving *again*?" she asks, worried, perhaps remembering the last move's chore of boxing up my father's books.

"Yes, but not yet. I must get the house ready, which will take a few months. Maybe before year's end."

Enedina reappears in the dining room carrying a silver tray with three bottles of beer and three glasses, and sets it in the middle of the table.

"I'll be on my way, Flora," says La Gallega, just as my mother pours beer into one of the glasses and sets it in front of La Gallega.

"Don't be silly! Stay and have a sip of beer!" my mother commands.

"Yes, this calls for a toast, young lady! To the beauty of our women!" My father winks at La Gallega and delicately pours himself a little beer, trying not create foam. They all raise a glass. Then my mother sets her glass down so hard that the foam splashes on the lace and embroidery of the white linen tablecloth.

Embarrassed by my father's attentiveness, La Gallega takes a sip or two of beer. "Thank you, Doctor," she says gruffly.

"Call me Gus! That's what my friends call me," my father says, sipping his beer with gusto.

My mother coughs artificially and fans herself with her hand. "My, isn't it hot in here!" she exclaims, pouring herself more beer.

La Gallega empties her glass so as not to offend my father, but she, too, puts it down on the table a little too firmly, maybe because she's so shy.

"So, we're going to live in Tutankhamen's tomb?" my mother asks, gulping down her beer.

"Hardly! It's a Spanish house! Or at least an imitation. My father was Basque, from Spain, remember?"

"Is there a garden to plant vegetables?" I ask enthusiastically.

"Yes, Bad Bug, you'll have a vegetable garden. I ordered them to remove part of the cement from the patio and fill in deep with planting soil," says my father.

He stands up, buttons his coat, and moves over next to La Gallega. He smiles at her, and leans in to take a sip of beer. La Gallega abruptly gets to her feet and stares at my father.

His eyes are half shut as he tastes the beer foam on his lips and mustache.

"Now, really, I must go, Flora!" La Gallega exclaims nervously, gets up, and almost runs out, without saying goodbye.

"You've become such a wet blanket! You won't let a girl enjoy herself," my father scolds my mother for the tension he thinks she's created.

Then he unbuttons his jacket to fish for something in his pocket.

"Enedina!" he calls, setting his beer glass on the table. Enedina appears in the dining room with a look of concern, thinking she might be scolded.

"Open your hand and close your eyes," my father says, placing in her outstretched hand a small square white box tied with a little red bow.

Enedina opens her eyes, stares at the package, and life comes back into her face. She unties the ribbon quickly and lifts a gold ring with a small diamond from the box.

"Doctor! Doctor! Thank you!" she cries out, hugging my father.

"*Bright lantern in the street, dark shadow in your own house,*" I hear my mother mutter between her teeth.

ON SATURDAY, as I leave the house in the morning, I notice that it rained overnight, and the soil from yards mingled with rainwater has run into the gutter and filled it with reddish mud.

At the curb, I find a boy playing with a stick in the mud and a chubby white mutt puppy watching him.

I approach, and the boy, squatting, looks up, green eyes in a face toasted by the sun. Drops of sweat glisten on his upper lip, where his mustache would be if he were a grown-up. His thick black crewcut, trimmed almost to the skin as if he were in the army, contrasts with the soft features of his face.

"I'm Andy. This is Kan, Dog of the Jungle. You're the new girl in the neighborhood?" he asks in a husky voice. Kan wags his tail when I sit on the curb next to Andy.

"What are you doing?" I ask, without answering his question.

"I want to build a great castle, but it keeps falling down, and there's not enough dirt," says Andy, who stands up, and so do I. He's not as tall as me, but he's burlier.

He wears khaki shorts and a sky-colored cotton shirt that shows his sturdy, sweaty, energetic neck.

"I'm going to show you something," he tells me, and, trailed by Kan, he walks over to the empty field next to his apartment building.

The field goes all the way to the other end of the block. A meandering path of red earth and white pebbles leads from one side to the other of this weedy field.

There are some small trees, but mostly it's choked with shrubs, wild plants, and yellow flowers covered in butterflies, both white ones and yellow ones with black stripes. The rough, bright, medicinal aromas of *romerillo* and chamomile are everywhere.

My socks begin collecting burrs and seedpods. Pulling these off carefully so they don't prick my fingers makes it hard for me to keep up with Andy. The boy is leading me to a white stone with a flat top under a mango tree with loads of fruit drooping from its branches, large green hearts with reddish spots.

"This is the stone where the Indians sit to talk war," Andy says, very serious.

"There are no Indians left on this Island," I point out pedantically.

"Be patient. You'll see them, too," the boy answers serenely.

We sit on the stone. Kan throws himself at his master's feet. I look Andy in the eye to decide whether he's stupid, or being a jackass and making fun of me. His gaze is serene. He smiles, and his white teeth contrast with the brown color of his face. He smells of sandalwood soap.

"They're those Indians from the movies. They come here to smoke the peace pipe and talk about war. The big chief has a headdress with so many feathers, it comes down to his knees."

"The Indians are discussing how to best wage war against the bird-men," I invent, contributing to his fantasy. It dawns on me that he thinks the way I do.

"For sure! They're hard to kill because they take off as soon as they sense danger. Arrows can't get to them," Andy replies enthusiastically.

I get up from the stone to explore the territory, and find chicken bones scattered throughout the terrain.

"You see these bones? The Indians have been able to kill some of the bird-men. From now on, let this place be called 'The Footpath of Death.'"

I approach Andy and shake his hand. "My name is Mercy, and I don't have a dog," I say, introducing myself according to my ceremonial protocol.

ALMOST A WEEK GOES BY. I sit on the little wall of the building where Andy lives on 12th Avenue, giving some thought as to how we might improve this neighborhood, since my father says you must do good for people. I've read about child soldiers who've died for their country, who've gone to war and even served as spies. The war's over, but maybe we can do some good for our neighbors.

I've noticed that the staircase of Andy's building has nice, clean, colored tiles, but they're not shiny. I hop down off the wall, climb the stairs to Andy's apartment on the second floor, and knock.

Wearing just shorts, Andy flings the door open with his usual energy. Kan barks and gets between his feet.

"Come outside. I have a proposition to make," I say mysteriously. His green eyes glow, imagining an adventure. This is what I like about Andy – his ability to imagine, and his courage. I always see him getting into punching contests with kids who are much bigger and stronger than he is. In this he's like me, but because he's a boy, everybody admires him, whereas I am despised, which I just ignore, and if some guy tries to assault me or disrespect me, I give him an uppercut to the jaw like I've seen boxers do in the movies. I know that boys' rules forbid them from punching females, but boys punch me like I was one of them, and when I win fights, it is by pure willpower, because I am very skinny and have no muscles.

"Wait a second while I put on a shirt," Andy asks.

I wait for him sitting on the little wall in the garden of his building, and in a jiffy the boy is sitting next to me, buttoning his sky-blue shirt, and asking me with his eyes what my plan is.

"We need to make the staircase of your building look prettier, and I think it should be waxed. But I need someone to help me. It's three floors and we must do it fast before anyone sees us."

"So where do we get wax?" he asks, showing that practical mentality that I'm finding so likeable.

I take him to the Cave of Ali Baba and lift the heavy metal lid. I point to the black wax at the edge of the lid, which is supposed to ensure that the lid closes hermetically and keeps the space waterproofed. With my thumbnail, I scoop the wax out and mold it into a ball. Andy scrapes the wax off on his side with a pen knife he keeps in his pants pocket. When we have several big balls of wax, Andy dries the sweat from his forehead and neck, and sits on the grass. He sweats more than I do, perhaps because he is male and stronger.

"You hide your balls of wax, and I'll hide mine. Don't tell anyone about this because I want it to be a surprise. Tomorrow, very early, we'll wax the staircase. I'll knock on your door about six in the morning. It's Saturday, and nobody's awake then to see us."

BY SIX O'CLOCK ON SATURDAY MORNING, Andy's already waxed the stairs to the third floor and is working on the landing of the second floor, scrubbing the tiles with one of the wax balls, then polishing it with a rag. Even though I don't like surprises and would have preferred that we start together, his dedication to work impresses me.

The tiles shine like gems.

"You finish waxing the second-floor landing and I'll start waxing the staircase, skipping every other step for you to use, then wax, so you won't leave footprints on the waxed steps," I say calmly, not bossily. "That way we'll finish faster."

As I imagined, people aren't coming and going this early on a Saturday, so we can work without being surprised or scolded. After a time, which seemed forever to me, we both get to the first floor just as a young woman is coming down the stairs.

She is beautifully dressed and wears high heels. As she passes me, the woman doesn't scold us but says, "Excuse me, please."

As a joke, I reply: "You pleased, me excuse."

Andy and the woman laugh at this word play I just made up. I've been playing with words lately, even creating them, because, how boring is it to use the same words the same way as everybody else? The problem is that sometimes people don't understand. Luckily, both Andy and the woman understand, and that makes me happy.

When the woman is gone, I stand back to admire what we've done. The stairs shine with the high polish of a palace staircase in the movies. I shake hands with Andy in gratitude and head home to write a story that occurred to me while we were waxing.

I MOVE QUICKLY PAST the door to my parents' room. My mother is snoring all by herself on their spacious bed. My father must have left early. I go to my room, which is empty. My brother's left, too. I'm alone. I take care not to make noise so that my mother doesn't hear me slip a notebook out of my bookbag. I write quickly in pencil:

> Two friends, Lilo and Lele, who had once lived near each other, met in a meadow by chance.
> Lilo asked about their friends in the old neighborhood.
> Lele told him that he did not focus on the past but on the future.
> "What do you plan to do in the future?" Lilo asked.
> "Go to the Sun!" Lele replied – could anything be more obvious?
> At that moment Lilo decided to go to the Moon. "I plan to go to the Moon. Why don't we get together in space to say goodbye?"
> Lele promised to meet Lilo in space, above the African continent, at three o'clock the next afternoon.
> Lilo had to take his dog to the vet and was delayed.
> Lele arrived on time, whiled away several hours contemplating the bright coast of Africa and the yellow waves of the desert's dunes. Then, tired of being kept waiting, he headed onward to the Sun.
> Lilo arrived as soon as he could, and remained forever waiting.

I close the notebook and hide it in my bookbag.

WHEN MY MOTHER WAKES UP, she informs me that she is taking me to the insane asylum to meet Uncle Adolfo. I've already heard stuff about this uncle, and the stories family members tell when they get together at Christmas or New Year's Eve have piqued my curiosity. What does a crazy person look like? How does he behave? Is a crazy person like a child? How does a crazy person speak and what is being crazy like?

When he was fifteen years old, out of the blue, my uncle Adolfo locked himself in the garage at Aunt Bella's house. He said he had to devote himself completely to an important project that required absolute concentration. His diet consisted of snacks that my aunt Chavela handed him when he cracked the door open. He did his business in a portable urinal that she would collect when it was full, then return empty. He slept on a cot in the garage.

A couple of days passed, and Aunt Isabel came to visit. When she heard what her brother had been up to, to find out what this very important project was, she ordered Adolfo to let her into the garage at once. Receiving no answer, she kicked in the door and found my uncle sitting at a table covered by a white cloth. There, he was placing every hair that he carefully pulled from his head in precise horizontal rows that now covered almost the entire table. Each time he set a new hair in a row, he would gauge its length with a measuring tape, then pencil the number in a booklet.

Isabel screamed in horror and phoned her doctor who, after talking to Adolfo, decided to commit him to a psychiatric hospital.

This psychiatric hospital is an old-fashioned white house with vast gardens planted in red roses, yellow daisies, and white lilies that have fine red lines. Scattered around the manicured green lawn are marble benches where patients and family can visit. We sit on one of these benches with Adolfo, who's wearing cotton pants, shirt, and alpargatas. They are all the same color – white. I try to find some trace of madness in his face, but it's normal, peaceful, a little sad and resigned. His long, thin hands move nervously, unbuttoning and buttoning the collar of his shirt, or straightening his sparse and graying hair. Hunched over, he patiently answers all my mother's questions. He doesn't look like a child, or like an adult; he's halfway between the two. He has the spontaneity of a child, the crystalline look, some of a child's quick gestures, but he also shows the solemnity of the adult: the wrinkled brow, the weight on the shoulders.

When I get home, alone and sitting on my bed, I decide to write my first poem in my school notebook:

> *White clouds*
> *Motes of cotton*
> *In the blue sky over*
> *The hospital patio.*
> *The wind pushes them.*
> *They flow quickly to other patios*
> *Where kids fly kites*
> *Between the white that escapes*
> *And the blue that remains.*

I finish writing this and immediately sense my mother behind me, not making a sound, spying on me.

"What are you doing, girl?" she asks, upset.

183

She yanks the notebook out of my hands to read it. I don't know what to say. I look at her in dread because I have no idea why she's so disturbed.

"Writing poems!" my mother screams. "How often have I told you that writing and reading 'literature' produces tuberculosis? Your Uncle Alexander was a poet, a writer, and he died of tuberculosis. And your Uncle Adolfo used to read novels, and you saw what happened there: he ended up in the insane asylum!"

My mother is pulling hair out of her head, her eyes are jumping out of their sockets, foam spouts from between her lips.

"What's wrong? *What is wrong?*" I ask, horrified. My mother throws the notebook on the bed, grabs me violently by the hand and drags me running into the living room, opens the door of the house wide, and gives me a great shove in the back to force me out into the street.

"Go outside and play! Go play!" she yells at me, her face red and swollen with anger, her eyes crazed.

I run to the sidewalk to get away from that monstrous face that seems a lot crazier than Uncle Adolfo's.

IT'S ALMOST NIGHT ON SUNDAY. My father still hasn't come home from his weekend "amusements," as my mother calls them.

She's playing solitaire at the dining room table.

Septimio, opposite my mother, is building a model airplane on a grubby white cloth, the purpose of which is to keep the glue he uses to connect the model's wooden pieces from dripping on and ruining the mahogany tabletop.

I'm reading the funnies sitting next to Septimio, impressed by the appearance of Prince Valiant with his sword and medieval costume. I have dreams like that. I use a sword with two hands and fight in battles, wearing suffocatingly heavy armor.

Other times, I am in a castle and through the open window of the room, I see the reflection of the full moon in the silver waters of a river.

"Louis XIV dined to music," announces my mother pedantically. "He hired French composers because it was bad politics to hire the Italians, although at that time they were the most famous and best of all the composers and musicians in Europe." She grimaces in disgust, as if she were an Italian composer shunned by the Sun King.

"What are you talking about?" I ask, irritated.

I am absorbed in worrying about Aleta, the wife of Prince Valiant, who's been imprisoned in a dungeon.

"Of course," my mother continues without answering me, "he built the Palace of Versailles and its extraordinary gardens because he was afraid of his nobles. He forced them to dress well by making them spend all their time at his lavish palace, and thus used up all the money they could have invested in revolutions. Oh no, Louis XIV didn't want mob rebellions instigated by the nobles. It's said that twenty-four violins played while he ate, in full view of everyone, as befits a king, as well as when he sailed on the Grand Canal in the royal barge.

"And here ends the morality tale for today."

Someone knocks at the door, and I get up to open it.

It's Andy and his mother.

The two of them have the same visionary green eyes, which now protrude so much that they are almost popping out of their heads.

Andy, behind his mother, lowers his head to look at the ground. His face is bright red, especially his ears.

The woman enters the house and, without greeting my mother, orders Andy in a loud voice: "Kneel down and beg forgiveness from this little girl! Apologize for accusing her of waxing the staircase of the building!"

I am about to laugh at the woman's performance, but Andy's unsmiling look as he kneels in front of me warns me that the situation is serious.

My mother gets up from the table and elegantly gestures to Andy's mother to sit in one of the armchairs in the living room.

The young woman sits, tucking her dark green knit dress under her thighs. She is pretty. Andy has inherited the harmony of her features.

"Tell me what happened!" my mother demands, surprised, sitting in front of her in the other armchair.

Andy gets up and stands next to his mother, with his head down. I go over and stand next to him in solidarity.

"My son confessed that he waxed the staircase of our building, but he says he did it because your daughter talked him into it. Saturday and Sunday several people fell down the stairs, including a pregnant woman and a man delivering a huge glass bottle of drinking water. They're both in the hospital."

My mother looks at me to see if this is true.

Andy's mother looks at me as if waiting for me to defend myself and say that her son is the only one to blame.

It's inconceivable to her that a little girl would do something like this. Girls play with dolls and are peace-abiding. They would never wax stairs for people to slip and fall.

"Andy told the truth," I courageously declare. "The idea was mine. I convinced him." The woman is aghast, and my mother smiles slightly. Andy raises his head and looks at me out of the corners of his eyes, like he's embarrassed. His eyes are swollen, if from rage or crying I don't know.

"Well, the two of you must kneel down right this minute, and pray that the people who fell recover quickly," the mother orders us.

Andy and I kneel and say an Our Father.

When Andy and his mother leave, I sit at the table waiting to be taken to task.

But my mother goes back to playing solitaire without saying a word.

My brother bursts out laughing.

185

"And here I thought we big boys were the neighborhood gangsters!" Septimio exclaims, after sitting quietly at the table through the whole drama, almost as if he has been waiting for this moment.

He goes on: "Yesterday I saw Mercy and Andy waxing the staircase, but it never occurred to me what havoc it might cause. When somebody asked who did it, naturally I kept my mouth shut. You little kids are the real menace, bona fide badasses!"

My brother can't stop laughing, and my mother looks at him, smiling.

"I just wanted to do something nice for our neighbors in that building," I explain, mortified and not understanding why my mother isn't killing me or something worse.

"Yes, my little girl, and that's why I don't scold you," my mother explains. "I know your intention was good, but next time, give some thought to the consequences of what you do."

16

NOW COMES THE FUTURE

MY MOTHER PUTS ON her cultured pink pearl necklace and tells me to come with her. Evidently, she wants to look elegant to discuss a serious subject. We sit on my bed in the bedroom I now share with my brother, who's out.

"You're seven years old now," she announces without preamble. "You have entered the Age of Reason. You can commit Mortal Sins because you're no longer a child. You're an adult with the ability to make sense of things."

Then she stands up brusquely and walks out, leaving me alone with Reason and Mortal Sins.

I look around. What's changed? The room seems normal, with its narrow twin beds. If I get up and look out the window, I see street lights in the bluish-gray darkness of sunset, and the well-lit patio of the Widow of Bermejo.

Nothing's changed, except that I've reached the Age of Reason. Yesterday my sins were venial, today they become mortal. Reason makes them mortal, deadly, fatal. I look at myself in the full-length mirror on the back of our door, smile, and see that terrible grin of childhood and old age: toothlessness. I've lost my baby teeth, and my real teeth haven't grown in yet, the ones that must last forever.

I lie down on my bed, while in the distance the clinking of dishes announces dinner. The room is almost dark, barely illuminated by the dim mauve twilight seeping through the window.

Reason amounts to examining what happens to me, having the ability to judge. Who is my mother in the light of Reason? My father? My brother?

What is this world that so far has only been days followed by other days, schools, homework, teachers, detention, classmates, friends, other people, things?

Who am I? The mirror reflects a pointed face, messed-up hair, toothless mouth, skinny body wrapped in a tiny white lace dress – shapeless body in a deluxe vessel.

I'm drowning in things. White socks, white shoes with the Buster Brown label showing a boy with a hat and a dog, white or colorful hankies, each with a different day of the week embroidered on it. Notebooks with fragrant, peach-col-

187

ored endpapers, a thermos with tomato juice in the mornings, and café con leche in the afternoons that sometimes tastes like printers' ink because my mother seals the thermos with newspaper around the cork so there's no leak.

"I'm in this new house, my birthday is over, and now comes the Future," I murmur. The Future will still be me, but seen from another angle, as if I were another person with me inside. On the outside, showing the importance of the years and their passing, toothless, sparse white hair, wrinkled skin like those of elephants. Inside, a girl dressed in lace, shapeless, trying not to smile so as not to reveal the black hole in her mouth, trying to keep her eyes from crying because of the powerful lights the photographer shines on her.

My mother, with her white turbans and her shoulder pads, and my brother, with his Doc Savage books and his orange-leather baseball gloves, are left behind. By merely getting out of bed today, I've entered the Age of Reason, where a mistake can be fatal and can send me to Hell. For the mistake of a second, an eternity of punishment. I've never understood the arithmetic of religion, but everyone argues that the mind is too limited to comprehend the profound mysteries of Catholicism, whether sorrowful or joyful. I would prefer, so long as we must have mysteries, the joyful ones, because when one is happy, one never asks questions, but when one is miserable, how can one not ask questions? Sorrowful mysteries are too much for me.

Suffering without understanding is beyond my nature.

As I sit down at the table, I serve myself very carefully from the dishes Enedina has placed there. My father has forbidden her to serve us, telling her that's the work of slaves. I take care not to spill the soup or the gravy from the roast beef on the tablecloth, I make no noise with the cutlery, I don't drink too much water, and, when I drink, I wipe my lips before and after with the napkin, so as not to stain the glass. One must be careful. Reason means this: taking care. Do not fall, do not trip, do not become confused. Live in a classical universe of harmonious proportions, of musical expression.

Sort of like making sure you don't generate bubbles when you're swimming, because they attract sharks.

I ARRIVE HOME LATE because I had to do yet another hour of detention for speaking out in class, and I bump into my brother in the living room, who is very well behaved now and always gets home on time, although he did, once, get detention for a week because they punished him for standing up in the middle of a math test while the school band was playing the National Anthem in the courtyard. The teacher told him that the class was excused from participating in the Civic Observance ceremony because they were taking an exam, but my hyper-patriotic brother Septimio replied, "The National Anthem is the spirit of the Republic, and when it is played, you must stand to show respect."

His classmates applauded him, but his teacher punished him.

Now, Septimio is doubled over laughing.

My father is wrestling with my mother in the dining room. My mother, her hair messed up and her face enraged, escapes from him and rolls up the sleeves of her white silk blouse.

Infected by my brother, my father bursts into gales, smooths his guayabera, shakes his wide-legged pants, and stops trying to restrain my mother.

"That great fat sow!" my mother yells, running out through the living room to open the front door wide. Standing at the balcony balustrade with her arms akimbo, she screams, "Laura Medinaceli de Alba! You smug nonentity! Monstrosity! You daughter of a rotten mother, ugly and worse!" She continues, looking to one side and gesticulating furiously. "You cockatiel! You basilisk! You great loggerhead turtle! Decrepit sybil! I hope you are struck by lightning!"

My mother stops to catch her breath and regain her strength.

Then, again she sets to screaming and waving her arms: "Laura Medinaceli de Alba! Come out so I can slap you to kingdom come! So, I'm nouveau riche, eh? I dare you to tell me to my face what you whisper behind my back!

"Hypocrite! Don't imagine you can hide now because you're afraid of your neighbors! You slattern! You viper-tongued, sly gossip! Lackey of dictators! You woman stuck to a gigantic nose! Come out! Even if you're naked as a jaybird!"

Laura doesn't appear, but when I go out on the balcony, I can see that almost the entire neighborhood has crept out terrified onto their balconies.

"Still hiding in your cave, craven slut? Come out and fight like the slinking bitch that you are! Repeat your gossip to my face, you long-tongued hussy! Conceited swine! Buttock-face! You bottom-feeder of all gossips!"

My mother, at this point run dry of epithets and gesticulations, stops to look at my father in his armchair, stunned and laughing uncontrollably.

"This one has to have fire lit behind her like the *macao* snail, to get her to come out!" my mother exclaims laughing as she comes inside, leaving the door open. Sitting in the chair opposite my father, she's bathed in sweat, out of breath, sated.

"That woman is public enemy number one," my mother goes on in a semi-normal tone. "She and her entire family! Those people have disgraced the country. They're bottom feeders, terrorists! How dare she talk about me, the fat-assed witch!"

"As Petrarch's verses say, 'Oh, if by such notes I could temper my sigh to soften Laura, making in her, reason, what in me is force'!" my father scoffs.

Our female neighbors gradually make their way into my house, to sniff out what's going on. My mother serves them coffee, and soon the living room is crammed with women chatting animatedly.

"How people talk, gentlefolk!" one neighbor exclaims.

Carefully, minding her manners, wary of getting on the wrong side of my mother and becoming the victim of her insults, she explains: "Laura says these things because she feels superior." Then this long-time resident adds, as if it really should go without saying, but maybe my mother, being new to the neighborhood, doesn't have all the facts: "You do know she descends from the family of the hero of the homeland, Roderico Acuña."

"What hero? That's nonsense!" my mother shouts in fury. "I descend from grandees of Spain, who could sit in the presence of the king and not be obliged to take off their hats!" I laugh to myself, wondering what advantage this confers in a republic where there's no king and people barely even wear Panama hats anymore.

"Well, Laura does descend from the Castilian kings of Spain," the same neighbor informs her, speaking carefully as one speaks to an angry lunatic.

"And *I* descend from the kings of Aragon! When Isabel rides, Fernando rides with her, and their thrones are of equal height!"

"Accusing Flora of being nouveau riche! Really!" another neighbor exclaims indignantly, to calm my mother down. "That woman has such a long tongue that she steps on it."

"So true!" another neighbor agrees, and the rest of the women nod, savoring the freshly brewed coffee they are being served.

My father looks at the women sardonically. After a while, he gets up with a dandy's gesture, smoothing his guayabera, flapping his wide trousers, and executing a graceful dance step with his two-tone shoes.

"Well, family, time to get moving!" he exclaims, smiling.

"What are you saying, Doctor?" asks the most talkative of the women, with a gesture between offended and proud.

"That's enough for today! End of the coffee klatch! Let's get moving, liberals of the parish! Clear out! Go for a nap in the park!" And he kicks them all out, making gestures like shooing flies.

Septimio, at the door, is laughing so hard he could be watching a Chaplin film. I'm slouched against the living room wall, not entirely sure what's going on.

When the women leave, my father drops back into the armchair and laughs himself sick. To my mother he says, "I'm making you my precinct captain. Get these gossips to campaign and vote for Prío for President, and we're set for life!"

We all laugh. My father combs his gray hair back, and his gold ring with the large aquamarine projects its blue light, clear as the sea at the break of day.

That night, my brother is reading another Doc Savage novel in bed, while I, in mine, can't get to sleep. It's not the light that Septimio reads by that bothers me.

"What happened today? Why did Mom insult Laura Medinaceli de Alba, since it's true that we've newly become rich?"

My brother sets the book down, and explains as if he were talking to a fool, "People call people 'new rich' as an insult when well-off people flaunt their money in a vulgar way."

"Well, we do, don't we? So why is this Laura a 'lackey of dictators,' and who are her family?" I inquire.

It's important to be unconcerned that Septimio despises me for my profound ignorance if I want to learn certain things.

"Mama thinks Laura and the entire Medinaceli de Alba family are in cahoots with Batista. Mom hates Fulgencio Batista because he kicked her out of the Ministry of Education when he was elected president of the Republic – she says he replaced her with some fool who worked on his political campaign. Although Batista was freely elected at the ballot box by the people and democratically handed over his government to Grau, Mom always calls him dictator and disgrace of the country."

"Oh, okay. Then, is it true that we descend from Spanish grandees?"

"Those are our relatives by marriage, the Nájeras. We do descend from the kings of Aragon. Mom rolls out all the family titles when she feels slighted and wants to give herself importance. Now stop asking questions and go to sleep!"

From the irritated tone of his last words, I know I must shut up and try to sleep. Luckily sleep captures me when I count the fifteenth black sheep jumping the fence of my imagination.

THE ABANDONED HOUSE on the corner of Fourteenth Avenue is protected by green-painted iron fences that frame a garden full of high grass growing over the sidewalk. The windows, cloudy with dust, hide the interior of this house from the curious gaze of passers-by.

I open the fence and try to force the old front door of cracked, unvarnished wood, but I can't. My hand gets covered with the green oxidation of the bronze doorknob and the slime of humidity.

A large pomegranate tree grows in the garden. I have fun thinking they could be hand grenades, and I imagine a battle throwing these fruits, a skirmish in the Island's war against Spain, or in the Allies' war against the Axis powers. I am now in favor of the Allies since I found out from Dieguín that Hitler was a vicious tyrant and that he sent Jewish children to concentration camps. I'm not Jewish, but I know what's criminal and would be deeply shameful anywhere in the universe. Dieguín told me I had better start reading newspapers and magazines and listening to the radio to keep up with national and international events.

I hurl pomegranates off into the high grass, and imagine them to be grenades bursting, spreading deadly seeds of dynamite over the Nazis, and try to visualize what Nelson, my favorite admiral (because he died in battle), might have achieved if he'd had explosive grenade trees growing on his estate.

I imagine how he might have captured the abandoned house, analyzing characteristics of the terrain, sources of provisions, weaknesses of the enemy. I dream that I'm on the bow of his flagship, using my telescope to examine the enemy fleet entering through the strait of the patio, as he did at Black Death Bay on Turtle Island. Then I stop being Nelson and become Yolanda of the dazzling black hair, daughter of the Black Corsair, shouting "Board now, me hearties!"

Sadly, I'm the only one who enjoys these dreams that lead me to exalted heights. My friends never want to turn themselves into different characters, or develop new situations and scenarios.

Next to this corner house is Adela's well-kept home, painted pink. I am dazzled by her garden that's planted with some crimson roses called the Black Prince. I like these roses because they are dark red, the color of clotted blood.

Adela, her white hair pulled back in a bun, smiles at me, raising her plump cheekbones. "I see you like to play pirates," she says from her garden. "When you're older, you should join the Girl Scouts."

"What's that?"

"It's an organization of girl explorers, who love action, just like you. What are you going to do when you grow up?"

"I don't know . . . maybe commander of our Navy? Or queen of England."

The lady finds my answer comical and laughs out loud with great vitality, showing perfect white teeth. Adela laughs at my fantasies, but I'm pretty sure she doesn't think I'm a criminal, or that I should be sent, like my Uncle Adolfo, to the insane asylum.

Dieguín, who's come up behind me without my noticing, says that the abandoned house is haunted, and that at night you can see the ghost of Chacumbele, the hero of a song of the moment.

The song's lyrics assert that "he himself killed himself."

His ghost lives inside the house and only comes out at night, to breathe fresh air. Some neighbors have seen it.

"You would never dare enter that house at night," he challenges me.

"Why don't you do it, then?" I answer, irritated.

"I've been several times, and I've seen him. Chacumbele glows in the night like a star." Dieguín plants himself in a brave pose on the sidewalk.

"I'll go if you go. I don't want to go alone."

"Are you afraid?" he asks, challenging me.

I can't violate the boys' code, or they'll never play with me again. No one can be afraid. Their regulations order them to die rather than show fear. I don't know any other code, because I don't know the rules of girls, or even whether they have any.

"No, I'm not afraid, but how do I prove I was there if no one sees me?" I say to disguise my fear. "No one would believe me. Not even you."

Adela, leaning on the fence of her garden, is listening, and shakes her head. "Children, children, don't ruin your lives by believing in superstitions!" she exclaims, worried.

The boy smiles like the hero of a hundred battles, ignoring her. He looks me over, top to bottom, like measuring the strength of my resolve.

"Tonight, at eight o'clock. In this very place." He points to the sidewalk with his index finger, to be dramatic. I smile dismissively, put my left hand on my shirt to look like Napoleon, and smack his outstretched hand with mine to seal the deal. These gestures give me the advantage of disdain and insolence.

"Okay. Don't chicken out, now!" I shout, to humiliate him.

I don't give him time to answer and duck into Andy's empty lot, next to Adela's house, which I've named "The Pathway of Death." Always, before confronting any danger, I enter that tiny forest and sit on the white stone of the Indians to ponder my strategy and, in advance, savor my victory.

AT EIGHT P.M. I'm waiting in front of the pomegranate tree. Dieguín isn't there. This means he is not going to keep his promise. He's always punctual. He says punctuality is the courtesy of kings. Maybe he thinks he's a king, or his parents have made him believe this because they are very well read and published college professors, as my mother says. Or he may not have come because he's afraid of ghosts, or because he thinks the whole thing is "childish," as he says dismissively when he doesn't dare do something. It's because of this phony superiority that boys don't play with him, apart from thinking he's a sissy. I don't care what their issue is. I like his intelligence and how well informed he always is.

Adela's out on her porch. A few moths flutter around the ceiling light, casting shadows on the walls. I open her garden gate and look at the moths. "These moths burn up in the light. They're different from butterflies in daytime," she says.

"I know how to hunt them by day," I announce boastfully. "I have boxes full of yellow butterflies. When I catch them by the wings, the dust comes off and colors my fingers yellow."

Adela goes back inside the house, and signals that I should follow her, sit on the living room sofa, and turn on the lamp. The room, painted light green, has a marine feel. Bamboo furniture and the many colorful cushions make me think of movies of the South Pacific Islands. Books and magazines are piled on the arms of chairs and on tables at either end of the sofa.

Adela disappears down the hallway, and in a trice comes back with a large illustrated book. She sits next to me on the sofa, which is upholstered with a thick, white cloth very rich to the touch that looks like linen. She opens a book full of photos and drawings of the world's most wonderful butterflies. I take the heavy book in my hands to see them better. I'm struck by a black one I've seen only once. It was impossible to catch. "I've seen that one," I say, pointing to the page with the picture. "It flew by one day and landed on a flower, but sensed me and escaped, flying so high that I couldn't go after it. It's even slipperier than zebras, those black-striped yellow ones, which I've seen and almost caught."

Adela laughs appreciatively and says, very seriously, "The black butterfly is impossible to catch. It's a rarity. It looks like the black moth they call 'the Widow' because they say it flies into houses when someone is about to die, and brings misfortune. Anyone who can hunt it down has supposedly lost the fear of misfortune and death. This is a superstition you shouldn't believe." She laughs as if she were ashamed to have become dramatic and superstitious.

"Butterflies are beautiful in books, but remember, when you think of hunting one, it feels pain, just like you," she cautions me kindly. "Also, we must treasure them because there will come a day when they disappear, along with all the animals on Earth. Respect life, revere it, because it's a miracle and a mystery. Everything that exists is sacred because we are part of an infinite organism without beginning, or middle, or end. Every birth enriches us, and every death diminishes us."

I don't understand what this woman is talking about. I put the book aside and go out to watch for Dieguín.

"When you come next time, I'll show you my collection of stones," Adela says. "It's fascinating to see a few crystals turn into canyons and precipices when you look at them through a jeweler's loupe. And I'll show you my books on flora and fauna, as well as the greenhouse in the patio where I grow flowers that give off the most exquisite fragrances and attract nightingales, robins, and mockingbirds – all those melodious songbirds."

I take off at a run because I'm afraid that this intimacy with an adult is too entrapping. I arrive at Dieguín's house out of breath and pound on his door with my knuckles, panting, after climbing three flights of stairs two steps at a time.

The boy opens the door and my ears are struck by a wisp of music something like what I used to sing when I was little.

"Why didn't you keep your word and come to meet me?" I ask him.

"Shut up and don't bother me," he cuts me dead. "We're listening to *Baquiana brasileira No. 5* by Villalobos." And, in one move, he slams the door.

FOR WEEKS I HAVE BEEN VISITING ADELA, despite my fear of the intimacy she creates, so she can show me her books and her greenhouse, and teach me how to identify perfumes. I have this feeling I must memorize everything.

"What's the importance of perfumes?"

"There are non-physical planes where perfumes awaken us spiritually and make us understand the true nature of mind. Your memory is prodigious, photographic. You must cultivate it. But you must also develop, I mean refine, all your senses, learn to differentiate all your perceptions. It's a good thing that you are creating a great store of knowledge from books while you are so young, but you won't achieve anything if you don't combine this knowledge with the sensual experience of life. In the future, you will recreate this world," the woman replies in a grave voice, as if she has gone through time immemorial and infinite space to find this answer. Her words impress me so, my heart seems to stop and I can't ask anything more.

17

AMONG THE ABNORMALITIES

I'VE AVOIDED DIEGUÍN ever since he slammed the door in my face. I don't understand why he did it. I suppose I made him look bad with his family when I ran away from the lunch table when my mother called, but it seemed the only thing I could do.

This afternoon, Dieguín's sister, Aurelita, is playing with Luisita, the new girl in the neighborhood, in the garden in front of my house. They are jumping rope. I try to join their game by jumping with my own jump rope, and Aurelita stops jumping, as if it bothers her to play with me.

Maybe it's because she's so different from me.

She is blonde with braids on both sides of her head and bangs over her forehead. Her face is round and her teeth even. She's always well dressed, unlike me. When I play, I always end up with bumps and scratches, and my clothes get dirty. When she jumps rope, Aurelita wears things like a woven light lavender short-sleeved blouse and a dark lavender pleated skirt, and she never gets dirty.

It wouldn't occur to me to dress like that, combining dark and light tones of the same color, to jump rope. And, unlike her, I can't have every hair in place all the time. Besides, usually I play with boys who couldn't care less about their physical appearance.

As she walks behind Luisita, Aurelita stops briefly, then continues walking. "Let's not play anymore," Luisita murmurs, coiling up her jump rope.

"I must help my mom prepare dinner," Aurelita says, carrying her very colorful jump rope, bought in the United States, up the stairs to her house.

My mother, who's been watching us through the window, goes out on the balcony. "Girl, come inside for a moment because I have a question."

Luisita looks at me in amazement, but she follows me into the house. My mother invites her to sit in an armchair in the living room. This perplexes me because she never asks my friends into the house.

"What did Aurelita say to you when she was passing behind you?" she asks Luisita menacingly. I find this weird, because I don't think Aurelita said anything, plus it bothers me to have my mother interrogating my playmates.

"Nothing. She said nothing to me," the girl protests, a little embarrassed.

"She did so say something to you. I saw it from the window. Don't tell lies, or you'll go to Hell. Would you like to have devils use hot tongs to pull out your tongue for lying? God punishes you if you lie. He sends you to be burned by devils who pour molten lead in your ears, and rip out your eyes and make you eat them."

"She told me not to play with your daughter, who is very nasty," Luisita answers, crying with fear and embarrassment.

"Ah, you see I was right!" my mother exclaims, answering the doubt she had not expressed in words.

AFTER A FEW DAYS, I feel like looking at the rocks that Adela forgot to show me because I was so interested in her books and her greenhouse. I open the gate to her garden. The squeak of the metal hinges brings her to the window. When I arrive at the door, Adela lets me in though I haven't touched the door knocker. I walk in without being invited and park myself on the couch. The woman smiles at me and looks younger. Her round, white face, framed by short curly white hair, puffs up a little at her cheeks. She's wearing a simple, immaculate white robe.

As if she's reading my thoughts, she tells me, "Wait till I bring you the rocks," and leaves the room, soon returning with a wooden tray full of stones and with a jeweler's loupe.

"Start with this group of yellow agates, which are used to protect the solar plexus, and continue with these green emeralds, which help the heart chakra," she instructs as she puts the tray on my lap and sits down next to me. "The chakras are centers of energy in our bodies. The solar plexus is near your stomach. Look at the stones through the loupe. Study them in detail."

It's true, as she said when she first invited me to see them, that these precious stones turn into mountain ranges, great crags with sharp peaks and deep gorges. Holding the agates against the light, I can differentiate shades of yellow – from the tender color of honey to the shriek of lemon. In emeralds, there's every shade of green, from the darkest ocean depths to the clear transparency of the shore.

In other groups, I am dazzled by the intense green of beryl, which helps develop intuition. The deep purple and delicate lavender of amorphous fluorite that forms crystals like skyscrapers – these develop the third eye. And the insect that flew millions of years ago and got stuck in the golden crystal of amber – this stimulates the chakra of the navel.

"The third eye, the eye of the psychic who sees beyond the material world, is located in the pineal gland, between your eyebrows," Adela explains. "We actually see very little with our regular eyes.

"There are so many lower and higher realities, visible in infrared and ultraviolet light, outside the spectrum our eyes perceive.

"Then there's the microscopic world, which can only be seen through the very powerful magnifying lenses in microscopes."

Seeing me dumbfounded at so much strange information, Adela gets up from the couch, goes to the kitchen, and comes back with a light bulb.

"You see this light bulb? Do you want to see me turn it on?" she asks me and, without waiting for an answer, holds it by its metallic base with the fingers of her right hand, and the light bulb lights up.

"How is that possible?" I shriek, astounded.

"I just concentrate my body's electrical energy on my fingers."

"I can't do that," I confess, frightened.

Adela goes to the window and talks to me from there:

"Come stand by the wall on the right side of the window." I get up from the couch and stand where she tells me, not knowing what she's up to.

"Penetrate the wall with your gaze and tell me what you see."

As I concentrate on the wall, it becomes something like smoky glass, and I see through it.

"Andy's riding his bike on the sidewalk," I say, uncertainly.

"So, you can't turn on light bulbs with your hand, but you can do other things that aren't normal for most people."

I'm afraid of this woman. Might she be a witch?

"No," Adela replies, as if she had read my thoughts, "I have developed these powers just by meditating."

"How did you know that I'd be able to see through the wall?" I ask.

"From your aura. The aura is the psychic light, electromagnetic light if you prefer, that surrounds your body."

I won't let her say any more, and I leave without a word.

EVERY SUNDAY my mother makes me wear nice clothes. It's almost always a satin-lined white lace suit, like the one I wore when they took my first color photograph. The photographer, who has a reputation for being the best, and whose studio is the most exclusive in the Capital, insisted that I smile, despite my missing tooth, and so there I am, forever dressed in white lace, sitting on a pink sofa, my white smile with a black space not quite in the middle.

After getting me ready, my mother puts on a white, draped dress and platform shoes that match her elegant white leather purse.

She's getting "all gussied up," as she calls it. She applies a layer of "pancake" to her face with a cotton ball. This is a light pink cream that dissolves with a little water, used to disguise the imperfections of her skin. Then she paints her lips bright red.

All this preparation is because we are going to church, apparently to be seen, not to pray.

I'm relieved to go to church after the scare I got at Adela's. The things they do in church are more familiar to me.

"What will they say about us if we don't go?" asks my mother very seriously. "That we're Jews? We must go. All the better people go, and we'll see painted statues

197

of saints, and we'll smell incense. Everyone gets down on their knees and people are very refined. We must go, above all because your father is a force to be reckoned with in politics, and because we have so much money. Just look at this!"

She opens her purse, pulls out a wad of bills, fans them out in her hands, and blows kisses at them, saying, "What colors! What smells! Look, my child, they're new bills, big denominations, a fortune. Touch them, because you may never see so much money together again in your entire life."

I don't touch them. My mother abruptly puts the money in her purse and closes it nervously. She combs her hair with my father's bone comb without noticing that it's covered in rosemary-scented brilliantine. Now, her hair is full of grease and separated into pitiful sparse strands on both sides of her face, but when she puts on her white turban, her sticky hair is invisible.

We leave the house and cross the almost empty streets. It's early and there aren't many people on the sidewalks. Maximino's bodega is closed, the metal grate rolled down. The church of St. Augustine, built on the sidewalk of the Friar, or of the Shadow, is illuminated by the sun in a near-mystical way, making its white marble glow.

We climb the great flight of steps to the church entrance and walk down the aisle between the pews and benches, where a small number of people sit: serious boys in long pants with shaved napes from recent haircuts, women with black veils and somber dresses or white veils and flowery silk dresses, a few grown men, well dressed, solemn, "Catholic Action" invisibly printed on their foreheads.

The altar boys' bells ring and the parishioners stand, kneel, sit down. The priest raises a gold cup, and all lower their heads, then he raises another round object of gold, and all lower their heads again. Kneeling on the hard bench hurts my knees. I sometimes fall climbing trees and walls, and my knees are full of bruises, scabs, and scars. But kneeling hurts more.

At length we sit and look up at the raised pulpit that sprouts from a column on the left side of the nave, where Father Piranelli, ascending in huge strides, emerges at the top like an exhalation.

Rubicund and chubby, brimming with warlike energy, he wears the white robe of the Augustinian order like a military uniform.

"There's lots of gold being spread around for luxuries and pleasures," he begins, declaiming his sermon in a foreign accent.

"But where it's most needed is for the Church! for the works of God! Politicking and gangsterism prevail in this society! No one takes time to do good! No one cares to practice essential charity!" he shouts from the pulpit. "Hypocrites! Misers! *Give all that money to the Church*!"

The congregants blush and lower their heads. My mother watches this like it's a movie, not something present in her life. Later I find out that's called "deliberately looking out-of-it" or "playing the crazy nanny goat."

Father Piranelli continues to fulminate. "One lady told me the other day, 'Father, when you pass the collection basket, you point it like it's a machine gun!'

Yes, I say! My offertory basket *is* a machine gun, meant to compel you to give money! To God I go pleading, and to you, the Islanders, with my whip flogging!"

The stained-glass windows vibrate with the priest's huge voice. My mother winces. Some women laugh nervously, but most of the congregation is staring at the ground, embarrassed. The priest descends from the pulpit and takes up one of the offertory baskets by its long handle. The altar boys follow him and spread out, holding them out to all the parishioners.

The clink-clink of coins is easily audible. "I don't want to hear clinking! No clinking! One-peso bills are fine, but five might be better!" Father Piranelli bellows.

Eventually, the priest himself is pointing the offertory basket directly at my mother's breast, and, with an air of importance, she drops in two five-peso bills.

The priest stares at the two of us, looks at my mother with displeasure, and says nothing. To the couple next to us who have donated the same amount, he gives thanks.

At the end of Mass, most of the parishioners remain on their knees, praying, but my mother tells me we are leaving.

"Why didn't the priest thank you?" I whisper. My mother doesn't answer, takes me by the hand, and we descend the great flight of steps.

Some pious women, arriving early for the next mass and climbing the steps with their heads covered by long black or white veils, give my mother indignant looks. Later, it occurs to me that they might have done so because my mother wasn't wearing a veil like those women, but one of her extravagant turbans.

HOME FROM SCHOOL, late as always because I've had hours of detention for speaking out in class, I take off my uniform, put on my brown overalls, and head to Adela's house. I haven't been by her house in days because I'm afraid. I've tried not to give importance to the things she says to me, but for some reason I can't stop thinking about them.

I don't like being afraid, and I always face my fears to get rid of them, but this fear is not physical.

It's emotional, or spiritual, which is harder to combat.

I realize, even though she scares me, Adela is the only person who explains strange things that happen to me and who doesn't threaten to send me to the nuthouse like my mother.

Adela is in her garden, tending to her plants with a large aluminum watering can. She smiles at the sight of me. It doesn't seem to bother her that I've taken to bolting without a word. She sets the watering can on the ground and waves at me to follow her into the house.

I sit on the couch, and she, in one of the armchairs.

"I have not meditated like you," I admit without preamble. "Why do these weird things happen to me? Am I crazy? Do I belong in the nuthouse? I never dare tell anyone what I see and what I can do because my mother says those are crazy people's things. Also, I hide what I write because she thinks writing gives you TB and what I write makes her really upset. And, for the same reason, I must hide not just *what* I read, but *that* I read. My mother thinks I'm going to turn out like my Uncle Alejandro, who was an intellectual and died of TB."

Adela laughs without any hint of mockery, as if she understands perfectly what's wrong with me. "You must have meditated in a previous life," she explains in a calming voice. "The meditation called *samatha*, which concentrates and calms the mind, develops these powers, which are transferred from life to life. The Catholic religion teaches that we live only once, but really, we have lived many – countless – times. You needn't fear these things, but you're right to hide them from your mother because you must not allow her to send you to a psychiatric hospital. Writing and reading are good – and, contrary to what your mother says, they do not pass on the TB bacillus! What your mother is afraid of is that you won't be able to make a living when you grow up if you dedicate yourself to things that aren't practical. You could study to be a teacher, which would let you keep writing and reading."

This enrages me. "They're all teachers in my family! I'm not going to be a teacher! Or a college professor! I *must* be something else!"

"Then, you can prepare for another career. What do you really want to be?"

"I like medicine and surgery."

Even though my experience with doctors hasn't been ideal, they never seem to become angry, and always have an answer for everything. I jump off the couch and walk around the room. I like to walk back and forth when I think.

Adela follows me with her gaze, but she doesn't move from her armchair.

"Fine. It's a good decision for you to dedicate yourself to healing others. And you can keep writing and reading literature. Chekhov, a famous Russian writer, was a physician, and he wrote plays and tales of great psychological depth."

"What are schools for?" I ask, suddenly very angry. "I go and get bored. They put me with the girls, and I only know how to play with boys, so I'm alone all the time. And the teachers just repeat the same things, over and over. I teach myself. I read my father's books, encyclopedias, newspapers, magazines. I listen to the radio. That's how I learn best."

Calmly, Adela says: "Schools are for normal children. You may learn faster than they do, and in this country, neither gifted children nor the developmentally delayed are given due attention. In America, and I know this because I taught in that country for several years, there are special schools for these two types of children, who benefit from being taught differently."

"My teacher says I'm retarded. The other students laugh at me when I answer questions."

"No retarded girl talks like you. There's nothing wrong with being gifted. It's an advantage for the child and for her family, if she can be educated. Why do you only play with boys? Is it because you have a brother?"

"No, man!" I answer, gesticulating as if it were the stupidest thing ever. "I won't play with my brother. When we lived in our house in La Sierra, he always wanted to be the chief. When it rained, we'd make a native hut out of armchairs covered by a sheet, and he insisted on being the chief. He said women were slaves with no right to tell others what to do. I stopped playing with him and since then, we each go our own way. I play with boys because it's more entertaining. Girls play with dolls and little houses. That's boring."

"Well, don't you think you should try to make friends with some classmates to find out what the girls at school think?"

"No. I don't want to gossip, and I hate to listen to it. Dieguín talks about the Sun and the end of the solar system – interesting. His sister, Aurelita, talks about the parents of her school friends, like whether they're rich, or poor. I prefer Dieguín. The girls at school are exactly like Aurelita – boring."

"What do *you* like to talk about?"

I get back up on the couch and look at the woman deep in her eyes.

"For example: Why are there always wars on this planet? I read in the history of the universe that there is always a war: the War of the Two Roses, the Thirty Years War, the First World War, the Second World War . . ."

"There is war because the ignorance and ambition of some men does not respect the territory or the rights of others. If we all respected others, there would be no wars, no soldiers, no policemen, no prisons."

I stare at her, and finally say: "How do you know all these things?"

Adela laughs, without mocking me, as if she remembers something nice.

"It's all because of Mr. Carter, the Englishman I married in America. He's been dead for a long time, and I'm a widow, but when I was young, he wooed me away from a poor boy, who could only offer me eternal love. Mr. Carter was rich and offered me a generous bank account. I chose him for that, because I wanted his money to travel and to be able to learn from different cultures of the world." She breaks off what she was saying. Then she adds: "Mr. Carter only lived five years after our wedding, and when he died, I began my journeys around the world, which taught me much more than the university I graduated from with a doctorate in education."

I feel a sense of urgency. This might be my only chance to ask someone who knows the world the answers to whatever questions I can think of.

"What's the worst thing that happened to you on your travels?" I'm surprised to be asking her.

"Hah! One night, in an African hut, I heard drums! Those drums paralyzed my heart. I had just reached an unexplored area, hoping to see lions, and at night the drums started. I called to my guide, who spoke English, and asked him what all that *tum, tum, tum* was saying. 'They say a white witch has arrived,' the African replied as if were not a big deal. 'An Englishwoman with evil spirits. They are agreeing to cut off her head tomorrow morning,' the guide said, without any emotion, as if this were the most common thing in their world. I said, 'No! No, you tell them with the drums that I married an Englishman, but I'm not English! I am

Latina, from the Caribbean!' I exclaimed, trying to disguise my terror. I said to him, 'We Caribbean people are like the Africans, there are many of you on our islands and we are all mixed together. Tell them I brought magical substances that produce dreams that reveal the future. If they visit me tomorrow, I will give these substances to them.'"

Adela pauses and breathes deeply as if to recoup her energy. "The guide got out his drum and was drumming back and forth with the other natives for almost an hour. The next morning, four tall, strong warriors appeared, shiny black and bright as obsidian, in front of my door. Ignoring their pointed spears and long knives, I quietly gave them several pipes and enough opium, which I had acquired in China, so that everyone would smoke and have a pleasant experience."

She adds, after a pause: "After this, no one else bothered me."

"What happened with the lions?" I ask.

"I couldn't find them. I later decided to go to Kenya on safari in a jeep, protected by an experienced English guide who knew where to find them. That's when I saw lions. And there I met Beryl Markham, the famous aviator and breeder and trainer of thoroughbred horses. Later, when I was in New York, the manuscript she was writing, which she let me read the first chapters of, was published as *West with the Night,* her fabulous autobiography. It was the book Ernest Hemingway could only have dreamed of writing."

"Did you have any other bad experience?"

"Oh, even worse! I became ill with malaria in the Bengal region of India, and no hotel wanted to admit me. I'd come in from the jungle where I'd been looking for the famous tigers, which is where I caught it. I had to sleep on the street like the Dalit. By a huge stroke of luck, I was found by a friend of Mr. Carter's, a millionaire duke who had been his roommate at Oxford. It was the duke who demanded that I be admitted to the best hotel in Calcutta. He brought me the doctor who cured me, and he paid for everything."

I've never had an experience like this before. An older person who talks to me as if I were a grown-up, who tells me the kind of stories I can only hear when I'm hidden and adults talk among themselves. Recalling her youth, Adela is transformed. She looks younger and encircled by light.

As she recounts the incredible anecdotes of her life, could she possibly be telling me lies?

"What was your best experience?" I ask to see if I can catch her in some misinformation.

"One of my most wonderful trips was my visit to the South Pole. I was in a bar in Buenos Aires when I met a group of scientists planning an exploration of Antarctica. They agreed to meet the following year at the same bar, on the same day and at the same time. I told them I wanted to go. They accepted me because we'd hit it off, there in the bar that night. Also, I mentioned that I had a second Ph.D. in geology, which might be helpful to them.

"The following year we met and went on a large icebreaker belonging to the Chilean navy to explore Antarctica."

This, clearly, is over the top. She's just piling on the lies now. I may be a girl, but I'm not stupid.

Adela, as if again reading my thoughts, and without any resentment of my suspicions, asks me: "Would you like me to show you the movie I made of that trip?"

Without waiting for my answer, the teacher goes to rummage in a back room for the film and projector.

She sets up the projector facing a wall that will presumably serve as a screen, mounts the reel on the projector, and threads the film through to the take-up reel. Still doubting, I think she is going to say the projector doesn't work, or the bulb has burned out, or the film is the wrong size or can't be projected because it's too frail. There's no way this woman went to the South Pole, or has had the experiences she's telling me about.

I see tall icebergs and penguins diving into a dark sea.

"This is me on the deck of the ship." She points her finger at a lady in a huge jacket, smiling as the camera focuses on her,

In another part of the film, whales blow spray into the sky, and the scientists come out of the house they have built on the ice to observe the southern sky, using strange instruments. I know what I'm seeing is the South Pole, and the woman wearing the bulky coat is clearly Adela.

My mother's voice comes through the window of the room, screaming my name and telling me to come home and eat. "I've never seen anything like this. Thank you, but my mother is calling me to dinner," I say, running to the door.

IN THE AFTERNOON IT RAINS, as it always does on the Island during the rainy season. The water falls on the schoolyard, darkening the glossy gray cement of its pavement. The black sky is gloomy, the barrel-tile roofs of the houses beyond the courtyard wall pour out dirty rivers that cascade down yellow walls. The volutes and arabesques of the silver bars outside the windows of our classroom sketch capricious figures on the landscape, wounding it, dividing it unpleasantly.

The teacher, sitting up there on her imposing professorial platform, speaks in a guttural voice. With black hair and olive skin, the teacher talks endlessly about the Gracchi, because this is our second-grade Moral and Civics Class.

"Tiberius Sempronius Gracchus and, later, his brother Gaius Sempronius Gracchus, as tribunes of the plebes, proposed laws on behalf of the humble, those who did not have Roman citizenship, as well as for the illustrious knights of the famous equestrian order," instructs the teacher in such a loud voice that it thunders against the classroom's ceiling. "But laws such as the distribution of land to the city's poor and to decommissioned soldiers, as well as the incorporation of knights into the courts that judged them, irritated the aristocrats."

I raise my hand to ask permission to go to the bathroom.

When she gives it to me, reluctantly because this teacher hates to be interrupted, I run through the halls of the school, slip without falling on the white marble floor that has veins of red and brown in it, careen down the stairs and across the courtyard towards the white wooden sheds with doors painted dark green.

The rain, by now pouring down in sheets, increases the weight of my school uniform, and sticks it to my skin. The raindrops pummel the tin roof of the outhouse, where I lock myself in with a gloomy clink.

On the concrete walls of the latrine, covered with a smooth dark gray film of plaster, there are, drawn in white chalk, hearts pierced by arrows, names of popular males, messages of love, vulgar words.

Through the opening over the door, I see the turbulent sky and faintly hear voices coming from the classrooms.

Everything suddenly stops inside me.

I sit floating in this shed impregnated with the smell of urine, deafened by the noise of the rain hammering on the roof and erasing the voices of girls answering questions and teachers explaining topics.

I can leave this shed, cross the courtyard to the entrance hall, stand for a minute protected from rain by the green canopy, and walk down the Avenue of the Presidents until I come to the sea. My bookbag, its bulging, greasy form, can remain behind in that classroom, along with its rough smell of leather, those colored pencils that transport me to other regions, especially the orange and blue green pencils. I can say goodbye to my bread-like eraser crumbs piled, seemingly edible, on my paper, and to the bitter taste of the blue ink leaking from the innards of my fountain pen, and to its iridescent case of green-veined beryl.

I can leave behind my name and my history, that card I must insert into the time clock every morning to print my arrival time and accuse me, in bright red, if I'm the tiniest bit late.

I can even leave myself behind, as if my body were a shell. All that's required is to take a walk and forget everything I'm leaving behind. Who am I, after all? Who is that name on that card? Who is that person who stands up tongue-tied whenever she's asked a question? Do I really live in that apartment with those parents and that brother? Or am I someone else, somebody who belongs to another world, a world of crazy speeds, of focused lights that penetrate everything, of instantaneous messages among the antipodes of the planet?

Now, everything is slow, slow, s-l-o-w. The walls of the shed begin to press in on me, and, like an iron maiden, they embed their daggers in my flesh. I can fly out, follow the wind towards the sea, float over this tin roof the way I do in dreams.

Without realizing it, my feet lead me back to class.

Everybody is looking at me. My uniform is soaked through.

"What were you doing in the bathroom?" the teacher asks, annoyed at the length of time I've been out of the classroom.

"I was busy. I couldn't come any sooner," I reply, very serious, sitting down at my desk without looking at anyone. I towel my hair dry with a white linen hand-kerchief embroidered with the image of a peasant milking a cow and the word *Thursday* cross-stitched in blue. Within minutes, I'm stunned to hear the strident bell ringing the end of morning classes throughout the school.

I'VE FINISHED LUNCH and I'm waiting on the sidewalk outside my house for the Baldor School bus to take me back for the afternoon session. On the opposite corner, standing on the sidewalk, the Paredes de Miranda Girl, wearing her wine-red uniform, is waiting for the bus from her school. Elena has told me she's rich and goes to Merici, a school that's even more exclusive than Baldor. This girl lives in the huge corner mansion with its very large patio. The entrance is obscured by tall, rusty, wrought-iron grilles covered by ivy and flowering climbers. The two-story white mansion hides behind huge windows veiled by white curtains of chiffon and lace. A port-cochere shelters the three steps, a white marble crescent with some gray veins that leads up to the front entrance with its imposing mahogany double doors covered in intricate carvings.

Chunky, with a protruding belly and blond braids, the Paredes de Miranda girl leaps down the steps, overflowing her Merici uniform, its fine white cotton shirt with long sleeves rolled up framed by its box-pleated red skirt with suspenders of the same color. I cross the street and walk up to her carrying my book bag, and, with my other hand, working a metallic-blue yo-yo I bought at Woolworth's Ten Cents. I throw the yo-yo with twists and turns. Not knowing who spoke first, nor how it happened, in a few minutes we're engaged in a trivial conversation, and she invites me to play in her huge patio when we get home from school at dusk.

AT SCHOOL, throughout the afternoon, I think of the patio garden belonging to the Paredes de Miranda Girl, which cannot be glimpsed through bars and foliage. What can this rich girl's life be like inside that enormous mansion, hidden behind walls and curtains?

When I arrive home from school, the Paredes de Miranda Girl is there, plac-idly waiting for me on the steps of her house, still wearing her Merici uniform. I run home to put on my brown overalls and hunt down Cristín, Ricky's brother, who told me he wanted to meet her. We follow the girl into her palatial residence.

The gray clarity of day penetrates through the open patio door on the other side of the foyer from the front door, lighting up the polished marble tiles of the foyer floor.

We pass a tiny alcove whose sole piece of furniture is a cot pushed against the wall. Rina, the maid, and oldest sister of The Twins, avoids looking at me as she meticulously stacks the clothes she's just ironed, placing them in a row on the cot where she will sleep, after delivering the piles of clean clothes, along with garments on hangers, to their Paredes de Miranda owners.

The Paredes de Miranda girl leads me and Cristín out into the enormous patio's garden. In the middle, a beautiful oval of dark tiles draws my attention, this garden's central feature, around a fountain with a life-size statue in gray marble of a beautiful naked woman staring at herself in the roiled water.

What must it be like for this corpulent girl to see this paragon of female beauty in all her glory, every day of her life?

On the far side of the fountain, outside the oval of tiles and the circle of velvety grass around it, there's all manner of flowering bushes, and, for exercise, a homely pommel horse and a swing set that includes a pair of rusty rings.

My guess is that not one of these objects has ever been used by the Paredes de Miranda Girl, who now urges me to ride her bike, which seems brand new. I climb on and take a turn around the garden, advancing in circles around the bushes, sometimes letting go of the handlebars.

Showing off his perfect teeth, Cristín laughs as he points his index finger at me. The Paredes de Miranda Girl doubles over with laughter. Every time I pass near Cristín, he mocks me.

I regret letting him tag along. When I'm playing alone with him, Cristín is a pretty, blond, blue-eyed boy, as peaceful as an angel. His games bore me because they are very passive, but I play with him because I felt sorry to see him playing little girls' games all by himself, or with his younger brother Ricky, who is also very feminine. But this side of Cristín, that of obsequious flatterer of a rich girl, is a surprise. He wants to entertain the Paredes de Miranda Girl so he can enjoy this garden, which has evolved into making me the monkey to his organ grinder.

I change tacks. I abandon the bike on the velvety grass and go to the rings to build strength. I do every exercise I can think of on the rings, trying to attain momentum as I hold on, even though my arms want to snap off and my stomach muscles stretch almost to breaking. I sweat copiously. I'm doing pull-ups on the rings. My hands hurt and become covered with a metallic-smelling brown liquid as my perspiration mingles with rust from the rings. My ears fill with the murmur of my pounding heart, but this doesn't keep me from hearing the laughter of the Paredes de Miranda Girl, enthroned on her white marble bench, clapping her plump hands, laughing as if I'm her court jester.

Cristín, next to her, works hard to ingratiate himself with this rich girl, making jokes and pointing his finger at me.

The enormous patio is transformed from an enchanted place where any kind of interesting game might be played, into a circus where the crazy fat princess applauds. As she claps, her crimson uniform's dye stains the underarms and then the rest of her white shirt. I see a sow marinating in red wine.

I abandon the rings and sit down beside her, to look at her closely and try to lift the veil of stupidity that covers her.

"Go ride the bike! Hang from the rings like a monkey! Be like a monkey!" the Paredes de Miranda Girl urges me.

"It's time to eat. I must go home," I answer. I walk up to the house quickly, but once I'm inside, I turn around. Cristín, riding the bike, does all kinds of pirouettes and circus tricks. Now he's the monkey. The Paredes de Miranda Girl continues to laugh and clap her flabby hands like seals' flippers.

I'VE BEEN ROLLER-SKATING ALL MORNING. I haven't seen any of my friends, but I can entertain myself. I've been all the way around the block at full speed, even though my mother warns me not to go that far, or that fast. It gives me a sense of freedom to go fast and have the wind on my face.

When I return to my building, I find the door to the stairwell closed. I take off my skates, and, carrying them in one hand, I open the door with the other. Sitting on the floor or squatting are Aurelita, Luisita, and some other girls I've not met. They all are holding dolls, and when I open the door, I can see that they've quickly changed positions, like they're hiding something.

"What are you playing?" I ask because I'm tired of skating, and it might be entertaining to play with them for a change.

"Nothing. We're not playing anything. We were all just about to go home," Aurelita lies with her characteristic hypocrisy.

I realize they don't want to play with me. I go to the balcony of my house, leave the skates on the floor, and sit on the little wall to wait for Luisita to come out. When I see her, I run after her and grab her by the arm.

"What were you playing at?" I ask her, assuming she's going to lie to me.

"We were suckling our dolls, and Aurelita told us that if you came, we had to cover our breasts, because you only play with boys." I let Luisita go and sit on the balcony wall, trying to understand what I've just heard.

WE ARE VISITING MARGARITA, another sister of The Twins. Margarita has black hair set in corkscrew curls, a long face that ends in a point, gray eyes, and finely curved eyelashes. She married a police officer and they live in a tiny apartment a few blocks from ours.

We're visiting because she just had a *curettage*, a word my mother closes her eyes and lowers her voice to say, as if it means something very ancient that everyone has forgotten, but which is sacred and makes the hair along your spine stand on end.

When my mother and I arrive, hand in hand, Margarita greets us from the bed. She's wearing a salmon-colored silk bed jacket adorned with white embroidery and bows. The rest of her is covered by a white sheet. Rina, her older sister, is sitting at the foot of the bed, massaging her legs under the sheet.

Margarita's husband comes home as we arrive, immediately removing his belt with its holster and regulation gun and hanging it on the back of a chair. His nightstick rests on the night table and looks like a small baseball bat with leather ribbons woven tightly around one end, the handle. These weapons smell of violence and lend the room a menacing atmosphere, as if the officer might suddenly start beating up or shooting people to stop a student demonstration, as we see on the newsreels at movie theaters all the time. However, the policeman, tall, thick, and fat as a barrel, squeezed into a navy-blue uniform so heavily starched that it creaks, looks like a chaste virgin when he is dispossessed of his symbols of power. Now he's just a husband consumed by worry about his wife's health – a beer-belly impotent in the face of female disease.

"Margarita, my dear girl, how are you?" my theatrical and Olympian mother asks, overpronouncing each word. She has come to pay a visit to the sister of her maid and wants to underline the democratic nature of her gesture. My mother, a woman of the people, worries about the ups and downs of her dependents, and guides them with a kind but energetic hand.

"Oh, Flora, you know how much it hurts to be a woman!" Margarita complains in a broken voice.

Rina cuts her sister a disdainful look. Rina, unmarried, is not a "woman," but a servant hardened by harsh treatment who detests whining and weakness.

My mother sits on the other side of the bed, opposite Rina, and holds Margarita's hands comfortingly. I stay standing, next to Rina.

"When did you leave the hospital?" my mother asks in a condoling tone.

"This afternoon. It was horrible, the hospital. Suddenly one is removed from one's house and handed over to strangers, like a cow led to slaughter. Luckily, my doctor, an overly affectionate bald man, treated me very well because his favorite flower is the daisy, the margarita, like me. I leave it to your imagination – a twice-married bald man!"

She laughs, her face contracted by pain, but with mischievous eyes. The policeman flits back and forth in the room like a gigantic moth. He doesn't seem to know what to do with his huge, plump, lily-white hands.

My mother laughs as if she knows the secret contained in Margarita's revelation. She, too, knows about doctors in love. When I had measles and almost died, the doctor, from so much visiting the house, fell in love with my mother and would come into the house carrying his black briefcase singing:

> *Woman! divinest of women! In your gaze,*
> *You have the venom that fascinates!*
> *Woman, alabaster figurine,*
> *You are the passion that vibrates*
> *in a sonata, in a sonatina.*

That was Agustín Lara's most popular song that year.

"Oh, but Flora, aren't nurses the devil's paw! Making dirty jokes all the time. They drink coffee all night long and tell the filthiest jokes you can imagine! With people dying of pain and screaming in the rooms! One woman had the most horrible illness: one of her breasts had grown so enormous, it reached her feet, and do you know what the nurses called her? *Mae West!* What people, girl!"

"Yes, well, but you're all right now, aren't you?" my mother asks, cutting off the hospital story. The last thing she wants to think about is hospitals. She's there to make a compassionate visit.

"Gregorio, do make Flora a coffee," Margaret entreats the policeman. "The poor thing, she's come to see me, with so many things she has to do."

Gregorio goes to the kitchen.

I've never seen a cop making coffee and I run after him to witness this spectacle, but my mother commands, "Stay here, girl! Do *not* bother Gregorio."

"That's right, Flora, be energetic with her! You don't want her to turn out like the Paredes de Miranda Girl," Rina says approvingly, happy to broach a subject that she has few friends to share with.

"The *Paredes de Miranda* Girl?" My mother is confused. She throws that question out like a hook to see what more there is, to investigate the case.

Margarita looks up at the ceiling like, "Must I hear this story *again*?"

"There are things that it's best not to repeat," says Rina demurely, looking at the ground to further incite my mother's curiosity.

Now, of course she must talk.

My mother beams at Rina, all ears, avid for gossip.

Rina demurs.

"Oh, for heaven's sake, just spit it out! What happened with the Paredes de Miranda Girl?" my mother finally explodes.

Rina moves her head as if in agreement, and looks at her hands, intertwined as the nuns say they should be when women sit down, to indicate modesty. Gregorio makes a noise like clearing his throat in the kitchen. Margarita plays with the laces on her bed jacket, sinking her chin into her chest as if it were a mountaineer's pike.

"The Paredes de Miranda Girl, every time she sees me, throws herself violently on my *breasts*." Rina pronounces this word loading it with meaning. Her cheeks swell and redden. She appears to be enjoying this moment greatly.

"But she's just a little *girl*!" my mother yelps, reproaching Rina.

"I don't like those abnormalities! In fact, I don't like them at all, not in the least!" Rina protests, reaffirming her revelation without contradicting my mother, who is erasing the image from her consciousness with a hand gesture that is, at the same time, like a medieval religious fanatic accusing someone of sorcery.

Gregorio transports the coffee in a tiny cup without a saucer under it. It looks ridiculous in his gigantic hand.

"Here, Flora," he says in a fluty, high voice.

My mother takes the cup delicately, curling up her little finger.

Rina stands up, and the space she occupied in this room collapses, because she is not going to be allowed to tell any more of her story. She slips out the door propelled by shame, saying goodbye to everyone with her hand.

"You look well, Margarita," my mother compliments her, relieved to be rid of a servant who criticizes her masters.

I sit at the foot of the bed, taking the place Rina occupied, in front of my mother. On the side where I'm sitting, the policeman drags the chair with his pistol dangling from it to the head of the bed, then sits down, pushing the gun to one side. He takes hold of his wife's hand as if to protect her.

His strength appears to grow when he is near that gun.

My mother looks at Gregorio and orders him: "Take good care of your wife, who is a treasure!"

Then, to lift the cop out of the inferior role she has put him in by giving him an order, given that she's a mere civilian, she adds: "Mr. National Police Officer!"

"Flora," Margarita says quietly and guiltily, "will you let me have a cigarette?"

"But of course, girl!"

My mother opens her purse and pulls three cigarettes out of their blue box, offering them to Margarita, who rolls over onto her side and sits up to take one of the cigarettes. Under her beautiful salmon-pink silk nightgown and bed jacket, I see a great bloodstain, bright red, expanding on the white sheet like the ring-of-snakes mane of a Gorgon.

Margarita covers the stain with her body when she lies back in bed. She lights a cigarette with the match that Gregorio brings close to her, and exhales the smoke through her mouth slowly, blinking quickly, lifting the tip of her nose, and pursing her thick, sensual lips.

"What pleasure!" she exclaims in a cavernous voice, her blue eyelids trembling as she squints through the smoke.

18

FILAMENTS PEOPLE WEAVE

IN THE MORNING I run out to the street because I'm afraid the apartment will imprison me. Lately I've been running from everywhere. Cristín even said to me, "You don't leave places. You escape." There's sun and yellow butterflies. Dieguín is throwing a wooden top on the ground. Cone-shaped, it's a bit smaller than his clenched fist, has a metal tip, and is painted a delicious lilac hue. The body of the top is wrapped in a cord, the other end of which passes through a squashed Coke bottle cap with a hole punched in its center, ending in a big knot. Without letting go of the bottle cap, Dieguín hurls the top and it spins solidly on the sidewalk.

"You, playing with a top?" I exclaim, astonished to see him doing something a normal boy might do.

"I'm studying its movement, its momentum, like Platón," he explains.

"Platón? A big plate?" I ask jokingly. Of course, I know about Plato.

"The ancient Greek philosopher. You need to read philosophy, because it will teach you to think. It's important to read what others have thought, but more important is *learning to think*. Information and knowledge are good, but wisdom is better. You can only arrive at wisdom if you know how to think."

Dieguín winds the string around the top, throws the top into the air, catches it spinning in the palm of his hand, flips a bit of the string around the top, and makes it walk spinning across the tense cord towards the palm of his other hand.

"Where on earth did you learn how to do that?"

"I learned it at school during recess. It takes lots of practice."

Cristín rides his bike past and waves goodbye with his hand as he chants:

> Bang, Bing, the fall of Berlin!
> Bing, Bang, the fall of Japan!

I wave back, but Dieguín glares at him without making any gestures. When Cristín is out of sight, Dieguín rewinds his top and hurls it violently at the sidewalk. The top spins elegantly in one place.

"What a jackass!" the boy exclaims in anger. "Babbling a stupid ditty about the destruction of Europe and Japan! Not to mention the beginning of the Atomic Era. It's a good thing the Allies won, but we'll never be able to sleep again without thinking that we might wake up vaporized by gamma rays, like Hiroshima and Nagasaki."

The child picks up his top and leaves without another word.

I find it strange that Dieguín cares so much about Europe and Japan because, for me, they are faraway places. Gamma rays! My mother would long ago have had that child committed to an insane asylum.

Yet the truth is, we have paid almost no attention to the end of the war. Of course, it's been reported in newspapers, on the radio, and in newsreels at movie theaters. But no one is dancing in the streets the way they are in Paris. Maybe it's because we weren't invaded by German soldiers. Or because war ended first in Europe, then Japan. Maybe, for greater impact, the wars should have ended everywhere at the exact same time.

Another thing: nobody's particularly worried about the atom bomb. It destroys entire cities and leaves them radioactive for who knows how many years. They say a new era has begun, but, in the neighborhood, everything stays the same. Meanwhile, my morning has been wrecked. My day has dropped off the balcony and can't be repaired. My afternoon gets more and more hollowed out, separating morning from night forever. When afternoon inflates itself like this, fixing objects in their places, it projects a glassy, hurtful, orange-hued glow over the houses, and it draws attention to the sounds made by cars, those phantoms on wheels that scurry around carelessly on the streets.

I feel as if I'm living in the afternoon of the end of the world.

My stomach is empty and my breath is panting. All our games have suddenly ended and no one is talking. Curfew has been imposed by the voice of Laura Medinaceli de Alba, Laurencita's mother, calling her home to take a shower and have dinner. That voice dropped like a lightning bolt into our group, destroying the illusion of the game, pushing us to go back to the homes and parents that we have wanted to erase from memory.

How can parents, adults, understand what they have done? How to pick up the thread of a game in which, at its climax, we had completely dissolved our very selves?

The damage is irreparable, and we end up watching cars, fascinated by the smoke that spews, reeking of gasoline, from the bazookas of those exhaust pipes.

We children sit, depressed, on the walls. With our eyes wide open, dry, unblinking, we look at the world that marches with an expression proclaiming life's unquestionable brevity, the most difficult fact of all to ignore, the most terrible to encounter head-on, and then dismiss with a game or a belly laugh.

Elena, sitting beside me, looks at me with her bright gray-green eyes and says, "Let's go. I have a surprise for you. Come upstairs to my house."

As discombobulated as a puppet with its strings cut, I don't have enough coordination to respond negatively. I've kept away from her for quite a while because I don't like her jealousy, her possessiveness, but, because it's easier than inventing an excuse, I get up and follow her upstairs and down hallways.

I walk through the door of Elena's house, stunned by the speed of her movements and the pointed, sparkling, sweet odor that greets me, produced by green guavas and yellow Filipino mangoes in fruit bowls, and pink roses with thousands of petals in vases. The fragrances of another family and other customs.

"I want you to watch me get my injection," reveals the girl, heroic and mysterious, raising her blond eyebrows and illuminating the taut skin of her cheeks from within.

I'm nailed to the floor in the face of this extravagant desire. I'm ashamed to witness such an act of intimacy, to watch her reactions, and, what's worse, to be required to appraise them, give them value. Her shamelessness bowls me over.

Elena jumps onto the bed, stretching out and bracing herself for the ordeal. Her mother, smiling and looking at me with complicity, plunges the needle into Elena's buttock with a graceful thrust and then inserts in the syringe a glass tube containing a yellow liquid that disappears into Elena's rump. The liquid gives off an acrid, oily smell, diffused by the effervescent scent of a cotton ball soaked in alcohol, with which the mother determinedly erases the tiny hole left by the needle.

I look out the window and let my eyes refresh themselves with the multitude of objects outside. The street and its people protect me against the strange emotions being put on display inside this room. I have participated in an act that is not for me. A fissure has been opened, and, wordlessly, I have been given a pass to enter another's life.

Elena leaps out of the bed like an acrobat, very pneumatic, bouncing off the bedspread and coming over to me, radiant. A crystalline glow dilutes her grey-green eyes, making them look blue. Her body smells of exercise, of good health.

As a response countering this overture, a paralyzing wall surrounds me, making my movements clumsy and my reactions uncoordinated, fusing my skin to the bones of my face, hardening the muscles around my lips as if they were made of steel.

"What did you think? Did you see how I reacted?" she asks me.

"Yes. You didn't cry," I reply, indifferent.

"That's not what I meant, silly. These are *oil* injections, and it's hard to get the oil under my skin. It's very painful."

I walk toward the door and am surprised that no one is stopping me. I'm glad to be freed of sticky emotions, entanglements in the filaments people weave around others. I don't utter a single word of farewell.

When the door closes behind me, I run down the stairs, filled by the great euphoria of freedom.

AT HOME, MY MOTHER IS WAITING for my father to pick her up so they can attend a banquet given by his political party.

Sitting on the sofa, dressed in beige silk with pleated shoulder pads, she's wearing one of her most spectacular white turbans.

At the end of her fingers there's a cigarette which she's raising to her mouth, painted a screaming red. A brilliant gaze and worried eyes. A white satin evening bag with a gold catch rests in the dip the dress makes between her legs.

On the sofa next to my mother, wrapped in white crinolines and wearing white shoes, Kika is reading Thomas à Kempis's *Imitation of Christ*. My brother, in khaki pants and a white cotton T-shirt with a V-shaped collar, is lounging in one of the armchairs next to the sofa. A lock of black hair falls on his forehead and his jaws play with a wad of tutti-frutti gum while he reads another Doc Savage paperback. I lie on the floor, bored on a rainy Saturday when there's no going out to play, bored by others' silence and reading. About six inches above the floor level, a hole left by removing a broken power outlet allows me to see what's going on next door, and even, if I press my ear against the opening, hear what they say. The white pants of the professional sailor, as my mother calls our neighbor, walk back and forth. He's a lieutenant in the Island's Navy. He's inspired me to imagine what I might become in the future, but I gave myself more stripes and gold leaf, and the rank of commander. The impeccably clean trousers, creased like sharp knives, keep pacing back and forth. From my observation post, I see the bottom of the golden sheath of his dress sword that hits his leg with every move. His military strides, from one side of the room to the other, make me think he's waiting for someone, or meditating on some problem of naval strategy. His figure, when I can see all of him, is imposing. Tall, black hair combed back with Brylcreem, feline smile, mustache trimmed in a perfect inverted vee, coconut white uniform with gold buttons, broad, arrogant chest, very straight back – he's the embodiment of military perfection.

And of nonsense, I think, after all my admiring, because his career is no more real than my games. The Island Navy is completely impractical. What war is it going to stand out in? He's no Nelson, nor is our Island England. His heroism is that of operetta, pure theater. Anyhow, I still admire these exercises in a vacuum, the demented military glory of a small country, now in peacetime, because World War II is over.

I set a mirror in the hole and, if I move it, I can see the reflection of his wife, who's running back and forth, getting dressed, putting perfume behind her ears, a little powder on her nose, a shawl over her shoulders. The naval officer sits on the couch at last, relaxing. His sword hits his shoes when he impatiently moves his crossed leg, producing a metallic sound as well as a golden glow when the scabbard reflects light. His coffee-colored eyes are fixed on an imaginary point in space. His gloved hands play with his officer's hat.

The woman grabs him by the arm and lifts him off the couch to dance a rhumba on their way to the door. The officer accompanies her out of the house, opening an umbrella. I run to the balcony to see them depart. They descend the building's little staircase, arm in arm, under a thin drizzle. When the lieutenant sees me, he smiles. His wife, flirtatious and smiling too, wags her head from side to side, agitating the permanent waves of her almost certainly dyed blonde hair. They are young, cheerful, light, champagne bubbles in the violet afternoon. I record them in my memory at this moment of triumph.

My exalted emotion is vaporized when my father telephones to say that his day has become complicated, that he doesn't have time to get to the house. He'll have to attend the banquet alone.

My mother, her face transformed by fury, goes to the bedroom to undress.

FIRE

19

Donald Duck
and the Gold Mine

WEEKS GO BY. My mother and I come home after watching *Atlantis*, which I found very strange. It's Saturday, around eight o'clock at night. Visible from the street, the living room glows with red, green, blue, and gold Christmas lights. A brilliant white star that crowns the tree almost touches the ceiling, and, from the sidewalk, it's a promise of happiness. The door opens, and the living room, with all those blinking colored lights and radiant glass tubes of red, green, blue, and gold liquid where bubbles go up and down, seems transported to another, happy, time, full of the promise of well-being. The atmosphere is mellow, the edges of furniture softened. The green manger on the white cotton snow at the foot of the tree, the sleeping infant Jesus attended by Mary, Joseph, three Wise Men, a cow lying down, a flock of sheep standing up complete the scene. Those painted plaster figurines and that stucco manger, backlit by a small blue spotlight I put behind the crèche, emotionally transform and dominate the house.

I go in and feel an uncommon joy in the air. My mother follows, flings her alligator-skin purse on the coffee table, stares transfixed at the Christmas tree as if she had never seen one before. In the dark, the lights softened by angel hair draped all over the tree give it an otherworldly appearance.

My father materializes from the shadows of the hallway with a glass of beer in his hand. He's wearing slippers, white dril 100 slacks. and a white guayabera.

"How was the movie?" he asks, turning on the light in the living room and settling comfortably in an armchair, crossing his legs.

"They showed an American film with that Dominican actress, Maria Montez, who makes her entrance in this huge, glitzy, shell-shaped bed, dressed as a mermaid with a tame panther at her side," my mother says, parking herself in another armchair, while I hop onto the sofa between them. "Asiatic luxury! She's queen of the lost city of Atlantis, which is found inside a sandstorm in the Sahara Desert by the French actor

Jean-Pierre Aumont, who plays a soldier in the French Foreign Legion. Of course, given his eyes, his seductive smile, and the exceptional luxury of María Montez, they fall in love. Like a new tale from the court of Louis XIV."

My father looks at her mockingly and settles into his armchair. Combing his grey mustache with one hand, he asks, "So, what are we talking about – 'Hollywood finds Atlantis in the Sahara at the court of Louis XIV'?"

My mother makes a gesture of exasperation. "Oh, don't start making fun of me! I meant it as a manner of speaking. Atlantis is just a pretext for the actress to wear out-rageous costumes in exotic locations. Who cares about Atlantis?"

After a pause, my mother continues with her usual passion, explaining as if she's talking to an idiot: "The elegant costumes, Montez's sensual accent, the French sol-dier's dazzling blond hair, all shot through a filter that makes their skin look lustrous, starry, a twilit glow on their noses – *that* made the film."

My father coughs. He stands up and takes a cigar out of the large humidor made of fine Spanish cedar that sits on the coffee table. When the humidor is open, its scent of cedar fills the air. Turning the cigar slowly to light it with his silver Zippo, inhaling and savoring the smoke voluptuously, he says to me, "How would you like to meet my boss, the new minister? Today is his birthday and I promised to stop by his new house, but I fell asleep after lunch, because it's so quiet without your brother. He's eating at a friend's house."

"Our esteemed president, Dr. Ramón Grau San Martín, should never have fired your friend, the scholar Dr. Luis Pérez Espinós, who was the only honest minister of education we've ever had," my mother comments. "But of course, around town they couldn't resist plastering all kinds of posters promoting Luis as our next president, and Grau doesn't want anyone eclipsing him. That's why he got rid of him and appointed that brash young senator, Dr. Diego Vicente Tejera, who decides he's one of the Three Musketeers, gets into a swordfight, and lasts six months as minister.

"And now you want to congratulate this new minister, Dr. José Manuel Alemán Casharo, who's slowly dying of inoperable cancer and doesn't care where he gets the money to give away to his friends. He's going to leave us all plucked, naked as jaybirds."

"Is there a reason you are suddenly giving titles and positions to everyone as if you were an informant for a foreign power?" my father asks.

"I want the girl to know what I'm talking about."

"Wouldn't you like to meet Alemán, Bad Bug?" my father asks me.

"Does he have anything to do with war? Aren't the *alemanes* the guys who lost the war?" My parents burst out laughing. For the first time in a while, they agree that something is funny.

"No, Alemán has nothing to do with the war. Those are others, the alemanes of Europe," my father clarifies as he takes off his slippers, pulls on his white socks, and steps into the two-tone wing-tip shoes on the floor next to his armchair.

I race to the bathroom to wash my face and get ready to see someone who's dying and who's my father's boss.

Enedina has left food in the fridge for dinner, but my mother, who doesn't want the house filled with the smell of re-heated food, gets up, goes to the kitchen, and comes back with a plate of ham and cheese. She sets the plate on the dining room table and eats with great appetite, rare in her. As my father and I are about to go out the door, she asks: "Do you want me to make you a bite?"

"No. I'll eat later," I say. Meeting my father's boss is much more important.

ALEMÁN'S MANSION, built around an interior courtyard, has two floors. My father tells me that in colonial times, the old family lived on the top floor and the servants, or slaves in earlier times, lived on the ground floor. But since the injustice of owning slaves no longer exists, the small, square, windowless room where slaves were punished first by flogging while they were chained to the wall, then by being fed only bread and water, now serves as a cellar for the wines that Alemán imports in large quantities from France. As we climb the stairs, my father informs me that the rooms on the upper floor are full of tapestries and elegant Louis XV furniture upholstered with luxurious pink brocades woven with gold threads in artistic floral designs, as well as fine glass cabinets full of Alemán's collection of Sèvres and Limoges porcelain, Baccarat crystal, and Meissen statuettes representing nobles and shepherdesses of the time of Louis XVI.

We go out to the inner balcony. The minister seems young, energetic, clean-shaven without a mustache, tanned by the sun, and very healthy. He wears the obliga-tory white linen suit of politicians, white shirt, and blue silk tie, as well as two-tone shoes, but with black tips. The near-black circles under his eyes and the peaks of black hair growing in on both sides of his forehead make him look a bit like the devil, and really alarm me.

Downstairs in the patio, his bodyguards, or "incompetent flunkies," as my mother calls them, are playing dominoes.

Smiling, Alemán asks my father, "What present can I give you, Augusto?"

"I don't ever accept gifts, Doctor. I don't want to be denounced in the press as a corrupt official. All I want is for you to take care of your health. The country needs you," my father replies sincerely. My father leans over to look at him more closely be-cause, although higher in rank, Alemán is much shorter.

Alemán laughs good humoredly, but there's pain in that laughter. "What a jokester you are, Augusto!" the minister exclaims. "This country doesn't need anyone, much less a politician like me. What do you want from me? Ingots of solid gold? A Cadillac? A furnished penthouse in the elegant part of the Vedado? An exclusive man-sion on Caguama Beach? A sugar plantation with a mill? A junket to India to visit the Taj Mahal? How about a pony for the little girl?"

My father turns fiery red.

His white trousers seem to get bigger and his light-brown leather belt rolls up and embeds itself in his premature pot belly. My father is no longer skinny.

"Don't be absurd, Alemán! I'm not an ass-kisser. Give it to your hangers-on down there!"

Alemán doesn't skip a beat, reaches for the crocodile-skin wallet in his back pocket, and pulls out the entire wad of high-denomination banknotes. "Here's your gift from Santi Clos, boys! Here's sweets enough for everyone, as President Grau says!" the minister shouts, flinging the bills over the balustrade.

The courtyard fills with the dead leaves of Republican pesos. The hangers-on noisily push and climb over each other like beasts in heat, punching and kicking as they grab at the bills. Alemán runs into one of the rooms, carries out more piles of money on a silver tray, tosses the bills from the balcony as if releasing pigeons. The free-for-all's screaming, punching, and kicking escalate.

"Throwing money away like it's straw! Not even Caligula dreamed of anything like this!" my father exclaims as he contemplates the crass spectacle.

"Not even Nero, Augusto," Alemán replies, excitedly. "I don't need to burn down the city. All I must do is toss out a little of the money I have too much of, and voilà, your Circus Maximus!" I lean over the balustrade of the balcony to see the melee produced by greed. The boss and his lieutenant, with the majesty of Roman emperors, coolly look down on the mob.

Suddenly, a shadow crosses my father's face. "Doctor, again, I must tell you to take care of yourself. You should be in bed at this hour."

The minister waves his hand with annoyance and enters one of the rooms that open on the balcony overlooking the courtyard, where the men continue stuffing their pockets with paper money. Nauseated by the men's greed, I follow my father, who's gone inside with his boss.

As we leave, I ask my father, "Why wouldn't you accept a gift?"

"Because 'he who bows a lot exposes his butt,'" he replies, and begins to sing a song about beautiful green eyes. "Also, I want to run for the Senate seat he used to have, which he knows, but I can't be indebted to him."

FRIDAY AFTERNOON, my pals and I tire of playing, and we sit on the little wall in front of the Twelfth Avenue building to watch cars go by. We count Oldsmobiles, my father's car, which I think is very elegant.

When we lose count, I want to rest, but Cristín and his brother Ricky want to go roller skating. The problem is, they only have one pair of skates, so they yell up to Andy to lend them his.

Andy comes out on his balcony with the skates in his hands.

"Come get the skates! The one who links bloozes!" Andy yells at them, swapping consonants as he sometimes does.

"Drop them!" Cristín yells back. In my imagination, I see the skates travel through the air and hit me in my scoliotic back.

I tell myself, "No, this can't happen. Those skates can't hit me on my back."

I don't feel any emotion because I think it's all a dream.

In a second, I feel a sharp blow to my spine and everything goes black.

IT'S NIGHT OUTSIDE when the black inside me clears up. I'm eating chicken noodle soup in the dining room. My mother, Andy, and his mother stare at me.

"What's up?" I ask. It's as if I were coming out of a dream.

"Andy threw his skates to you and they hit your back. I could tell it was serious from your sobs and screams when Cristín and Ricky carried you home."

My mother turns to look at Andy's mom. "Mercy never cries. It must be something very terrible for her to scream and cry. We took her to the hospital and they did an X-ray." Looking at me, my mother says, "You don't have a single broken bone. It's as if nothing happened to you. Are you in pain?"

"No. I don't remember screaming, or going to the hospital. I don't have any pain in my back."

"A pair of heavy, four-wheeled iron skates lands on her back and she doesn't even have pain! It's God's miracle!" Andy's mother exclaims.

"Are you sure this happened? I don't remember a thing," I say.

"I made Andy pray for you the whole time, and it worked," Andy's mother tells me quietly. "Remember what happened with that staircase you kids waxed? The people who slipped and fell didn't suffer serious injuries and recovered soon. The pregnant lady who fell didn't have a miscarriage and was able to leave the hospital that very day. That's how powerful children's prayer is."

My mother looks at her with mocking eyes, but doesn't contradict her.

ON SUNDAY, MY MOTHER TAKES ME to the Rex Cinema to forget the incident of the skates. Now that my father makes a lot of money and we've won the lottery, we can go to this movie theater downtown in the Capital and see cartoons with the rich kids – "the spoiled brats," my father calls them. Septimio, now eleven, thinks cartoons are kiddie stuff and never comes with us.

Driven by Seboruco in his own car, which my father hires for our personal use, we cross the Almendares River, as usual full of the tons of red silt that turn the water light brown, or "carmelite," as we Islanders say because the water is the color of that monastic order's habits.

The river is lined with cottages and small docks with sailboats and motor launches tied up. I dream of someday visiting one of these two-story houses, sleeping on the second floor overlooking the river, hearing the water flow by at night through my open window.

I also dream of hoisting sail and escaping out the mouth of the river towards the freedom of the sea.

We pass through the Vedado, a neighborhood of new houses and some grand old houses, all painted and clean, and we continue at full speed until we reach the center of the Capital where the colonial-era buildings are adorned with brightly-colored stained glass windows. Seboruco drops us in front of the cinema and tells us to telephone him to pick us up when the cartoons are over. Under the marquee announcing upcoming attractions, we get in line for the box office, a glass aquarium where an older woman with wrinkled arms and drooping skin spins a roll of red admissions tickets and gives us two.

When we push open the theater's glass door, the chilled air suffuses our throats and noses with an ice-cold sensation. The architectural style of the theater is Art Deco, my mother observes, and everything shines. I savor the intensity of the blue, red, and gold colors, lit by many lights.

I am surprised to see so many children floating in the air for joy, boys in dress shorts and girls in gauzy dresses full of ruffles, all smelling of scented soaps. This spectacle transports me to a paradise of perception involving the bright-red painted lips of mothers and their tinkling gold bracelets, their perfumes composed of musk, lilies, orange blossoms, and gardenias, as well as fathers, freshly-shaved, still showing white traces of soap and talc, and smelling of colognes with lemon, amber, sandalwood, vetiver, and cinnamon ingredients.

Everything comes to a strange visual, auditory, olfactory, and tactile climax when I put my head in the highly polished, silvery metal water fountain, and drink water so cold that it passes through my nose to the top of my head like a painful electric shock.

And opening the fleshy red velvet curtain at the entrance to the auditorium feels like a caress and produces an inexplicable paroxysm of joy in me.

The shadows inside are filled with children and giggles of happy anticipation. We sit comfortably in the plush red seats. After a few minutes, the first of the afternoon program's multicolored cartoons fills the large white screen.

The face of Goofy the dog appears to announce that he will be the star, and all the children cheer.

For the next cartoon, Mickey Mouse's face appears, and the kids in the audience stamp their feet and kick the seat in front of them before settling down to watch the show.

Then, Donald Duck's head emerges against a brilliant blue background. Golden beams radiate from his white feathers and yellow beak, and the children go berserk, making the theater shake with their cheers.

Donald Duck and the resplendent, edible colors of Technicolor make me jump for pleasure in my seat. Donald Duck, for some reason, visits a gold mine. As the gleaming yellow molten metal is poured into molds that transform it into glittering ingots, golden rays with red tongues or spikes radiate outward from the metal and wrap me in a net of sensations that fill my senses to overflowing.

Suddenly, Donald Duck trips and falls into one of the molds and sinks all the way up to his beak, becoming a large ingot.

The children stamp their feet and laugh hysterically.

I jump out of my seat and flee from the excess of this scene, which suddenly seems to me to bode evil. My mother catches up with me at the theater exit. I am grateful to her for not asking me why I ran out of the horror-filled theater, saving me from having to provide a logical explanation.

IT'S ALMOST NIGHT. Even after the long ride home on the last bus from school, my hand feels like it's going to fall off after writing "I must not talk in class" numberless times. I rip off my uniform, put on my overalls, and run to Adela's house.

She's in her garden pruning her rose bushes.

"I have questions," I blurt out. Adela takes off her gardening gloves and leaves them on the grass beside her pruning shears. I follow her to the living room and sit on the couch. Adela pulls one of the armchairs over to sit close to me.

"The other day somebody threw a pair of heavy metal skates from a balcony. They fell on my back and everything went black. When I woke up, I was having a bowl of soup in the dining room. They say I walked all the way home, crying and screaming, helped by Cristín and Ricky. My mother tells me she took me to the hospital, where they X-rayed me. I have no broken bones. I woke up with no pain and don't remember a thing about what happened. How can this be possible?"

Adela smiles. She's wearing one of her white cotton dresses printed with pink and yellow flowers. She looks like an affable aunt with her big, light-blue eyes, her fresh, healthy face, and her benevolent smile.

"What happened before the skates fell?" she asks.

"I saw it in my mind, but I thought it couldn't happen. It felt like a dream."

"Aha!" Adela exclaims, slapping her thigh. "There's your answer. For an instant you accidentally penetrated the true essence of reality. What's the most important thing about dreams?"

"That they are bizarre and meaningless?" I ask doubtfully.

"That they have no consequences!" Adela exclaims. She answers as if this were the most obvious thing in the world.

"But I'm telling you it *wasn't* a dream! It happened! And with tons of witnesses! I'm not imagining things. I am *not* crazy."

"It happened in the continuous dream of reality that is nothing more than a collective dream seen through lenses colored according to one's level of understanding," she explains, speaking slowly, as if to make it easier for me to hold it in my memory. After a long pause, she adds: "And, before you dash away from my house without saying goodbye, I must tell you something. There's going to be a big change in your life. From now on, we will communicate in a place in space created by the minds of many people on the path to enlightenment. It is a cathedral illuminated by the violet flame. Imagine it before bed, and you will be able to enter it. I'll be there to answer all your questions."

"I have a few more questions," I say, rising and walking back and forth.

"What are they? This is the time to ask them," she says in a restful voice, sitting with the palms of her hands facing upward, on her lap.

"How do vowels differ from consonants?"

"Oh, that's easy! They differ in the difficulty of producing sound. Vowels are easier to pronounce than consonants."

"I've always been confused about additions, subtractions, multiplications, and divisions using zero. Zero terrifies me."

"Aha! That's because the Hindus called the zero *sunya*, 'creative void'. They were the first to use it as a symbol and as an idea. You sensed the mystical meaning of zero. But it's wrong to teach arithmetic operations in elementary school using zero to give a product of zero. It's absurd. You must understand its meaning. Without zero, we would have no physics or engineering. It was thanks to Newton and Leibniz, who developed the calculus, that zero was fully understood," she adds after a pause.

"Why are you so understanding towards me?"

"Because I know you have a type of autism, not as severe as other cases, but I recognize it," the woman replies with regret. "One of my grandchildren has it. In the late 1920s, coming back from India, my husband and I went to Moscow.

"There, we met an extraordinary psychiatrist, Dr. Grunya Efimovna Sukhareva – not, by the way, a Communist, but so good they let her alone – who identified and described this range of mental development problem that make communicating and relationships with others very trying for some children.

"Above all, she demonstrated that they happen in girls, not just boys. Also, that it's not insanity – not in the least."

I don't want Adela pointing out my problems anymore. It scares me.

"Besides, I know you're not from here," Adela continues, smiling and ignoring my grunt of dismay. "You're from another galaxy. There are only twelve places with intelligent life, like ours, throughout the galaxy and I know the vibration of their inhabitants. I don't know your vibration."

"Why do I always want to punch kids who disrespect me?"

"You're a warrior! You are a *kshatriya*, as the Hindus call you. Your lama, or spiritual master, will also be a warrior. You've had many incarnations as a warrior, and you've killed a lot of people because you had a great fascination for seeing bloodshed. Now, that's only manifested in your predilection for the color red."

"Have I really killed lots of people?" I ask, horrified.

"Don't worry. Everything has been paid for. From time immemorial, all living beings have been our mother several times, so we must value them very much, keep them from suffering, and make them happy."

She adds: "The best way to help them is by enlightening ourselves."

"How can I lighten up?"

She laughs gently. "Become '*en*lightened.' You will receive initiations, teachings, and methods, but for now, you must say, in a low voice and as many times as you can, the mantra of Chenrezig, the Buddha of Compassion: *Om, Mani, Padme, Hung*. 'Mantras' are words or phrases, sound vibrations, which summon different Buddhas and protective energies of the mind. They all produce benefits, but the benefits of saying this mantra even once are so many that even the omniscient Buddhas cannot know them.

"Also," she adds as a serious warning, "you should endeavor to be very alert all the time, and pay very close attention to everything you think, say, or do."

20

THE MOVE TO ORFILA

AS THE BALDOR SCHOOL BUS limps up the small hill, Rigoberto, the driver, shifts into first with a gearstick that looks like a tall, thin, red-headed mushroom dressed in a white knit baby bootie. The vehicle lurches to a stop not even close to the front of my new house. Rigoberto has never seen my house, so I tell him it's the one with the red tile roof and the black lanterns but it's okay for him to leave me right where he's stopped the bus. He moves the handle at his right, causing the bus door to screech open like a cat howling. I hop off the bus's step, navy blue with its center unpainted and silvery, polished by the friction of many jumps and scarred by the scrapes of many shoes. From the sidewalk, I stare up as the bus door closes. Behind the iron rods in the windows, the children have stopped paying attention to me. Now they laugh and smack one another on the head, or turn around to tell jokes to the kids sitting behind them.

Today we moved to the Orfila quarter and into our brand-new Spanish-style house, which, my father has, finally and at great expense, decorated and furnished.

I didn't say goodbye to anyone in Almendares, but that hasn't bothered me the way it did when I moved from La Sierra to Almendares. Leaving is worse if you say goodbye. My friends and the old apartment have disappeared in the distance, vaporizing behind the clouds that get lost behind the rooftops at the end of Columbia Avenue. Only Adela remains in my memory, in the cathedral illuminated by violet light, where I may or may not be able to find her before I fall asleep.

In our last conversation, I asked her, "What should I do in the future?" She answered: "Create the maximum freedom for the greatest number of people of the most distant future. And always tell the truth. If you do so, your word will create the reality. Hear the voice that speaks within you: it is the voice of your inner being. In the future, you will be given the keys of the spiritual world. They will reveal mysteries to you . . ."

"What is the secret of existence?" I asked to keep her away from the personal.

But Adela gestured with her head, indicating that everything is related, that the personal and all of existence are intimately related. "The subject, object, and action are parts of a single whole and at the same time interdependent," was the last thing she revealed to me. As she predicted I would do, full of fear at hearing her strange words, I ran out of her house without saying goodbye.

FOR THE FIRST TIME, I enter a house that is our very own. We won't pay rent every month. The rent collector won't be showing up his little checkerboard shirt, wiping the sweat from his neck with his wadded-up handkerchief. This house is forever, like a barge that one boards to float down a river until it reaches the sea and never touches land again.

Today doesn't seem like yesterday. Yesterday I was sleeping in an apartment and today I'll be sleeping in a house. The eternal house that does not need to be paid for, which is our own and is paid off. My father has had a lot of luck with money, and earns enough to lay out fifteen thousand pesos without blinking. Neighbors will see me grow up and the neighborhood children will be my friends for life.

Facing us is the white mansion of Ansola, the Minister of Commerce, with its elegant, paved, horseshoe-shaped driveway that's wide enough for cars to pass each other, and gardens that adorn an esplanade and end almost at the front door. There, I imagine, this minister of commerce markets the Island's products to foreigners. He's a merchant on a grand scale. That's how he takes care of the country. He doesn't need to have a store like little people. I imagine that all the furnishings in his home have price tags, in case any foreign minister wants to buy them. Almost certainly his patio is full of sacks of sugar, for the same reason.

In the garden, Willy, Minister Ansola's son, is playing catch with their uniformed chauffeur. My father, who's been going over to our new house for months to check up on the changes he thought were needed, has told me that Willy is a spoiled brat and is never allowed out of the house. The new houses and their inhabitants mean nothing to me. I haven't seen any kids yet, apart from Willy, but I'm over seven years old, and I know that at least *some* kids must be allowed to play in the street.

I push on our silver gate that still smells of paint and enter our garden, planted with areca palms, decorative ground cover, and bougainvillea. The porch, the red-and-white wooden armchairs, the white table of the same material in the center, and the red tile floor, all welcome me. On opening our front door, which is not locked, I'm facing an archway in front of a hallway. The wall over the arch is adorned with a picture of the Heart of Jesus and, below, a square white flag with a triangle of red silk in the center: the symbol of Changó. The two religions of the house: Catholic and Yoruba.

My mother says she's Catholic, in her way, and believes in religious images.

My father, although so white that he looks like a newly-arrived Spaniard, believes in the African religion of Blacks because they are the ones who make up his political base and were his childhood friends in the poor people's neighborhood of Jesús María where he grew up.

The new living room has influence from Doctor Alemán's house: furniture upholstered in a pink brocade woven with gold threads in floral designs, an Art Deco table of mahogany carved in the shape of a kidney and protected by a glass top, and, as a centerpiece, a pink crystal ball.

This is filled with sand that anchors long, dry stalks with yellowish plumes. Also on this table is a tinted photo of me, smiling without an incisor.

In the hallway, a small staircase leads up to my brother's room over the garage. He even has his own bathroom up there. I share the first bedroom with my mother. My father's is the more spacious second bedroom, and the three of us share the bathroom in the middle.

My parents have come to yet another agreement not to sleep together.

The entrance hall ends in the large dining room, full of Spanish furniture, its dark wood carved into faces of conquerors wearing pointy helmets. To the rear on the left, there's the kitchen, and, at the end of the hall, a door leads to a rectangular patio, with a strip of gardening soil ready for me to plant my vegetables and flowers.

The patio is enclosed by a yellow wall a little taller than I am. From there I can study the two-story house next door, which has a large garden with not a single plant growing in it. "Can this possibly be a house inhabited by children?" I wonder with curiosity, but without anguish.

There's a crackle of a pan frying something in oil, and the breeze brings the aroma of foods heavily seasoned with garlic. There's the distant sound of radios along with racket from kitchens and dining rooms.

Despite these noises and smells made by living beings, I can't see any of them.

I go back inside the house and head to the bathroom to take a shower. I want to remove the memories of the other house, which stick to my skin like dirt. After a while, I'm lying down and ready to fall asleep, and the horn of a distant train wounds my ears. I imagine the bright rectangular windows of the passenger cars steaking by like flares in the blackness of the hot night. Inside those cars, clowns in red, blue, and green wigs hold multicolored balloons in their white-gloved hands.

SATURDAY, BEFORE SEVEN O'CLOCK in the morning, I'm already out on the street of our new neighborhood. The areca palms in the garden of my house, heavy with dew, move their fronds with the gentle breeze of sunrise.

Our old apartment has been locked in a box and set in the attic of my memory. Somehow, I think it's healthy that the past can be erased in this immediate way. Just by putting a little distance between us, apartment and neighbors of Almendares disappear, along with all the problems they created, such as Aurelita's intrigues; Cristín's and Ricky's mother's forbidding them from inviting Zaro to their children's parties just because he is Black and the son of a laundress; the refusal of boys to play with Cristín, Ricky, and Dieguín because they are rumored to be fairies; the taunts of the Paredes de Miranda girl; the gossip about her that Rina, her maid, passes on to us. You can't go back, and if you carry forward doing good the way I tried with Andy, you are in danger of going down the Road to Hell, according to my mother.

Life may be like that: a mountain of boxes where people, houses, and events of the past, good or bad, are put in storage. In this way we are cleansed, purified, so that we can receive the future when it turns into the present. Now the street of the new house glows under an anemic sun hidden behind a screen of clouds, and the air smells of pavement, of new masonry. There are no empty lots full of weeds here, no butterflies jumping from flower to flower, no Pathway of Death full of chicken bones and bare skeletons of fish. Nor do black vultures circle in the sky like finger rings under the white of the clouds, whenever they smell a dead dog lying on the grass, its teeth bleeding, its lips deformed by a sardonic smile.

At this moment in my life, I dream that a ship will take me to the Future and deposit me there, without my having to make the slightest effort. I merely need to wake up and go to sleep, get dressed and go to school, link the ideas that my head stirs up, array them single file and capture them like butterflies –stealthily – when they fold their wings up and cover their legs, wings, and proboscises with pollen. Then, put these ideas in a box, a display case, sort them according to size and color, organize them, judge their importance.

I can't hunt real butterflies anymore, after Adela told me they felt pain just as I do. Ideas don't feel pain.

I don't want to ride my bike because it would destroy the thrill of this moment: an exploration on foot of the territory. There would be something immoral about introducing speed, whipping by these houses that I have not yet carefully studied. Walking will let me see, at a measured pace, these people who do not yet have faces, who might be dangerous or mocking, and who, perhaps already, are spying on my every movement through their almost-closed Venetian blinds, judging who I am and whether I have any right to invade their lives. or walk in front of their houses. Or push them around, to make room for me.

Almost no one's on the street at this hour – just a few adults going up and down the steep sidewalk in front of my house and disappearing down streets and avenues. Continuing uphill on the sidewalk where my house is, there is a two-story house painted green that stretches out into a large porch and, above it, a large balcony. I imagine that's where the King of the Block lives, and that he would speak to his subjects from that wide balcony.

Following my mother's fantasy, maybe he's Louis XIV.

The next house, to the left, has only one story, painted blue with a porch that has brick columns painted pink and light blue. On that porch, lying down on a cot, there's a boy who looks like a conehead, like those statues on Easter Island but pale, with amber eyes and hair, and covered in freckles. One of his legs looks way too wide. Maybe he's one of Louis XIV's victims, recovering from a bout of torture in the Bastille.

The child wears blue-and-white striped pajamas, the right pants-leg cut open to make room for his real leg, encased in a plaster cast. An open checkerboard sits atop the plaster cast, and the child is fully focused on playing against himself, stretched out like a tame animal on the white sheet, with his upper body sitting up because the cot is adjustable, thanks to a crank that raise and lowers the head.

I'm a little disturbed by this boy's face. It's white as a frog's belly, splashed with freckles. His open pajama top reveals his scrawny chest and protruding ribs. The plaster cast is full of words of encouragement written in ink. The stiff cotton mesh matrix that sprouts from the plaster looks like white eyelashes at his groin and foot. So absorbed is this child that, like the Chinese emperor with the mechanical nightingale, he doesn't notice when I sit down, very quietly, at the foot of his bed. I move a red checker, and his startled jump almost sends the board flying.

I introduce myself as Cardinal Mazarin, and the child smiles.

"My name is Tito," he announces simply.

"Do you like to play alone?" Tito moves his head negatively like a bell. His cats' eyes darken, and suddenly his face seems to be filled with humiliations and rejections, the acts of the past multiplying around him, like Furies yanking his hair.

"No. It's just that no one wants to play with me," he replies, lowering his head weeping, and looking at the board. What am I seeing? A boy crying? This makes me want to smack him, but it's against my code to hit a cripple.

"How did you mess up your paw?" I ask lightly to cut the drama.

"Oh, that was long ago! I was jumping with Kit. I slipped and hit a wall."

The shadow on this porch has a pleasant odor. Outside, the sun is going down spinning, splashing, dripping off the roofs of houses, jumping over silvered gates, beating the dust from the leaves, making them jump in the sharp glow of its rays. But here in this portal, the shadow dallies, like a mother who cares and cradles as a consolation for a person's being handicapped.

There is order inside this house. I can see it and smell it through the porch window. I breathe the pine scent of the spotless floors and know that on the wood of the furniture my fingers would glide over the wax like velvet. I sense that the father and mother are responsible people, and that their house is well run.

I inhale this normality like a perfume. "Who's Kit?" I ask.

"My older brother. He's very strong, and very good at sports. He's nine years old and he's in fifth grade!" he says, smiling proudly.

What a pain to have a brother in fifth grade! My brother is in sixth and I'm in second grade, so I know the separation, and sometimes hostility, that this can cause. But Tito seems to admire his brother just because he is in fifth grade. As he speaks, his eyes glow and his face stops having the beaten-dog look that seems natural to him. Tito uses the emaciated bone of his jaw to catch the collar of his striped pajama top with his chin and laughs as he bangs the checkerboard with the black checker in his hand.

"What's so funny? Why are you laughing?" I ask him, upset.

"I'm laughing because I was going to ask you to play checkers, but of course ladies – *damas!* – must know how to play checkers – *damas!*" Now he laughs with great guffaws, showing his teeth, pointed as an organ grinder's monkey's. Is he crazy? It's odd to have a pajama leg cut off, and to be lying on a cot at seven in the morning, playing checkers by yourself. Maybe he has a screw or two loose – "bats in the belfry," as my mother would say.

"Since you're a lady, you should know how to play," he repeats seriously, trying to restore order.

"Lady?" I ask, looking down at my brown corduroy pants. Am I wearing a ball gown? What's the story on this nut? I'm a *girl*, not a lady. "Hey!" I exclaim, whacking the cast on his leg to be more dramatic. "I'm a champion of damas/checkers, not because I'm a lady, but because I learned how to play when I was this tall!"

I lower my open palm to almost touching the ground. To my surprise, Tito tosses the black checker on the board, backhands the other pieces, scattering them everywhere, and falls back on his cot, bursting into sobs. Tears stream down his milky cheeks, between his freckles.

An older boy appears at the door banging his chest with his fists clenched and shouting, "Sanmangariiiiii!" –Tarzan's cry. As broad-chested as Super Mouse under his white cotton T-shirt, this boy wears khaki pants like me, but he has a black belt with a gold buckle. His almost round face shows indentations in both cheeks that old ladies call dimples. His black locks fall on his high, somewhat protruding forehead, his eyes are like black balls and very bright. His body projects adventure, the image of explorer, Magellan circling the world, James Cook exploring New Zealand, Vasco Núñez de Balboa discovering the Pacific. He demonstrates the whiteness of his incisors and canine teeth in a threatening animal smile, which is almost a challenge. I stand up to better resist his thrust. He's my height, but older and much stronger. His developed biceps bulge under his shirt like a sign saying "Stop. You better mess with someone else."

"This is Kit," says Tito, unnecessarily.

"Tarzan, King of the Apes!" Kit shouts, leaping and landing on the blue tile floor.

"And this is Jane," Kit adds, dragging a girl by the hair out of the shadows behind him. Later, she tells me her name is Ofelia, and she is their sister. She, too, has a round face, but with brown eyes and brown hair. The girl wears a white cotton dress with blue flowers of the same color as the tiles.

"And who am I?" I ask, guessing I'm somehow in the film he is cooking up.

"You are ... Cheetah the Monkey!"

He collapses laughing, as does Ofelia/Jane.

Tito is crying loudly and banging a checker on the game board.

This is my moment. If I let this insult pass, there will be a chain reaction. The humiliations will multiply and become increasingly cruel. Kit really will be King of the Jungle, and I will need to keep my mouth shut, defer, cry like Tito, hate the world, open a hole in the ground, sink into it and never come out.

"Your mother, faggot!" I yell at him, stomping on his right foot with all my might. Kit grabs his foot with his hands and hops around on his left leg, his eyes bloodshot with pain and rage. I turn my back on him and sit on Tito's cot.

Turning your back is a gesture I've learned from cowboy movies, where the best gunman turns his back on the enemy, knowing that at any moment he can be shot through the lung. It's essential to make this gesture of contempt, because it puts things in perspective, establishes differences, clarifies doubts, reduces the enemy to dust. No matter what Kit decides to do, turning my back on him is a gesture of supreme grace, though it could end up being a joke I tell with my head on the executioner's block.

At least Tito has stopped crying. I am no longer a toy that he defends with tears, but a possible ally. I feel the vibration of the ridiculousness of the instant, the theater of my actions.

Kit disappears inside the house, followed by Ofelia. I don't feel his hatred behind my back. Instead, something begins to clear up, like a day that cuts through the gray clouds and brings out the sun. Tito's eyes are lost on the street, maybe dreaming that someday he will be able to run, roller-skate, or ride a bike. Suddenly he grabs my hands in his, which are as bony as bird claws.

"At night my leg itches and I can't scratch myself, I can't scream, and nobody comes to pull me out of this plaster cast," he says. Then this invalid mysteriously asks, "Have you seen the face of the night?"

"No."

"It's green and never laughs," he whispers as if he were scared. As if he thought an enemy were eavesdropping on him.

From inside the house comes Kit's voice singing, mockingly, with double meaning:

The múcura is on the ground, and mama, I can't handle her.
I bring her up to the head and mama, I can't handle her.
I really can't handle her! Mama, I can't handle her!

VERY EARLY SUNDAY MORNING Tito is not on the porch of his house. Maybe he's still asleep. But the King of the Block is on his balcony. Seen from the sidewalk, the King of the Block is smaller than I imagined, with very white skin, brown eyes, and light brown hair. Through the balustrade I can see that he's wearing a white short-sleeved shirt with red checkers and navy shorts. He gives the impression of being very clean and careful with his clothes. "Why don't you come down?" I yell to him from the sidewalk.

He replies in a loud, squeaky voice: "They don't let me play in the street. Why don't you come up?" I don't need any more encouragement and I run up the stairs, taking the steps two at a time. The boy, named Dick, opens the door himself.

I am disillusioned to find that he is shorter than I am, and moves with delicate girlie gestures as he takes me to the terrace where he has a Parcheesi board open on the floor. I think he, like Tito, must mostly play against himself.

"Why aren't you allowed to play in the street?" I ask, as if I've known him forever.

"My mom says children are full of germs, which would give me diseases. Also, they could punch me."

"What if you get sick *and* get punched? Haven't you ever punched anyone? Haven't you even climbed a tree?"

"No . . ." Dick replies in a fearful voice. I show him my knees full of scars.

"I've fallen many times and been in fights, but I haven't died. Does your mom think you're made of glass?" I ask.

That's when I realize that the mother is standing behind us, watching us.

She is energetic in appearance, tall, well-built, blond with metallic blue eyes.

She asks curtly, "Are you the girl who just moved in?"

"Yes."

"You're welcome to come and play with Dick. He may *not* go down and play in the street. I do not want him mixing with the boys here, who are really violent."

The mother says all this in an unpleasant, authoritarian way, reminding me of the despotic tone in general use at my grandmother's house. Dick listens sitting on the ground, passive, his face well-washed and placid. I'm sitting in front of him, with the Parcheesi board between us. I am suddenly infuriated by this child's lack of freedom. As soon as his mother is back inside the house, leaving us alone on the terrace, I say, "You are a man, and you need to get stronger. You must be able to handle other boys. You can't be alone on this balcony all the time like an invalid." To emphasize my words, I punch him in the shoulder, which another male would have taken as a gesture of camaraderie, but which he receives as a sign of hostility.

"I don't want to fight! I don't like fighting!" he confesses, sobbing.

It occurs to me that I have moved to the block of crybabies and cowards, none of whom respect the masculine code I follow.

However, Dick makes me think, for the first time, that maybe those rules are stupid. In fact, where is it written that boys must beat each other up?

"Why don't you like to fight?" I ask, curious.

"Because they could hurt me."

"Well then, how are you going to defend yourself?"

"By not getting into fights. I don't want to get into fights. That's why I don't go down to the street, so I don't get into fights," he says in a very thin voice.

I look at him with pity. He's missing out on childhood because of this protectiveness. His house is a prison. And yet, I'm torn, because a part of me thinks he may be right not to want to fight, and I should imitate him. Of course, life is more pleasant if we don't hit other people, and those other people don't hit us back. But that's also more boring. I decide to play Parcheesi with the King of the Block and not waste any more time debating about violence and freedom.

During the game, I notice that Dick, King of the Block, concentrates hard on the dice because he wants to win. This makes me want to laugh out loud, because I know what he doesn't: if you want the dice to obey your thought, you cannot concentrate like that. There can't be any tension in your mind.

I feel for this crybaby, who does not speak or respond to my attempts to engage in conversation, and I drift into a relaxed state of mind, willing him to win.

In the end, of course, Dick wins. I think there's very little salt in the grinder, as my mother says, because he doesn't know how to disguise his joy with elegant detachment, as is my style, but boasts of his triumph and calls himself a genius.

"This is a game of chance, Dick. Intelligence has nothing to do with it. Give thanks to luck." When I say this, I get up and go to the door to leave.

His mother, behind my back, says to me in a greedy voice: "Come play with Dick every day. I want him to win at Parcheesi all the time."

21

PROTESTANT CABBAGE AND THE GREAT BEYOND

WHEN I GET READY TO GO TO SLEEP, I remember Adela's words. I try to visualize an ancient cathedral with spires and ribbed vaults. I enter without paying attention to the details of the façade and find myself surrounded by great darkness. A small amount of colorful light comes in, tinted by the numerous stained-glass windows. I hear a choir singing music that fills the cathedral. My eyes gradually adjust to this medieval interior. Adela is coming towards me, garbed in a white tunic.

"I see you didn't doubt," she says, well pleased. "Not everyone believes they can discover this cathedral, and very few find their way here."

"How is it possible that reality is a dream?" I ask her.

"It's a collective dream," Adela explains calmly. "Of course, the consequences of your acts are very real. If you stick your hand in fire, you'll burn yourself, but if you've really grasped the mental nature of reality, you can manipulate the laws of the physical world at will. The great masters, the enlightened, have limitless powers."

"Am I also a dream?" I ask, mistrustingly.

"Your ego is. The mind is not, but the mind is not individual. Everything is mind. I use the word 'mind' not for 'the brain,' but for what's inside you, what sees through your eyes, and hears with your ears."

Listening to these words, I fall asleep and dream of the Lone Ranger riding into the desert, shouting "Hi Ho, Silver, away!" to his pure white horse.

NOW THAT I LIVE in the Orfila neighborhood, which is a long way from the Baldor School compared to our Almendares apartment, for an entire week I am the last to be dropped off by the school bus. This means that, by the time I get home, it's dark. Of course, that's because every day I have hours of detention for speaking out in class. When I arrive on Friday night, my parents are sitting in the living room, waiting for me.

"Now do you understand? The child arrives home from school so late she doesn't even have time to do homework!" my mother complains.

"I can't send my driver to pick her up. He always needs to be available for Ministry matters," my father says apologetically.

"Yes, I know. I'm not asking you to do that," my mother clarifies.

The two of them stand up and follow me to my room, where I take off my school uniform and put on a short-sleeved white cotton shirt and khaki overalls. My father and mother continue talking, keeping their eyes on me, as if seeing me inspires them to develop the ideas they're expressing.

"She needs to go to a different school," my mother decides. "I'm told the Buenavista School is nearby and she can even ride there on her bike. It's a Protestant school, but the girl isn't a fanatic Catholic, or even very religious."

"I don't want to change religions!" I shout, annoyed.

"Oh, hush, girl! Protestants are Christian, too!" says my exasperated mother.

"They are heretics." Sticking his head in when he hears the argument, my brother contradicts her with a mocking smile on his lips.

"That doesn't matter, they believe in Christ Jesus. They're not Hindus, or Buddhists, or Mohammedans," my mother protests.

"Protestants are *so* the same that Catholics killed thousands and thousands of them on St. Bartholomew's Eve," Septimio ironizes.

Even my father shakes his head, as if it will take more to convince him that I must go to Buenavista. I think my mother is deliberately dragging him out of his important political problems, forcing his brain to change gears, as if he were a car. "You might want to consider that the girl has friends at Baldor and it could be traumatic for her to start at a new school not knowing a soul, let alone when classes have already started," he says.

"The girl made friends here right away. Why wouldn't she do that at school? She cannot keep coming home after dark. This can't continue!" My parents go to the living room to continue discussing the matter, but I know they are going to change schools on me, because once my mother gets an idea in her head, that's that.

I don't like changing religions. I don't know what Protestants are like, and it's been drummed into my head in Catholic religion classes that it's a mortal sin to consort with heretics and expose yourself to their heresies. What can I do? Maybe I can ask Baldor's religion teacher for help, but I know she'll tell me she can't oppose the will of my parents. That's what they always say, because it's the parents who pay.

My brother looks at me from the door with laughing eyes and I decide to ask him: "What are Protestants like?"

"They don't believe in the Virgin Mary or the Pope's authority, and they don't permit images in their churches," he replies in a serious voice and without his usual malicious look, so I don't think he's misleading me now.

He leaves, maybe to keep me from asking him more questions.

I plop down in bed, disheartened. It's bad enough having to make new friends in the neighborhood, without being forced to do the same thing at school.

The first few days in any school are always unpleasant, but they're the worst when you start late and have a different religion. The only thing that comforts me is that I won't need to complete the hours of punishment I have accumulated at Baldor, which by now will take me until I get old and gray. I imagine myself wrinkled and white-haired, sitting at my desk, writing a thousand times in my notebook: "I must not speak out of turn in class. I must pay attention to the teacher."

At last, with joy, it dawns on me: I'll have a clean slate, a new account.

My mother comes in, triumphant. "It's all decided! Tomorrow I'm going to Buenavista to enroll you, and I hope you can start as soon as possible. Your cousins Titi and Toni go there, and you can talk to them for the first few days so you don't feel alone."

"I don't want to change religions!" I insist.

What really upsets me is that my cousins Titi and Toni are the daughters of my father's brother the dentist, a disapproving witness at my grandmother's house in La Víbora when I threw up pigeon soup consisting of beautiful doves that I thought had been given to me to be pets.

"At first it'll be hard for you to adapt, but you'll get used to it," says my mother, impassive. And with these words she leaves the room again, removing my Today, leaving me alone to face yet another Unknown Tomorrow. I go to my father's room to find the book of biographies of famous men, and again read about Napoleon's terrible childhood, which always makes me feel better at times like these.

IT INTRIGUES ME that the two children who live in the house on the corner of Avenida de Columbia always play by themselves on their porch, and never go out on the street. I decide to visit them, to see if they must set themselves apart because they have an authoritarian mother, like the King of the Block, or because they think they're better than everybody else.

Materializing at the entrance to their porch, I say: "Hi! I'm the new girl on the block. My name is Mercy. What are your names, and what games do you play?"

They sit there, gaping at me. I sense that they have no idea how to respond. Are they slow-witted? Are they shy? What is wrong with the kids in this neighborhood? I, who enjoy my freedom so much, can't bear that these scaredy-cat children haven't the nerve to leave their homes and explore the wonders of the world.

"What a bore!" I exclaim, not imagining that I might offend them.

The girl seems to be about my age, almost eight, and the boy maybe seven. They are sturdy, rather fat children, with white skin, black hair, and black eyes. Not pretty, not ugly, but "of the heap," as the great jokesters at Baldor School would say. Both kids are sitting on the floor in front of a large toy house with no back wall.

After a long pause and in a trembling voice, the boy responds: "My sister's name is Molly. I'm the youngest. My name is The Bebe. We play House."

"What game is that?" I ask, pretending I'm ignorant to force him to speak.

"We play furnishing our house. See these pieces of furniture? Well, we put them inside, and then put these dolls in the rooms," the boy says shyly. Molly shows me the dolls, which can be made to sit on the chairs and the couch by bending their legs. Father, mother, and baby, all made of rubber.

"We entertain ourselves like this," Molly replies, defensively. "My mom doesn't allow us to go outside, so this is how we play."

I decide to go along with the little play-house activity to avoid upsetting them. But, as a game, it is incredibly boring, because it ends as soon as we place the father in the armchair next to the hearth in the living room, the mother making dinner next to the stove in the kitchen, and the baby inside the crib in a room on the second floor.

"Are we going to play this game *again*?" I ask, exasperated.

"What else can we do?" Molly answers, resigned.

"If you have another doll, we can make him a gunman, kidnap the kid, knock the father over the head with a stick, and abuse the mother," I suggest, to animate the game.

"I don't like that game!" The Bebe howls. We end up staring at one another.

I'm beginning to think it's nearly impossible to play with kids who reject action, even if it is imaginary.

"We could make the father win the Lottery and walk to the kitchen to tell the mother, while the child cries in the crib," Molly proposes.

"No! Not the Lottery!" I protest, disgusted, remembering the chaos of reality when my family won.

"What do you suggest, then?" asks Molly equably.

"Why don't we go inside your house and play Hide-and-Seek?"

A moment of stupor goes by while the siblings give each other fearful looks.

Finally, Molly opens the front door to their house and The Bebe and I go inside to hide. My plot is that we are both spies, and that Molly is the head of the secret police hunting us down, because we've stolen the blueprints for an atomic bomb that explodes like bubblegum and sticks everybody together.

Even though the ideas are mine, Molly embraces them with great enthusiasm, as if they were her own.

After the thrill of tension that lasts for quite a while, Molly discovers us and drags us to the police station for questioning. That's when I decide it's time for me to go home, and, without saying bye-bye, I escape through their patio door, which we had opened for fresh air to enter, and abscond over the short wall that surrounds their house.

MY FATHER MAKES ME LATE when he gives me a ride to school in his car because he's been dealing with political problems since dawn.

It's my first day attending Buenavista, the Protestant school. Sitting next to me in the back seat, my father reviews Ministry of Education documents he must deal with.

When we drive up to the school, I jump out of the car without saying goodbye because I can hear they have already started singing and I must run to the chapel. Later I find out that what the whole chapel was singing was Psalm 23:

The Lord is my shepherd: I shall not want. He maketh me to lie down in green pastures: He leadeth me beside the still waters. He restoreth my soul: He leadeth me in the paths of righteousness for His name's sake. Yea, though I walk through the valley of the shadow of death, I will fear no evil: for Thou art with me; Thy rod and Thy staff they comfort me. Thou preparest a table before me in the presence of mine enemies ...

This language moves me deeply. I am prepared to avoid being convinced by Protestants to change religions, but I am totally disarmed to be received on the first day with these words set to music. My hostility lessens. Also, how great is starting the day with singing, rather than classes or litanies! Here, children sing naturally, without putting on their "goodness" faces as in Catholic schools. The altar is very simple, with only a gold cross hanging from the ceiling, and no statues of saints. When I see that the girls aren't wearing veils, I'm relieved. Everything is informal.

After chapel, I go to the second-grade class, the teacher introduces me, and the girls laugh at my last name. I've gotten used to this. I must stand up and correct the teacher's pronunciation, which causes greater hilarity among my classmates. "Cut what? Cut heads?" they ask. I might have wanted to cut these heads full of little curls having so much fun at my expense about an unusual last name that I didn't pick, that's not my fault, and that my cousins Titi and Toni have already unveiled. I decide to ignore their laughter and sit at the desk the teacher points to.

Now I observe that this teacher is short and fat, with short, dark-blond, very curly hair. Just like Baldor's teachers, she has broad hips and bulging buttocks.

Before she turns around to write on the blackboard, I look at her oval face, black eyes, and flat nose that shines with sweat that reminds me of a pig's. There's something silly and violent about this teacher that repels me. Her aggressive, squeaky voice contributes to this negative impression: she speaks by shrieking.

Soon I can see that the class is working on some types of arithmetic problems that we had already studied at Baldor. I whisper this to the student next to me.

Without missing a beat, the chubby, dark-blue-eyed girl stands up and says: "Miss, the new girl says that what we're learning she already studied at her old school."

With malice, the teacher smiles and says, "Well, if you've already learned what we're doing, then come to the board and show all of us how to solve these problems."

I have no choice but to go to the board. The eyes of the entire class are on me. The blood buzzes in my ears and I can't think. My mind has gone blank. I try to do some additions and subtractions that I then erase. The minutes stretch out endlessly. I feel the looks of all the girls on my back as if they were flames. At last, to end this shameful situation, I confess: "Sorry, I can't remember how to solve them."

"Ah, you *can't* remember? Then you didn't learn well, did you? What you *can* do, then, is get back to your seat, shut up, and learn well, for once and for all!" the teacher shouts in a victorious voice, amid the laughter of the whole class.

I take my seat, upset, humiliated, and furious with the girl who gave me away, and who looks at me now with a satisfied expression, as if I had received my just desserts thanks to her. This incident reveals to me on the first day the personalities of my teacher and of my classmates. From now on, I vow, I will not talk to anyone and will be suspicious of this teacher who, paradoxically, is called Love.

I'M A DAY STUDENT AT THE SCHOOL, meaning I stay at noon for lunch. I'm glad my parents didn't place me as a boarder to get rid of me. I imagine the sadness of the girls who are boarders and must live at the school, as if they were orphans, because I remember the pain I felt when my brother lied and told me I was adopted. For these girls, school becomes a prison. At least my prison is partial.

At the end of the morning classes, I walk through the central courtyard of the school to wait for the bell that calls us to the cafeteria for lunch.

After the tattle-tale episode, I reaffirm my pledge not to try to befriend anyone and, alone, sit on the swing and rock, listening to the piano that comes from the music room, which has the only class that continues through lunchtime. From the swing I can see girls gathering in small groups. They talk in loud voices and occasionally laugh.

My cousin Titi, in a group of big girls, comes over to me. I'm afraid she'll scold me for being alone and send me to play with girls my age.

But Titi's not interested in my isolation.

"Do you have a peseta to buy a soda and a chocolate bonbon? I left my money at home." She asks me this in a friendly tone, standing right next to me. I see seriousness in her black eyes. She is very tall, and has sun-toasted skin and long, straight black hair, with bangs. She's thirteen or fourteen.

I think for a moment and consider that I owe her a favor.

Recently she pulled me out of the water at the Yacht Club beach when her brother Papón, who is the same age as me, seven, but weighs three times as much, sat on my back while I was snorkeling. There was no way I could get to the surface with that fat hulk on top of me. Within seconds, the sea water turned bright green with stars, and the hum of water in my ears became distant music of flutes and violins. I was drowning, yet my inability to breathe made me very calm, at peace, as if winged creatures were carrying me. The light became more intense, the music more melodious, and I felt great joy that I was about to be able to fly.

At that moment, Titi pulled me out of the water and tore into Papón for trying to drown me. I was mad at Titi, though I didn't show it, for plucking me out of the happiness I'd felt on the sea floor. Then I realized that she'd done me a favor. Now, when Titi asks me for a peso, I feel I owe her my life and must give her what she asks for. I take the coin out of my uniform pocket and put it in her hand. Titi smiles, surprised, as if she expected me to be flat broke.

"Say, thanks!"

I don't answer and keep floating on the swing until the lunch bell rings.

I have no idea where the dining room is, but follow the other girls thinking that's where they must be going. This is confirmed by the smell of boiled cabbage, which intensifies as we approach the dining room. This odor is very exotic to me because in my house they cook Creole food such as chicken and rice, black beans, picadillo, meat-and-potatoes. This meal involving cabbage is from the United States. The menu of the day is roast beef, mashed potatoes, and boiled cabbage.

I sit at the table that I'm told to, and the big girl who presides must serve me because suddenly I'm stunned by the memory of almost drowning, and I don't know what to do with my hands. The others laugh when the big girl puts the napkin in my lap, but since I don't know any of these girls, I don't care.

The food is tasteless and I miss the delicious seasoning of Toñita, our mulatta cook and our distant relative, descended from one of the Black slaves that my great-great-grandfather had on his cane plantation.

My great-great-grandfather, who was his wife's first cousin and who had to go to Rome to ask the Pope for a dispensation so they could get married, after years fell in love with this beautiful slave and had many children by her. The children swore revenge on the white side of the family, which was never willing to recognize them as relatives. One family story said my great-great-grandmother had died of chagrin from her husband's infidelity, and another said her death was caused by the slave, who was a *santera* and used witchcraft to murder her rival. My Aunt Bella says that every time there's been a misfortune in our family, a descendant of that slave woman has been working in the house of someone on the "white" side of the family tree.

All this seems to me the stuff of radio soap operas. I treat our cook, my relative, normally, which means as an equal, because it annoys me when I am treated as an inferior.

When I'm almost done eating and bracing myself for a future of lunches with disgusting boiled cabbage, a commotion forms at the adjoining table. The big girl who presides over our table gets up to see what's happened there. A representative of the school's administration arrives to intervene and restore order.

When the big girl comes back to our table, I ask her what caused the furor. "A little girl brought in a pressure cooker and said that from now on we had to steam the cabbage with vinegar and capers or fry it, instead of boiling it, or she'd change schools."

I think that's absurd, but I laugh because it's a protest. That takes courage.

DAYS LATER, Titi again comes to ask me for money when she sees me flying back and forth on the school swing, waiting for lunch. She gives me the same story: she forgot her lunch money. I'm pretty sure she's taking me for a ride again, and I tell her I don't have it, looking her dead in the eye.

In my opinion, it's not immoral to lie to a liar.

Titi leaves without saying anything. I thought she might try to coerce me and I was prepared for all sorts of arguments, from sentimental to menacing. None of this happened, and I ended up with all that adrenaline inside and no fight to use it up on. Bored and with a bitter taste in my mouth caused by Titi's little game,

I get up from the swing and go to the music room to enjoy the piece a student with whom I have made a superficial friendship is practicing for a recital. She gave me all the information: it's the second movement, the "Andante cantabile con espressione" of Mozart's *Piano Sonata No. 8,* K310. I find it intensely dramatic.

It makes me dream of passions I might have as an adult.

When I am most enraptured by this music, two little girls walk down the corridor near me, holding hands and speaking quietly with great enthusiasm. I decide to follow them because this is weird. Usually girls are by themselves, like me, or in groups talking very loudly.

Today, the two little girls duck into the bushes planted inside the large wall that protects the entrance of the school. I think I should report them because it's forbidden to go there, but something stops me. They're younger than me, so I could reprimand them, behave like a "big girl," but that disgusts me. Why shouldn't they be able to hide from others if they like? I hate laws that prevent people from doing things that don't harm others and give them a sense of freedom. I admire these little girls' spirit of independence. When they stand behind a mango tree so they can't be seen from the street and kiss each other on the mouth, I stop looking at them, because I think that's violating their privacy.

The bell calls us to lunch, and I follow the big girls towards the dining room. This time I know how to behave. I even bring a silver napkin ring, inscribed with my initials, to roll up the napkin inside.

The menu consists of the usual dishes, potatoes, cabbage, and meat, but this time the potatoes are boiled. While I'm being served, I turn my face to the left to say, "That's enough, thank you," and feel something strange filtering through my hair, down my scalp, like dirt.

It's grains of salt.

"Are you the person who poured salt on my head?" I ask the girl on my right.

"Me? Good heavens, certainly not!" the girl replies, with theatrical innocence. Her long, white face glows pink, and her eyes, golden with green streaks, reflect the light of fear. She's the only one who could have poured the salt on my hair, yet she denies it. For a few days now I've been finding salt on my head and couldn't imagine how it got there. By dumping so much of it on me all at once, it's clear.

I say nothing, but decide to get even.

As we leave the dining room, the students who belong to the school orchestra gather in the patio where, every Friday, the civic act and the pledge to the national flag take place. The orchestra plays a sappy march by Schubert, the brass being particularly damaging to the ears. The entire piece is played so badly I must ask the pianist what they are playing. As far as patriotism goes, it is ludicrous by comparison with John Philip Sousa's *Stars and Stripes Forever*, played brilliantly at Baldor for the same occasions.

This school hasn't Baldor's military discipline or violent atmosphere, nor does it have the repressive air of nuns' schools. Baldor inspires patriotic heroism with civic observances that pay tribute to the warriors who won independence for our Island. Convent schools create hypocrisy with their sick obsession with sex, expressed even in the way religion is taught.

But this "Protestant" school is disappointing me. What new thing does it offer? On the first day of school, I thought everyone was going to be in meetings critical of Catholics. Because they were Protestants, I assumed their main purpose was to protest. I did notice, after a bit, that there were no religious prohibitions, threats to be sent to hell, derogatory comments about sexual intercourse, or calls to patriotic heroism.

What does this school have? Liberty. I'm not used to this liberty and I feel lost without the straitjackets of the other schools. And yet, something deep inside me responds favorably to this absence of tyranny. This something-inside-me decides not to tattle on the little girls who hide in the patio, and never to accuse anyone of anything. I hate tattle-tales like my brother. Isn't it ironic that in this I'm following the masculine code of conduct? In other words, you ought to die before you rat somebody out, even if it's your cousin who's always asking for money.

As I leave school riding my bike on my way home, I see my mother hiding behind a column at the corner store. I pedal towards her and exclaim in a loud and angry voice: "Don't ever let me catch you spying on me again!"

"It's because you're so little," she explains in a voice full of shame. "You could be kidnapped. If someone tries to pick you up at school, *do not* go with that person. Go only if it's your father or me."

"Nobody's going to kidnap me."

"Put your bike in the trunk of the Dodge and come home with me," she begs.

And there is Seboruco, in his black Dodge that's usually parked in front of our house for my mother to be able to go shopping or do errands or come pick me up.

"No! I'm a Protestant now, and this is my first protest. I'm going on my bike and I'm going all by myself!" My tone is categorical and I pedal away as fast as possible.

THE NEXT DAY, at morning recess, I look for the girl who poured salt on my head. She suspects something when she sees me and runs until I corner her, almost at the school gate. Without a word, I empty on her head the entire contents of a salt shaker I brought from home. The salt courses through her hair and down her face, piling up on the white sailor's collar and black kerchief of the school uniform. To my surprise, the girl starts screaming like she's been hit.

The big girls arrive to march us up to the office of Mrs. Campbell, the school principal, a white-haired American woman of medium height and slightly overweight. However, she has a sharp and energetic face.

Mrs. Campbell turns to the other girl first to ask what happened. The girl presents herself as an innocent victim of cruel aggression. I explain that she's been dumping salt on my head for days, thinking they'll let me go because my action was taken in self-defense.

"When something like this happens, do *not* take matters into your own hands. You must report it to a teacher or to me," the principal says in very American English. "You both are grounded in my office, and will stare at the wall for one hour."

I laugh inside because I know that reporting things to a teacher or to the principal never solves a thing. Also, I find the punishment ridiculous. At Baldor I would have been sentenced to an hour a day for an entire month for something like this, regardless of whether I'd been the instigator of the chain of events.

This punishment is more of a reward because it frees me from the classroom and allows me to spy on the principal, who only speaks English, but since I am way ahead in that language, I find out everything that's going on when teachers come to the principal's office to ask for a new blackboard or a day off for personal needs, but mainly to discuss wayward, unruly, problematic, or underachieving students.

The fourth-grade teacher comes in to make a complaint about Olivia, a student who spends all her time reading in class. I know who she is because she has braces on her legs from polio, and I asked to know her name because she'd caught my eye. Mrs. Campbell suggests to the teacher that she ask Olivia questions in class about the lesson being taught, to embarrass her out of her inattention. I'm surprised she doesn't suggest confiscating the books Olivia reads, as would have happened at the nuns' school, or at Baldor. I remember the day a girl brought a pornographic magazine to Baldor's second-grade class and the teacher confiscated it when she saw us reading it. I was lucky because the teacher first asked Lourdes about it, and Lourdes, an expert liar, said some boy had thrown the magazine from the second floor down to the playground. When I was interrogated, of course I corroborated Lourdes' version because I didn't want to serve hours of punishment until the day of my death for telling the truth. Even so, we were punished by taking away our morning and afternoon recesses for a month.

After the hour, Mrs. Campbell lets us go back to our classes. At the exit of the principal's office, the salt girl looks at me complicitly and smiles. I smile too, and know she'll never dump salt on my head again.

THAT NIGHT I WASH MY HAIR to rid myself of any remaining salt, and, before I fall asleep, I think of Adela and decide to visit the cathedral in my imagination. This time the architectural details are clearer and remind me of pictures of the Cathedral of Toledo that I've seen in *The Treasure of Youth*. I recognize its tower and its apse, as well as the great arch of the main facade. I enter and encounter the primordial darkness of the interior, pierced by iridescent, sea-blue, fire-red, and sun-gold rays of light from a large stained-glass window. The music of two organs thunders against the high vaults of the nave, and from the great censer wafts the heavenly scent of sandalwood.

As my eyes adjust to the gloom, I see Adela in a white robe approaching, and she stops in front of me. "What is life?" I ask as a manner of greeting. "Why are we born and why do we die? So much suffering. I don't get it."

"Life is the play of mind or consciousness," Adela explains with a smile.

She goes son: "We have always been, and we will always be. Birth and death are products of the ignorance of consciousness that, like our eyes, cannot see our Self and realize our true nature."

"That makes utterly no sense!" I protest.

"I don't expect you to understand now," Adela replies patiently. "Anything I tell you will mix with your dreams, and, like a seed planted in a fertile furrow, will bear fruit in the future." When Adela says this, I fall asleep suddenly and dream that I am in a field made of lapis lazuli, whose dark blue contrasts beautifully with the yellow of the golden road that crosses it. The turquoise sky is filled with humming-birds flitting around, showing off their resplendent emerald green and indigo blue plumage, while cardinals with plumage and chest of solid crimson deliver songs that teach about the true essence of life, and that touch my heart.

SATURDAY MORNING, Tito is on his porch, stretched out on the cot as always, but with a smile on his lips. We've played checkers several times in the past few days and I noticed that he was very somber. But now he's smiling.

I sit beside him on the cot's mattress, and say, "What're you smiling about?"

"They're taking off my cast in a couple of days," he answers, struggling to sit up on the cot beside me. He takes this as a personal victory, as if he had healed himself.

"Be careful," I warn him.

"Be careful of what?"

"Don't fall again, or, more to the point, don't let somebody push you and make you fall." Tito looks at me in disbelief. He doesn't understand what I'm saying.

He smiles again, and says, "No I won't, because my grandmother's going to help me walk. I'm not going to walk alone the same day my cast is removed, but eventually. My leg has been greatly weakened," he says with great confidence.

"I'm just asking you to be really, really careful," I say, weighed down by a prem-onition. Tito, annoyed, turns his face to look at the street, furrowing his brow in a deep frown. I know this gesture very well because it's what I do when I give good news to my mother and she makes some negative comment about the news, or drags in some irrelevant, illogical thing. This always makes me furious – and makes me sorry I told her anything at all. In fact, the less I talk to her, the better off I am. That way I protect myself from fits of anger that it's pointless to manifest, since my mother will continue to react irrationally or negatively. My anger does not make her logical or positive.

"I am glad your cast is coming off, but I don't want you to have an accident in the first few days," I explain calmly.

"Accident! What accident? I can't stand another minute in this bed, and fi-nally I'm getting out of it. I don't want to hear another word!" he yells at me, furious.

He lies down on the cot, covers his ears with his hands, and puts on a pouty face, as old ladies say. He's about to burst into tears.

"Now, don't start crying," I say, without getting angry. "You're a *man,* and you must be strong. Crying doesn't solve anything, and people will make fun of you.

You're not going to be able to play with boys if you cry about any old thing. They will say you're a sissy. When you feel like crying, think of something that makes you really, *really,* mad, to control your tears."

Shame, for the first time, stops his sobs. He stares at me, hurt by my words, but at the same time comforted, because he senses I want to help him.

"Don't you cry?"

"No."

"But you're not a man."

"No, but I've played with boys all my life, and if I'd cried, I wouldn't have had a single friend. They'd despise me for being a weak little girl, a crybaby. Besides, I know crying makes things worse, or at least it doesn't fix them. Crying is effective only when you play with girls, but even when I play with girls, I've gotten used to holding back tears and I don't cry."

Tito throws his head back on the pillow and looks up at the porch roof, as if what I just said really irritated him. "*You* don't need to lie in this bed without ever being able to get up. *You* can play with whomever you want! *You* don't have *any* reason to cry!" the invalid reproaches me.

"I can play with whomever I want, and yet I come to play with *you,*" I try to reason with him in a comforting tone. I get up to leave because the conversation is becoming too dramatic and I'm tiring of it.

"Don't go! I have something to ask you."

I sit back down on the cot.

"Don't you see things at night?" he asks, quietly and with an air of mystery.

"What things?"

"Things, people, green plants."

I laugh, remembering my nights when I was very young. Now I'm older and I suspect these things are hallucinations. I remembered the day I woke up in the other house, the one in Almendares, marveling at what I had seen during the night. The trees and flowers had been spectacular, the small creatures had made all sorts of mischief. Of course, I assumed everyone in the house was going to talk about this over breakfast, but nobody said a thing. I realized then, with a shudder of fear, that I was the only one who saw these things and was afraid that they would think I was crazy if I talked about them. Since then, I've decided not to see anything at night and never to talk about this to anyone.

"These are children's dreams," I say. "They don't exist in this world. Now that you are older, you need to watch out. You mustn't talk to anyone about this."

I stand up, determined to leave even if Tito calls me back. But he keeps quiet.

He looks at me with a fading light in his eyes that reveals to me the mistake of ever talking to others about my premonitions.

HAVING NEW FRIENDS is an exciting experience, but I'm saddened at being forcibly separated from my friends in the other neighborhood, especially from geniuses

244

like Dieguín and Hugo. Therefore, I'm very happy when my father tells me that Elena, she of Almendares (and not of La Sierra), has moved here, to another private house like ours and not to an apartment like before. Her family has risen in the world and can afford more expensive housing. Her father is no longer a subordinate of my father's, and enjoys the confidence of the Minister of Education, perhaps, says my mother, thanks to having brought so many cafés con leche to the minister's secretary. In the end I avoided playing alone with her, but now I'm glad to continue our friendship of several years. My brother is also pleased that they've moved, because Elena's brother, César, is a friend of his. Septimio never talks about his feelings or his daily life, and in this he follows our house's style of impersonal communication, but I sense that he has missed César, as I have Elena.

On Elena's and César's first visit, I try to convince Elena to transfer to my school because it's closer to her house. I tell her that it's very relaxed, and they let us out at three in the afternoon. Also, they teach English well because it's an American school. I don't tell her it's Protestant. That doesn't seem important because she's never seemed a devout Catholic. I remember how hard she laughed when I confessed to her, ages ago, that I wanted to become a Claretian, a Missionary child of the Immaculate Heart of Mary, so that I could go to the Far East and convert the infidel. I laughed with her—what else could I do? I didn't dare tell her I was serious. Besides, this wanting to be a Catholic missionary thing might have been an early sign of insanity. I don't want to end up like my uncle, counting the hairs on my head in a sanatorium.

This first day that Elena and César visit us, my brother insists on showing them the movie projector the Three Wise Men brought me for Christmas, which Septimio liked more than I did. We all go to my room and Septimio projects a cartoon about Thanksgiving Day in the United States. I'm not at all interested in re-watching that ship crash into Plymouth Rock, or those turkeys running while the English pilgrims shoot them with blunderbusses, and especially not that turkey scalped by buckshot, leaving only three feathers in its tail. I escape to the garage to fix the chain on Elena's bicycle, which she complained was very tight. After a while, her bike is as good as new, oiled and tuned, all of which I learned to do by watching my brother fix his.

When Elena comes out of the "projection room," I list, with my fingers covered in black grease, everything I did to her bike, but she doesn't say thank you. I wipe my hands with a handkerchief and offer to accompany her home riding my bike. Halfway there, Elena tells me to go back home.

"Because you are not a man, you need to be careful," she counsels me with an adult air. "You mustn't run around alone all the time."

"Okay," I say to humor her, but how odd that it's only now dawned on her that I am not a man, just a little girl. At this halfway point we talk about superficial things. I feel something has ruptured in our relationship, which used to be, at its best moments, a kind of complicity.

Back home, I find Pablito leaning against the gate. Pablito is a child who lives in the so-called riffraff part of the neighborhood. He frightens me because he thinks and speaks very quickly. Then, too, he threatens to punch me when he gets angry, and he spies on grownups through their Venetian blinds.

The only thing I like about him is that he shares with me his English-language magazines that publish articles with photographs of weapons used by the U.S. Army and by the henchmen of organized crime who machine-gun people on the streets of Chicago and New York. He also shows me erotic postcards and explains them to me, laughing rudely, because at first, I didn't know what he was showing me. Pablito has also given me books about sex that describe everything adults do, but in refined language. When he talks about sex, he puts his hand inside his pants and rubs. This doesn't upset me, because he doesn't touch me.

His sister Rita is as fast as he is, and as weird, but at least she doesn't threaten to punch me out. Ever since the King of the Block made me see that it's not civilized to hit people, I can't, for that very reason, smack Pablito when he threatens me with his fists. He's smaller than I am and skinnier, so I could kick his butt easily, but I think the time has come for me to stop being violent.

So, whenever he threatens me, I smile at him, make a joke, or walk away without answering him.

This holding back, unnatural in me, makes me feel afraid for the first time.

"Who was that girl with you?" Pablito asks me with interest.

"My friend Elena, from the other neighborhood."

"I want to meet her when she visits you again."

I find that odd, because little boys never want to meet girls. This makes me realize that Elena, who is now thirteen years old, has grown quite a bit in recent months and has become very pretty. I didn't notice this right away because you always see familiar people as unchanged. More to the point, although he's very short in stature, Pablito is also thirteen years old and may have already entered the age of "dating."

"Have you fallen in love?"

"In love with what? That's complete bullshit," the kid says with an insulting laugh. "I just want to put my hand up her skirt."

I'VE WOKEN UP with a big mess inside my head. I think it's awful that boys and girls live in Bombay, Kenya, or Tokyo, but I have no way to communicate with them. Would they be interested in poets and ancient philosophers? I feel terrible that there are so many millions of people in the world at this precise moment when I exist, and I will never know them. There's no way for us to communicate.

If I could only talk with Dieguín in some cathedral in space, as I do with Adela, I'm sure he'd tell me how this *will* be possible in the future precisely because now, today, it's *not* possible.

I would like to be able to communicate with university professors in the United States, as they are so far ahead in that country, and ask them what city it was that Xenophon passed through, in his retreat to the sea, where people did in public what the Greeks did privately, and in private what the Greeks did publicly. Xenophon does not make this clear in the *Anabasis: Retreat of the Ten Thousand,* nor does he specify why they were doing it.

I imagine toilets *al fresco* and orgies in the public squares. I can't find the answer in *The Treasure of Youth,* or in my father's books, and I can't ask anyone here because this kind of question is not normal for a girl.

Only Dieguín or Hugo might know the answers.

By myself, I just feel weak and stupid.

I can't punch Pablito, or anyone else. I have no one to talk to. I am bored. I think about Alexander the Great, ancient Macedonian warrior, conqueror of the world then known, educated by Aristotle. I'd love to talk to him, and suddenly I'm very upset that I can't read his diaries the way I can read the letters Julius Caesar wrote during his expeditions in Gaul.

Alexander, who described his campaigns in detail, ran out of words about his later life. Time covered his mouth, erased his thought.

Fortunately, my family is not home this Sunday. Everyone's gone to visit my grandmother in La Víbora, because she's sick. When my mother woke me up so I could go too, I pretended to have a migraine. My mother has these headaches, so she respects me and lets me sleep. I'm alone with the maid and the cook, who's our Black relative. They don't mess with me, and I don't mess with them. Because I never repeat the nasty comments they make about my family when they've gone out, they speak freely in front of me and do not rat me out to my mother, but I don't feel like listening to their gossip today.

It's much more exciting to be able to write without fear of being caught.

I find all our books mentioning Alexander the Great, pile them up on the dining room table, and sit down. After reading them to refresh the information in my memory, above all to mimic the style, I write in my composition book:

I thought I would stop writing diaries when I felt I had conquered the world. But I did not want historians to write about the big or small events of my life or my kingdoms without me dictating their thoughts, so I decided to continue to write. I thought that all that remained for me was to become part of the world of the gods and to have my story sung in temples during religious ceremonies. That was before the fever attacked me. Although I have been in agony ever since I was wounded in India by a spear that breached my lung, I was able to ignore the pain by throwing myself into the work of managing the kingdom, and by planning the conquest of Arabia. But this fever is something else. Perhaps, as happened to my father and my divine ancestors, I must leave this body. I must die. I had doubted this until now because I survived all my battles and recovered from all my wounds. I did not confide this intimation of my immortality to anyone, least of all to my friends, because I knew they would laugh. They do not follow the Eastern custom of accepting the word of kings as divine revelation, although they dare not say this in public. They are very Greek in their predilection for independence, the equality of all men, and rationality. When I ordered that I be deified in Macedonia, my order was obeyed, but I know that in the privacy of their homes my subjects laughed at me.

India's Brahmin prognosticators tell me I have little time left to live, but I don't believe them. I feel the energy of youth in my limbs and the thirst for conquest in my chest. It is not possible that this torrent of energy and desire is about to be extinguished. The Brahmins also prophesy that nothing written about me by my friends and generals will ever become known, nor will my diaries or letters come down to posterity. Not one witness of my exploits will be able to transcend the oblivion of time; I, who carried out those exploits, will remain speechless. But I do not believe this. How can that be possible? How can they steal my glory like that? If, after every battle, I have always given the spoils of war to my generals (about which my mother constantly reproaches me in her evil letters), it is because I care nothing about the gold or the lands or kingdoms I conquer. Only the glory of my exploits will keep me alive in centuries to come, when all that reflects me are the songs about my deeds. Is that not what happened with Achilles? Did he not preach the glory of war and prefer an early death to restful old age and a life of luxury and power in obscurity?

"Alexander, please try to focus. I come from the future to write your thoughts. Tell me about your death."

"Is it you, Hephaestion, the bravest and most beautiful of warriors? You're alive? Ah, like Achilles, how much I would give to be a dog, alive, rather than Alexander, dead!"

"Alas, no, I am not your friend Hephaestion. I live in the future. Now that you are in Hades, you probably know how you died. It is speculated that you were poisoned by your generals, by murderers sent from Macedonia, by your wife Roxane, or that your liver became so weak from drinking that it killed you. Or perhaps the cause was malaria, Nile fever, or infection from your lung wound."

"Among all these deaths I choose the one that seems the most artistic to me: Nile fever," says the conqueror of the known world, with regret.

I hear our car pull up, and my family is about to enter the house. I race to put back the books from my father's library, and climb in bed to read about Alexander's campaigns in *The Treasure of Youth*.

22

CARNIVAL

I DECIDE TO TAKE PABLITO and his sister Rita over to Molly and The Bebe's house because my mother is forever saying, "Sharks bathe, but they also splash," which I take to mean "You should share."

Of course, what she's probably referring to is rumors that Grau, the President of the Republic, and Alemán, the Minister of Education who's my father's boss, steal from the people and pass the money on to their friends.

My father, who likes to take whatever point of view is the opposite of my mother's, always replies that this is "calumny concocted by political enemies," that Alemán's wife is a multi-millionairess, meaning he has no need to steal, and that Grau is "too much of a philosopher to stain his hands with peculation." I must look up "calumny" and "peculation" in the dictionary to understand what they are talking about. I must do this very often when there is talk about politics in my house, which, lately, is most of the time.

Molly and The Bebe are slower than I am, so I'll feel more comfortable and have more fun at the speed of Pablito and Rita.

The game between the five of us starts to get very interesting, so we go inside because we need more room than the small porch where Molly and The Bebe are supposed to play. Pablito comes up with a game involving corsairs and privateers, and we make capes out of towels and swords out of umbrellas. We tear around the house and, for the first time, I hear Molly and The Bebe laughing out loud.

"The Devil take the hindmost!" I yell, running in a circle and tipping over the chairs in the dining room. I'm enjoying the game immensely, when Pablito announces that he and his sister want to leave. Maybe Molly and The Bebe's slowness bores them. I don't want to be alone with the two of them, and that's why I leave, but I have the feeling this game isn't over.

At home I find that the Mexican charro costume I picked out in a costume house to wear for Carnival has arrived. My Aunt Isabel has invited me and Septimio me to participate in the parade in a borrowed *calèche*. My brother explains to me, as if I were a fool, that a calèche is an old-fashioned open carriage used by the viceroys of New Spain so Mexican natives could lay worshipful eyes on their reputedly immortal European rulers.

"And what other purpose could a calèche have?" I answer, and run to put on my Mexican *charro* suit and its black hat embroidered with silver threads.

It's a spectacular costume, in my opinion, and when I'm all dressed, I go out to show it off to Molly and The Bebe. The back door of their house is open and I hide behind the little wall to surprise them when they go out into the patio. There's a big commotion in the house because Molly and The Bebe's mom has just arrived home from a shopping trip.

I've never met her, and she's screaming at her kids.

This is particularly upsetting to me after the exciting games we invented and the euphoric feeling they produced in us.

"What's this? The house is upside down! I told you never to let that Mercy set foot inside this house! She's a savage and out of control! I don't want her dragging the chaos of her house into ours!" the mother shouts.

Molly and The Bebe mumble excuses in shaky, whiney voices. In that instant I realize that they are just as much prisoners of their mother as the King of the Block is, of his mother.

There's no way to fix this. I feel wounded at the accusation of being savage and unruly, because all I wanted was to bring life to these children with my joy of living. I leave without anyone seeing me, filled with shame. When I get home, I sit outside on the garden wall. I can't enter the "chaos" of my own house after hearing that I've passed it on it to my friends' house.

Now, Chaos-Made-Animal crosses in front of me, taking the form of my rooster Omobono, stomping down the middle of the street as if it belonged to him. When he was a young cockerel, I fed him capsules of beef liver extract because I thought the poor thing was too skinny. After several months of this diet, when he got to be about the size of a large adult turkey, Omobono left our house to travel the world. Now, it looks like he's back.

I jump off the wall in my charro outfit and carefully walk towards the rooster. Omobono gives me a malicious look and charges towards me. I sense his bad intentions. Fearing his tremendous spurs, I break into a run to get away from him and climb the wall on one side of my house. Omobono jumps up to attack me, but fortunately he's too fat to reach me. Each time he lands after a jump, the alley's layer of concrete shakes.

What happened to this rooster that I raised with such loving care? Did the liver extract go to his head and drive him crazy?

The window in my room, which faces the wall where I'm perched, is partly open. I can see and hear my mother complaining to my father's sisters.

"You must intervene," my mother begs in a tormented voice. "Augusto has other women and is spending everything he makes on them. He's making me and the children suffer and keeping us from enjoying the fortune that he's been able to earn and lucky enough to win."

After a pause, she adds: "It all has to do with books! I want to run into the street and built a pyre with all his books!"

"Flora, my brother's books have nothing to do with this, and we absolutely cannot intervene," says Amelia, very irritated. "This is a matter between you and him. Speak to him frankly."

"I'm afraid he'll get violent," my mother replies, fearfully.

"You must take that chance," Amelia insists.

Omobono stomps off in an imperial huff when he realizes that I'm going to remain on top of the wall until he goes. I finally get down when I see him head out into the middle of the street.

I don't want to continue listening to this conversation. I'm ashamed that my mother is complaining about my father to my aunts, his sisters. In my opinion, you shouldn't talk about what's going on in your own house with other people. I sit back on the wall at the entrance to the house, very angry, waiting for my aunts to leave so I can go to my room and change out of my costume.

I'M SITTING ON THE SOFA in the living room, reading the comics in Saturday's paper, when my mother charges in, her face all discombobulated, wanting me to search my father's closet.

"Go to your father's room and look in the first drawer of his wardrobe," she orders me, incensed.

I don't know how to take these words. I have never searched through my father's things, except to look for books in his library.

"Why should I do that?" I ask angrily.

"Go and look, girl! Go see what your father has in that drawer!" she yells at me, even angrier.

So I go to his wardrobe, pull the drawer open, see a small box upholstered in navy velvet, and open it.

The white satin lining surrounds a gold ring with a ruby in the center, encircled by tiny diamonds. The ring is small, for a girl's finger.

I gently lift it out of the box and show it to my mother, who's right behind me. "Put it on and see how it looks on you," she commands, furiously.

I put it on and it fits my ring finger. I really like rubies, but my father would have given it to me on my birthday if it had been meant for me.

"It fits me perfectly," I say, afraid my father will be angry that I took it.

"Yes, but it's *not* for you. It has to be for one of his mistresses' daughters."

"*Not for me!*" I cry out, pulling it off and putting it back in its box.

My mother comes over and shakes me violently, squeezing my arms with her hands, hysterical. "You want him to give it to his mistress? That ring belongs to *you*, his only legitimate daughter."

I look at her with consternation. I hate it when she gets upset and crazy-eyed. It scares me to death.

"Tell your father you just happened to find the ring, and simply thank him for buying it for you," she now suggests, suddenly peaceful.

I hear the front door open, and my father comes in with Santana and Pancho Pistola. I put the ring on again and go out into the hall to greet him, showing him the ring and laughing with joy.

"Thank you, Papa, for this lovely ring!" I cry, hugging him.

"How did you find it?" he asks me, serious and cutting.

"By chance! I was sniffing your colognes to make a perfume for you by mixing them, and I thought you were going to give it to me, and I tried it on to see if it looked good on me. It's perfect!"

My father smiles at me, but shoots a very serious glance at my mother, standing behind me. I know he doesn't believe this story, but I must keep up the charade to stop them from declaring all-out war.

My father heads for his room. His bodyguard and assistant pull up chairs at the dining room table, and they each ask Toñita for a cup of black coffee. My mother goes to my room. I follow her, set the ring back in its box, and stash it in my wardrobe, between my trove of school handkerchiefs. My mother lies down on her bed to smoke.

I slip out to the living room to hear what my father has to say, now that he's sat down to have coffee with his assistant and his bodyguard. I stay out of view in the big armchair in the living room. They've forgotten about me and speak freely.

"There's talk on the street that Emilio Tro is after El Colorao, to rub him out," murmurs Pancho Pistola in a truculent voice.

"What the hell! They're already implicated in more than fifty incidents, between bombings and assassinations, like just the other day they shot Lino Mancebo Rosell as he was coming out of the Business Arcade," Santana says.

"That happened because they pinned the death of that hick, Niceto Pérez, on Mancebo," the bodyguard growls in a sinister tone.

"The Federation of Farm Workers campaigned nationally to have Niceto Pérez's death prosecuted, and the trial was about to start. Couldn't they just wait for the verdict?" the assistant asks.

"Who waits for anything here? The streets are on fire!" Pancho Pistola exclaims, sounding uncharacteristically frightened.

"That's exactly why *you* need to prepare better than you ever have," my father points out to his dour bodyguard.

THE NEXT DAY, in the morning, I take a dining room chair to my father's room and set it in front of his chifforobe. I'd watched my father put something wrapped in a handkerchief on top of the cabinet. I stand on the chair and find on top a large clear crystal wine glass full of water. Under the wine glass are two cards from the

Spanish Tarot deck: the Ace of Swords and the Ace of Pentacles. Beside these, there's something swathed in a handkerchief. I unwrap it: it's my father's .45 caliber Peacemaker. I pick it up with both hands because it weighs a ton, and am aiming at one wall of the room precisely when my mother walks in.

"Look! A gun!" I cry out enthusiastically, pointing the gun at her. My mother flattens herself against the wall, opens her arms in the shape of a cross, and stands there livid, shaky, speechless. After a few seconds, costing her every ounce of courage she has, she says in a wobbly voice that pretends to be calm: "Girl, aim the gun at the ceiling, take your finger off the trigger, and gently put it right back where you got it from."

I do what my mother tells me to, but I'm surprised at her fear. I know what a pistol can do. I don't understand why she thought, even for a second, that I was going to shoot her.

I LONG FOR THE EXCURSIONS WE USED TO MAKE to La Puntilla, when my father was just a primary school teacher. Also, I miss our visits to the Jaimanitas beach restaurant, where we ate seafood and listened to *danzonetes*. Now, on weekends, my father invites his politician friends to lunch here, at home.

It's good because my father's home, but bad because he talks to his friends all the time, ignoring us. Paying attention to these conversations, I hear about big gangs and little gangs and gunmen and political groups who have all vowed to annihilate one another.

These groups identify as IUR and MSR, and the R in both cases stands for "Revolution," not "Republic."

I ask my mother what these initials mean to understand what they're talking about. She tells me to shut up and she'll explain later. When we're alone, my mother sits at the dining room table, lights a cigarette, and exhales a puff of smoke. I sit as far away as possible so as not to breathe her smoke, which irritates my throat.

"During the struggle against the Machado *dictatorship*, before our *republic*," she says in her teacherly voice, "several leftist revolutionary groups were founded that continue to this day, in our republic, as gangs of gunmen, some with ideals of freedom and others with no scruples at all, only lust for power."

I try to ask her a question, but she shuts me up with her hand indicating that I will understand if I let her continue her story.

"Trying to appease them, our current President, Grau, who was then one of five men in the Pentarchy, gave Government positions to the main leaders of these groups," she says, exhaling with pleasure a huge puff of smoke towards the dining room ceiling.

"At first," she goes on, "what Grau did was thought to be a veritable Judgment of Solomon. But then it turned into an excuse for the groups to try to destroy each other and grab full control of the government. They haven't been able to do so, and now, some of these groups have turned against Grau and the officials working in his government. This includes your father."

THIS SATURDAY, MY MOTHER takes my brother with her to call on her sister Isabel, leaving me alone with my father. He is having lunch with two friends and his executive assistant from the ministry, the Black Santana. Everyone dresses as if they were about to attend a big political rally, wearing the obligatory white dril 100 suit, fine white cotton shirt, blue or red silk ties, and two-tone brown-and-white shoes. Every man has a .45-caliber revolver on his belt, even my father, although he's eating at home and the leather holster at his waist must be uncomfortable. I'm listening to them from the living room armchair that lets me see them.

"It's not a lie that's being spread," says one of his friends, the smallest, most fragile-looking of them. "I think the MSR is preparing a major attack. I don't think it will be the president, but it might be Minister Ansola, who lives up the street from you."

"No way! Why would they mess with Ansola, who's in very good standing with the government?" my father contradicts him with contempt.

"That's why it's going to be a major attack, Doctor! The MSR must exact revenge, and who better to go after than Ansola, a prominent member of their enemy, the UIR. I'm sure they think UIR is responsible for the attacks against them."

My mother already explained to me that the Revolutionary Insurrectional Union (UIR), which Emilio Tro founded and directs, is the gang most despised by the Revolutionary Socialist Movement (MSR), as well as the strongest supporter of Grau.

A bunch of UIR members are active political supporters of my father.

What I mainly understand about this mess is that it all started a long time ago, before I was born, when the dictator by the name of Machado was in power and some college groups armed themselves and made and planted bombs to drive him from power. It's great that we don't have a dictator now, but it's horrendous to think that MSR gang members are now police officers and even functionaries in the Ministry of Education. My father explained to me that's why he must carry a gun on his belt to protect himself from any attacks these guys might make on him while he's performing his duties. It's horrible that even children's education is so mixed up with violence.

From the armchair I ask, although I already know the answer: "So the restaurant bomb was to kill *us*?"

My father rises sharply from the table.

"Do *not* eavesdrop on grown-up conversations! Go to your room and read!" he yells at me, furious.

JUST BEFORE NIGHTFALL, I go by Tito's house and am surprised to see him walking on the arm of a white-haired lady who, I assume, is his grandmother. Tito laughs with joy at proving he can walk, even though it's slowly and with the old lady's help. With his cast off, I can see how emaciated his leg is, like those of prisoners in photos of Nazi concentration camps.

"Look how well I can walk!" Tito yells at me, euphoric.

I smile and wave goodbye with my hand.

I enter the patio of the King of the Block's building to run and jump over walls. I want to see if I can make it around the block through backyards, because that will be my escape route from the house should we be attacked.

When I get to the pink house's patio, I must run on tiptoe because a woman who lives there screams whenever she spots me. As I turn the corner, I bump into Pablito spying. He's sitting on the concrete floor of the passageway and peering under the blinds, which aren't completely lowered. He signals me to keep quiet and sit next to him.

I forge ahead stealthily on my path and discover that all the patios are connected and, yes, it is possible to escape this way.

SOMETHING ABOUT ALL THE POLITICAL CONVERSATION in our house makes me go to the drawer in my father's wardrobe where I know he keeps his French colognes. They are very expensive and their scents make me dream, but they are not unique, because you can buy them in stores.

I know that my father should smell differently from other men to distinguish himself. His own fragrant atmosphere should be part of his political image.

I take the bottles of cologne out of the drawer and start mixing them in an empty bottle that I've washed in hot water and let dry to make sure it has no scent.

I start with a small amount of orange-scented cologne that makes me dream of gardens of white citrus blossoms. White and orange combine in my mind and produce a subtle fruit scent, peach palpable as velvet.

Then I add some drops of a cologne having an aroma of spices like cinnamon and anise. These are very powerful and I only use a little to produce a background scent, like musical accompaniment of a main instrument, the way drums can dampen the high-pitched sound of strings.

This ground adds safety and firmness to the scent. I then add a few drops of sandalwood cologne, sparkly, loving, attractive.

I shake the bottle to mix all the colognes, then sniff the result. My sense of smell goes to a party, a dance of fragrances that swirls pleasantly around my nose. This, indeed, is the perfume of my father, suiting him perfectly: a fragrance of power and money, but also of sympathy, personal attraction, and generosity.

My father comes back from the bathroom half dressed, after taking his morning shower, and I hand him the bottle of his individual perfume.

"This is the cologne I created for you," I proudly announce.

My father sniffs the cologne and smiles.

"What a wonderful scent, Bad Bug. Where'd you get it?"

"I told you, remember? I was going to mix a few of your colognes to make a unique fragrance. It smells of fortune! Empire! Napoleon!" I declaim, inspired, as I hand him the red silk tie I've chosen for today.

I FIND IT SO HARD TO GET UP EARLY on the days I must go to school, but on weekends I wake up before six in the morning, without anyone having to prod me.

On those two days, I am seized by a sense of adventure, excited by what the day might bring, above all on Sundays when a special silence reigns, perhaps because people go to church. Since my mother has given up the habit of going to church, and my father and brother never go, I decide not to go either.

I'm a Protestant now, but I don't feel the need to look for a Methodist church to attend on Sundays because, I think, surely, it's enough to go to chapel every weekday. Besides, my devoutness consists in reading the Bible, protesting everything, researching everything.

I think Protestantism is about this: Catholics shouldn't know anything and Protestants should know everything. What gave me this idea? Nobody talks about religion at school or tries to convince anyone to become a Methodist.

I've been walking our empty street from one end to the other for several minutes, and now, arising from the place where the morning sun shines first, and blinding me with the light that a halo produces, a figure emerges, mounted on a bicycle. The brilliance of the light stirs me like a religious apparition. When the figure reaches me and I discover it is Elena, my hands are still trembling.

This seems to be a moment in my life when any strange visual or auditory phenomenon moves me because it reveals something subtle that hides behind things. This happened to me when I was younger, but to a lesser degree.

Now, everything seems intensified because I feel great agitation in the atmosphere, as if things floated or had the lightness of dreaming. Occasionally the hairs on my arms stand on end, while electrical energy runs up and down my spine.

Elena is haloed in golden light and when she comes to a stop beside me, dressed in yellow, her skin glowing and her blond hair tousled by the wind, I think I can't be awake.

Adolescence has taken hold of her. She's no longer a little girl like me. She has the majesty of youth, while I'm still stuck in the inferiority of childhood.

"I decided to get some exercise and ride my bike a little," Elena explains unnecessarily. "You fixed it very well for me and I like to ride it."

We go to my house so she can leave the bike in the garage.

"Look how I've fixed my nails," she says, showing me her hands.

"Did you do them yourself?" I ask because I don't see anything different about her nails.

"No, my mom took me for a 'manicure,'" uttering the latter word with an affected English accent. I stare at her and let out a silly laugh because I don't know how to talk to this new person who gets her fingernails painted by someone else.

A heavy, embarrassing silence develops between us.

"Do you still like the Protestant school?" Elena asks me with a laid-back air that slightly lessens my unease, this straitjacket that I feel trapping me.

"Yes, and I even get home early, but then there's no one to play with. Because I ride my bicycle to school, at three, when I come home, the sun heats things up so much that I spend hours in the bathroom with my head boiling under cold water."

"My mom went to sign me up. I convinced her because you were going," Elena explains, with the air of a queen.

Pablito opens the garage gate and comes into the yard walking like some tough cowboy. As usual, his sister Rita is right behind him. Without glancing at Elena, he despotically announces: "Today we are going to play hide-and-seek!"

"And who are you?" Elena asks imperiously, looking down at him as if he were an insect.

Like me, Elena is much taller and stronger than he is.

"Listen up, do you want me to punch you?" Pablito answers. He closes his fists and stands with his legs far apart, like a boxer, in front of Elena. I stand stock still, because if he hits Elena, I must beat Pablito to a pulp, and that will put me back in the world of savagery and break my promise to civilize myself.

"I double-dare you!" Elena yells at him, facing him down fearlessly. Pablito makes some feeble threatening gesture and ends up walking off with Rita.

Elena has won the showdown, but I feel deflated. I wonder if my passivity is at its root cowardice. Elena, with no one to vent her annoyance at, looks at me with contempt and gets on her bike without saying a word.

"Come see me once in a while," she finally says. "I don't like your neighbors."

WHEN I GET HOME, I don't go inside, but sit out on the porch because I can hear my father in the living room talking with Pancho Pistola.

"They shot El Colorao while he was walking along the Ayesterán highway," the bodyguard growls out hoarsely. "He was very lucky because he wasn't killed, but it's going to be blamed on Emilio Tro."

"Grau did the wrong thing, placing Tro and Salabarría in the police," my father criticizes, annoyed. "There's been bad blood between those two bosses of rival gangs for a long time. For sure, there's going to be payback. Colorao is with Salabarría."

"We're going to have fireworks very soon," the bodyguard agrees somberly.

"Make damn sure keep your eyes and ears wide open!" my father commands threateningly. "Act first and think later."

"Yes, you need to have guts of steel," Pancho Pistola agrees.

CARNIVAL'S COMING. I had forgotten about it, after the day my giant rooster Omobono went after me. My mother tells me I need to put on my Mexican charro costume because Aunt Isabel will be along to pick me up soon. In minutes I'm dressed and sitting on the porch between the bodyguard and my father's driver. They have machine guns and .45 caliber pistols, but I've got a couple of six-guns that shoot caps hanging from my cowboy belt with its fake ammunition. I am glad I insisted on renting this costume, against the will of my mother and the sales-woman, who preferred the costume of a Mexican peasant girl, which is the female version of the charro. They couldn't convince me because the last thing I wanted to wear is a colorful dress with lace and petticoats and no guns. Besides, I like my big charro hat. The bodyguard and driver look at me and I hear one of them whisper that I'm going to follow in my father's footsteps and wear a sidearm.

My aunt shows up in a rented chauffeur-driven white Cadillac convertible, not the promised calèche, which was probably another of my brother's lies. It still isn't clear to me why people dress up, put on masks, and throw streamers and confetti, or why Carnival is supposed to be cheerful. It can't just be that the people love King Momo, monarch of Carnival who looks like a clown.

When I climb into the convertible, I get the feeling that my aunt is taken aback by my costume, but she makes no comment. My cousin Gisela and her boyfriend, disguised as the Egyptian gods Isis and Osiris, don't pay any attention to me because they're whispering sweet nothings to each other and holding hands.

Osiris attracts my attention because of what I've read about Egypt and its gods in *The Treasure of Youth*. I'm almost done reading what interests me in this compendium of all human knowledge in twenty volumes, because I want to learn. Yet again, it seems to me that in school, they don't teach us anything, only how to waste time. I should know much more about Isis and Osiris, but I can say that this Osiris is tall and thin; Isis seems petit and buxom next to him. My Aunt Isabel isn't wearing a costume of any kind. My brother returned his Lone Ranger costume days ago because he had to prepare for an exam.

We head in the convertible over to Bella's house to pick up my cousin Nadia, one of the Three Little Girls. When we get there, she's on the sofa, disguised as an American cowgirl in a skirt that's mostly leather fringes and a cowboy belt like mine with a couple of cap guns in holsters. Nadia tells us, with regret, that even though she's all dressed in her costume, she's decided that she had better not go. The evening is a little chilly, and she's afraid it will make her cold worse. Nadia has had trouble with her lungs, and to strengthen them, for months she's been breakfasting on one raw egg in a glass of port wine, which, in my mother's view, is the best restorative. Nadia rested in bed for months because everyone was afraid the same thing would happen to her as to her mother, who died of tuberculosis.

No other family member can be convinced to come with us, and we leave Nadia sitting on the living room sofa, all dressed to play a role in a Western movie.

In the convertible I sit next to Aunt Isabel, who, after looking askance at me yet again because of my costume, pulls out the cellophane tubes containing colorful streamers and the bags of confetti, places them all around her as if she were a guard dog, and gives each of us one streamer roll.

"Save streamers," she admonishes us.

This, I think, is nonsense. During Carnival, aren't you supposed to free yourself from everything, be spontaneous, cheerful, almost crazy? Streamers and confetti are bought to be thrown, not saved! I keep my thoughts to myself so as not to spoil the joy of this party, which is just as well, because as it turned out, she knew from experience why to do this.

As we drive along the Malecón, we see the floats, trucks with wooden platforms on top, adorned in the most imaginative ways. There is a float with a crescent moon hanging from a reproduction in wood and papier-maché of the Arc de Triomphe in Paris. On the moon sits a woman in a bathing suit who shows off her chubby white flesh, which shudders like custard as the float progresses.

Moving suggestively and adoring her are two ballet dancers with huge mustaches wearing rhumba costumes of skin-tight pants and exaggeratedly ruffled sleeves, frenziedly playing maracas. Another float transports three spinning heads with eyes that keep opening and closing. These are the Three Wise Men.

The most spectacular float is titled "Tropical Hell." In cardboard cauldrons, flames of red cellophane blown by fans roast nearly naked old men, fat old ladies dressed in fake tiger skins, young dyed blonds, and almost-naked mulattas with scarlet stars stuck to their nipples.

Presiding over this float is a great Devil dressed in scarlet sequins, his horns, tail, and silvery pitchfork all covered in tinfoil. The Devil's job is to inflict wounds on the Damned, who twist among the black-and-red cardboard rocks in the embrace of crepe-paper pythons and anacondas.

The Devil lets out an ear-splitting cackle and starts messing with the participants who've come in convertibles.

As he passes us, he yells: "Today those who know how to steal are enjoying themselves! Tomorrow they will be crying in these cauldrons!" I'm stuck staring at him terrified, never having seen anything like this.

"Ma'am, your mask is very good!" the Devil yells at my Aunt Isabel, who isn't wearing a mask. "Take it off when your husband gets into bed! Enjoy!" the Devil howls, while pricking with his pitchfork the enormous bottom of an elderly woman in the crowd, who lets out a sharp cry. In our convertible, no one comments, but the driver accelerates to get us away from this Devil who shouts insults.

We all breathe with relief when we see the *comparsas*, groups of dancers wearing beautiful costumes, performing on the street. On one side of us, a *comparsa* of Black dancers dressed as kings, queens, and nobles in the time of Louis XIV, with enormous white wigs, dance a minuet, as in the movies. The music comes from a car equipped with a loudspeaker.

After this, the performers are dancing the *comparsa* called "The Dead to the Hole and the Living to the Gold," in which men dressed as skeletons carry their own tombstones, accompanied by nearly naked, beautiful young people of both sexes rubbing against each other as if they were making love.

I find it strange that my aunt isn't scandalized by this show, but she makes no comment. Gisela and her boyfriend throw a few streamers every now and again, but really, they only have eyes for each other. My aunt gazes at everyone with an aristocratic air, and seems completely out of place among all these out-of-control, vulgar people.

I, too, throw streamers from time to time. One of my streamers fails to unroll and hits one of the Dead, who sets his tombstone down and comes over to me. He stares at me with black, bright, malevolent eyes from behind his black-and-white skeleton mask. The Dead opens his mouth in a big, dark smile, as if he were a beast about to devour me, then spits in my face. I have no time to raise my hands to cover my face and scream in terror. The Dead runs off without his tombstone, disappearing among the Living who are happily frolicking.

Aunt Isabel, who hasn't seen what's happened, complains: "You can't take children anywhere." But I found out why she was being so frugal with the streamers. This carnival is grotesque and I regret coming, but I take comfort in thinking that soon the summer holidays will arrive and we will be off to Varadero, the best beach on the Island.

23

VARADERO

SEBORUCO DRIVES US, me, my mother, my brother, my cousin Cleo, and our maid Kika, in his car to a tongue of sand that stretches out into the sea, the beach of Varadero. A friend of my father's has loaned us her summer house. My mother told me yesterday that, like my father, this friend is a Doctor of Pedagogy, which finally I've figured out means "expert in the teaching of children," and she has a son who looks a lot like my brother.

"If you see that boy when you're grown up, don't even think of falling in love with him," she warns me, very perturbed. "I'm positive he's your half-brother."

"But how can I have half of a brother?" I ask, confused.

"Your father must have slept with his mother," she replies impersonally.

Cleo, sitting next to the driver, whips around to tell us all about her volunteer nurse work. Septimio and I, squeezed against the windows on the outsides of the back seat with my mother and Kika separating us, ignore her. When I stick my head out the car window, the wind keeps me from breathing, but I don't care because the freshness of the air fills me with energy. The wind is like a huge hand slapping my nose, each finger delivering a different smell. All of these are dominated by the bittersweet scent of the cane fields and the sharp odor of horse droppings, already dry and disintegrating into yellow litter on the road. It's a world of strange voices that we are passing through, of trees whose branches crisscross overhead, their canopies forming a tunnel of purest air perfumed by leaves and flowers.

As we pass through the villages, ads on the fences announce "DRINK JUPIÑA" or "DRINK IRONBEER/OR DON'T DRINK AT ALL!" The Ironbeer ad shows the arm of a muscular boy lifting a black weight with iron balls at both ends. Men in white guayaberas that flutter in the wind are strolling along the narrow sidewalks; women in dresses of cotton printed with colorful flowers timidly cross the streets. The houses, painted light blue, dark green, and *mamey* red, their narrow porches encased in large wrought-iron cages, pass dizzyingly before our eyes. This is "the Interior," or "the Field." It makes no difference whether you are in a town or in the countryside;

anything outside the capital is "the Interior." And "the Interior" means these houses, side by side, with people sitting on porches watching cars go by, and corner stores with signs posted at the door: "No CREDIT TODAY. COME BACK TOMORROW."

Occasionally you hear a *guaracha* and, sometimes, this popular song:

> *Silverio, Silverio Pérez,*
> *Toreador, spin and twist,*
> *You great Aztec Spaniard!*

I'm amazed that there are landscapes, houses, children, women, and men when we leave the Capital. I know this country is very long, but being able to *see* it astounds me. And every new thing I see and feel makes me understand *life* more deeply. I live in the people, the trees, the houses, in the white clouds that are bluish at the bottom, as if the indigo sky behind them had faded and stained them. I breathe deeply and joy fills my chest to overflowing. I am alive and I am superior to the dead – to the millions of dead of all ages, so many that if placed one on top of the other they would reach and pass the moon. Alexander is dead, Napoleon is dead, Caesar is dead, powerful conquerors of the world before whom people trembled, all dead. None of them can breathe, but I can. At this fleeting moment I can pull life towards me, seize it to fill me with triumphant, joyful, exalting tremors.

When we get to the valley of the Yumurí River, in Matanzas province, we pile out of the car to admire the landscape from the bridge that crosses the river. Below us, the valley unfolds, green and blue, and the thin river that runs through it glitters and undulates, a snake-shaped mirror among the peasant huts with their pointed thatched roofs scattered across the plain.

We can hear guitars accompanying a baritone voice singing:

> *She is my life*
> *My pretty* guajirita,
> *The loveliest little thing,*
> *My dark-skinned girl.*

Another male voice, higher and melodious, sings:

> *Come here, passionate girl*
> *Nothing inspires me now,*
> *Not even birds singing*
> *As they sail the blue.*
> *Come brighten my hut,*
> *Even the river bed*
> *Grows gloomier*
> *Because you are not here.*

A few farm workers with machetes tucked in their belts, wearing white guayaberas, khaki pants, and leather boots, ride their horses in a stately procession.

262

Along the river bank, from the huts' doorways, the women wave farewell.

It occurs to me that this is a show prepared for tourists at this lookout point. It's just not possible to catch people in situations that are so typical. It's like a postcard titled "The Interior" and meant to remind us of the War of Independence from Spain over half a century ago. Now, the war with Spain is over, no Spaniards dominate the Island, they just own bodegas and get rich.

"What a beautiful sight!" I exclaim, unaware that I might sound fatuous.

"Ah yes, behold the valley soaked in blood," replies my brother Septimio, with great anger. After a pause, he adds: "Here the Spanish conquerors carried out a huge massacre of the aboriginal people."

Cleo steps ahead of us, stands in front of the wall and, as if to erase my brother's lugubrious words, with her arms outstretched, she sings to the valley in a marvelous voice:

Come, oh my love, to the banks
of this river of gold
with your arrows and your hut.
Come and you'll see how the river
and its waters sigh with
the protests of the Siboney.

We climb back in the car in silence and drive very fast through fields planted in cane and corn, with, always in the background of the landscape, the tall, slender, distinguished royal palms, the Island's symbol, swinging their unruly green plumes at the whim of the breeze.

ON ARRIVING AT PEACEFUL VARADERO, we take possession of a traditional white villa built of wood that smells old and locked up, but also of wicker furniture and freshly painted walls. White mosquito netting hangs from the ceiling, hiding the beds in the four bedrooms. The doors and windows are insect-proofed by fine gray screens. There's running water, but in the courtyard a relic remains from the ancient era in which the villa was built: a rusty pump which can still draw water from a walled well. There's no phone.

My mother decides we must explore the environs. Seboruco has gone back to the Capital in his car, leaving us with no means of transportation.

A horse-drawn carriage drives past the house, we stop it, and are on our way to town to buy swimsuits. The driver, a skinny man with a big moustache, is called Cirilo, after Cirilo Villaverde, the father of our Island's vein of *costumbrista* novels. He tells us that his mother gave him this name because she was a passionate reader of those novels.

We sit in the seat looking at the coachman's back, my mother and Cleo facing us. Kika sits in front next to Cirilo, who joggles the reins to get the horse moving at a gentle trot. At the tourist shop, Septimio and I buy fins and masks for snorkeling, a red one-piece swimsuit for me, blue swim trunks for my brother, and a pair of green shorts, a blue cap with a visor, and a yellow sports shirt for me.

Green, blue, and yellow, the colors of Paradise.

Kika is accompanying us because our actual maid, Almaviva, had to stay in the Capital to take care of her sick mother. Kika refuses to come into the store to buy anything, and says she'll stick to wearing her white cotton uniform because she thinks it's out of place for her to look like a beachgoer. It's fine for American tourists and the Creole gentry, but not a maid.

My mother tries to convince her that she is not a maid but our companion. Still, Kika insists she won't go in, and stays outside talking to the coachman. Maybe she hasn't any money.

Cleo also stays behind talking to the coachman, but after a few minutes she comes in to buy a straw hat.

"Nobody but Americans come to this shop," says Cirilo when we climb back into the carriage loaded with packages. "I always bring them here. They like horses, too. But then, you're almost Americans, being from the Capital."

"Americans?!" My mother laughs. "No pick inglishss! We imitate them, we copy their movies. Did you see *Gone with the Wind*?"

"No, ma'am, but I did see what it brought," Cirilo replies, laughing. This is an ancient joke and I was betting he'd use it.

"You're a clever man, Cirilo. Why do you work as a coachman? There are opportunities galore in the Capital," my mother says, eager to help him. She never misses a chance to enlighten people. Already she is imagining how she will radically transform this coachman's life.

"No, ma'am, I'm a communist. I believe in the country, the Field, the Interior, not the City. What's more, I don't believe in cars, only in horse-drawn transportation. Mechanization is the ruination of everything."

My mother takes off her sunglasses to get a better look at him.

"A *communist*!" She gawks at him with astonishment. "Are you *really*?"

"Yes, ma'am, a card-carrying member of the Party."

"A *Party* member!" she shouts again in a paroxysm of wonder. "Look, Cirilo," my mother says, staring in disbelief at the coachman, "since the coup that overthrew the dictator Machado, I have not laid eyes on a communist. I mean, not one who claimed to be in such a chic way! Oh, you must come to the house one day to have coffee!"

Cirilo smiles but keeps his eyes on the road, giving the horse gentle taps with his whip. Now we head to the butcher's because my mother has a craving for steak. Cirilo takes us to the butcher that sells the best meat on the beach, and my brother and I climb back into the carriage with a pile of thick, red steaks wrapped in waxed brown paper.

The sea isn't visible from the road, but I can feel its presence in the air, smell its odor of iodine, salt, seafood. The joy in my legs and arms, the appetite that awakens with fury and hits my stomach, also reveal the nearness of the sea.

My mother puts on her sunglasses and waves at the people going by in the other carriages. "Clowns! Freaks! Tourists!" my brother and I yell, laughing and ducking for cover behind the retracted canopy. Our obnoxiousness no doubt mortifies Kika, sitting primly in front, and Cirilo launches into a song that fits in with the clop, clop, clop of the horse's hooves meeting the cobblestone street:

> *We, who were so sincere*
> *From our very first glance*
> *Loved each other*
> *From our love we made*
> *A wonderful sun,*
> *A romance truly divine.*

Dropping us in front of the villa, the coachman hands out his business card and tells us to find him whenever we want to go downtown again. His house is nearby, he says. All we must do is walk a little way down Central Street in the direction of the Capital.

"We *will* visit you," my mother promises regally as Cirillo helps her down.

THE FIVE POINTS OF A STARFISH slog forward underwater on the sandy bottom. The starfish, its dark yellow conspicuous against the lighter-colored bottom swirling around it, seems to be under a spell as its five legs and their dozens of pinkish tube feet trudge along.

I pick it up by the tips of two of its legs and the tiny tube feet dance frantically and uncoordinatedly, like wheat spikes swirling in the wind. In the center, a hole like a lint-lined eye watches me.

I set the starfish down on the sand, it raises one leg, and, after making some confused turns, it waddles off towards the sea.

After a few seconds I regret letting it go and pick it up again to put in a jar of seawater, so it can go back to the Capital and live with me.

Some distance behind me, Cleo perches on top of a metal table under an umbrella made of dry palm fronds. There isn't much sun. What's left is just half a reddish egg yolk floating in the indigo of the ocean, against the horizon. The rays filter through cirrhus and cumulus clouds, huge pearly masses, a rainbow of violet, red, yellow, and green, a peacock in the sky radiantly reflected in the water. Cleo, who didn't bring her new straw hat thinking the sun wouldn't be very strong at this hour, raises her hand like a visor to protect her eyes from the blackish sun, and crosses her legs. She's wearing tight green clamdiggers and a sleeveless blouse with red, white, and blue horizontal stripes, like the flag of France.

Everybody in the family will be going to the beach tomorrow, but I just can't wait. I tell Cleo I want to watch the sun go down in the sea and feel ridiculous saying it, when my mother, overhearing me talking to Cleo, exclaims: "What sunset? What are you talking about? What's to see? Just water!"

Cleo says she'll come with me, and we leave before my mother can utter another word.

On the way to the beach, I try to reconstruct the landscape in my mind, the sea with its waters of green bands ranging from light sea green to luminous emerald, ending in the dark green of imperial jade, as I once read in a book on gemstones. The sea with its waves where fish loll on their backs, staring at a crystallized sky with orange and purple veins. Fish covered in algae, bearded with silt, bubbles streaming out of their stupefied open mouths. In each bubble there is one letter, written on a tiny, wrinkled bit of paper, a letter that shoots up, explodes, and falls on the water. I see a small, bubble-blowing snapper playing a violin with its fins. The fish approaches the sand and walks out of the water on dozens of tube feet, like those of the starfish.

"It's a shame my feet aren't perfect. They'd be better if I had fewer of them and they were bigger," the snapper laments, then dives back into the water.

Or have I thrown him? I've brought him out of my head, my eyes have put him in the sea and made him walk. I throw him into the sea, and his double in my imagination penetrates my eyes.

There, it all fits.

Inside my eyes, no one can see, no one can say, "These things are ridiculous. They don't exist." It goes without saying that they don't exist. I take them out of my eyes to give them air, walk them, so they don't fill my mind with sounds and laughter when I want to sleep. Also, to keep them from doing me harm.

Once at the water's edge, I spend time observing the movement of the waves, listening to the seagulls' cry, breathing in the bracing salt air.

In the end, the sun is a finger of blood on the horizon sinking into the blue-green waters of the sea. Minutes later, it's almost night, because nothing is left of the sun but a golden afterglow in the sky, a death-rattle of light before it expires in the shadows. The water, covered with a layer of melted gold, now looks gelatinous. The coconut palms behind me laugh with every gust of wind.

Cleo gets up from the table and stands behind me, her hand on my shoulder. I see her oval nails, their red enamel clotted with a pink crescent at the root of each nail. In sinister letters I can't bear, they unite to say "Let's go!"

The landscape closes like a theater curtain. It's getting cool. I'm hungry.

"WE HAVE FILET MIGNON!" my mother shouts from the kitchen, as she makes a great display of showing me the meat that Septimio and I had gone into the butcher to buy. Enjoying this dinner before it happens, she adds: "The best grade of meat on the Island, found only in the finest restaurants. Very expensive. Look and marvel, my child, filet mignon!" Happy to be away from the violence of the city, my mother stabs the thick-sliced steaks with a huge fork and tosses the pieces on top of each other, causing the meat to produce a soft, moist, slapping sound. The steaks, red and nicely marbled, squirt watery blood across the glossy brown paper they came wrapped in.

"Ma'am, how would you like these prepared?" Kika asks in a frosty voice.

"You must fry them in olive oil, but make sure the center stays raw, *sanglant* as the French say," my mother instructs her, completely forgetting that she invited Kika to come with us as a companion, as a member of the family, not as a cook. When she says *sanglant*, my mother passes her tongue over the edge of her upper teeth, and her eyes light up with a special glow. In her white cotton shorts and blouse of the same material with black-and-white vertical stripes, my mother looks very athletic.

Cleo has gone to her room. Bored watching food being prepared in the kitchen, I cross over into night on the porch, where my brother is reading yet another Doc Savage paperback under the high-watt bulb hanging on a cord from the ceiling fixture. The book's cover shows the sun-roasted explorer standing in a short-sleeved white safari shirt, his Man of Bronze biceps bulging.

Up on the second-story terrace of the house next door, the wooden deck shakes as the children jump and dance, making a thunderous racket as they sing:

> *Carmelo, up there in heaven,*
> *Leans over to watch you,*
> *King of the* trincherazo.
> *Toreador, you twist and spin . . .*

The little faces belonging to these high-pitched voices rise into view along with their necks each time they jump. But their bodies stay hidden behind the terrace wall, and I imagine that Carmelo, a bullfighter as famous as the Silverio Pérez of the song except that he is dead, is the only one who can see these kids' entire bodies since he is watching from the sky. My brother growls with exasperation at the kids' racket, which he can't silence the way he did Dieguín's parrot, by slamming a window shut and stomping out of the house, so he keeps reading his pulp novel under the yellow glare of the ceiling light.

The jasmine bush in the garden accentuates the boredom of the moment with its monotonous sweet smell. Crickets noisily rub their wings together. I always believed that they sang as they chewed, that their jaws clashing together produced their shrill chirping, but then I read in *The Treasure of Youth* how this noise happened.

I must read about everything in books because I no longer believe anything I'm told. Too many people have tried to fool me. Adults don't talk like books, direct and fact-based. Instead, they laugh, wink, refuse to talk, invent some absurd story to hide their ignorance, or make fun of me. I forge my way through books the way ants move along a path, advancing through every letter's section, retrieving breadcrumbs. When I have enough of these, I chew on them and feel good.

As for textbooks, they're like guns put to your head. Arid and inaccessible, nevertheless they must be understood and memorized if you want to pass tests. One time I asked my mother to explain the lesson I had to learn in my Natural History textbook. She didn't understand it either and said she'd ask my brother's tutor, a man with several doctorates whom my mother calls the Brainy Black Guy because he's not white and she doesn't want him to get all full of himself around her. Despite this, she does recognize his brilliance and takes him my textbook to decipher. The tutor reads the lesson several times, then shakes his head as if in despair, and says, "This, nobody can understand. Either they write like this to seem cultured, or it's a bad translation from English."

Everybody in the beach house is doing something. Cleo listens to the radio in her room, Septimio reads on the porch, Kika cooks in the kitchen, my mother in the pantry tells stories from the 1920s and '30s to Kika.

I hear it all. My mother says I have the hearing of an invalid with tuberculosis.

I pass through the house again and go to the patio by the kitchen door. Through the open window I hear my mother: "Baloney!" she exclaims. "The freedom that women had after the Great War, the First World War I mean, we haven't had since. In the Twenties, women set themselves free from all narrow-mindedness, cut their hair, wore short skirts, felt the equal of men at work and in life. The flapper was a free spirit. After the Great War, during the 'dance of the millions,' our Island was flooded with dough, paper money printed in the US with pictures of our national heroes – the streets were awash in 'Patriotas'! The price of sugar went through the roof on the world market, and a whole lot of people here were just rolling in money. Women became very independent then. Those were the days when dirty old men would throw rolls of hundred-peso bills onto our porch just to get my sister Bella, who was barely eight then and gorgeous, to go outside and scoop them up. All just to see this child for a minute!"

Meanwhile, out in the patio, I've decided to get water out of the well. By the light coming from the bulb over the kitchen door, I try to move the rusty pump handle. I jump up and press down with all my strength, and finally the pump handle gives, the spigot burps out a mouthful of water and wets a patch of ground that still has a little grass, a circle dying under the spout.

NIGHT HAS FALLEN. The sky reminds me of my mother's black sequin dresses, splashed with shiny silver dots. There's no region of the sky that isn't blinking brightly, bursting with white bubbles. I might touch the sky just by reaching my hand up to harvest those resplendent clusters, scrape off that glittering dust. In the Capital, I've never seen anything like this. I'm overcome by profound awe.

A tiny frog jumps on my foot. She's breathing agitatedly, inflating then deflating herself. Carefully, I pick her up with my fingers. She's slimy and cold. Her black eyes, which I imagine to be compassionate, gaze at me fearlessly. I caress her soft, cold, viscous belly. "You shouldn't be walking alone at night. A lot of crazy dogs run loose around here," I admonish, setting her down on the grass. She sits, quietly staring at me, as if to ask me something. Between the frog and the starry night sky, there is communication of some kind, having to do with me but not with the busy inhabitants of this house, something I don't know how to explain to myself.

I pump more water out of the well and wash my hands, red with rusty metal, splashing some on my head and face. My mother is still talking: "The Charleston! I couldn't dance with anybody because I'm five feet ten inches tall! and the whole dance hall is full of short men! The band is playing the Charleston, and all those tiny people dancing! Luckily, I met Gus, who's over six feet tall. When we got married, my boss at the Ministry of Education said our kids would grow up to be balcony inspectors!" My mother shrieks with laughter.

I can see her through the window, sitting at the dinner table and drinking her ice-cold beer, her *sudadita*. With the huge fork, Kika is flipping the steaks in the frying pan. Squealing, they give off smoke and the appetizing odor of fried meat.

MY MOTHER AND I HAVE WALKED for what seems the length of the isthmus to Cirilo's house, and, for some reason, I'm surprised that it has a thatched roof. The outer walls' siding boards, painted turquoise blue, sit on top of each other like eyelids, an earlier coat of lime green paint showing through gaps in the light blue layer. The windows, opening outwards, are decrepit and dangle by their lower hinges. A small dirty green towel serves as a doormat.

Cirilo's wife opens the door and stands aside to let us in. She is small, with angular shoulders and sunken chest, and wears a filthy pink housedress that's too big for her. She stares at my mother as if transfixed by the splendor of civilization.

Inside, above the door, a large print of Saint Teresita dominates the scene. Her head crowned with pink roses, her eyes gazing upward, her hands clutching some very white lilies lend the house a mystical touch. Under the print's frame, a plaster-of-Paris half-vase painted the color of strawberry ice cream is nailed to the wall and is filled with three plastic white roses. On both sides of the print, like radio antennas, are the dried palm leaves the church distributes on Palm Sunday.

Upon entering the living-dining room, I am surprised at the tamped-earth floor and a smell of urine that's strangely enhanced by the sparkling perfume of Florida Water. My mother takes me by the hand and steers me to a wicker chair with barely enough woven seat to keep my bottom from falling through.

"We've come to see Cirilo," my mother immediately announces, to dispel the possible misconception that she's the First Lady of the Republic, there to do charity work. "I'm his customer. We like to travel in his carriage."

Without being asked, my mother makes herself comfortable on the rocking chair next to me. Though it still has a seat, its paint has mostly peeled off and it goes crick-crack when my mother rocks back and forth. The small table that separates us has an ashtray made from the bottom of a beer bottle that retains part of its Hatuey label. My mother lights a cigarette with a dramatic gesture, then examines the woman with the gaze of a military inspector. Cirilo's wife, her sad face's cheeks drooping from premature old age, her sharp chin framed by her long, tousled black hair, looks at my mother as if she is waiting to be invited to sit down in her own house.

"Do you mind if I smoke?" my mother asks, belatedly.

"No, Cirilo smokes too. He says he learned it from tourists. I don't. I don't smoke because I don't know when to exhale," she says, laughing to excuse her lack of sophistication and revealing yellow teeth, several of which are missing.

My mother looks at her with surprise, but quickly abandons the idea that this peasant woman's laughter doesn't fit the image of witlessness she has formed about her. In an instant she buries her surprise and smiles with a worldly air.

"Where might we find Cirilo? We have come to detain him, to apprehend him and take him downtown."

"To *detain* him?" the woman asks with a start.

"I'm joking, ma'am. I am not the police," my mother says, raising her head and aiming a puff of smoke at the ceiling. "In the Capital, as you can imagine from the recent disturbances, we talk like this. We're always making morbid jokes. But here, you lead a natural life, full of the little green lights of fireflies and crickets chirping at night. You will be our saviors, of us fools in the Capital. You are the hope of our nation, the country dwellers!"

My mother sings out these last words lyrically, stubbing out her cigarette in the beer-bottle ashtray. Cirilo's wife has no clue how to react to my mother's histrionics, or even how to behave in her own home. Maybe she is searching her memory for the right words, her gaze clinging to her meager possessions, shipwrecked in a sea of her own making.

"Well, Cirilo should be here shortly. If you'd like a little coffee . . ."

"The black nectar of the white gods! The juice of the coffee bean! That delight of the palate, that Asiatic luxury!" my mother declaims.

Seeing the surprise on the face of the peasant woman, she adds: "Yes, ma'am, we'd be most grateful, thank you."

My mother keeps using lofty-sounding words, making expansive gestures, ravaging this house with the cyclone of her dreams. Might she be making fun of her audience? For my part, I can't help doubling over with laughter, not because I'm making fun of this unfortunate woman's confusion, but because I find my mother's ability to keep piling on one exaggeration after another mind-boggling.

Of course, my mother ignores my laughter, taking it to be yet another negative aspect of theatrical performance that she must put up with.

The peasant woman scoots into the doorless kitchen behind my chair, and I turn to see how she fills a strainer of white cloth until it's swollen like an udder with very aromatic ground coffee, then sets water to boil in an aluminum pot over a single burner. In a few minutes, the woman carefully pours the boiling water over the strainer, which turns dark brown and gives off a sensual aroma that reverses the tension of the situation and makes everything soft, almost gentle. She holds this udder over one of two small, crude white cups and the coffee squirts out, black and steamy, then repeats this process with the other cup, then places both little cups on a green ceramic plate.

"This coffee smells marvelous. It's not like ours in the Capital. It's fresh. I'm sure you grind it fresh right here in this house," my mother says with admiration. "How happy you must be, señora! You have this little house that's a paradise and a husband like Cirilo, who's quite the man! I'm quite sure you raise piglets, too!"

"No, madam, we do not raise pigs," the woman replies, setting the small cups very delicately on the table, leaving the green plate in the middle, and sliding the ashtray closer to my mother.

Then she sits in an armchair covered with pink plastic on the other side of the room, far from us. It bothers me that she sits all the way over there, like we're dogs ready to bite her. My mother ignores this and picks up the tiny coffee cup, savoring the liquid with a great show of delight. I pick up the other cup and drink the coffee without making a fuss.

"Well, we do, but only for Christmas Eve," the woman says, as if she suddenly remembers. "In December we fatten one up with palm nuts, corn cobs, food scraps, even coffee grounds. And as many fruits and vegetables as we can get. On Christmas Eve morning, Cirilo stabs it over and over with our widest kitchen knife. I cover my ears. Oh, ma'am, how those damned pigs squeal!"

When she talks about pigs, the woman reveals an odd dignity. She's in her element. She knows all about pigs, and we don't. My mother seems to respect the country-dweller's experience on this subject and humbly cedes her the floor.

"Pigs are the worst thing you can see. They're filthy and will eat anything. They like to wallow in mud and muck. But they look at you with such sad eyes," the woman suddenly blurts out with deep compassion.

A long silence ensues.

After a while, when we have sipped the last drop of the coffee and set the empty cups on the green plate in the middle of the table, and when my mother has smoked several cigarettes, left the butts in the ashtray, and exhausted all her talking points, Cirilo comes in, stamping his heavy boots loudly.

The coachman is startled to see us. "Emilia," he says, looking at his wife with eyes wide, "I didn't know we had visitors!"

"They have been waiting for you for half an hour. I gave them coffee."

There's no clock in the dining room or kitchen, and Cirilo's wife doesn't wear a wristwatch, so I have no idea how she could figure that we have been in her house for half an hour. My mother would surely have told me it was by the sun's rays, even though little light comes into the room.

That's because it's blocked by curtains made from pieces of bedsheets that cover the windows.

"I can see they've been waiting," Cirilo replies, glancing at the empty cups. The coachman drops like a heavy bale onto another rocking chair that has a sturdy seat, next to the armchair where his wife is sitting. He smooths his hair with his hand, scratches his cheek and tilts his head a little to one side.

"So, to what do we owe this surprise?" the coachman asks after a pause, his eyes squinting at my mother with curiosity and a little mistrust.

"We came to kidnap you, Cirilo," my mother says, laughing. "We want to go to town, and we can't walk that far."

"Ma'am, I'm not the only coachman in Varadero. Why did you walk here?"

"Didn't you give us your business card and invite us to visit your house?" my mother asks, irritated, then continues in a kinder tone: "And besides, we want to go with someone we can talk to. Apart from that, Cirilo, aren't you interested in making more money?"

"Yes, ma'am, but I didn't think you would come. People from the Capital tend to have poor memories," he explains warily.

He sits thinking for a few seconds and continues in a friendlier voice: "You want to go into town? Are you sick of the beach already?" The coachman thumps on his stomach like a bongo. "See how the rich tire of eating acorn-fed Spanish ham!" the coachman exclaims, not intending to be insulting.

My mother cuts a glance at him, and then smiles. "See here, Cirilo, there's only one person eating ham right now, and that's President Grau," she replies jovially. "We are just trying to keep our heads above water."

My mother pauses as if considering how to say what's on her mind. Contracting her face intensely, she now looks at the coachman, nailing him to the couch with her eyes.

"Do you know anything about the house we're staying in? I mean, is there a legend? Any stories?" She asks these questions in a very concerned voice.

Emilia stares at Cirilo, and then at me, as if she's alarmed and asking something. Cirilo settles into his armchair, fussing with a wrinkle in his trousers that's bothering him.

The jute curtain, yellowish and worn out, which separates the living-dining room from the room that may be giving off the bitter scent of urine, sways slightly in the morning breeze arriving from a window open somewhere.

"Well, ma'am," says Cirilo clearing his throat, scratching an eyebrow, and exhaling through his mouth, as if for the first time he can relax, "there's a kind of ugly story about the house. We all know it. It happened a while ago, but here everybody knows everything, and nothing is forgotten. You'd think country people had nothing better to do. Gossips!"

"Cirilo!" my mother scolds him impatiently. "Cut the suspense and tell me what happened in that house!"

"Actually, it's a long story. Do you have time to listen to it?"

My mother nods.

"This all happened before the lady doctor bought it," the coachman goes on, taking his time. "She doesn't believe in these legends. She's an educated woman and might even get to be a senator one day. She talks about a lot of things when she takes my carriage and that's how I improve my mind. I learn by talking to my passengers from the Capital and from our Party comrades with university degrees. It sticks to you. Well, before the doctor, nobody wanted to buy the house because, here, everyone is stupid. I'm not. I believe in science, not ghosts."

My mother gives him a furious look for keeping her dangling. Cirilo seems to enjoy the suspense of this moment when all the attention is focused on him. His wife takes a deep breath. She feels her husband's pride vicariously. She is the frame around this man who is now monopolizing the conversation, and therefore she participates in his importance.

"To cut to the chase, ma'am, a jealous madman lived in that house," the coachman says at length, perhaps fearing that my mother will scold him again in front of his wife. "The man believed his wife was cheating on him with every other man on the Island. One day he couldn't take it anymore and cut off the woman's head with an axe. Later he threw her body down the well.

"At that time, the well had a wall around it and was open to the air. It didn't have a pump the way it does now – you had to draw the water by lowering a wooden bucket. Afterward, the madman set her head on an altar in the small bedroom in the back. He fantasized that this was really the head of Saint Barbara, who, as you know, was beheaded by her father. Late at night the man would beat a *tumbadora*, the largest bongo drum, because this madman was also a *santero* and Santa Barbara is the god Changó.

"The neighbors complained about the noise, the police came, they found evidence of the crime, and the husband ended up in the nuthouse. After that, people said, the woman's ghost appeared at night to torment anyone who lived in the house."

My mother comes out of the trance Cirilo's tale has put her in as if it were a nightmare. She shakes her head and seems to be organizing her ideas like a poker hand.

"And you believe this story?" she asks at last in an emotionless voice.

"No!" Cirilo answers forcefully, as if it hurts him to deny it, because deep down he has doubts. "I don't believe any part of this story. These are superstitions of illiterate hicks! Their stories, their fears mess with my head!"

Cirilo suddenly stands up and his boots creak. He opens the front door and goes outside, as if to spread his wings.

In the house he cannot even stretch, he feels reduced to domesticity, the world of women. I see him framed by the door with the trees and the sky in the background, making a declamatory gesture and pointing to the sky.

"Look at that sky!" he shouts from the doorway. "That's what I like to see, that sun up there, nailing us to the ground. And the clouds so close, you think you can spit at them."

He tucks his thumbs into his wide leather belt and breathes deeply, taking in all the air as well as the landscape with its pine trees in the distance seeming to evaporate in the heat.

Cirilo's horse, half asleep in the street, lifts one hoof, then strikes the pavement with its shoe, producing a brief metallic sound.

My mother, exasperated by the coachman's exhibitionism, gets up and commands, "Take us to town, Cirilo! We're in a hurry now."

BACK FROM OUR TRIP IN THE CARRIAGE, my mother tells Cleo and Septimio what Cirilo said about the house. But she decides not to tell Kika, who's in her room with the door closed. "Black people are very superstitious," is the explanation she provides for hiding this story from Kika.

As the night goes on, the fear of falling asleep becomes noticeable among family members. The image of the headless woman has come to life in our imagination. Even Cleo thinks she sees her moving, gauzelike, from the kitchen to the living room. Septimio, fed up with this female hysteria, announces that he's off to his room to go to sleep. He intends to make clear that he finds laughable the fears of the weaker sex, but as he goes into his bedroom, I see him turn pale. Kika, who knows nothing, has been asleep all by herself in her room for a while. My mother decides to move into Cleo's room, which has two beds, one of which I've been sleeping in since we got here so I wouldn't have to breathe my mother's cigarette smoke.

Now I must give my bed to my mother and share a bed with Cleo, as well as resign myself to smelling cigarette smoke. We turn off the lights, and the darkness is lit only by the rabbit's eye of my mother's cigarette, a tiny red Mars in the bedroom's black sky. We haven't let the mosquito nets down since the first night because no insects bothered us then, and the nets turned the beds into Turkish baths.

Likely the mosquitoes come later in the rainy season, when their larvae thrive in the stagnant water of puddles gown to the size of ponds.

My mother's guttural contralto voice breaks the darkness by introducing sounds from the everyday world into this chaos of primordial shadows.

"This Cirilo is a little on the sinister side," she says. "I've never heard a peasant talk like that. Might he be a Russian spy?" my mother says, trying to fish out what Cleo's feelings are towards the coachman.

Cleo bursts into gales of laughter that cascade like rows of green dragon scales over the blackness of the room. I can feel, rather than see, in the darkness the wounding white of her sharp incisors. The mouth half open, the three-line crows' feet at the corners of her eyes, allow me to touch her laughter, which hardens in the gooey air of late summer with facets like a diamond inside an invisible setting.

"Don't listen to him," Cleo answers, seeming indifferent. "He's just a malicious peasant." Cleo says this as part of the crescendo of her laughter, drawing it out and playing with it musically.

"So, I take it you like this 'malicious peasant'?" my mother exclaims in an insinuating tone.

"Oh, please stop!" Cleo says, beginning to sound annoyed.

"Then why do you laugh at him? I saw very well he way he looked at you. Why did you stay outside to talk to him when we went to the store the first day?"

"He's just a dumb hick! As if I'd pay him the slightest attention!" Cleo defends herself.

I feel a strange struggle beginning between my mother and Cleo. I have no idea how they became entangled in this battle. It's as if I am nailed to the bed, silently begging them to end this game, stop hurling their words full of sharp edges and booby traps. Nothing has happened, nothing has been said, but behind every sound and silence, I imagine absurd things hidden.

A huge bug sails around the room, its buzz like a hoarse whistle, monotonous as the ticking of a clock.

Outside, the chirping of crickets rubbing their wings together accentuates the silence. I can see the clouds have dissipated and slivers of light from the full moon come in through the half-open slats of the Venetian blinds, lighting up the floor, illuminating the room with a diffuse silver glow.

My mother puts out her cigarette with a cynical snort.

"Don't you dare kick me in your sleep," Cleo warns me. "I won't put up with kicks," she adds, covering herself with the sheet and giving off a scent of soap and cologne. Between these two odors sprouts another that at first is very subtle, but gradually increases.

It's the smell of ripe fruit, open, fallen from the tree, of a young and healthy woman.

A pause takes shape in the room, arresting the movement of things. The furnishings, protected by the anonymity of shadows, fix themselves in their places.

I try to fall asleep by recalling a painting. I imagine I'm walking down a dusty path that ends where a cypress in a cemetery evaporates upwards in volutes, turning into a sickly green-and-blue sky. The sun, a ball of pumpkin flesh, pours down on the wheatfields lining both sides of the road, and crows like heavy eyebrows fill the sky with upside-down vees.

Several voices move around inside my head like frogs trapped in a box.

"Your father wants us to come here and live so he can be free to sleep with the doctor," my mother complains in this recollection. "I need to have another chat with his sisters. This man is driving me crazy with his cheating."

My bed moves in a gentle rocking motion. Cleo changes her position. After a squeaking of springs and a hollow feeling of void, sleep arrives. As I'm drifting off, near the surface of consciousness, I see Cleo, naked, in the milky glow of the moon. Without putting on underwear, she quickly pulls on a pair of pink clamdiggers and shoves her arms into a red-and-white checked shirt, and as soon as she finishes dressing, she hurries out of the room, but then comes back to get something out of her suitcase. It's a green bar wrapped in tinfoil, and with it she draws a line under her ears. The scent of cologne swiftly fills the room.

THE NEXT MORNING, we have a quick breakfast. Cleo seems rested and calm. Did I dream she dabbed perfume under her ears and went out last night?

When we finish our coffee and bread-and-butter, my brother is the first to shoot out of the house for the beach. He has a light blue towel hanging around his neck to complement his navy-blue trunks, I'm wearing my red swimsuit and I have a big white towel in my hand, and we both have our own snorkeling gear. We want to swim in the morning sun which, according to my mother, "is the richest in ultraviolet rays, which prevent rickets, promote vitality, and nurture growth."

Under the sun's fierce rays, the street we cross seems to end in a mirage of shimmering light, and it exudes a pungent smell of tar.

We hop quickly over the boiling asphalt to keep from burning our feet. Walking on the grass next to the street, which is cool and pleasant on our feet, I ask Septimio, "Which way is north?"

"Now what? You think you're Mungo Park, looking to discover the source of the Niger River?"

"I'm not Mungo Park, nor John Speke, who found the source of the Nile. I want to orient myself. You should always know where the cardinal points are," I answer, annoyed.

"Instead of orienting yourself, you better pay attention to the sand while you're in the water. There are holes in the bottom where you could disappear."

BEHIND SOME DELICATE DARK-GREEN PINES, the sea suddenly spreads out before us, horizontal, shiny as a blue herring. Its flat waters, not a wave in sight, turn a little cherry-colored when they reach the shore and mingle with the pink coral sand. This powder sticks to my feet and ankles, and I can see how Septimio's "disappearing" holes of underwater quicksand might exist. I decide to take care when I go in the water not to get sucked into one of them suddenly.

Through the transparent water, which is various shades of green, I can see the pinkish-yellow bottom. I put on my fins, mask, and snorkel, and dip my head into the gentle, warm water to look for these sinkholes.

Cleo swims up to me and asks, mockingly, "Are you looking for pearls?"

"I don't want to disappear into an underwater sinkhole."

"What? Oh! There aren't any of those here. They're at the beach at Santa María del Mar," she says, amused.

My brother is off swimming in the distance, generating lots of foam from his powerful kicks with the fins. Too bad he's not around to crack him over the head with a coconut. Cleo swims away with great style. I push the mask on top of my head and just float in the water, contemplating the white clouds in the vast blue of the diamond sky, seemingly so close I might touch them with my hand.

Something crashes into me and I see a school of yellowtails. Thin and bluish, with a bright yellow band that runs from their heads to their tails, the fish are swimming so fast, they leave trails of bubbles in the water. I put on my mask and swim deeper to get away from the school of fish, and am surprised to see, hidden among some white corals, a phosphorescent angelfish, turquoise with spots and tail yellow as the sun.

I wonder if fish have mirrors to be able to see and enjoy their own incredible beauty. In some strange way, this moment has been underlined by someone, as if I myself, many years from now, already an adult or even old, were swimming on this very same beach, already having the panoramic vision of this moment and having the whole of my life in front of my eyes. Every move contains this weight of the future, this pain-filled clarity that makes me feel spied upon, and this deep emotion that nearly paralyzes my heart.

We are all in the water, even Kika, who has finally put on the white swimsuit Cleo loaned her, which contrasts beautifully with her light-chocolate skin. My mother, in her black bathing suit, gets into the water wearing a straw hat because the sun bothers her.

Every gesture, every word has ceremonial dignity and, at the same time, a lightness. I attempt to put my thoughts in order: I'm on vacation at the most beautiful beach on this Caribbean Island. I revel in this privilege. I'm with my family, we have more than enough money, and my father is powerful. Everything seems to be full speed ahead with the wind at our back, especially on this beach, the extreme opposite of the Capital, so quiet that the City's helter-skelter life seems part of another, distant world. I am somebody on this beach, showing off my red swimsuit bought at the village store. I'm here as a tourist, like a rich American, to have a good time. The boring classes at school are done. I'm enjoying the freedom of summer vacation.

The whole world believes the future holds greater happiness, everything will be better, better, and better. But a strange feeling makes me distance myself from this happiness, as if I were watching a movie.

AT NIGHT Cleo grabs me by the arm and drags me into our room, closing the door carefully behind us. Septimio is sitting on my mother's bed, smirking, while my mother stands with her arms crossed, leaning against the wall.

"We all must go to bed early," Cleo says quietly, hunched over and flashing impish looks toward the closed door.

"What is going on?" I ask, alarmed.

"Cleo is the Devil's Paw!" my mother exclaims.

"Shhh! Don't let her hear us," Cleo says quietly and continues to speak to me in this low tone. "We're all going to bed now. Kika is bringing in the porch chairs, and when she's done, you must tell her to go to sleep."

"Me? Why do I have to be the one to tell her?"

My mother stretches out on her bed. Septimio is sitting there at the foot. She shakes her head, laughing disdainfully as if Cleo was beyond redemption.

"I hope nothing happens to Kika. If she has a heart attack, you'll be responsible," my mother warns.

"Oh, do shut up, Flora! Don't spoil the joke," Cleo scolds. "The plan is for Kika to go to bed. After half an hour, when the whole house is quiet, Septimio is going to pull her sheet off with a thread. When Kika gets up scared, he's going to grab her feet. Septimio is going to be under Kika's bed and, Mercy, you must make Kika believe Septimio is in his own room."

Cleo says this staring straight at me, as if doubting I can do it.

In the distance we hear the racket of Kika dragging in the heavy porch furniture.

I take off my clothes, put on my pajamas, open the door of our room, and stand in the hallway, where some light from the patio bulb filters in through the kitchen window. Kika is on the porch, and through the wide-open street door, the porch light projects a yellow box on the floor.

On tiptoe in white stocking feet, Septimio sprints away from our room, slips into Kika's room, and quietly closes the door.

Kika drags in the last rocking chair, pulls the front door shut, and collapses on the chair. I go to the living room. The dark skin of Kika's face is completely covered in drops of sweat, which she tries to wipe away with her hand.

"It's hot," she sighs, I guess just to say something.

"Yes, but at least there aren't mosquitoes." My voice seems to be coming from a radio. There's something mechanical and false about my tone.

A thing inside me doesn't want to take part in this joke and says, "Don't get involved!" Another part goads me on: "It's going to be a great joke." Another voice, feeble and hidden, says: "Resist this stupidity! Tell Kika what's being planned!" But this last voice sounds completely irrational to me.

I can't understand it. This is my family. I was born to live among them. Everything is being done with lightheartedness, with no desire to hurt anyone.

And yet, this situation has divided me into several parts.

"I'm going to read for a while before bed," Kika murmurs, getting up and giving me a little pat on the shoulder as a farewell. Maybe she doesn't want to stay in the room and talk. She goes into her room and shuts the door.

The clear yellow light from the front porch now pours in through the window, passing through the floral designs of the wrought-iron grille and projecting Chinese figures on the floor. In the shadows, the furniture smells more strongly of humidity. The fragrance of the sea lives inside, is part of the furniture and the house's wooden walls. The crickets chirp and the lemon trees in the courtyard rustle in the breeze, emphasizing the void created by the shadows.

I'm glad I didn't say anything to Kika. I don't want to be involved in this joke. It's producing a bitter taste coming from my stomach. I turn off the porch light and, taking care not to make the wooden floor creak, I slowly make my way to Cleo's room. I open the door carefully not to make noise but it can't be helped: the moan of old wood sounds like thunder by contrast with the night's silence.

The room is dark. On one side, a reddish star reveals my mother's cigarette. I close the door in slow motion. Feeling my way in the dark, I come to the surface of a hard object. I trace the object and conclude that it's part of Cleo's bed. My hand continues to explore until I reach the soft oasis of the mattress covered by the smooth, soft sheet. I lie down in the bed while the fiery eye watches me from afar. I try to fall asleep.

After quite some time counting sheep jumping fences, I hear a woman scream, over and over. Then: "Have mercy! Mercy! Little yellow butterfly!" The screams jerk all of us out of the dark lethargy and dreams that have invaded us. The cries shatter the night on multiple levels, the first being unspeakable fear and the last, studied mockery.

I don't know which scream to respond to, which tone or intent.

Cleo, in her blue-and-white striped pajamas, jumps out of bed violently.

She turns on the ceiling light, and in almost the same movement turns on the hallway light, opens Kika's bedroom door, and turns on that light. I run after Cleo and see Kika, in her white nightie, standing in the middle of the room, hugging herself, face ashen, eyes popping out of her head, standing stock still.

"Come now! What's all this?" Cleo asks, stifling her laughter. I step to one side of the door so my mother can get into the room.

Kika remains motionless, looking at a point in space. My mother throws her arm around Kika's shoulder, leading her off to the kitchen. Cleo follows, turning on more lights. I'm the only one who sees Septimio sneak out from under the bed. He's livid, with white lips and a lost look. He walks past me not looking at me, not saying a word, and slips into his room, closing the door quietly.

I head to the kitchen. Sitting at the table, Kika looks cadaverous.

My mother turns on a burner and sets a pot of water on it to prepare a cup of chamomile tea for Kika. Cleo and I sit down at the table.

The water boils in the pot and my mother turns off the burner. Kika, motionless, arms folded, looks at us in amazement.

"What happened?" Cleo asks again, this time seriously.

"Let her calm down, Cleo!" my mother chides.

Through the window the lemon trees shake their leaves, illuminated by the electric light of the patio. Beyond that, there's nothing but shadow. The waning moon sits high in the starless night, mostly covered in clouds.

"Ma'am, you won't believe me. I'm Catholic and I don't believe in those things. I'm not a superstitious ignoramus."

I look at my mother and laugh, remembering what she'd said before about Black people. Abashed, she ignores me, places the cup of tea in front of Kika, who sips carefully not to burn her lips.

Then she sits down facing Kika, glaring at Cleo reproachfully because she doesn't seem contrite enough. Cleo's big, black eyes with dark circles under them have not lost their malicious light.

Kika drinks her tea, plays with the tablecloth, smoothing imaginary wrinkles with long fingers that have short unpainted nails. She won't look us in the eye.

"What frightened you, Kika?" my mother asks when the young woman seems to have calmed down.

"I fell asleep right away," she says in a shaky voice, "I don't know for how long. I was dreaming about the nuns at school, when I felt something start rubbing my thighs. I waited to see if it happened again, if it was just my imagination. In a little while it happened again. The sheet started to slip away. They were taking my sheet off! I opened my eyes a little and there it was, on top of the chifforobe! Right there, looking at me! A woman's head! Almost all eaten by worms, but the head of a woman. Definitely. Blood was dribbling down the chifforobe. All eaten by worms and still bleeding!"

My mother looks at Cleo as if to say, *Who is playing a joke on whom?*

"That's not real," she says in a calm voice.

After a pause, she adds: "You're very high-strung and you imagined that. Go back to sleep and don't give another thought to chopped-off heads."

"That's right, Kika!" Cleo exclaims, laughing. "What head could there possibly be on top of the chifforobe? You dreamed that. You thought you were awake and you were dreaming."

Kika takes another sip of chamomile tea, a little relieved to be returning to the prosaic world where severed heads can't possibly sit on top of the furniture. This certainty gives her courage. She smiles.

"That's crazy, isn't it? To see that! Yes, it must have been a dream," she agrees, ashamed of her fear.

"Of course! Tomorrow you'll see. You'll feel better. It was just a nightmare. Your imagination! It can happen to anyone," my mother reassures her, in solidarity, trying to project security in her voice, produce calm.

Somehow, everyone feels taken in.

Words are spoken as if we are on stage in a theater, to produce an emotional effect on another actor. Only Kika seems real, with a truth to tell, a horrible experience to forget. When she finishes drinking her tea, Kika goes to her room smiling, as if apologizing for having woken up everyone because of a dream. She closes her door, and for a moment there is silence.

"'Have mercy ... mercy ... little yellow butterfly,'" says my mother in a low voice, mulling over what just happened. "That's what they say on that radio soap opera when they're scared. Kika got it from there, of course."

Cleo looks at my mother like she can't believe how stupid her aunt is.

"The radio? Really? Flora, can you truly be that foolish? Can't you tell when people are pulling your leg? The joke's on us! A *severed head*, bleeding?" Cleo laughs scornfully and gets up to go to her room.

"Yes, God has punished us! This is the punishment of God!" my mother exclaims, making the sign of the cross. Then she adds, in a very low voice, so that only I hear her: "The worst part is that I saw that very thing on our first night here, before I asked Cirilo about it, when I looked into Kika's room."

RAIN HAMMERS THE ZINC ROOF of the beach house with a metallic sound. Dawn has brought us a sky with bloated thunderclouds being shoved around by capricious winds. The shapes in the clouds multiply: gray tigers and bears join black butterflies and dragons. Then the landscape vanishes behind the cloak of a downpour.

The bluish rain rakes the stout palms, shredding their fronds, strewing long leaves and red-and-orange palm seeds all over.

My brother tells me that Varadero is an isthmus, that is, a tongue of land surrounded by water everywhere except for the one place that links it to the rest of this Island. In my view, Varadero is surrounded by water everywhere but *two* places: the one that connects with the mainland, and the one above that connects to the sky. My brother guffaws at this observation, the same way he thought it was so funny when I told him that if you multiplied 20 times 0 the result had to be 20, because the original 20 could not just disappear. I've stopped paying attention to him, along with getting used to people making fun of me. Still, the thought of being so exposed to the sea and sky terrifies me.

The rain outside with its metallic patter revives my ancient fear of the Flood. Now, water is pouring down on this earthly tongue.

What happens if it doesn't stop raining? If it goes on raining forty days and forty nights? A gigantic wave will rise!

In my imagination, this is how it starts: I'm on the beach gazing at the horizon, and the enraged sea backs up, as if gathering up her skirt as she runs away into the distance, leaving the sand littered with fish: silver fish, red fish, blue fish with yellow stripes, yellow fish with black stripes, all hopping on their tails in the sand; confused starfish lumbering around in all directions; white corals with green algae dripping in tangles from their calcareous fingers; small pod-like marine plants filled with sticky liquid stranded between mollusks and snails.

All left behind by the sea, treated like rubbish.

Then, in an instant, at the horizon line where the sea has curled up her tail, the crest of a great wave rises in a gigantic hand sculpted from gray water and white foam. When it reaches me, it is as tall as a mountain but concave, sucking in its stomach as if to hold its breath, preparing to collapse on the shore like a cyclopean fist, crushing everything.

Often, I dream that I'm in Atlantis, contemplating the opulent palace of Poseidon surrounded by rings of water, canals filled with barges so luxurious they're like floating castles and small, lightweight boats that conduct trade. The gold-and-ivory temple that glows with sun-red flames is unforgettable. Occultists say that, centuries ago, our Island had great temples like this, now submerged under the deep and vinous sea.

Cleo appears in the door of our room. I am hiding under the sheets, trying to block out the rain and wind, the howling of the royal palms and the coconut palms. "Come to the dining room. We're making coffee," she says enthusiastically, as if she's over and done with the severed head incident.

I jump out of bed, pull on my green shorts and yellow jersey, and run to the dining room without brushing my teeth. I grab my cup of coffee and sit at the table facing my mother, who's lounging sideways in her pink nylon robe that's open on both sides of her crossed legs. She's already finished breakfast and is smoking a cigarette. Cleo has on blue clamdiggers, a red short-sleeved cotton blouse, and, on her head, a red kerchief printed with black flowers.

"I repeat, Flora, not one iota of that is true, there's no dead woman," Cleo says, sounding like she's talking to a child as she sits down at the table to drink her coffee.

My mother looks at her distrustfully. I study my mother's face, without makeup a little gone to wrack and ruin, her unkempt hair covering her forehead and watery eyes, their yellowish whites crisscrossed by tiny red veins.

"There's something to this," my mother says. "It's not that I give it any credence...but there's something, because otherwise this makes no sense. How did Kika know the thing about the woman? That wasn't a joke."

Cleo laughs and shakes her head as if baffled by such naïveté. The dark circles under her eyes expand like a curtain and the black fuzz on her upper lip fluffs up. Her perfectly oval face and heart-shaped mouth suddenly darken.

"Don't you remember, when we were in town on the first day, we all went into the store, but Kika stayed outside, talking to the coachman?"

"Yes," says my mother, drawing back in surprise. "What's *that* got to do with it?"

Cleo shakes her head again as if my mother is completely clueless. There's a spark of freshness in this gesture, something operatic about the mental power of youth.

"*That* was when the coachman told Kika the story, and she's been taking us for a ride ever since," she says. "We wanted a laugh at her expense and she ended up laughing at us. How could you not have figured that out?"

My mother slumps back in her chair, eyes open and huge, creating a path in the air, opening the way to some remote place where maybe she parked her ability to see, like Kika, beyond material things.

I finish my coffee, get to my feet, walk over to the front door, and grab the doorframe with my hand. I stand on one foot, the way I've seen some chickens sleep.

The doorframe's wood is deeply scarred. The many coats of white paint over these rough splinters have raised and hardened them, and they prick my fingers.

Kika, dressed all in white, is knitting a pink sweater, rocking back and forth in one of the chairs on the porch. My brother, in another rocking chair, studies the morning rain through a magazine he's rolled up into a telescope. The porch's cement floor is wet at the outside edges, and the cement's gray looks darker there. Where the pools of water are shaped like pyramids and semicircles, lit by a feeble sun behind a mask of clouds, the floor becomes shinier, taking on a pearly appearance.

Some force keeps me at the door. Kika and Septimio together form an impassable blockade, immersed in his and her private worlds. Their thoughts have created an electrical barrier of loneliness on the porch.

Inside, in the living room and the bedrooms, all the mirrors are covered with sheets, because my mother is convinced that reflective objects draw lightning. Having to shroud the mirrors now makes them look like ghosts, like white stains standing out in the gloom of the house.

In the kitchen, shrunken in the distance, my mother continues to sit at the table smoking. Behind her, the patio looks even darker because of the door's metal screen, and the rain continues to pound the yard's lemon trees and deafeningly beat up the bananas, their broad leaves torn into fringes that look cut with scissors. The wind now moves each section of a banana leaf toward a different compass point. The bananas, like swollen fingers, present their yellow backs among the green of the leaves.

I figuratively kick down the psychological barrier that's been erected on the porch and abruptly enter. Kika looks at me alarmed, then resigned, to the inevitability of my entering her space, but she continues to work her white plastic knitting needles, churning out row after row of interlocking pink yarn.

"Let's go to the beach," I say to Kika.

I pick a white umbrella out of several in the golden metal umbrella stand by the door and hand it to Kika, because I don't care if I get wet. Then I hop down the walkway's cement slabs that are separated by gaps where pink and white flowers sprout. They're phlox, I think, because I've watched my mother make eye drops by boiling the petals of these flowers.

Kika follows me, sheltered under the umbrella. I take off my shoes, carrying them in one hand and, barefoot, run across the street. I advance down the narrow path of wet sand that leads to the beach, avoiding those tiny pine cones that are full of cutting edges, like diamonds in the rough. Sometimes my feet hurt from stepping on burrs or the small thorny stalks and leaves of a certain plant that has a scented sap, but even though I'm surprised and upset, I just curl up my toes and keep going, barefoot, to be able to feel the different surfaces that my feet land on.

The rain soaks through my shorts and jersey, and my hair is dripping wet, like I've gone swimming.

Kika keeps up with me while taking care not to get wet in the rain and not to ruin her dress that now glows mysteriously in the gray light of day.

At a turn in the path, the perfidious sea suddenly appears like a slap in the face. Enraged, the dark green, gray, and black waves leap high. The thatch umbrellas double over in the wind, and, vibrating under them, the small white metal tables, imprisoned by concrete plinths hidden in the sand, produce a monotonous metallic roar. The pine trees behind me emit loud moans that end in deep murmurs. There's not a soul on the beach.

I leave my shoes on one of the tables and, feeling like Admiral Nelson, I run to the water's edge and whip out an imaginary sword, shaking it at the waves that are preventing me from launching my ships to conquer great glory for the English Crown. It's of the utmost importance to prevent the mongrel Corsican from becoming emperor and tyrant of all Europe. "Damnation! The sea is against us!" I scream, skillfully wielding my sword to slay this maddened liquid monster. I sink my sharp blade into the shore's tamer waves.

After a while, being Nelson bores me, and I transform myself into his enemy, Napoleon. I find myself in the primary school the Corsican attended, at the time when he was scorned by his classmates. I walk around the cloister of the school, my right hand inside my jersey and my left behind my back. I construe terrible plans of destruction. My fellow students see me stride by and mock my seriousness. They have no way of knowing that I will become emperor of France. Soon they'll be made to regret all the insults they have heaped on me.

I throw my sword into the sea, along with my Corsican hat, my imperial crown, my laurel wreath. The cavalry, the cannons, Nelson's squadron, all are lost in the waves. I walk over to Kika, who mockingly applauds my performance.

I sit next to her, on the metal table, after tendering a sharp military salute.

The sea continues to rampage in violent, disordered waves.

Suddenly a lightning bolt hits the water, throwing off a hissing whistle, like the sound a piece of meat makes when dropped in the boiling oil a frying pan, but infinitely louder. Instantly we hear a deep, loud, rumbling sound, as if somebody had let an elephant-sized iron bank vault fall on the sand from outer space.

The sound's vibration makes us jump onto the table. "Holy blessed Saint Barbara! Changó!" Kika screams, making the sign of the cross for Changó, the Yoruba god of lightning.

A smell of violets sprouts from Kika's dress. Her round, bright face and her slightly chubby cheeks seem compressed as if being made to cross a narrow passageway between two worlds: her Black and her white heritage.

Another lightning bolt hits a royal palm farther off. By chance I'm staring at that palm and see the thread of light, a bright yellow snake, spiral around the palm tree's trunk, coil in on itself, and dive deep into the earth beneath the tree. As it penetrates the earth, the bolt shakes us with a huge, dry whack, a deafening noise like hundreds of lions roaring as one under the sand. We quake at the sparks and reverberation. The palm's incinerated crown looks like the smoldering stump of an arm, and the burnt leaves give off a sulfureous smell. Kika makes several signs of the cross and shouts "Changó!" again.

After one more terrifying thunderbolt, Kika grabs me by the hand and drags me running with my shoes in my hands toward the house. Along the way, pine cones and sharp pine needles, treacherous thorns and burrs among the mangrove roots, even dried leaves, everything, gets a second chance to lacerate my feet. The worst torture comes from small yellow spheres with hard prickles and thorns, which pierce the soles of my bare feet and cling tenaciously. I let go of Kika's hand to pluck them out, hopping on one foot to try to keep up with her.

At last, we emerge on the street between us and the house. Kika composes herself emotionally and opens the umbrella. We are so wet the umbrella's almost a joke, but the gesture symbolizes a return to the safety of everyday life.

NIGHT HAS FALLEN. Rocking in one of the chairs on the porch, I can hear the others chatting in the living room, paying no attention to me. I close my eyes and focus on Napoleon Bonaparte.

It's the time period after his loss at the Battle of Waterloo. "Your Majesty, I do not call you General because, although I am sad you lost your throne, for me you will always remain Emperor," I whisper so they can't hear me inside the house. A surprisingly cordial and pleasant male voice responds:

> Yes, it vexes me when people call me General, but the English insist on that title out of perversity.

What made you go to England when you were overthrown?

I was not "overthrown." Wellington had a stroke of luck and won because he had nowhere to retreat in the battle. His rearguard was blocked, and Lady Luck favored him. I tried to go to England because my friends convinced me that it would be better for France if I left, and I agreed that it was better to surrender to the English than to French monarchists. Above all, I did not want to be shut up in the Bastille, which we ourselves had razed, in great part.

I come from the future. Where are you now, Emperor?

We have just passed the Cape Verde Islands in the Atlantic Ocean. I am aboard the Northumberland *near the Equator and heading for the island of St. Helena, farther south relatively, near the Tropic of Capricorn. As we passed the latitude of the Sahara Desert, I was forced to go belowdecks to protect myself from the hot, sandy wind that comes from that fiery land.* (He goes on, disconsolate:) *They are sending me to die miserably in the tropics.*

Yes, you've already had the taste of Egypt in your youth, Your Majesty.

I can't stand the unhealthy heat and fumes of those latitudes. (There's a moment of silence when I think I've lost communication, but Napoleon comes back with interest in his voice:) *You say you are from the future? What century?*

From the twentieth century, where a global war has just ended. Tell me, Majesty, what does it feel like to lose an empire?

I never wanted an empire! I was the ruler who worked the hardest in the history of indolent France! I wanted to transform all the French institutions, but I was not in power long enough. I was not favored by luck.

From the door Kika asks: "What *are* you doing? Talking to yourself?"

"I'm reciting the rosary," I say.

THE FOLLOWING DAY the children next door jump and skip around on the veranda outside my field of vision, their bodyless voices singing:

> *Let it rain,*
> *let it rain,*
> *Our Lady of the Cave!*
> *The birds are singing,*
> *the earth's arising,*
> *Our Lady of the Cave!*

They're always singing and jumping, and all I can see is heads and hair. From time to time, they peer over the railing and stare at us: eyes and faces of children, just for an instant, and then more singing and jumping behind the railing.

I take this as an insult. I could have had a lot of fun with these kids who, I'm pretty sure, are about my age. The days in Varadero really drag, particularly since the rain has reduced my world to humorless adults and their endless conversations. I include my brother as one of those adults, and I pace, bored, from the porch to the yard, from the yard to the porch.

My mother, sitting at the kitchen table, wears black shorts and a sleeveless black silk blouse printed with pink roses and green buds. She also has on a white visor cap of Septimio's, which would shade and ventilate her face, if there were any sun. Cleo, facing her, eats fried shrimp, picking them up by their greasy pink-and-red tails. Because somebody forgot to buy napkins, she dries her oily fingertips on the lace-bordered white cloth covering the table. Kika, next to my mother, continues to knit her pink sweater. And I sit on a wooden stool beside the stove.

Septimio comes in, bouncing a red ball off the ceiling.

"Do you mind? Go play on the porch! You're staining the ceiling red. That ball leaves marks," my mother scolds. Septimio catches the ball with the gesture of a major league pitcher and sits across from my mother and Kika.

The pieces are all here together for the adults to begin another of their creepy chess games, the kind that never end well. Since we arrived, we keep coming together and disbanding in small groups, ever changing, setting up all possible combinations. Now, all five of us are together in the kitchen, stretching the air tight as drum leather. There's no oxygen.

The rain is picking up. Outside, the rain may be the plants' salvation, but inside, it's the people's prison. The rain may cool, but it prevents escape.

"What finally happened with the head?" Septimio asks, tongue in cheek.

"What head do you mean?" Cleo asks, in turn, maintaining a superficial tone as she delicately places an uneaten shrimp tail on her plate.

"The woman's head," my mother clarifies.

"The woman without a head! The woman without a head!" I cry excitedly.

"Oh, stop, you. Nothing's happened. Kika never saw a thing. Right, Kika?"

Cleo doesn't wait for an answer and goes on: "This is local lore, country legend. Superstition. Maybe somebody told us this to make us nervous. That Cirilo is a trickster."

Kika stops knitting and stands up, arranging her knitting needles and pink yarn to carry them in her skirt, like a tray. Then she vanishes into her room without a word. "You can't broach the subject with her," my mother whispers quietly, gesturing with her thumb toward Kika's small room.

"We are all going to end up seeing bloody heads," my brother says, laughing and spreading his legs to bounce his ball on the floor.

"Septimio, tell what you saw! Did you see the bloody head?" I ask, very clearly remembering his livid face.

"No! Nobody saw any heads! Drop the subject. I'm sick of this!"

My brother goes out to the porch, throwing the ball against the ceiling.

"I don't like mysteries. Things should be light, and chocolate dark. It seems to me the entire world is telling me lies. Even my own son!" my mother whines, as if seeking to be consoled.

Cleo stands up with her dirty plate, scoops the shrimp tails into the small garbage bin next to the sink, and holds the dish under the open faucet, soaps it, rinses it, and turns off the faucet. Drying the dish with a cloth, she puts it away carefully inside the kitchen cabinet.

Sitting down again at the table, she cleans her teeth with a toothpick from a small white holder, sucking with her tongue to remove bits of shrimp meat from the gaps between her teeth.

"I'm going to tell you what I think," Cleo says. "I think we're creating this story to entertain ourselves, but, I'm with Septimio – I'm getting tired of it. Shall we play Parcheesi?"

I run to bring the board with the box of pawns and the cup with the dice. I arrange everything on the table and choose the four red pawns. After all, I'm for the Capital baseball team, and our color is red.

I drop the dice in the cup, shake it, and blow on the dice to give me luck.

And then I hear a weak, trembling voice, almost cracking, from Kika's room: "Ma'am, ma'am! Come and see! Quickly, come and see!"

My mother and Cleo look at each other, perplexed. I dump the cup out on the table, and the dice come up double sixes.

We run to the room and see Kika standing propped against the wall next to the bed, covering her eyes with her arms crossed. The small room is half lit by the leaden gray day outside seeping through the partly-closed Venetian blinds.

"Look at the chifforobe! The chifforobe!" Kika shrieks, her body trembling. My mother, Cleo, and I, standing at the door, all turn our gaze to the piece of furniture.

On the chifforobe's antique wood front, a red liquid is cascading in rivulets towards the ground and making large scarlet rosettes on the white tile floor.

"Blood! All full of blood!" my mother exclaims, nearly vomiting, her face compressed into a look of disgust.

Cleo walks purposefully towards the dresser, swipes across the dark dribbles, and shows us her hand as it drips a horrid garnet liquid. Then, leaving no time for us to stop her, she sticks out her tongue and systematically licks her hand.

I double over in disgust, my stomach ready to come out of my mouth.

"This ketchup isn't bad," Cleo says indifferently.

"Ketchup!" Kika shouts.

"Yes, tomato sauce," Cleo clarifies unnecessarily, giving us a mocking look as she leaves the room, and gently nudging my mother, paralyzed at the door.

We follow Cleo into the kitchen, and Kika follows us.

Cleo rinses what's left of the tomato sauce off her hand and dries it with a dish towel. Kika sits in a chair, still shaking. My mother, across from her, is white, shrunken, caved in on herself. I fill a red plastic glass with water, and, standing there, before I take a sip, I peer through the glass at the scene, and see my mother, as red as if she were in hell.

"What is the meaning of this?" my mother asks Cleo.

"It means one joke deserves another. Keep a close eye on what your sweet little son does. I'm sure he poured the ketchup on the cabinet," Cleo replies, unconcerned that Kika is listening to this. My mother is stunned.

"While you all went to the beach, Septimio came in the kitchen and opened the refrigerator," my mother says as if coming out of a dream. "I thought he was going for a drink of water or milk and I didn't pay him the slightest attention. I was too busy thinking about the 1930s and Russian spies."

Cleo laughs and sits down next to my mother, who passes her hands over her face in exhaustion. Everything is sweating inside the house. There's no air, just suffocating steam. I stop peering through the red glass, drink the water, and put the glass in the sink. Outside, the rain has let up a little, and the horizon widens in my field of vision. The pinks and blues of nearby houses reappear.

In the patio, the banana trees are completely back in focus, outlined in phosphorescent green. The kitchen, lit by fluorescent light, is like a white cube between the gray and the green of the landscape.

I imagine I'm looking through the window, watching a scene of family intimacy in a kitchen. Three adults and a young girl. Living from one moment to the next is a major achievement just now. The atmosphere presses down like lead.

Kika's expression is inscrutable.

"How would you all like me to make you some coffee?" Kika says, as if to get us to forgive the abject fear she's just shown.

And at once she stands up to put the pot on the burner.

"Well, I think, here endeth the grotesque story of the severed head!" Cleo exclaims, laughing joylessly, and giving Kika a suspicious look.

SOMEONE KNOCKS AT THE STREET DOOR. I open, and there, framed in the doorway, haloed by the sky's gray light, Cirilo has materialized.

My mother sticks her head out into the hall and tells him to come on in. After smacking and tapping his boots with his hands, Cirilo walks towards the kitchen. I follow him.

The coachman's khaki pants, as well as his Brylcreemed black hair, are sopping wet from the rain.

"I can smell I've come at coffee time," says the coachman jovially. He marches into the kitchen, greets my mother with a nod, and takes a seat at the table without being invited.

"It's always coffee time, these past few days," my mother says happily, revitalized by the arrival of a new person. "Given this dreadful weather, what's there to do but drink coffee and chatter endlessly?"

"I barely have any work with this rain. The tourists don't go out. I was just passing by, and I said to myself, wouldn't it be a fine idea to stop and say hello to Madame Flora? After all, we are nearly neighbors."

I remain standing, slouched against the kitchen wall.

"For heaven's sake, Cirilo, you don't live nearby!" my mother protests.

"Come now! I live right there, down where the road turns. You yourself went on foot with your daughter!"

Kika strains the coffee and serves it in demitasse cups. She serves Cirilo first, because although he is a man, he is privileged by being our visitor. Cirilo takes the tiny cup handle in his brown hands, his fingers full of calluses, gnarled from handling the reins all day. Then she gives the other cups to Cleo and my mother, and retreats quietly to her room.

"I know we can go walking, but judging by distances in the Capital, you're hardly a neighbor. People in the Interior have no concept of distances. Everything is 'right over there' and then one comes to discover that the place is miles away," my mother points out, without meaning to be critical.

"For just that reason, I never go to the Capital. You all think you know everything. Have you ever even seen a pig killed? I'll bet not!" Cirilo says in a joking tone, smiling as he sips his coffee, making theatrical gestures to show how much he is enjoying the delicious Arabic coffee that is the Island's national pride. Cleo makes a dismissive gesture, and my mother glances up at the ceiling as if to say, "Do we have to talk about killing pigs?"

"Of course, we've seen pigs, Cirilo. And we've seen them killed, too," my mother replies in a condescending tone.

Cleo looks at Cirilo jokingly, but at the same time with interest. She seems to think he's a character in a novel, so tall and so skinny, with so many wrinkles on a young face.

"Ah, that's true! You all have cars in the city and can go to the Interior and then you've seen it all. Absolutely true," the coachman replies seriously, as if something very important had slipped his mind.

I GET TIRED OF STANDING UP and head for the front door. It's still raining. Septimio is in the street examining Cirilo's carriage, parked in front of the house.

The workhorse, a black-maned chestnut with a huge, powerful rump, flicks his tail, shows his teeth, and strikes the pavement loudly with the iron shoes on his hooves. He seems worn out from the burden of his heavy, complicated carriage harness made of leather that, soaked with the animal's sweat and the rainwater, gives off a sharp, but not offensive, odor.

The slavery of this animal strikes me like a punch in the chest.

The automobiles that from time to time go by on the wet street look like metallic monsters compared with the simple beauty of Cirilo's horse and carriage.

I go up to my brother and say, "Did you put the ketchup in Kika's room?"

"Of course not! Ask Cleo, she's in charge of practical jokes," he snaps.

Behind the pine trees, towards the sea, it's clearing up. On both sides of the street, following the curbs, rivers of red water run, laden with earth and leaves.

Everything smells wet. The porch awnings, secured on their rollers, also smell of humidity. Bored, I go back to the kitchen and sit at the table.

With his index finger Cirilo pushes back his nonexistent hat, then, realizing how absurd this gesture is, he scratches his wide forehead.

"The country is lost, ma'am!" the coachman exclaims. "There we have President Grau!"

My mother and Cleo shake their heads and sigh as if the last thing they want to discuss is politics.

"So many illusions he gave us in his youth," the coachman continues as if inspired and looking at my mother. "The brain of the Pentarchy that ruled the country! For five days, Grau made jokes at the Presidential Palace: Five leaders mounted on the same administrative bicycle! Then the Pentarchy was done. We had faith in that clown."

Cirilo seems to suffer personally when he recounts the evils of the Nation and now looks up at the ceiling and heaves a sigh, as if to say that the country is beyond salvation. "Now that Grau is president of the Republic," the coachman informs us unnecessarily, "he provides us with gangsterism, crime, payoffs, nepotism, corruption, immorality. He steals right and left. Even the diamond belonging to the National Capitol, which they say was the property of Russia's last tsar and has magical powers, disappears! stolen from the Capitol, one of the most heavily guarded places in our country! then, mysteriously, reappears on President Grau's desk!"

The face of the coachman contracts, the smallpox scars on his skin deepen, and the color of his cheeks turns yellowish, bilious. His eyes, on the other hand, display great vitality. His chestnut-colored corneas grow brighter and give off a greenish light. To underline his words, he pounds his thighs, making a sound like the snap of a whip against his starched khaki pants.

"You don't understand Grau," my mother replies in a teacher's tone. "The old man is a philosopher who tells Creole jokes, who uses the *choteo* to tell us the bitterest truths. What's going on in this country? Disrespect for law, corruption among government officials, gangsterism! Criminal gangs are the heritage of the revolutionary socialists of the 1930s. All the politicians and gang members of to-day were young revolutionaries who fought to overthrow the dictator Machado. Communists and socialists. People of inconceivable ruthlessness, that's what we have now: Policarpo Soler, Orlando León Lemus alias El Colorao, El Extraño, El Manquito, El Turquito, the University Bonche, not to mention the gunslingers of the University Student Federation. Pure Chicago gangsters."

Then she adds: "My husband says Grau tried to emulate the Greek state by incorporating troublemakers into the so-called paramilitary groups to control them." She pauses to let Cirilo think about this, then continues: "The trouble is, Grau and his followers forgot that this Island is not ancient Greece ...."

Suddenly it's very quiet. My mother crosses her legs. Her black shorts reveal white thighs with the purple and green bruises she calls "black-and-blue marks."

Even since we've been sitting here, she's inadvertently bumped into the kitchen table several times, while Cleo and Cirilo slowly sip their coffee avoiding looking at anyone. My mother lifts the coffee pot Kika has left on a low flame, serves herself what's left of the coffee, turns off the burner, and sits down to enjoy it.

I see through the open door that it's stopped raining. A double rainbow, almost transparent, throws its semicircles of colors up into the cloudy blue sky. Red, yellow, and green stripes embrace in the luminous space. This represents God's sacred covenant with humanity that He will not send another great Universal Flood.

That's reassuring unless it means, instead, that the Earth runs out of water.

Cleo, her elbow on the tablecloth, rests her cheek in her hand. Her eyes fix on Cirilo, as if to memorize his features.

"Ma'am, I didn't know you were for Grau," says the coachman, opening his arms and pushing his chair backwards.

"I am not 'for' Grau any more than I am 'for' Christopher Columbus, but one must live, Cirilo," my mother replies, vexed. "What do you want? Here we are in Varadero, supposedly on vacation, but, really, we are avoiding kidnapping or assassination because my husband is high up in the Department of Education and coming to be known as a politician. We left our house in the Capital because it's rumored that El Colorao's people are going to machine-gun us all because my husband hasn't handed over to them the millions of pesos they say he stole, which he did not!"

After a pause to catch her breath, she adds: "Imagine, all of us with more holes in us than a colander! My poor children lying there on the floor, shreds of meat in pools of blood! Oh well! These days, that's just life!"

Then she adds: "But right here, in the closet of my room, I have a pistol and I will shoot anyone. One has to survive!"

The coachman looks at her in shock. Cleo laughs and covers her mouth with her hand coquettishly. "Don't you believe a word, Cirilo. She trembles at the sight of a gun. She's just trying to impress you," Cleo explains.

My mother rearranges her hair and decides it's beneath her to contradict her niece.

"Well, I think it's a horrible way to live!" Cirilo exclaims.

"As long as we have a democratic president that we can remove from office every four years, we'll be fine," my mother lectures the coachman, staring at him. "The unhealthy thing is dictators and tyrants that no one can get rid of. Yes, the Republic is in trouble. Gradually our problems will be solved – after all, we haven't even been independent for fifty years yet!" She takes a sip of coffee and says, "What do you want? To have us all be idealists like my brother-in-law, Alejandro de Nájera? To have us all die of tuberculosis while organizing a strike against a dictator so that the communist paradise can be born?"

Cirilo lets his gaze drift down the hallway as he struggles to disguise his astonishment and awe at learning that we are connected, if only by marriage, to Alejandro de Nájera, co-founder of the Island's Communist Party. "It's an honor to know you, ma'am," the coachman says after he's recovered, with an emotion in his voice that he can't disguise.

After a moment, he adds: "Alejandro was one of the pure ones, one of our martyrs, who never failed us."

"That's as may be, but he died repentant and feeling guilty," my mother says, savoring this opportunity to deflate the coachman's balloon of innocence. "Alejandro saw the real Russia of Stalin when they sent him to a sanatorium in the Caucasus to cure his tuberculosis. What he witnessed there made him realize that communism would cause the destruction of the world. He returned to the Island knowing that he was dying, but determined to lead the strike that would overthrow Machado. Running a high fever, during the day he hid in the clinic of his friend Dr. Almanzor, and by night came out to lead the rallies that galvanized the working classes.

"He was fortunate to die in his own bed," she goes on, "because ultimately the comrades would have killed him, by orders of Stalin, the 'Little Father' the old ladies who sweep the streets of Moscow worship," she says.

"And the apparatchiks are still here on the Island, buying up the corruptible, duping the idealists. Let's hope we never get our own 'Little Father' in the future, because when the cancer of communism strikes, it is intractable, impossible to cure," she grimly concludes.

Cirilo cannot disguise his fury at my mother's words, but he dares not contradict her. He squints his eyes at her doubtfully, suspecting that she is lying.

A peach-colored light filters in through the door and seems to levitate objects. The white of the kitchen walls melts into that soft, almost amber glow. Words vibrate in the atmosphere like the flutter of pigeons, leaving the trace of their echo in my memory. This moment, not because of what is said, but because of its profound resonance in consciousness, is happening in various worlds at the same time, multiplies in other dimensions, and piles up in an infinity of time and space, taking on a strange resonance.

"Your brother-in-law lived before his time, ma'am, but nothing is lost in this world. The future will be different," the coachman says to recover, somehow, from the impression that my mother's revelation has made on him.

"The future will bring us a military dictatorship and the communism of Russia," my mother predicts with a mocking laugh. "All backed by the Yankees so we don't make problems for them with riots in the street and bombings at their embassies and consulates all around the hemisphere," she adds in a mysterious voice.

Cirilo looks at my mother as if she were crazy, but decides not to answer, though the muscles of his chin and arms contract in rage at this woman's absurd ideas.

"I saw the orders from Stalin, from 'Comrade Steel,' sent to and received by Party Headquarters on the Island," she says, nailing Cirilo with a furious look. "This Island will be the beachhead for Russia in the Western Hemisphere. Wasn't it Humboldt who said we are the key to the Gulf of Mexico?"

And she goes on to answer her own question: "Well, we're also the key that opens the Pandora's Box of communism in America."

After a few minutes of tension and silence, the coachman rises, making noise with the heels of his boots and bumping against the table as he gets up.

"The coffee was very good, ma'am. Now the rain's stopped, and I must be on my way," he says, a bit curtly.

Cleo and I follow him down the hall. Cleo accompanies him to the sidewalk and they talk for a while, while the coachman pats the horse's neck affectionately.

My brother, sitting in a rocking chair on the porch, watches them mockingly, while I spy on them from the doorstep. Cirilo makes wide gestures, owns his central zone and its periphery. Cleo seems captive in that circle, flying like a moth around a lamp.

Cirilo walks toward the garden, takes a yellow bellflower and tucks it into Cleo's hair. In doing so, his fingers graze her breast.

In a quick gesture, as if he had gone too far, he leaps into the carriage, gives his horse a gentle nudge with the whip, and disappears among the few cars on the street.

Cleo seems lost in the orange glow of the sky. The golden edges of this scene are attenuated by the green of the pines in the background. Cleo shrinks, in my imagination, lost on the sidewalk watching Cirilo's carriage disappear, the way you see, in films, the size of people remaining on a train platform shrink as the train pulls away and races off at great speed.

Inside the house, my mother's resonant voice comes from the kitchen, where she is all alone: "That peasant believes communism is going to be better than democracy. There's no blinder man than the one who doesn't want to see. Communism is going to plunge us into the deepest of all hells."

AFTER ANOTHER WEEK OF SUN and very pleasant temperatures, going to the beach every day, and having lots of fun, without tension or boredom, we get up early and haven't even finished breakfast, when my father unexpectedly arrives, driving our car himself. The lady Doctor is with him in the front seat.

My father tells us seriously, without his usual jokes, to pack quickly because we are going home a few days early.

The lady Doctor explains that her aunt, who lives in Miami, has arrived out of the blue to spend a few weeks at the Varadero house. "I'm so sorry," says the lady Doctor, who reminds me of Ingrid Bergman in *For Whom the Bell Tolls*. She wears a cotton shirt with red checks and khaki slacks and has short blond hair, as well as the graceful walk of the famous Swedish actress. I am surprised to be asking myself, have she and my father split up? I don't believe the "rich aunt" story. It makes me insecure to think that my father has a lover, but on the other hand, I like that he's not a perfect man.

"Go get your stuff, Bad Bug. We're leaving right now!" my father tells me, smiling.

"How are we all going to fit in one car?"

"The doctor is staying here to wait for her husband, who's coming from the Capital, and I'm going to drive our car. You should study physics! You're always so interested in how things fit together."

I run to the patio. On the windowsill is the glass jar with the starfish that I caught when we first arrived at Varadero. When I open the jar, the stench fills my lungs with vomit and misfortune. The starfish has died and is disintegrating, slimily, in the seawater.

How could she die in seawater? I throw her on the grass and she crumbles completely, becoming gray gunk. I feel her death personally, this starfish, her agony at being enclosed in that bottle, suffocated, unable to move. When the flare of death touches life, it lights up life's contours and shadows in bright and blood red. I double over from the pain of having killed her, and vomit. Then I pump some water out of the well to wipe my hands and rinse off my nose, which retains a trace of the ghastly smell. Too late I remember Cirilo's story of the headless body the jealous husband threw down this well. I'm surprised that water even comes out, instead of blood.

My mother calls to me as she drags our bags out of the house and piles them up in the portal. Kika, always diligent, helps her with the packages and suitcases. Cleo complains at not being given a chance to say goodbye to Cirilo. My brother puts on his eye-rolling, cynical face. Upstairs in the house next door, the children sing raucously:

> It was your eyes or your mouth, it was your hands, it was your voice,
> it was probably impatience, waiting so long for you to arrive.
> I know no more, can't tell you how it happened,
> but I fell in love with you.

The Doctor, blond and luminous, smiles on the porch. Her face takes in the freshness of the breeze, and she relaxes with the calm of one who has returned home. My father, by her side, dressed in a starched white guayabera, his silver hair flaring from his temples like Clark Gable's, also smiles, displaying his gold teeth.

Inside, the activity of leaving; outside, the enjoyment of the instant.

As we all run in and out of the house in furious commotion, my father and the lady Doctor sit on the porch, calm, united in an aristocracy of power and wisdom. They have read the same books. They deeply care about ancient Greece and ancient Rome, Socrates, Cato, Epictetus, Cicero. They talk about these things while we remove our "gear," as my brother calls it, and "stow" it in the car. A classic and triumphant atmosphere envelops the couple, separates them from the triviality of us stupid mortals.

My mother is immersed in France, in Louis XIV, Madame Pompadour, Cardinal Mazarin, Fouché, Talleyrand, fascinated by that whole other world of hereditary autocracy. I'm not sure which of these worlds will win, in the end.

But I have no doubt, now, that my mother's jealousy is fully justified.

When everyone is finally inside the car, the kids next door chant:

> Pumpkin Heads, Pumpkin Heads,
> every one of you Pumpkin Heads
> take your silly selves home.

24

RETURN TO ORFILA

AS SOON AS WE RETURN from Varadero, the air begins to choke up with one veiled conversation after another. Mostly I overhear my father talking in detail with Santana and Pancho Pistola about a member of El Colorao's gang, Police Captain Rafael Ávila, and his attempt to assassinate Emilio Tro by machine-gunning his car.

This happens a little over a week after we get home from the beach. Tro got away unharmed, but then, a couple of days later, he took his revenge by shooting Captain Ávila at a bar in the Vedado.

I would give anything to go back to that quiet, that freedom of vacation, sea, rides in Cirilo's carriage. Our time there seems like a year in Paradise.

On the Monday in September that vacation is over and we are all supposed to go back to school, I can't bring myself to get ready. I'm overcome with disgust at the idea of going every day just to be bored in classes and pestered by stupid questions. Just imagining the strain of sitting for hours at a small wooden desk makes me want to walk, run, jump, breathe fresh air.

I imagine a classroom and see a prison.

And, when I consider how many years I will have to spend in that prison before I graduate from university, I want to pull a sheet over my head, go back to sleep, and never wake up again.

Why can't we study like the Peripatetics, wandering the gardens of the Academy in ancient Athens, gazing up at the Parthenon on the Acropolis, listening to and debating with teachers like Socrates and Plato?

Also, I would enjoy being free of the feeling that somebody wants to kill us. What would that take, I keep asking myself?

A YEAR LATER ON THAT FATEFUL DAY, it's still coming back to me: my mother asleep in the other bed in my room, me dressing myself very quietly in khaki pants and a red-and-white-checked shirt and slipping out into the living room, my brother, Septimio, in his Baldor School uniform bolting down the stairs from his bedroom with, because he thinks it's childish to use a bookbag, all his textbooks under his right arm tied together by an old leather belt. Also, because he thinks school buses are for little kids and he's a thirteen-year-old "man," he rides to school with friends, who are now honking the horn out front, all of them apparently oblivious of the dangers I perceive – such as threats to kidnap Septimio, which our father is still nagging his bodyguard to do something about.

I think Septimio's going to school with a bunch of friends might end up with all of them being kidnapped. But at least it's become old news to say that the big advantage of my switching from Baldor to the Buenavista School is that I'm no longer the "kid sister," meaning now girls of a certain age don't make friends with me just so they can sidle up to Septimio, who's so popular with the girls at Baldor.

When I think of how that school day began, something makes me connect it with Andy and the incident of polishing the staircase, maybe that Almaviva was dry-mopping and polishing the hall floor when the whole incident started. But then I come back to Toñita brewing the fresh pot of coffee, an aroma that fills the entire house every day, and the horror when Septimio, as usual skipping breakfast, leaves the house slamming the front door behind him – a sound that, now, always makes me jump.

And it makes me start re-playing this day, over and over.

I head to the patio to find Pompadour the Pullet, the fine young hen my mother got for me when we came back from Varadero as compensation for my having to go back to school. The reason I called her Pompadour the Pullet: my mother had been prattling on about Madame de Pompadour instead of obsessing about Louis XIV, when we got back from Varadero. My mother had entered a phase of theorizing that for a woman to attain real power, she had to become the mistress of a king. Madame de Pompadour was the mistress of Louis XV. I tried arguing with my mother that, if for a woman to attain real power, she had to become the mistress of a king, women now would have zero chance of power since kings no longer exist in our part of the world. Of course, I was pretty sure that what my mother had in mind was mistresses of much less exalted figures than kings in the present era.

My mother then turned the whole concept upside-down and prophesied, "Just you wait – a woman is going to save this country when it falls into darkness."

The time of darkness that's coming to the Island was my mother's new tangent, probably as a reaction to her conversations with Cirilo the coachman. Now, every time she starts ranting about "the time of darkness," my brother and I give each other nervous looks and hope that Almaviva and Toñita aren't listening. We're worried that they'll think she's crazy.

Anyway, out of this "time of darkness" theme came Pompadour the Pullet, and at the time of the debacle in Orfila came Almaviva telling me that she was sick of cleaning up poop everywhere. So I was going to build a chicken coop for Pompadour and a nice rooster, so they could produce lots of chicks and we could have lots of hens and I could start a business selling fresh eggs in our neighborhood, and none of us would starve, darkness or no darkness. And we would make none of the chickens into soup.

So, when I scooped up Pompadour on that fateful day and headed for the porch, where Armando the driver and Pancho Pistola the bodyguard were lounging as they waited for my father and discussing his political prospects as they sipped beer, I set Pompadour on the floor, stretching her neck a little to hypnotize her, and watched her lying there, quietly asleep, under that gray sky full of dark clouds, her down gently lifting in the coolish, watery breeze that foretold rain. And that was when I noticed the black car cruising past, which meant *this might be the day.*

Inside the black car cruising, here were two men in front and one in back, all dressed in black and wearing sunglasses with super-dark lenses, trying to look scary, and seemed even scarier when they went by again minutes later and I stood up to get a good look. Pancho Pistola was already on red alert holding his machine gun.

Clearly, this was going to be the moment everybody had been muttering about. I had even prepared for it when we first moved to Orfila. What I did was explore our block and devise a plan. This was: get out of the house through the patio, jump over the wall, and make my way through the backyards of houses to a safe place. The plan covered any number of potential events, obvious or unforeseen. My plan included taking Pompadour the Pullet with me, tucked securely under my arm.

But then, my mother came out of our room and my half-shaven father came out of his room, and my father yelled "Take the girl and run, right now!" to Almaviva, and I ended up tossing Pompadour on the floor when Almaviva grabbed my hand and dragged me, running, out of the house. And among the terrible things that happened that day was that Pompadour the Pullet ran away and, unlike Omobono, never returned, and I don't know why.

I re-examine this moment in my life obsessively and am completely aware how damaging it is to actually "witness history." At first, not dying, escaping unharmed, made me happy, but then, it just got worse and worse, because I realized that relief at escaping the death suffered by others is a barbaric kind of joy, fit for a savage.

It's uncivilized to feel unconnected to others, to consider one's own person as the most important thing. Molly and The Bebe's mother accused me of being a savage, but I dispute that assessment.

I've read more than other kids my age. I've tried to create an ethic, a way to behave. Supposedly this isn't normal in a girl, but when my mother started asking me for advice when I was three years old, I had to make myself think and reflect my way out of the placid stupor of childhood.

I've learned from Greek philosophers and the Latin classics, such as Socrates and Seneca, that one must have standards of conduct, protocols, and adhere to them. I read these writers before I found out that they were important and that they were taught in universities. I wasn't awed by them, or afraid of them. They made perfect sense to me. Now, I consider them friends, counselors.

I used to think my exploration of the past would clarify new things about my life. But now, I still don't know who *I* am, or why I'm here with *this* family, with *these* people, on *this* violent Caribbean Island. I still don't know what to do.

I'm not sure there's anyone who can answer all my questions.

The Christian religion has offered answers, but I don't believe them. I don't believe that an old man created the world, or that humankind has been made to suffer continually because Adam and Eve ate an apple. Those are children's stories. You must go along with adults to keep them from punishing you, but I don't believe the stories in the Old Testament.

Excepting those of the Babylonians. I would really have enjoyed watching King Nebuchadnezzar eating grass in his palace garden, and Nimrod trying to shoot an arrow into the Sun.

And, although the wise woman, Adela, answered all my questions, I don't yet understand all her answers, and since we last saw each other, I have thought of so many more questions. It seems a cruel joke to say life is just a dream when there's so much death and suffering.

Now, in my room, ruminating on the horror of that battle a year ago, I know I've drawn a curtain over the past.

Tomorrow's sun will shine light on another person, and Death, whom I now imagine to be a tall, thin young man dressed as a clown who plays chess with his most beloved victims, and performs his macabre dance when he inevitably beats them, will come closer and closer to me, keeping an eye on the sand of my life trickling through the narrow waist of the hourglass, watching for the last grain of sand that will close my eyes forever.

The horn of a distant train, that most desolate sound in the world, interrupts my thoughts. I imagine the train has passed through snowy mountains and arid plains in faraway lands, through fields of wheat whose blond manes shiver in the wind, and traveled over oceans of near-black water. Inside the train's cars, clowns dressed in white satin trimmed with black sequins play marimbas, saxophones, and bugles.

25

DEFENESTRATION

IN THE YEAR SINCE "THE INCIDENT," I've become almost as tall as some of the big girls at my school. I've focused on getting good grades and making friends, if only because the political situation has meant doing nothing but attending school and coming right home to do homework. Also, I've sneak-read everything I can get my hands on, most recently "The Fall of the House of Usher" by Edgar Allan Poe, which gave me the creeps.

Carlos Prío Socarrás has been elected president, and, although my father campaigned day and night for him, that apparently didn't matter, because President Prío appointed as Minister of Education a man called Aureliano Sánchez Arango, who for some reason hates my father. My father says he doesn't care because he has a new position from which it would be difficult to fire him, but will give him time to mount his campaign for the Senate.

At home, none of this is discussed openly. I've had to deduce the whole thing from bits of conversations between my parents.

Today is Saturday, and the sun beams down brightly on our street, but no longer can I banish the gloom inside our house by going out to play with Pablito and his sister. Recently, when I saw Pablito, he said, "Our block has gotten so boring. The bloodbath made everybody move away."

I go out on the porch. My father is sitting by himself, a rare moment of ease, while his bodyguard – Pancho Pistola – is enjoying his lunch inside at the dining room table. My father no longer seems at all concerned that a car might drive by and mow him down with machine-gun fire.

I sense I must take a photograph of him. I want to preserve this moment when, despite the occasional threat, his loss of power, and his reduction in salary, he is happy to be living in the house of his dreams – and owning it outright, as he does, thanks to that freak of winning the lottery. It's not hard for me to talk my father into posing on the porch, enthroned. But, as I now know, things have a way of changing from one moment to the next.

In the photo I'm taking, my father is wearing white dril 100 pants and a fine white cotton shirt, sleeves rolled up, open collar and no tie. He looks toward the garage, then smiles at the camera the Three Wise Men brought me last Christmas. I connect my father's relaxed smile to his being pleased that he's an important figure for his daughter, as opposed to the reporters and photographers who used to chase after him at school openings and political rallies.

Campaigning to become Senator has taken the place of having to be constantly on the go for the Ministry of Education. Now, mapping out what he hopes to do as a Senator keeps him engaged, and lets him behave as if the firefight that took place just a block from our house a year ago never happened, and he is oblivious to the craters in the walls of the besieged house and the slowly fading bloodstains on the sidewalks and in the street. We are all trying to be oblivious, but it's not easy.

When I get to the last frame in the roll, he says, "That's enough, Bad Bug. You'll get to take plenty of pictures of me when I'm elected." He smiles and waves farewell to the camera.

I can't resist taking advantage of this rare moment between us, and, pretending to be one of those people he can't stand, a reporter, I say jokingly, "And now, sir, tell me about your new job!"

Instantly, he looks irritated, as if I have somehow betrayed his trust and become like everybody else, a "journalistic maggot" wanting something from him he cannot give. But then, it's as if suddenly he realizes he has a chance to say something, to get "off his chest" something he wants me to know, but not for anybody else to overhear.

He leans forward, and says, so seriously that, at first, I assume he is kidding, and so low that only I can hear:

"My job is to listen to the self-important, over-educated men who are supposedly the managers of the school districts of the Island.

"They want people to believe they have our country's children's best interests at heart, and they tell me what they want our President Prío to think they are doing for the schools they are responsible for, and just how much money they are spending to do this. Santana takes notes, then later types up the minutes of these meetings on mimeo forms, I sign them, we deliver the original of these reports to my boss, who gives them to the Minister of Education, and we keep copies in a filing cabinet in case our President or anybody else ever asks him to see them."

"Do you enjoy this job?" I ask, thinking that I haven't seen any of the ebullience and bonhomie, two words I've just learned that mean good nature and good humor or so.

"What do you think?"

"Well, it lets you go everywhere and understand everything. It sounds wonderful, sort of like being an angel, or a ghost!"

My father laughs out loud, so hard that he gets red in the face. Then he gets very serious. "Well, let's hope I don't become an angel or a ghost anytime soon! Just remember what I said about meetings, because you are going to have lots of them when you grow up. Philosophy has proved that it's not possible for anybody to tell the complete truth. People who rise high enough to be included in meetings have learned the trick of presenting mountains of what may look like facts while never telling the truth.

"Also, they have learned that it's dangerous to challenge each other's lies. Be very careful with that.

"Sometime, read Cicero's *Tusculan Disputations*, where he quotes Pythagoras, the inventor of mathematics, who says something along the lines of:

> *So, we come from another life and another nature into this one, in the same way that people move from one city into a crowded marketplace. Some of these people want glory, and others want money, and a very, very few consider all that nothing but dross, just garbage, and only care about looking into the nature of things. Those are the people called philosophers, students of wisdom, which is the very best thing you can be: a person who observes, not one who acquires. While you are alive, contemplate things, understand them: that's better than any other activity to which you may devote yourself.*

"I'm sure that's not an exact quote, but I have the idea Cicero might help you understand something of what is happening right now – and how to look at it."

THE NEXT MORNING, I head down the hall to the patio and catch my mother lurking in the doorway to my father's room.

"Gus, why won't you tell me what's going on?" she asks anxiously. "Just because you were too proud to be on the take and suck up to Ali Baba – sorry, I mean your ex-boss Alemán, the minister of education who stole the most in the history of this unfortunate country and now has fled to Florida –"

He cuts her off. "Flora, this is the last time I'm going to say it: Alemán is in Florida undergoing cancer treatments. If Prío's people were able to prove that Alemán misappropriated public funds, they would be extraditing and prosecuting him. I asked Alemán for one favor, and one favor only: to find a way to get me appointed as Secretary of the Superintendency of Schools, because Prío, on becoming President-elect of the Republic, would name his own Minister of Education, who would name his own person as head of Primary Instruction, etc., as part of the so-called 'clean sweep' against Alemán."

He adds, with a great deal of self-control, "The Secretary of the Superintendency of Schools is a complete nonentity, which as far as anybody on this planet is concerned, might as well not exist but will never go away."

Growing more and more irritated, he goes on, "The whole point of becoming Secretary of the Superintendency, as you know, was to *not* get fired in the transition, and above all to have an 'unimportant' job that lets us make ends meet while I'm running for the Senate."

"You're an idiot!" my mother shouts. "Who was going to fire you? You were – still are – the most popular official in the Ministry!"

My father flies out of his room in a rage, bellowing at my mother, "Stop sticking your nose in things you know absolutely nothing about!"

His fury shuts my mother up and she flees to my room in terror.

I follow her and sit on my bed, while she drops on hers and lights a cigarette. "Your father refuses to admit they demoted him to humiliate him. He thinks he became 'Secretary of the Superintendency of Schools' the same way they gave Alemán the title 'Minister without Portfolio,' which just means 'Man with No Ministry,'" she says, puffing out smoke and waving it away with her hands.

"Or maybe Papa was demoted because he wouldn't accept Alemán's gifts."

"Oh, of course the idiot should have gotten in on the take," my mother says sarcastically.

"But that wouldn't be legal or civic-minded," I protest fiercely. Then, as an afterthought, I add: "This pilfering is going to destroy the Republic! 'O times, O customs!'"

"Where are you getting these ideas, girl?" she asks suspiciously. I don't answer, because the last thing I want her to know is that, now, I'm reading Cicero, and that's where I'm getting my ideas.

I shoot out to the dining room at the very moment when my father sits down at the table with Santana, who is still his aide, despite my father's "demotion."

They are waiting for Toñita to serve them breakfast. Pancho Pistola stands behind my father, watchful and discreet.

I slip into the living room and sit where my father can't see me, so I can hear the conversation clearly.

"Well, Alemán might not have embezzled public funds, but he's gone to Miami with enough money to buy himself a shedload of properties. It's rumored he even bought an island in Biscayne Bay," Pancho Pistola blurts out.

Pancho Pistola's been listening to my father's conversations with Santana and, apparently, thinks he can presume to argue with "the Doctor," now that my father has this new "inconsequential" job. He continues: "The new guy says cleaning up the Ministry of Education is going to be like Hercules running a river through the stables of King Augeus, to clean the manure out in a hurry. But they will have to extradite Alemán from the US to get the money back – if in fact he stole it."

"I do not want you fueling rumors that Alemán stole," my father replies angrily. He turns around to stare menacingly at his bodyguard for being a rumor-monger and aping his boss's manner of speaking, even down to his classical references. "If Alemán stole, then he must be charged in court. I know I didn't steal, even though those gangsters must think so, since they keep on trying to squeeze money out of me to 'protect my son from kidnapping.' If I'm on the take, why don't I abscond to Miami? Why doesn't anybody believe that Alemán went to

Miami for cancer treatments? Why do I stay and continue in politics, instead of bolting like so many others?"

My father pauses, then adds: "And where did these hoodlums get the idea that I can find a million pesos to pay them, hmm?"

"Doctor, why don't you try to talk to President Prío? If you had his protection, these thugs would stop pestering you," his aide Santana suggests naïvely.

My father laughs, and Pancho Pistola laughs even louder.

"You watch too many American gangster movies, Santana! President Prío can't even protect himself! To keep the gangs in line, he's given important positions to all the gang leaders, after blaming Grau for doing exactly that! The two of you must figure out how to protect Septimio as well as my whole family. What sons of bitches, threatening to kidnap a boy!"

THE NEXT MONDAY AT LUNCHTIME at school, I race out to buy an Africana, which is a vanilla cookie covered in chocolate, and a Coca-Cola. They're sold at a snack bar in the middle of the school patio. I'm starving, but I can't abide the thought of that dreary, eternal, stinky cabbage lunch, even if now it's steamed or baked, not boiled.

I just found out that my mother has enrolled my cousin Barbara – she who chases her brother, Emilito, with a baseball bat – at my school, and we are paying her tuition. Now I'm worried about how Barbara, who has never set foot inside a school of any kind, is going to behave, and I'm afraid that any negative action of hers will reflect badly on me. Thus far, I've managed to stay detached from everyone so as not to get drawn into nasty situations, but Barbara might make me the target of taunts or cruelty from the girls at school.

From the snack bar, I look over and see, among the big girls, not Barbara, but Elena. This is even more unsettling.

I approach her and exclaim, in all sincerity, with a big smile: "I'm so glad you've transferred here, Elena!"

"How are you?" she answers coldly. The big girls around her eye me from head to toe because, no matter how tall I am, I'm still a "little" girl.

I don't answer, turn my back on her, and walk off eating my Africana and sipping my Coke. It takes me a few minutes to finish eating the Africana, suck the chocolate off my fingers, and dump its lavender-colored wrapper and the empty Coke bottle in a trash can, during which time I determine never to speak to Elena again. I regret trying to persuade her to come to this school. She makes me feel embarrassed, ridiculous, clumsy.

To console myself, I rocket higher and higher on the playground swing.

Katie Queen, an American girl my age who just entered my English class, sits on the swing next to me. Katie doesn't know any Spanish, and, although all the girls in the school know how to read, write, and speak English, no one ever talks to Katie. I think this is just as stupid as big girls' contempt for little girls, whites for Blacks, rich for poor, men for women – and Elena for me, just because her breasts have started to show.

I speak to Katie in English, and I admire her, both for being unmoved at being excluded, but also for being amazing at the gymnastic rings that hang from the metal pipes that support the swings, which, until Katie came to this school, I hadn't touched since my brief turn as a monkey in the Paredes de Miranda Girl's backyard. Not only can Katie do pull-ups, but she can hang parallel to the ground with her arms outstretched as if she is flying. She can even hold herself upside down. No one has ever practiced on these rings before for lack of strength, and her enthusiasm for sports is far more interesting than the affected daintiness and fragility of the other girls at the school.

I've decided to play with Katie all the time. Now, I walk down the halls of the Buenavista School not wondering what the "natives" talk about. Now, my only friend is Katie, because although I like to talk about music with the piano student, I don't consider her a friend but an acquaintance. With Katie, I talk about everything, but most recently about Laurence Olivier's movie of *Hamlet,* which both of us thought was amazing. Also, we talk about explorers, like Amundsen, my favorite, who reached the South Pole first because he had planned his expedition so carefully. For example, he brought lots of dogs, which pull your sleds but if you start to starve, you can eat them and even feed them to the other dogs. As a Norwegian, Amundsen knew more about surviving and getting across the ice than Scott, his British competitor, who died in the enterprise. Katie, being from the United States, is partial to Scott, so we change the subject back to her physical prowess. She isn't just good at rings, she's a tremendous athlete. She's been trying to teach me several sports, but I can't concentrate enough to excel at any of them. Also, physical exercise annoys me, because I always end up so sweaty, I feel like a fruit compote. My Aunt Isabel calls girls like me "juicy."

When I arrive home, I get to hear what my cousin Barbara, who decided to go to the Protestant school because of things I told her, did on her very first day.

Because she's never been to any school before, even though she is a year older than me, Barbara was placed in the second grade with Miss Love, that teacher who looks like a piglet.

The moment the teacher started in with her mean tricks, Barbara lit into her, calling her a dead dog and a few other choice epithets. Miss Love told the office she was sending Barbara home. This makes me ecstatic. Not that Barbara got sent home, but because, seriously, what wouldn't I have given to call Miss Love a dead dog!

But I had to keep my mouth shut to avoid getting kicked out of school permanently, because, ironically, I am passionate about reading and writing, so school appears to be my destiny, and, at this Protestant school, I've learned not to protest, but to be a hypocrite, though not a flatterer. I don't defend myself against bad teachers by flattering them, the way other girls do.

My strategy is simple: I never open my mouth in class, so I never get called on. I am boring, but safe.

By contrast, the story of the never-before-schooled Barbara gets better and better. My horrified mother informs me that, after sending Barbara home, the inaptly-named Miss Love telephoned Barbara's parents, my aunt Chavela and her husband Emilio, to complain about their daughter. The next day response: Chavela and Emilio accompanied Barbara to school and, to Miss Love's chagrin, Aunt Chavela told the teacher in front of the whole class that, given her pig-like face, she had no business teaching children but should tend animals.

Then they left with Barbara, never to return.

I cannot suppress my cries of joy at the courage of my family. I had to stop myself from peering into Miss Love's classroom to stick my tongue out at her. I don't dare because I'm doing very well in school. I'm in fourth grade in Spanish and fifth grade in English because they found out I knew too much English to stay in fourth grade. Classes are taught in Spanish in the morning and in English in the afternoon, and although I cannot possibly know more English than Spanish, I accepted the promotion because I've gotten used to not arguing with teachers and grown-ups. As I said, I've turned into a tremendous hypocrite.

Unfortunately, this "advanced" class in English is all about Columbus and his voyages, which I've already learned about in Spanish endless times, and am sick to death of. Every time the teacher says the name of Don Francisco de Bobadilla, the Spaniard who replaced Columbus and who is always cast as the villain in this B-movie about the New World, I happily imagine embedding the axe of a Carib cannibal in the teacher's head.

Fortunately, my father's books deal with all different topics, but I must read them without any discussion, so my mother doesn't send me to the psychiatrist.

I must be like my grandmother's terrible saying: "There's Mary Jane's cat, throw the stone and hide your hand." I never talk anymore about what I know.

Once I showed, to a classmate who sits next to me, part of a letter Seneca wrote to his friend Lucillus: "Virtue, in fact, never leaves a void in the soul; it fills it all up; it alone dispels all sorrows, for it is the beginning and origin of all good." This little girl looked at me like I was crazy when I recommended that she buy Seneca's book "because he writes really interesting things about friendship." At the time, I thought the Latin classics were the work of lesser-known contemporary writers whom I could help by giving them publicity so their books would sell more copies.

The noise of the bell calling everyone to lunch takes me out of my thoughts, and I head straight to the lunchroom because I can tell by the odor that we are not having cabbage.

Nobody pours salt on my head anymore.

I know how to ladle the goop we are served onto my plate, and I use a fork and knife very deftly.

Above all, I have an inner life, or so my cousin Gisela says, which has obliterated the threats, betrayals, and put-downs of others.

ONE DAY I ARRIVE HOME from school, and my mother shows me some purple veins in her arms, and says my father is giving her injections while she's asleep.

"What's he giving you shots of?" I ask, trying to disguise my skepticism.

"Drugs. He injects me with drugs to turn me into a drug addict so he can sneak off at night with his girlfriends."

How can he inject her without waking her up?

I shut up. I've learned not to argue at school or at home. Also, I've figured out that going to the movies is a distraction from my mother's detours into a very dark world, and that one big advantage of our house in the Orfila neighborhood, apart from its being our own property, stable and private, in which succeeding generations will be born, is that it is within walking distance of the Cine Avenida. This movie theater charges adults a peso and kids fifty cents for a double feature that changes every four days, a much better deal than other theaters that, only every two to three weeks, change features for which they also charge more. Another benefit of this theater is that it combines English-language features with ones in Spanish – dramas starring the incredibly beautiful Hedy Lamarr, with Mexican Westerns starring the charismatic actor and singer Jorge Negrete, American Westerns with Mexican comedies as well as dramas, all lightened up by shorts in English about a man who's very clumsy and smashes his fingers while trying to hang pictures, or drinks beer from a glass with a hole in the bottom and gets his pants wet.

The audience always laughs, but to me, these are mean, devilish stories about someone who's not right in the head – sort of like the way things go in my house.

I'VE DISCOVERED THAT MOVIES are as necessary for my mental balance as sleeping or dreaming, not least because my mother is always ready to take me. She says that, for a peso and a half every four days, when the movies change, she can stop worrying about politics for four hours. I don't dare go alone, even though I ride to school on my bike, because I fear the darkness of the theater.

Just today, we saw Dorothy Lamour in *The Hurricane*, a decade-old black-and-white movie with excruciating scenes of flattening wind and horrendous flooding, which I think the theatre shows every year at the beginning of hurricane season. The American actress represents an aboriginal woman who lives on the invented island of Manakoora and who wears nothing but a sarong, a kind of shift that's open on one side, and a lei, which is a necklace of flowers. It's about this romance between her and another native on this island in the South Pacific.

When the movie ends, my mother tells me that she doesn't mind the movie being old, because, "After all, the hula-hula dance never goes out of style, and South Seas Islands scenery never changes."

But she doesn't stop there: "They should show more films like this – touristic – with assassinations in the Taj Mahal, prostitution in Macao, drug trafficking in Nepal, not to mention heroic Polish cavalry officers brandishing swords to defend Poland against Nazi panzer tanks! Tragic action in exotic places! But not to forget to have a June Allyson film, because what's a movie without a woman and a love story? Like June Allyson's first hit, *Two Men and a Girl*, or something of the sort! But enough of movies like *Battan Patrol*, all soldiers, men alone dying like flies! That's like making a movie in prison – an abnormality!"

Coming out of the theater, we run into my friend Elena.

She's wearing bright red lipstick, pink rouge, and a red-and-yellow dress with frilly sleeves. She looks like the proprietress of a saloon in a Western.

A young man is holding her hand. He's her boyfriend, she informs me without my asking. Elena is headed into the final stretch, dizzyingly leaving childhood in the dust. The lipstick and rouge make her look artificial, a Hans Christian Andersen doll. She has lost her athletic energy, her spontaneity, and whatever she had left of sincerity.

"Come see me whenever you like, but I can't visit you. I'm very busy with exams," she tells me apathetically, showing off in front of her boyfriend. I have exams too, but is what she's saying worth thinking about? This creature who pushes open Cine Avenida's glass door, leaving behind the relief of air conditioning, is unrecognizable – she's Coppelia, a mere mannequin.

Once we reach the sidewalk where Elena can't hear us, my mother exclaims, "What garish colors that girl wears! She looks like a parrot!"

My mother wears turbans and sequined dresses but, she says, she avoids lots of colors so she won't look like a parrot. In my opinion, parrots are gorgeous, but I keep my mouth shut.

THE NIGHT, LIT UP WITH NEON SIGNS, dazzles us, and the heat claps its sweaty hand over our mouths. It makes me want to throw up.

When we get to our house, my mother shuts herself in our room, saying she has a migraine. I sit down at the dinner table to eat with my brother.

My father always comes home late because he eats out at some restaurant or other. More likely, says my mother, he eats at his concubines' houses.

Toñita is quick to serve us her specialty, chicken breasts roasted in wine and seasoned with oregano and olives stuffed with red pimientos, accompanied by black beans and white rice.

"We went to see *The Hurricane* by John Ford. Cine Avenida is putting on a festival of great film directors," I say, to break the awkward silence between me and my brother.

"Where'd you get that, Delgadina?" Septimio asks crankily.

"From the program they handed out at the box office, jackass," I snap.

"Always watching movies! Why don't you read Doc Savage books, so you can educate yourself?" my brother continues gruffly, because this seems to be yet another of those days when everything irritates him. My mother is now defending Septimio constantly with the excuse that he is at "the age of mortification," whatever that is.

"Because I'm reading *The Twelve Caesars* by Suetonius, jackass!"

"What could you possibly understand about that book, Messalina!" he exclaims, sneering.

"More than you think, Nero. It helps me to understand that we're not the only family with problems. Ancient Romans had it much worse than we do. That's very comforting."

Septimio makes an irritated gesture, then brusquely leaves the table without finishing his dinner so he doesn't have to listen to me.

WHEN I ARRIVE HOME FROM SCHOOL THE NEXT DAY, my mother is in my room with an ancient mulatto of small stature, dressed all in white except for a red bandanna on his head. The little man, whose name is Nino, smells faintly of horse manure, and is painting a cross on my mother's forehead with something that looks like fat, but which I'm told is *corojo*, lard made from red palm oil that's used to beg the *orishas*, the Yoruba gods, for protection.

To make this cross, Nino must raise his arm because he is much shorter than my mother, and this reveals a half-moon of sweat in the armpit of his white shirt. Nino is a *babalao*, a high priest of the Yoruba religion my father follows, and he is giving my mother a spiritual cleansing. I decide that his strange horsey smell must emanate from the herbs he keeps in his shirt pocket.

"Now you must cleanse Mercy, Nino, because she picks up things, and she walked in just as you were cleansing me," my mother says with concern.

"Why are you doing a cleansing?" I ask cautiously, because I never know when my questions are going to provoke a fight or a drama.

"Your father just broke off from his *madrina,* and I'm afraid she's put a curse on us," she explains calmly. Nino nods as if that goes without saying.

I'm surprised to see this scene, because my mother has always been against my father's religion. She considers it the superstition of the lower class – that is, Black people, although she claims she harbors no racial prejudice.

What's made her a convert so suddenly, when she has always been ashamed of the flag of Chango that hangs inside our house, facing our front door?

"Yes, clearly, this girl must be protected," Nino says, looking at me with very kind eyes. "She's a European spirit. She has a very fine spiritual aura, you know what I mean? a lot of psychic power, you know? She's a daughter of Yemayá, goddess of the sea, but Obatalá has her head.

"You must give great thanks to Obatalá, because this child is an *abicú*, a bird of passage, you know, and it's amazing she's managed to stay alive this long." He ends with a laugh.

My mother listens without contradicting or ridiculing the *babalao*.

"Obatalá is *la Virgen de las Mercedes*, the Virgin of Divine Grace, very pure. Everything affects her. That's why the girl collects so much, you know what I mean?" he asks with another giggle. The *babalao*, who speaks in a fluty, mellifluous voice, approaches me, then brushes my body all over with the redolent herbs from his shirt pocket. Then he passes half a coconut and a white dove over me from head to toe. The pigeon is very tame, and its breast is warm and throbs against my cheeks. Nino finishes the protection by painting a cross on my forehead with the *corojo* lard, just as he did to my mother.

He stares at me through squinted eyes for a few moments, then pronounces: "The evil spirits closed off from this girl all but one womb, one that wanted to kill her, you know? Someone cursed her before her birth and took poison so she wouldn't be born, but she was born after eleven months, and had long, black hair, and could stand up soon afterwards. And, out of mercy, she didn't kill her mother, you know what I mean?

"Although that's what the doctors had predicted," he adds after a pause, with that same silly giggle.

I glance at my mother to see if she is laughing at the mulatto, but her face is whiter than coconut meat.

"Well, I must leave now," I announce, and take off at a run to avoid witnessing my mother's distress. I want to breathe fresh air out on the street and not feel suffocated by her anguish.

FLEEING IS THE BEST SOLUTION when situations get thick and sticky with intense emotion. Also, no one's out on the street at this hour. It's the moment when the sun shines strongest on the city's streets and kids who go to Catholic or public schools still are in classes.

Only Protestants are free. I find this a bad thing – we're not learning enough. We're ignorant as donkeys, compared to kids who go to the other schools.

I walk to the corner house that's almost at the top of our hill, and contemplate the luxuriant garden, now neglected by its owners, where roses mingle with tiny yellow and blue wildflowers, and weeds and grass grow tall and exude a scent of adventure.

"Do you want to go inside the garden?" asks a friendly voice coming from a skinny man of medium stature and tanned skin.

He wears wide-legged white linen trousers, a white short-sleeved shirt, and a black belt. A silver keychain hangs from his belt in a semicircle and disappears inside his trouser pocket.

"Yes!" I answer enthusiastically.

I am thrilled to find a grown-up who can guess my wishes.

"Then I'll take you," the man offers smoothly, smiling.

"What if they see us from the house?"

"They won't. Nobody's there," the man says, still smiling.

"In that case, I can go by myself."

"Okay, but there's a really mean dog that bites kids. If you go in with me, I'll protect you from the dog," explains the man with a softness that inspires confidence.

I agree to go in. The man leads me by the hand into the garden.

Then, unexpectedly, he picks me up and carries me in front of him, against his thighs. He takes a few steps and begins to rub me against one of his thighs. I sense something odd that I don't like, and I make a gesture to get him to release me.

But the man has me in such a strong grip that, now, I'm terrified.

"Don't let go! Don't let go, or the dog will bite you! The dog will bite you!" he whispers, frightened.

I keep quiet and let him finish rubbing against me because I'm afraid he'll do worse if I try to get away. After a few minutes he wets his trousers and relaxes. I free myself from his powerful grip and run as fast as I can, fearing he will catch up with me, but I manage to escape from the garden. I look back, and he isn't following me.

I sit on the garden wall of my house, because I don't want to go inside and encounter the *babalao* again.

Even so, I sense that the *babalao*'s cleansing has saved me from something very bad, and I should thank him. I think about what the man in the garden did and cannot understand it. Something awful, but I don't know what.

But this experience validates my decision to be on my guard against grown-ups, including, or perhaps above all, those who understand the feelings of children.

26

RAINING
WHILE THE SUN SHINES

NOW, ON A SATURDAY MORNING, the garage fence scrapes open and in comes a young man. He's my cousin Paco, the son of my maternal Aunt Dora who died of tuberculosis, and the brother of the Three Little Girls. I'm surprised he's visiting us because he never has before, and we only ever saw him at my Aunt Bella's, because none of us visited him either.

Paco is in his thirties, he's tall and thin, has black eyes and hair and very white skin, and is very distinguished looking, but the best thing about him is his smile. My mother told me that, when she was in the hospital having one of the many hemorrhages caused by my pregnancy, the other patients in her ward would go nuts when Paco came to visit her. "Such an interesting man!" they would say as Paco was leaving. "He looks just like that Hollywood actor, Tyrone Power!"

Paco dresses elegantly in a grey suit, fine white cotton shirt and navy-blue silk tie. He's working for a major insurance company now, and he handles his leather portfolio as if it had important work papers inside.

Paco flashes a beautiful smile and shakes my father's hand when he rises reluctantly from his porch chair to greet the young man. "How are you, Doctor? I've been working in this area and decided to drop by and say hi to the fam—."

"Flora has a migraine," my father cuts him off.

"In fact, I came to see you, if you have a few minutes to chat."

My father waves him brusquely toward the other armchair and moves the one he was sitting in to face Paco, who lays the leather portfolio on the coffee table between them. I perch on the top step to hear the conversation.

"It must be interesting to be so close to political power. You must feel very powerful, but also under lots of pressure." Paco smiles affably at my father.

"What brings you here, kid?" my father asks guardedly.

Paco sits back in the armchair uncomfortably, but keeps on smiling.

I feel sorry for him because my father is being so rude. My father has never liked any member of my mother's family because he thinks they're all conspiring against him, fanning the flames of his wife's jealousy to make her feel insecure so they can pressure her to force him to give them jobs and scholarships. He's already had to help several of her relatives.

"Doctor, I've come to bring you peace of mind. Within walking distance of your home, a tragedy not long ago has left many families feeling unprotected. How important are your precious children and faithful wife to you?" he asks, drawing attention to me with the palm of his hand.

"So where is this question coming from, touching on things that are none of your business?"

I am stunned at the way my father insultingly rejects these kind words about our family.

"I'm just assuming your wife and children are the most important things in your life," Paco forges on, looking at me and clearing his throat nervously. "Just now, they are fine, they have a house, a car, the kids go to private school. But what if, one day, you aren't here to earn the daily bread and protect them? Your wife and kids will be helpless.

"I've come here," he continues, "to hand you the money that will guarantee that they will be able to live in the comfort they've enjoyed up to the present time. For a small monthly fee now, I guarantee that your family will be well off in the future."

I find it astonishing that, by paying "a small monthly fee," we might live luxuriously for the rest of our lives.

My father squints to take the measure of this individual who, though part of the family, has up to now been almost a stranger to us.

"How can I 'one day not be here'? I'm not planning any trips."

"Well, Doctor, we *are* all mortal, and in this ephemeral world we need to take care."

"Well, thanks for bringing that elephant into the room."

"Doctor, should you die, your children will not be collecting your current salary," Paco brutally clarifies, lowering his voice presumably to keep me from hearing him, and growing desperate at my father's resistance. "Do you sincerely believe they will be able to get along on nothing but your pension?" he whispers.

My father studies him through slitted eyes and finally says, "Look, kid, take your damned portfolio and run along back to where you came from."

My father gets to his feet abruptly as if to punch him.

Quickly, nervously, Paco picks up the papers he's laid out and with great alarm shoves them into his portfolio, then takes off, tripping over a leg of the armchair.

"Come here to announce my death, have you, you vulture! Hyena! Harbinger of doom!" my father yells from the porch.

As Paco runs off with his tail between his legs, which is the phrase my mother would use, I stare at my father perplexed. I am terrified that he will die, but what Paco has proposed seems to me to be very practical and I completely agree with him. My father does need to insure himself. I find his reaction irrational and stupid, but by now I've become used to this sort of absurd and illogical outcome in my house.

"Don't worry, Bad Bug. I'm not going to die," says my father with a fake smile intended to reassure me. Instead, it alarms me. It makes me completely aware of what we would need to lose in order to gain that money.

PACO'S SISTER, my cousin Chiquitina, comes to visit us one Sunday afternoon soon afterward, when my father happens to be away. We call her Chiquitina because she's the smallest of the Three Little Girls, completing the trio with Cleo and Nadia, all already in their late twenties.

When Chiquitina was born, the girl's mother grew so weak that she died of tuberculosis, and Bartolo, the girls' father, always harbored a grudge against her for contributing to his wife's death – or so my mother said.

In my opinion, Bartolo treats Chiquitina the same as his other daughters.

From the moment she turned fourteen, Chiquitina attracted more boys than her sisters because she is identical to Elizabeth Taylor. Also, I like her better because she's so natural and always listens to me while other grown-ups ignore me. Also, once on the beach at Santa María del Mar, without realizing it, I swam to a place where it was too deep for me to stand up.

My relatives, as usual laughing and making jokes, didn't hear me scream, except for Chiquitina, who heard, and saw, and came to rescue me.

I think it's very interesting how Chiquitina always moves both hands at the same time. When she scratches her shoulder with her right hand, with her left hand she scratches thin air. They say it's because she had eclampsia while giving birth to her only daughter.

But the thing I most like about Chiquitina is that she is psychic. She talks about the future as if it's something she's seen with her own eyes.

Recently, like her sisters, Chiquitina hasn't been to visit at our new house in Orfila because it's such a long way from her home. Today, she's here to tell my mother a dream. She wears a cotton dress printed with violets and looks very young and springy, but the expression on her face is one of worry. My mother invites Chiquitina to sit in one of the big armchairs in the living room, while she sits in another.

I stand, slouching against the hallway wall, where I can see both of their faces but they can't see me. My brother is locked in his room over the garage, reading the latest Doc Savage book, or doing homework.

"How wonderful to see you, Chiquitina? It's been ages! How are the Little Girls?" my mother asks, with real interest.

"Well, Flora, everybody's just fine. You've moved so far away, it's hard for us to visit you. But I had to come because last night I had a very strange dream."

My mother makes a gesture indicating that she is bracing herself for one of Chiquitina's spiritualist rants.

"I'm sure you're about to tell me!" she exclaims, ironic.

"I know people don't believe in these things, but I must tell you this dream."

My mother rises from her armchair without a word, walks right past me, and comes back from her room with a lit cigarette in her mouth. She drops into the armchair and takes a couple of deep drags. Maybe she needs the distraction of smoking to keep from kicking Chiquitina out of the house.

"I dreamt I was in this wheat field," Chiquitina begins bleakly. "This man wearing polished silver armor and mounted on a white horse is galloping towards me. As he gets closer, I recognize him as the Archangel Michael when he violently draws his sword. 'One of your family is going to be mowed down,' he says, cutting the tallest spike of wheat with his sword.

"Well, Flora, I think that's Augusto, because, out of our entire family, he's the one who has reached the highest position."

I tear out of the house because I don't want to hear any more of this fateful prophecy. This house is imprisoning me. Lately I have felt as if its walls are trapping me inside. Outside, the afternoon is wonderful, the sun is shining, the sky is sapphire blue, the clouds are white as lilies.

Except that it's raining.

I look up at the sky to see where this rain is coming from, but there's not even one dark cloud. My hair stands on end, and I have goose bumps. This rain is coming from nowhere! I try to calm down and not give it any importance. I could be imagining things. There's not a soul on the street and, on the sidewalk, in this strange rain, I keep a steady pace to exercise and clear my head.

As I walk past the building where the King of the Block lives, I hear him yelling at me from the terrace: "It's raining while the sun shines! It's raining while the sun shines! The devil is getting married!"

SITTING ON THE LIVING ROOM SOFA, through the window I watch night's blackness cover the garden shrubbery. I'm alone in our house with my mother, who's about to serve dinner. This is a unique moment of solitude, where most of the time people are milling about.

I hear my mother preparing dinner in the kitchen, but, out in the living room, I'm all by myself. I've always thought of solitude as a good time to give important things some thought, because being with people drags me down.

Now, there's this big void in my life that I can't fill with what I'm taught at school, or with the things I study on my own, or what I learn from my family.

I really, really miss Adela, the sorceress of Almendares, who answered all my questions and looked me straight in the eye.

She made me feel that I was able to learn from someone, able to communicate with someone.

Suddenly, I become aware that I'm dreaming. It gives me great joy because I am conscious and can do whatever I want in my dream, but at the same time I'm afraid this joy is going to wake me up.

I calm down so I can observe what's going on.

My mother glides into the room with that loathsome sneaky walk of hers that's meant to catch me at something. She sits in the other big armchair. I suspect she's about to begin one of her crazy-making monologues about Louis XIV.

"Your father is the disgrace of this house," she says in a tragic tone. "We have money, not as much as before, and yet we're not happy. He goes out with his women in the street and comes in late to sleep. If he died, we would be happy. Someone must kill him, but I don't have the courage to do it. It has to be someone very brave."

"We would lose the money from his salary," I point out to arouse her greed and drive the idea out of her head.

"Well, all I can say right now is, no amount of money in the world could make us happy. But, if he's dead, we'd have his pension as well as the money he has in the bank, which he now spends on all his sweethearts," she replies coldly.

"Whoever kills him will go to jail," I point out curtly.

"Not if it's planned well. There are many crimes that are never discovered. I read about them every day in the crime section."

"No one has any right to kill another person," I pronounce firmly to get her to let me alone, because I suspect she wants me to be the one who kills him.

Through the window, wafting in on the cold breeze, a huge black moth flaps around the room.

I race to the bathroom for a towel to frighten the moth away. I chase it around the house, forcing it to leave where it came in.

"Take her with you, water wind!" I shout, glaring at my mother reproachfully. "Begone, evil omen! Shoo, black widow moth, harbinger of misfortune!" Screaming and punching the mattress, I wake up.

TWO DAYS LATER, again I wake up screaming and bathed in sweat. This time I dream I'm driving an antique race car around a track at top speed, when suddenly I realize there's no steering wheel. I blame myself for not noticing this before the start of the race, and the thought of how, with no controls, I'm going to be able to take corners, terrifies me. Instinctively I lean right to edge the car off the track, then brake and come to a stop. Miraculously the race cars bringing up the rear don't crash into me.

My mother materializes in the doorway looking worried.

"You're screaming like a soul in Hell!" she shrieks.

"I was dreaming," I say, not wanting to share details.

"Don't listen to your cousin Chiquitina and her silly superstitions. I'm not falling for that rubbish of hers about the Archangel Michael predicting Gus's death. She hasn't been right in the head since Dora gave birth to her. Don't believe her fortune-telling."

I don't answer, and jump out of bed to get dressed and avoid talking to her. If she shows me the purple bruises from the veins in her arms one more time and accuses my father again of injecting her with drugs, I'll move to Aunt Bella's.

I throw on some clothes and run out of the room. My mother follows me, but gets sidetracked and goes to the kitchen to tell Toñita what to prepare for lunch.

I really don't want to leave the house this early because none of the neighborhood kids are up yet, and I'll be stuck with looking at images of the desert that haunt me lately when I have no one to play with. They're like dreams, but I have them while I'm wide awake. I don't know why I have these memories. They can't be mine because I've never been to the desert and I've never seen or read anything that might produce these fantasies. The images always begin the same, me staring at the black night from the balcony of a palace and contemplating the blue moonlight shining down on golden minarets and white marble domes. I smell the fragrance of night-blooming flowers, listen to music produced by water coming from jets and fountains, and tremble at the chilly breeze on my skin.

In the distance is the desert. I walk among the dunes, my feet sinking, leaving phosphorescent, bluish footprints in the moonlight. In the light of the full moon, the desert looks like a sea of diamonds. There's a booming silence, and the sky teems with glittering stars. I breathe in the sweet air that's shot through with the scent of flowers of thorny, rough desert plants.

This instant is full of controlled strength and infinite possibilities, as if the walls that trap me inside myself have collapsed. In this space of porous waves of sand, everyone is alone, has self-worth, finds his innermost face, discovers the fragility and dignity of being human.

THE NEXT NIGHT I have my recurring dream about attending the circus. After any number of trapeze artists in purple tights, puppies in tutus doing cartwheels, lion-tamers stuffed into braid-covered jackets with epaulettes, and clowns in green pants with red polka dots riding unicycles, comes the main attraction. A great silence ensues when the lights go out. I can hear the anxious breathing of the audience awaiting the surprise.

Suddenly, in a blinding circle created by spotlights, a small Black boy dressed in bright colors of every hue appears carrying in his hand an object that emits light and, from a distance, looks like a lamp. As the boy approaches my bench, I can see that he is carrying a golden birdcage with a tiny sun floating inside it. In that instant the entire audience recognizes, to its horror, that what they are looking at really is the Sun, shrunken and confined in a cage, and that outside, forever, shadow awaits.

Late that afternoon, I toss my school bag on the bed, take off my uniform and quickly pull on my overalls and T shirt, to fly out of this house where we all live like trapped mice. I want to breathe the outdoors, see the sun shining, discover new horizons. Despite the many lamps with pink bulbs producing pleasant light, despite the expensive furniture and the fussy authentic Spanish decor, the house seems dark and dilapidated.

I'm playing outside with Pablito and his sister when my father arrives home, sick. His driver must help him into the house as he walks hunched over with what seems to be a terrible stomachache. I say goodbye to the kids, run to the house, and go to his room to see if he really is sick — but he seems fine, he's got the same smile as ever. Still, there he is, in bed, covered by a sheet.

I think maybe this sickness thing is an excuse to lie down and rest, to avoid having to get up early every morning to go to work, or to "campaign." I have no idea what "campaigning" is like, but I imagine it's giving speeches and picking up and kissing babies and shaking hands. I've seen this in the newspapers and in the movie news. My father still laughs, but now he can't campaign because he's in bed.

My mother, concerned that my father is refusing to go to the hospital, has sent for her family's doctor.

When this doctor comes into his room, my father shouts, "What I have is a simple case of indigestion, which I don't need any doctor to tell me."

"Augusto, you always think you have indigestion and solve everything by taking laxatives," my mother retorts angrily.

My mother's family's doctor grimly warns, "This stomach pain might be appendicitis, Doctor. Taking a laxative could cause peritonitis, which can be fatal."

He says this very emphatically.

"Medical doctors can't see beyond their own noses," my father replies, irritated. "I just have a case of indigestion from eating fritters at Madrina's."

The doctor leaves after carefully feeling my father's stomach and recommending absolute rest until he sees what this develops into. I go to my father's room to look up *appendicitis* and *peritonitis* in the medical dictionary, and find out they are very serious things.

My mother walks into my room, closes the door so my father can't hear her, and almost shouts: "Imagine, eating at that witch's house after he got into a fight with her! Without a doubt, she put something in those fritters!"

IT'S VERY EARLY IN THE MORNING and I wake up to the sound of two female voices in the hallway of the house. My mother is screaming and Almaviva is whining. I jump out of bed in my pajamas and open the door.

"You killed him! You killed him!" screams my mother in her nightgown, her hair a mess and her eyes coming out of their sockets as she shakes Almaviva, who cries like her heart is broken.

"I didn't know, ma'am! The Doctor asked me for a laxative. I didn't know!"

"I only fell asleep for half an hour! Couldn't you just say 'No'?"

"Ma'am, you never once warned me not to give him a laxative!"

"I told you, damn it! I did so tell you!" my mother screams, shaking the maid even more violently, pinning her against the wall.

"Ma'am, you may have *thought* to tell me, but you *didn't* tell me," Almaviva protests, sobbing. "I can't read or write and that's why I have a great memory. You *never* warned me not to let him have the laxative!" Almaviva lets herself be shaken by my mother as if she were a puppet, while she tries to hide her tearful face in her hands.

"You killed him! You killed him!" my mother keeps screaming with such rage that now I am afraid she will try to kill the girl.

I take my mother by the arm to stop her from shaking Almaviva and continuing to accuse her.

At the touch of my hand, my mother stops, calms down, and goes to sit at the dining room table.

"Now we must call the hospital. They must come get him," she murmurs. Staring at nothing, she looks like she's waiting for somebody to pick up the telephone and call for an ambulance. After a few minutes she gets up and makes the call herself. Meanwhile, I wake up my brother and we get dressed. Watching the attendants lift the stretcher with my father lying there covered by a sheet, his face serene but unsmiling as they carry him into the ambulance, to me it all looks like a prank played by my mother.

How is it possible that my father asked Almaviva to give him a Pluto Water laxative, his favorite remedy for an upset stomach, when he knew that what was wrong with him might be appendicitis? I read in the medical dictionary that taking a laxative could do something like explode the very thin membrane of the intestine, causing a sepsis that would lead to his death.

My father isn't stupid, he's a Ph.D., he knows the Greek and Latin classics, he's a well-known government functionary and "good" politician, he's running for Senator. How could he do something so stupid?

My mother tells Almaviva to stay in the house until we get back. Neither my father's driver nor the bodyguard has arrived yet, so we don't get into our car, but we call Seboruco to come get us in his car, which he always does immediately, and we follow the ambulance.

When we get to the hospital, I'm told to stay in the waiting room, while my mother and brother walk into the emergency room with my father. I sit in one of the empty armchairs, unaware that it's directly across from the sofa where sits my father's brother, not my uncle Papo, the beloved delinquent, but my uncle the dreaded dentist.

Of course, my mother telephoned him before we left the house.

Staring straight at me, my uncle says to the man beside him, whom I've never seen before: "Right there where you see her, so serene, so modest, sits a savage!" And pointing his finger directly at me, he goes on: "She plays with boys, gets dirty, tears up her clothes, smashes the furniture of her house, and answers back as if she knows more than anybody else. She's got the devil in her body!"

I look at my uncle with astonishment. I have never seen him in my house. He has never visited us. I only ever remember seeing him once, eating pigeon soup when my father and I were living at my grandmother's house in La Víbora.

What can he know about how I behave now?

My own parents have never said anything like this to me. Why is he accusing me to a stranger? Maybe it's because it's characteristic of my father's family to hate my brother and me, possibly because they are envious of my father's success, or because they don't like my mother.

I stare at the white tile floor in silence. This is not the time to respond to my uncle. My father is in the emergency room, behind a cloth wall, lying on a stretcher, and that is all I care about.

As we are leaving the hospital, my uncle asks us for the keys to my father's car.

My mother refuses to give them to him. "The car is ours. We'll need to sell it to pay the hospital bill," my mother says, controlling her anger.

My uncle is incensed, though why he feels he has a right to my father's car is a mystery. He leaves us without saying goodbye.

As we walk to Seboruco's Dodge, my mother tells us we'll stop by our house just to pick up some clothes, and then go on to Bella's. She says she won't be able to sleep in that house ever again, and we are never going back.

Armando, my father's driver, Pancho Pistola, his bodyguard, and Santana, his assistant, are sitting on the porch hoping to hear that my father is doing better, and to find out what orders he may have for them. My mother tells them that the hospital and its doctors and nurses are doing everything possible for my father, but the recovery may be longer than expected. They will receive checks in the mail to tide them over during his convalescence, or until the Ministry finds them new assignments.

My mother tells Almaviva and Toñita, who have just arrived, to go home because they no longer have jobs, and she pays each of them three months' wages so they have some money until they get another job.

I go to my room and put a few clothes in a small suitcase, then walk out to the yard and notice that the corn I planted when we moved in already has cobs. I open a couple of them, and they are completely dried out. My garden is dry because, despite seeing Adela do it over and over, I didn't think I had to water the plants regularly or fertilize them.

I find that I don't care about the corn or about the other vegetables I planted that didn't prosper.

I walk out to the street to look at all the houses for the last time.

As I pass by Tito's, I notice that his cot is no longer on the porch. The front door is wide open, and, instead of furniture, there are cardboard boxes scattered around the living room.

Pablito walks past me and, almost without stopping, tells me: "They moved out. Tito broke his leg again. His brother accidentally pushed him as he ran after his sister. And Molly and The Bebe moved. I'm moving too. Everybody's moving."

I have no answer, but Pablito turns his head and looks at me with a pitying expression that makes me think he knows my father is in the hospital.

I return to the house just as my mother and brother emerge carrying suit-cases. I go to my room, pick up the small suitcase where I had packed my most essential clothes, and lift it into the trunk of the car parked in front of the house.

My mother tells Seboruco that this is the last trip he'll be making for us, that my father won't be hiring him anymore. The driver doesn't ask why, and seems happy with the money my mother gives him to help him get by.

27

THE WHITE BIRDS

BELLA WELCOMES US at her front door and tells us we can have The Little Girls' room, which is empty because they've moved to a house in Almendares with Bartolo, their father, who now has a job that pays a lot. We lug our bags to the room, which hasn't a stick of furniture, just three mattresses on the floor.

I leave my things and set off to find Barbara and Emilito to play with. But they are busy with their own business and pay no attention to me now that I'm like a refugee in their house.

My mother says she's going to the hospital again to spend the night with my father, and leaves with my brother in tow.

I head to the porch to sit and watch the sun go down. It all seems like a dream and I don't want to think about what's happened, or feel any emotion. Seeing the sunlight graze the top of the trees gives me a sense of peace.

The warm breeze protects me from the icy air I felt inside our house. I clutch at this breeze and its light scent of leaves and flowers of the shrubs and trees planted in front of this mansion in La Sierra.

I WAKE UP FEELING my mother lower herself down to my mattress, with a sad look on her face.

"Today you're going to get to see your father," she announces, pausing as if to answer questions.

"Okay," I say, impassive.

I sense my mother is waiting for me to put on an extravagant, embarrassing display. What can I say? It's bad enough to be obliged to play-act the comedy of childish stupidity every day, without having to keep up this role in critical moments.

"This is coming to an end," I think.

Never mind the mystery surrounding my father's illness, I can make logical deductions. In an instant it's clear what has happened. How can I not know? The facts are there. I just must put them together and draw a conclusion, but, for the first time in my life, I do not want to think.

We arrive at the hospital without my realizing it – staring without looking – and suddenly I'm walking down a huge, long hall that smells of chloroform.

White doors on one side of the hall open and close with a squeak of hinges.

I hear a voice in my brain saying: "Pay close attention, remember all the details, because this is the last time you'll see your father." My mother takes me by the hand, squeezing my fingers, like trying to give the moment a drama it doesn't have. It's all so simple. We're at the end of something. I just need to watch it unfold. Nothing else. As I push the door open, I see my father at the end of the room, on the right, lying on a white metal bed and covered by a sheet with a big bulge in the belly region. My father smiles and I try to ignore this mound under the sheet. He thinks I'm going to ask him what's the matter with him, but I won't. It is possible that he doesn't know, but I do. He's on the doorstep of Death. I try to make him laugh, to offer some of that droll lightness that has always been his gift and that everybody is doing their best to take away from him now, when he needs it most.

My mother, perched on one of the white metal chairs against the wall, no doubt thinks the way I'm behaving is owed to the ignorance of childhood. My father laughs at my antics, and plans our future. I can't tell whether this is to make us feel better, or to hide how he feels.

"Everything's going to be different. We'll take a trip, all four of us. We'll sell the house and sail on a transatlantic liner to Europe," he says.

When he laughs, the circles under his eyes grow darker, the mound under the sheet moves up and down, the silver metal table next to his bed, full of glasses of water and juice, clinks. Everything smells of rot and disinfectant.

SOME TIME AFTER THIS, today, Sunday, December 4, the day of Saint Barbara otherwise known as Changó, Barbara and Emilito and I are sitting in the armchairs on the porch at Bella's, when my cousin Nadia invites me and my cousins to go for a ride in her swimming-pool-green Ford parked in front. It looks like a Studebaker, this year's most popular car, but it's just a copycat Ford. Bartolo, Nadia's father, is driving and she's in the front seat next to him. Emilito sits in the back, between me and Barbara. My mother and brother are at the hospital visiting my father, but Nadia tells me we're not going to that hospital, but to another, where the father of the little girl next door is dying. I don't know this girl, but I imagine her barefoot, slouched against the wall, her big hazel eyes and her angular face distraught. They're very kind to be going to see the father, because I guess no one visits him, as the people next door are very poor.

Nadia says to Bartolo coolly, without feeling, "The man is dying in pieces. The doctors tried to operate on him and just closed him up again. There's no cure."

We drive through the tree-lined streets of La Sierra. Buses move along, huffing to a standstill at each bus stop and at the red sun of each traffic light. We drive past the Arenal Cinema, and I remember all the Sundays I spent there watching movies with my mother, then eating chocolate ice cream at the soda bar.

"I have no idea what's to become of the wife," Nadia continues in the same tone. "Because, you know, she's half crazy. Thanks to him, she's muddled through, though she didn't realize it, fool that she is, always seeing ghosts on the walls, like every jealous woman. And the girl —" she cuts her eyes at Bartolo— "is so sickly, rickety, thin as a skeleton, she might die of tuberculosis. And the boy, so arrogant. I don't know what he's going to do without his daddy."

Barbara and Emilito are quiet, looking out the windows. Bartolo doesn't speak a word either. It's hurtful, what she's saying about that family, destroyed like that. Such mean words about that little girl I don't know! Why do grownups talk like that, with no thought for the people left alone in a room by a broken father?

Nadia's face shows no emotion. She's been speaking not with hatred but with scientific objectivity. Her blonde mane flows with the wind and her perfect white skin gives off a subtle fragrance of orange blossom. But once upon a time, she had been a little girl locked in a room with a mother dying with florid tuberculosis, as the doctors called it. I assumed people with florid tuberculosis would have flowers sprouting from them when they died, but my mother said no, they called it that because the sick person was standing, working to the very end, looking healthy with their cheeks flushed. In Nadia's mother's case, my Aunt Dora was hunkered down in bed, reading, to the very end, so her sisters nicknamed her "Lazybones" because they had no idea that she was dying. Every time they passed by her room, they would shout, "Five children, and such a slacker!"

Though Dora pretended not to pay attention to them, of course it must have hurt her, and she would tell my mother, "Florita, I feel like I'm a ship on the high seas and all I want is to get to port."

When we drive up to the hospital, I jump up in my seat with surprise. "But this is where my father is!" I yelp, not understanding.

"Why yes, he is in the same hospital," Nadia explains in a kindly voice. "Almost everyone comes to this hospital because it's one of the best in the city." When we park, Nadia and Bartolo slide out of the car and close their doors delicately, while we children pile out and slam the doors hard.

"You stay down here, kids," Nadia orders, winking at Barbara. "The little girl won't care to have other children see her father."

Nadia and Bartolo enter the hospital. For the first time I notice how big this building is, with lots of windows and several terraces, surrounded by a garden shaded by almond trees and poplars and who knows what other kinds of trees. Cars pass in front of the hospital without honking the way they do everywhere else in the city. This must be because inside, people are dying, and you aren't supposed to make noise.

Behind the houses on the opposite side of the street, elegant violet clouds with pink edges pile up in a golden sky that sheds its light on the mysterious and somber treetops. Maybe because people die inside that place, the trees seem so solemn, as if they've been scolded for something.

For some reason, today I feel that organizing play is my job, that others expect it of me, so I propose we play hide-and-go-seek. Emilito and I hide behind the trees. We run out and scream when Barbara discovers us, but she can't catch us because we're skinnier and faster. We don't bother to follow the rules of the game that say once we're discovered, we've already lost.

Barbara shouts insults at us, stamping her foot on the sidewalk and crossing her arms, looking mad as hell. I answer back in kind.

Then I see my mother emerge on the terrace, her face distraught, followed by my brother whose face is disfigured by rage. We're close enough to see every detail of their expressions.

"Septimio! Septimio! Come down to play!" Emilito calls to him, excited and mocking, making faces, jumping up and down.

My brother peers over the balcony wall and calls back, his voice furious: "Shut up! All of you! Just shut up!"

I sit down on the curb. I don't want to think. I'm dumbstruck. I can't escape realizing that something has broken. If this hospital is one of the best in the city, how can the father of that poor girl next door afford it? This is a hospital for people who are well off. And it happens to be where my father is.

"Let's keep playing, Mercy," Emilito says, grabbing my arm.

"Let me be!" I answer violently, shaking myself free.

Now, I feel as if my games and my shouting are an offense. How can I be playing here, on this cold Sunday in December, right in front of this hospital where people are dying? How can I scream and yell, with the fresh life of childhood in my hands, while the lives of those inside fly away like doves? A sound of storm, of water crashing into reefs, erupts in my head.

Through the balustrade on the terrace, I can see my brother sitting on the floor with his legs separated and his head in his hands. Behind him, my mother, white as a ghost, sits in a wicker armchair, completely absorbed in her thoughts. Nadia and Bartolo, with serious faces, reach the terrace and say a few words to her.

Several clouds materialize and the sliver of sun that had been dallying on the roofs of houses disappears, swallowed by the city.

The treetops and roofs of houses are plunged into a sudden blackness that overtakes all the streets.

I can't bear to see the sun go, but don't know how to retrieve it. Cars go on passing by slowly, now with their headlights and red taillights on.

I look up at the sky. Night has fallen, though the stars aren't yet out. All is darkness. Still, something luminous grows inside me. With the strength of my imagination, I make the black birds that have ushered in the night turn in the sky, fly in the opposite direction, and become the white birds that will bring the day.

Someone on the terrace thinks to switch on the light.

ABOUT THE AUTHOR

MERCEDES CORTÁZAR (Havana, Cuba, 1940) became a naturalized citizen of the United States in 1970. Shortly after arriving in New York, she became a founder of the literary magazine *Protesta* (1962), only one issue of which could be published. In 1968, with a group of Puerto Rican poets and Cuban writers in exile, she launched *La Nueva Sangre*, published regularly for many years. Her own writing was recognized with the CINTAS fellowship for Literature 1971-1972. In 1973, Farrar, Straus & Giroux enlisted her as poetry consultant for the English translation of José Lezama Lima's novel, *Paradiso*.

Writer, then editor-in-chief of *Fascinación* in Miami in the late 1970s, she became founding editor-in-chief of *Mar Abierto Revista Náutica Internacional* in 1980, then founding editorial director of *Marine Business Journal*. In 1990, she moved to Atlanta and was until her retirement founding editor-in-chief and editorial director of *Apparel Industry Internacional*, then, publisher of *La Bobina*.

During this period of commercial publishing, Mercedes Cortázar continually contributed poems, essays, and short stories to the print and virtual literary magazines of Latin America and Europe, including such prestigious publications as Spain's literary magazine *Turia*, Mexico's famed *El corno emplumado*, Paris-based *Mundo Nuevo*, cynosure of the writers of the Latin American literary boom, and many others. (A more comprehensive literary bibliography may be found on *academia.edu*.) Her essay in *Enciclopedia del español en los Estados Unidos* (Cervantes Institute and Editorial Santillana, Madrid, 2008), pointing out that writers who wrote in Spanish in the United States were being blocked from publication in Spain, provoked such a stir that major Spanish book publishers began to award literary prizes and book contracts to Spanish-language writers who resided in the United States. Recently, her remembrance of Cuban artists, writers, and intellectuals in New York of the 1960s appeared in the monograph *Zilia Sánchez: Soy Isla* (Yale University Press/The Phillips Collection, 2019).

A selection of her poems is available in Spanish (*Orbes 1959-2016*, Ediciones La Mirada, 2017) and English (*Orbs: Collected Poems*, PPI, 2019); selected literary prose, in English (*Images of the Divine Bird: Stories and Autofiction*, PPI, 2020).

ABOUT THE TRANSLATOR

ANDRÉE CONRAD (Caracas, Venezuela, 1945) has translated works by José Donoso, Victoria Ocampo, Robinson Rojas Sandford, and others, as well as Mercedes Cortázar's *Orbs: Collected Poems* and *Images of the Divine Bird*. While associate editor at Farrar, Straus & Giroux, she edited the translation of José Lezama Lima's *Paradiso* and other books originally written in Spanish, Italian, and Portuguese. Her translations have been published by FSG, Alfred A. Knopf, Harper & Row, David R. Godine, and PPI.

SPECIAL ACKNOWLEDGMENT

The author and the translator
wish to express their heartfelt thanks
to M.R. Mathews-Haney,
wife, mother of Generation Alpha daughter,
and when school is in session, inner-city guidance counselor.
She managed to accomplish her meticulous reading
of the manuscript of *Infancy in Paradise*
during one of the most fraught periods in this country's history,
in which the worlds of children and parents alike
were turned upside-down by the Covid pandemic.

www.ingramcontent.com/pod-product-compliance
Lightning Source LLC
Chambersburg PA
CBHW020841020726
47497CB00005B/1203